MOONDYNE JOE

A STORY FROM THE UNDERWORLD

BY

JOHN BOYLE O'REILLY

P. J. KENEDY & SONS

NEW YORK

TO

ALL WHO ARE IN PRISON

I Dedicate this Book.

JOHN BOYLE O'REILLY.

CONTENTS.

Book First.

THE GOLD MINE OF THE VASSE.

		Page
I.	The Land of the Red Line	1
II.	The Convict Road Party	5
III.	Number 406	11
IV.	Bond and Free	15
V.	The Koagulup Swamp	19
VI.	The Bribe	21
VII.	The Iron-stone Mountains	25
VIII.	The King of the Vasse	30
IX.	A Dark Night and Day	34
X.	On the Trail	40

Book Second.

THE SANDALWOOD TRADE.

I.	The Mate of the *Canton*	49
II.	Countermining the Miner	59
III.	The Sandalwood Agency	63
IV.	The Teamster's Tavern	66
V.	In Search of his Sorrow	73
VI.	The Door of the Cell	76
VII.	Millbank	84
VIII.	Sir Joshua Hobb's Convict Mill	94
IX.	Mr. Wyville	99
X.	The Upas-Tree	107

Book Third.

ALICE WALMSLEY.

		Page
I.	Miserere!	120
II.	A Flower in the Cell	129
III.	Following a Dark Spirit	141
IV.	Mr. Haggett	148
V.	Two Heads against One	156
VI.	Female Transports	159
VII.	After Nine Years	162

Book Fourth.

THE CONVICT SHIP.

I.	The Parliamentary Committee	166
II.	Harriet Draper	175
III.	A Captain for the *Houguemont*	184
IV.	Captain Samuel Draper	188
V.	Koro and Tepairu	193
VI.	The Child's Grave	198
VII.	The Sailing of the *Houguemont*	204
VIII.	Face to Face	207
IX.	How a Prisoner might break a Bar	212
X.	Dead-Sea Fruit	221
XI.	The Fever	228
XII.	Husband and Wife	234
XIII.	Woman's Love and Hatred	239
XIV.	The Darkness of Desolation	245
XV.	The New Penal Law	248
XVI.	A Prisoner at Large	254

Book Fifth.

THE VALLEY OF THE VASSE.

		Page
I.	Alice Walmsley's New Home	257
II.	Sooner or later a Man must face his Sins	262
III.	Walking in the Shadow	268
IV.	The Meeting	275
V.	Mr. Wyville faces a Storm	283
VI.	The Valley of the Vasse	290
VII.	The Convict's Pass	298
VIII.	The Bush Fire	304

MOONDYNE JOE

THE GOLD MINE OF THE VASSE

I.

THE LAND OF THE RED LINE.

WESTERN AUSTRALIA is a vast and unknown country, almost mysterious in its solitude and unlikeness to any other part of the earth. It is the greatest of the Australias in extent, and in many features the richest and loveliest.

But the sister colonies of Victoria, New South Wales and Queensland are famous for their treasure of gold. Men from all lands have flocked thither to gather riches. They care not for the slow labor of the farmer or grazier. Let the weak and the old, the coward and the dreamer, prune the vine and dry the figs, and wait for the wheat to ripen. Strong men must go to the trial—must set muscle against muscle, and brain against brain in the mine and the market.

Men's lives are short; and unless they gather gold in the mass, how shall they wipe out the primal curse of poverty before the hand loses its skill and the heart its strong desire?

Western Australia is the Cinderella of the South. She has no gold like her sisters. To her was given the servile and unhappy portion. The dregs of British society were poured upon her soil. The robber and the manslayer were sent thither. Her territory was marked off with a *Red Line*. She has no markets for honest men, and no ports for honest ships. Her laws are not the laws of other countries, but the terrible rules of the menagerie. Her citizens have no rights : they toil their lives out at heavy tasks, but earn no wages, nor own a vestige of right in the soil they till. It is a land of slaves and bondmen — the great Penal Colony of Great Britain.

"There is no gold in the Western Colony," said the miners contemptuously ; "let the convicts keep the land — but let them observe our Red Line."

So the convicts took the defamed country, and lived and died there, and others were transported there from England to replace those who died, and every year the seething ships gave up their addition to the terrible population.

In time the Western Colony came to be regarded as a plague-spot, where no man thought of going, and no man did go unless sent in irons.

If the miners from Victoria and New South Wales, however, had visited the penal land some years after its establishment, they would have heard whispers of strange import — rumors and questions of a great golden secret possessed by the Western Colony. No one could tell where the rumor began or on what it was based, except perhaps the certainty that gold was not uncommon among the natives of the colony, who had little or no intercourse with the aborigines of the gold-yielding countries of the South and East.

The belief seemed to hover in the air; and it settled with dazzling conviction on the crude and abnormal minds of the criminal population. At their daily toil in the quarries or on the road-parties, no rock was blasted nor tree uprooted that eager eyes did not hungrily scan the upturned earth. At night, when the tired wretches gathered round the camp-fire outside their prison hut, the dense mahogany forest closing weirdly round the white-clad group, still the undiscovered gold was the topic earnestly discussed. And even the government officers and the few free settlers became after a time filled with the prevailing expectancy and disquiet.

But years passed, and not an ounce of gold was discovered in the colony. The Government had offered reward to settlers or ticket-of-leave men who would find the first nugget or gold-bearing rock ; but no claimant came forward.

Still, there remained the tantalizing fact, — for, in the course of years, fact it had grown to be, — that gold *was* to be found in the colony, and in abundance. The native bushmen were masters of the secret, but neither bribe nor torture could wring it from them. Terrible stories were whispered among the convicts, of attempts that had been made to force the natives to give up the precious secret. Gold was common amongst these bushmen. Armlets and anklets had been seen on men and women ; and some of their chief men, it was said, wore breast-plates and enormous chains of hammered gold.

At last the feeling in the West grew to fever heat ; and in 1848, the Governor of the Penal Colony issued a proclamation, copies of which were sent by native runners to every settler and ticket-of-leave man, and were even surreptitiously distributed amongst the miners on the other side of the Red Line.

This proclamation intensified the excitement. It seemed to bring the mine nearer to every man in the colony. It was a formal admission that there really was a mine ; it dispelled the vague uncertainty, and left an immediate hunger or greed in the minds of the population.

The proclamation read as follows:—

£ 5,000 REWARD!

The above Reward will be paid for the discovery of the Mine from which the Natives of the Vasse obtain their Gold.

A Free Pardon will be granted to the Discoverer, should he be of the Bond Class.

No Reward will be given nor terms made with Absconders from the Prisons or Road-Parties.

By Order,

F. R. HAMPTON,

Governor.

Official Residence,

Perth, 28th June, 1848.

But nothing came of it. Not an ounce of gold was ever taken from the earth. At last men began to avoid the subject. They could not bear to be tantalized nor tortured by the splendid delusion. Some said there was no mine in the Vasse, and others that, if there were a mine, it was known only to a few of the native chiefs, who dealt out the raw gold to their people.

For eight years this magnificent reward had remained unclaimed, and now its terms were only recalled at the fires of the road-making convicts, or in the lonely slab-huts of the mahogany sawyers, who were all ticket-of-leave men.

II.

THE CONVICT ROAD-PARTY.

IT was a scorching day in midsummer — a few days before Christmas.

Had there been any moisture in the bush it would have steamed in the heavy heat. During the mid-day hours not a bird stirred among the mahogany and gum trees. On the flat tops of the low banksia the round heads of the white cockatoos could be seen in thousands, motionless as the trees themselves. Not a parrot had the vim to scream. The chirping insects were silent. Not a snake had courage to rustle his hard skin against the hot and dead bush-grass. The bright-eyed iguanas were in their holes. The mahogany sawyers had left their logs and were sleeping in the cool sand of their pits. Even the travelling ants had halted on their wonderful roads, and sought the shade of a bramble.

All free things were at rest; but the penetrating click of the axe, heard far through the bush, and now and again a harsh word of command, told that it was a land of bondmen.

From daylight to dark, through the hot noon as steadily as in the cool evening, the convicts were at work on the roads — the weary work that has no wages, no promotion, no incitement, no variation for good or bad, except stripes for the laggard.

Along the verge of the Koagulup Swamp — one of the greatest and dismalest of the wooded lakes of the country, its black water deep enough to float a man-of-war, — a party of convicts were making a government road. They were cutting their patient way into a forest only traversed before by the aborigine and the absconder.

Before them in the bush, as in their lives, all was dark and unknown — tangled underbrush, gloomy shadows, and noxious things. Behind them, clear and open, lay the straight road they had made — leading to and from the prison.

Their camp, composed of rough slab-huts, was some two hundred miles from the main prison of the colony on the Swan River, at Fremantle, from which radiate all the roads made by the bondmen.

The primitive history of the colony is written forever in its roads. There is in this penal labor a secret of value to be utilized more fully by a wiser civilization. England sends her criminals to take the brunt of the new land's hardship and danger — to prepare the way for honest life and labor. In every community there is either dangerous or degrading work to be done : and who so fit to do it as those who have forfeited their liberty by breaking the law ?

The convicts were dressed in white trousers, blue woollen shirt, and white hat, — every article stamped with England's private mark — the Broad Arrow. They were young men, healthy and strong, their faces and bare arms burnt to the color of mahogany. Burglars, murderers, garotters, thieves, — double-dyed lawbreakers every one — but, for all that, kind-hearted and manly fellows enough were among them.

" I tell you, mates," said one, resting on his spade, "this is going to be the end of Moondyne Joe. That firing in the swamp last night was his last fight."

" I don't think it was Moondyne," said another; "he's at work in the chain-gang at Fremantle; and there's no chance of escape there——"

" Sh-h !" interrupted the first speaker, a powerful, low-browed fellow, named Dave Terrell, who acted as a sort of foreman to the gang. The warder in charge of the party was slowly walking past. When he was out of hearing Dave continued, in a low but deeply earnest voice: "I know it was Moondyne, mates. I saw him last night when I went to get the turtle's eggs. I met him face to face in the moonlight, beside the swamp."

Every man held his hand and breath with intense interest in the story. Some looked incredulous — heads were shaken in doubt.

"Did you speak to him?" asked one.

"Ay," said Terrell, turning on him; "why shouldn't I? Moondyne knew he had nothing to fear from me, and I had nothing to fear from him."

"What did you say to him?" asked another.

"Say? — I stood an' looked at him for a minute, for his face had a white look in the moonlight, and then I walked up close to him, and I says — 'Be you Moondyne Joe, or his ghost?'"

"Ay?" said the gang with one breath.

"Ay, I said that, never fearing, for Moondyne Joe, dead or alive, would never harm a prisoner."

"But what did he answer?" asked the eager crowd.

"He never said a word; but he laid his finger on his lips, like this, and waved his hand as if he warned me to go back to the camp. I turned to go; then I looked back once, and he was standing just as I left him, but he was looking up at the sky, as if there was some'at in the moon that pleased him."

The convicts worked silently, each thinking on what he had heard.

"He mightn't ha' been afraid, though," said low-browed Dave; "I'd let them cut my tongue out before I'd sell the Moondyne."

"That's true," said several of the gang, and many kind looks were given to Terrell. A strong bond of sympathy, it was evident, existed between these men and the person of whom they spoke.

A sound from the thick bush interrupted the conversation. The convicts looked up from their work, and beheld a strange procession approaching from the

direction of the swamp. It consisted of about a dozen
or fifteen persons, most of whom were savages. In
front rode two officers of the Convict Service, a sergeant, and a private trooper, side by side, with drawn
swords; and between their horses, manacled by the
wrists to their stirrup-irons, walked a white man.

"Here they come," hissed Terrell, with a bitter malediction, his low brow wholly disappearing into a terrible ridge above his eyes. "They haven't killed him,
after all. O, mates, what a pity it is to see a man
like Moondyne in that plight."

"He's done for two or three of 'em," muttered
another, in a tone of grim gratification. "Look at the
loads behind. I knew he wouldn't be taken this time
like a cornered cur."

Following the prisoner came a troop of "natives,"
as the aboriginal bushmen are called, bearing three
spearwood litters with the bodies of wounded men.
A villanous-looking savage, mounted on a troop-horse,
brought up the rear. His dress was like that of his
pedestrian fellows, upon whom, however, he looked in
disdain, — a short boka, or cloak of kangaroo-skin, and
a belt of twisted fur cords round his naked body. In
addition, he had a police-trooper's old cap, and a heavy
"regulation" revolver stuck in his belt.

This was the tracker, the human bloodhound, used
by the troopers to follow the trail of absconding
prisoners.

When the troopers neared the convict-party, the sergeant, a man whose natural expression, whatever it
might have been, was wholly obliterated by a frightful
scar across his face, asked for water. The natives
halted, and squatted silently in a group. The wounded
men moaned as the litters were lowered.

Dave Terrell brought the water. He handed a pannikin to the sergeant, and another to the private trooper,
and filled a third.

"Who's that for?" harshly demanded the sergeant.

"For Moondyne," said the convict, approaching the chained man, whose neck was stretched toward the brimming cup.

"Stand back, curse you!" said the sergeant, bringing his sword flat on the convict's back. "That scoundrel needs no water. He drinks blood."

There was a taunt in the tone, even beneath the brutality of the words.

"Carry your pail to those litters," growled the sinister-looking sergeant, "and keep your mouth closed, if you value your hide. There!" he said in a suppressed voice, flinging the few drops he had left in the face of the manacled man, "that's water enough for you, till you reach Bunbury prison to-morrow."

The face of the prisoner hardly changed. He gave one straight look into the sergeant's eyes, then turned away, and seemed to look far away through the bush. He was a remarkable being, as he stood there. In strength and proportion of body the man was magnificent — a model for a gladiator. He was of middle height, young, but so stern and massively featured, and so browned and beaten by exposure, it was hard to determine his age. His clothing was only a few torn and bloody rags; but he looked as if his natural garb were utter nakedness or the bushman's cloak, so loosely and carelessly hung the shreds of cloth on his bronzed body. A large, finely shaped head, with crisp, black hair and beard, a broad, square forehead, and an air of power and self-command, — this was the prisoner, this was Moondyne Joe.

Who or what was the man? An escaped convict. What had he been? Perhaps a robber or a mutineer, or maybe he had killed a man in the white heat of passion; no one knew — no one cared to know.

That question is never asked in the penal colony. No caste there. They have found bottom, where all

stand equal. No envy there, no rivalry, no greed nor
ambition, and no escape from companionship. They
constitute the purest democracy on earth. The only
distinction to be won — that of being trustworthy, or
selfish and false. The good man is he who is kind and
true; the bad man is he who is capable of betraying a
confederate.

It may be the absence of the competitive elements of
social life that accounts for the number of manly characters to be met among these outcasts.

It is by no means in the superior strata of society
that abound the strong, true natures, the men that may
be depended upon, the primitive rocks of humanity.
The complexities of social life beget cunning and arti-
ficiality. Among penal convicts there is no ground for
envy, ambition, or emulation; nothing to be gained by
falsehood in any shape.

But all this time the prisoner stands looking away
into the bush, with the drops of insult trickling from
his strong face. His self-command evidently irritated
the brutal officer, who, perhaps, expected to hear him
whine for better treatment.

The sergeant dismounted to examine the handcuffs,
and while doing so, looked into the man's face with a
leer of cruel exultation. He drew no expression from
the steady eyes of the prisoner.

There was an old score to be settled between those
men, and it was plain that each knew the metal of the
other.

" I 'll break that look," said the sergeant between
his teeth, but loud enough for the prisoner's ear; " curse
you, I 'll break it before we reach Fremantle." Soon
after he turned away, to look to the wounded men.

While so engaged, the private trooper made a furtive
sign to the convict with the pail; and he, keeping in
shade of the horses, crept up and gave Moondyne a
deep drink of the precious water.

The stern lines withdrew from the prisoner's mouth
and forehead; and as he gave the kindly trooper a
glance of gratitude, there was something strangely gentle and winning in the face.

The sergeant returned and mounted. The litters were
raised by the natives, and the party resumed their
march, striking in on the new road that led to the
prison.

"May the lightning split him," hissed black-browed
Dave, after the sergeant. "There's not an officer in
the colony will strike a prisoner without cause, except
that coward, and he was a convict himself."

"May the Lord help Moondyne Joe this day," said
another, "for he's chained to the stirrup of the only
man living that hates him."

The sympathizing gang looked after the party till
they were hidden by a bend of the road; but they were
silent under the eye of their warder.

III.

NUMBER 406.

SOME years before, the prisoner, now called Moondyne Joe, had arrived in the colony. He was a youth
— little more than a boy in years. From the first day of
his imprisonment he had followed one course : he was
quiet, silent, patient, obedient. He broke no rules of
the prison. He asked no favors. He performed all
his own work, and often helped another who grumbled
at his heavy task.

He was simply known to his fellow-convicts as Joe,
his other name was unknown or forgotten. When the
prison roll was called, he answered to No. 406.

In the first few years he had made many friends in

the colony — but he had also made one enemy, and a deadly one. In the gang to which he belonged was a man named Isaac Bowman, one of those natures seemingly all evil, envious, and cruel, detested by the basest, yet self-contained, full of jibe and derision, satisfied with his own depravity, and convinced that every one was secretly just as vile as he.

From the first, this fellow had disliked and sneered at Joe, and Joe having long observed the man's cur-like character, had at last adopted a system of conduct toward him that saved himself annoyance, but secretly intensified the malevolence of the other. He did not avoid the fellow ; but he never looked at him, saw him, spoke to him, — not even answering him when he spoke, as if he had not heard him.

This treatment was observed and enjoyed by the other prisoners, and sometimes even adopted by themselves toward Bowman. At last its effect on the evil nature was too powerful to be concealed. With the others he could return oath for oath, or jibe for jibe, and always came off pleased with himself; but Joe's silent contumely stung him like a scorpion.

The convicts at length saw that Bowman, who was a man capable of any crime, held a deep hatred for Joe, and they warned him to beware. But he smiled, and went on just as before.

One morning a poor settler rode into the camp with a cry for justice and vengeance. His hut was only a few miles distant, and in his absence last night a deed of rapine and robbery had been perpetrated there — and the robber was a convict.

A search was made in the prisoners' hut, and in one of the hammocks was found some of the stolen property. The man who owned the hammock was seized and ironed, protesting his innocence. Further evidence was found against him — he had been seen returning to the camp that morning — Isaac Bowman had seen him.

Swift and summary is the dread punishment of the penal code. As the helpless wretch was dragged away, a word of mock pity followed him from Bowman. During the scene, Joe had stood in silence; but at the brutal jibe he started as if struck by a whip. He sprang on Isaac Bowman suddenly — dashed him to the ground, and, holding him there like a worm, shook from his clothing all the stolen property, except what the caitiff had concealed in his fellow's bed to insure his conviction.

Then and there the sentence was given. The villain was haled to the triangles and flogged with embittered violence. He uttered no cry; but as the hissing lashes swept his back, he settled a look of ghastly and mortal hatred on Joe, who stood by and counted the stripes.

But this was years ago; and Bowman had long been a free man and a settler, having served out his sentence.

At that time the laws of the Penal Colony were exceedingly cruel and unjust to the bondmen. There was in the colony a number of "free settlers" and ex-convicts who had obtained land, and these, as a class, were men who lived half by farming and half by rascality. They sold brandy to the convicts and ticket-of-leave men, and robbed them when the drugged liquor had done its work. They feared no law, for the word of a prisoner was dead in the courts.

The crying evil of the code was the power it gave these settlers to take from the prisons as many men as they chose, and work them as slaves on their clearings. While so employed, the very lives of these convicts were at the mercy of their taskmasters, who possessed over them all the power of prison officers.

A report made by an employer against a convict insured a flogging or a number of years in the terrible chain-gang at Fremantle. The system reeked with cruelty and the blood of men. It would startle our

commonplace serenity to see the record of the lives
that were sacrificed to have it repealed.

Under this law, it came to Joe's turn to be sent out
on probation. Application had been made for him by
a farmer, whose "range" was in a remote district. Joe
was a strong and willing worker, and he was glad of
the change; but when he was taken to the lonely
place, he could not help a shudder when he came face
to face with his new employer and master — Isaac
Bowman.

There was no doubting the purpose of the villain
who had now complete possession of him. He meant
to drive him into rebellion — to torture him till his
hate was gratified, and then to have him flogged and
sent to the chain-gang; and from the first minute of
his control he began to carry out his purpose.

For two years the strong man toiled like a brute at
the word of his driver, returning neither scoff nor
scourge.

Joe had years to serve; and he had made up his
mind to serve them, and be free. He knew there was
no escape — that one report from Bowman would wipe
out all record of previous good conduct. He knew,
too, that Bowman meant to destroy him, and he resolved to bear toil and abuse as long as he was able.

He was able longer than most men; but the cup
was filled at last. The day came when the worm
turned — when the quiet, patient man blazed into
dreadful passion, and, tearing the goad from the ty-
rant's hand, he dashed him, maimed and senseless, to
the earth.

The blow given, Joe's passion calmed, and the ruin
of the deed stared him in the face. There was no
court of justice in which he might plead. He had
neither word nor oath nor witnesses. The man might
be dead; and even if he recovered, the punishment
was the lash and the chain-gang, or the gallows.

Then and there, Joe struck into the bush with a
resolute face, and next day the infuriate and baffled
rascal, rendered ten-fold more malignant by a dreadful
disfigurement, reported him to the prison as an absconder, a robber, and an attempted murderer.

IV.

BOND AND FREE.

THREE years passed. It was believed that Joe had
perished in the bush. Bowman had entered the convict service as a trooper, but even his vigilance brought
no discovery. Absconders are generally found after a
few months, prowling around the settlements for food,
and are glad to be retaken.

But Joe was no common criminal nor common
man. When he set his face toward the bush, he
meant to take no half measures. The bush was to be
his home. He knew of nothing to draw him back,
and he cared not if he never saw the face of a white
man again. He was sick of injustice and hardship—
sick of all the ways of the men he had known.

Prison life had developed a strong nature in Joe.
Naturally powerful in mind, body, and passions, he had
turned the power in on himself, and had obtained a
rare mastery over his being. He was a thoughtful man,
a peacemaker, and a lover of justice. He had obtained
an extraordinary hold on the affection of the convicts.
They all knew him. He was true as steel to everything he undertook; and they knew that, too. He
was enormously strong. One day he was working in
the quarries of Fremantle with twenty others in a
deep and narrow ledge. Sixteen men were at work
below, and four were preparing a blast at the head of

the ledge, which ran down at an angle of fifty degrees, like a channel cut in the solid rock. The men below were at the bottom of the channel. A pebble dropped by the four men above would have dashed into their midst.

Suddenly there was a cry above, sharp, short, terrible, — " *Look out, down there !* "

One of the half-filled charges had exploded with a sullen, mischievous puff, and the rocks at the head of the ledge were lifted and loosened. One immense block barred the tumbling mass from the men below. But the increasing weight above grew irresistible — the great stone was yielding — it had moved several inches, pressed on from behind. The men who had been working at the place fled for their lives, only sending out the terrible cry to their fellows below, —

" *Look out, down there !* "

But those below could only look out — they could not get out. There was no way out but by the rising channel of the ledge. And down that channel would thunder in a quarter of minute the murderous rocks that were pushing the saving stone before them.

Three of the men above escaped in time. They dared not look behind — as they clung to the quarry-side, out of danger, they closed their eyes, waiting for the horrible crash.

But it did not come. They waited ten seconds, then looked around. A man stood at the head of the ledge, right before the moving mass — a convict — Moondyne Joe. He had a massive crowbar in his hands, and was strongly working to get a purchase on the great stone that blocked the way, but which actually swayed on the verge of the steep decline. At last the bar caught — the purchase was good — the stone moved another inch, and the body of the man bent like a strong tree under the awful strain. But he held back the stone.

He did not say a word — he did not look below -- **he**

knew they would see the precious moment and escape. They saw it, and, with chilled hearts at the terrible danger, they fled up the ledge, and darted past the man who had risked his own life to save theirs.

Another instant, and the roar went down the ledge, as if the hungry rocks knew they had been baffled.

Moondyne Joe escaped — the bar saved him. When the crash came, the bar was driven across an angle in the ledge, and held there, and he was within the angle. He was mangled and bruised — but life and limb were safe.

This was one of several instances that proved his character, and made him trusted and loved of his fellow-convicts.

Whatever was his offence against the law, he had received its bitter lesson. The worst of the convicts grew better when associated with him. Common sense, truth, and kindness were Joe's principles. He was a strong man, and he pitied and helped those weaker than himself. He was a bold man, and he understood the timid. He was a brave man, and he grieved for a coward or a liar. He never preached; but his healthy, straightforward life did more good to his fellows than all the hired Bible-readers in the colony.

No wonder the natives to whom he fled soon began to look upon him with a strange feeling. Far into the mountains of the Vasse he had journeyed before he fell in with them.

They were distrustful of all white men, but they soon trusted him. There was something in the simple savage mind not far removed from that of the men in prison, who had grown to respect, even to reverence his character. The natives saw him stronger and braver than any one they had ever known. He was more silent than their oldest chief; and so wise, he settled disputes so that both sides were satisfied

2

They looked on him with distrust at first; then with wonder; then with respect and confidence; and before two years were over, with something like awe and veneration, as for a superior being.

They gave him the name of "MOONDYNE," — which had some meaning more than either manhood or kingship.

His fame and name spread through the native tribes all over the country. When they came to the white settlements, the expression oftenest heard was "Moondyne." The convicts and settlers constantly heard the word, but dreamt not then of its significance. Afterwards, when they knew to whom the name had been given, it became a current word throughout the colony.

Toward the end of the third year of his freedom, when Moondyne and a party of natives were far from the mountains, they were surprised by a Government surveying party, who made him prisoner, knowing, of course, that he must be an absconder. He was taken to the main prison at Fremantle, and sentenced to the chain-gang for life; but before he had reached the Swan River every native in the colony knew that "The Moondyne" was a prisoner.

The chain-gang of Fremantle is the depth of the penal degradation. The convicts wear from thirty to fifty pounds of iron, according to their offence. It is riveted on their bodies in the prison forge, and when they have served their time the great rings have to be chiselled off their calloused limbs.

The chain-gang works outside the prison walls of Fremantle, in the granite quarries. The neighborhood, being thickly settled with pardoned men and ticket-of-leave men, had long been deserted by the aborigines; but from the day of Moondyne's sentence the bushmen began to build their *myers* and hold their *corrobborees* near the quarries.

For two years the chain-gang toiled among the stones, and the black men sat on the great unhewn rocks, and never seemed to tire of the scene.

The warders took no notice of their silent presence. The natives never spoke to a prisoner, but sat there in dumb interest, every day in the year, from sunrise to evening.

One day they disappeared from the quarries, and an officer who passed through their village of *myers*, found them deserted. It was quite a subject of interesting conversation among the warders. Where had they gone to ? Why had they departed in the night ?

The day following, an answer came to these queries. When the chain-gang was formed, to return to the prison, one link was gone — Moondyne was missing.

His irons were found, filed through, behind the rock at which he worked ; and from that day the black face of a bushman was never seen in Fremantle.

V.

THE KOAGULUP SWAMP.

WE arrive now at the opening scene of this story. Eight days after his escape from Fremantle, Moondyne was seen by the convict Dave Terrell, on the shores of the Koagulup Swamp. In those eight days he had travelled two hundred miles, suffering that which is only known to the hunted convict. When he met the prisoner in the moonlight and made the motion to silence, Dave Terrell saw the long barrel of a pistol in his belt. He meant to sell his life this time, for there was no hope if retaken.

His intention was to hide in the swamp till he found an opportunity of striking into the Vasse

Mountains, a spur of which was not more than sixty
miles distant.

But the way of the absconder is perilous; and swift
as had been Moondyne's flight, the shadow of the
pursuer was close behind. No tardy step was that of
him who led the pursuit — a man with a terribly
maimed face — a new officer of the penal system, but
whose motive in the pursuit was deadlier and dearer
than the love of public duty.

On the very day that Moondyne Joe reached the
great swamp, the mounted pursuit tracked the fugitive
to the water's edge. A few hours later, while he lay
exhausted on an island in the densely-wooded morass,
the long sedge was cautiously divided a few yards
from his face, and the glittering eyes of a native
tracker met his for an instant. Before he could spring
to his feet the supple savage was upon him, sending out
his bush-cry as he sprang. A short struggle, with the
black hands on the white throat; then the great
white arms closed around the black body, and with a
gasping sob it lost its nerve and lay still, while Moondyne half rose, to listen.

From every point he heard the trackers closing on
him. He sank back with a moan of despair. But
the next instant the blood rushed from his heart with
a new vigor for every muscle.

It was the last breath of his freedom, and he
would fight for it, as for his life. He sprang to his
feet and met his first brutal assailant, a native dog, —
half wolf, half greyhound, — which sprang at his
throat, but sank its fangs in his shoulder.

A bullet through the animal's brain left him free
again, with steadied nerves. Even in the excitement
of the moment a thrill of gratitude that it was not a
man that lay there passed through him. He flung his
pistol into the swamp, and dashed toward the log on
which he had gained the island. Beside it stood two

men, armed. Barehanded, the fugitive flung himself
upon them, and closed in desperate struggle. It was
vain, however; others came and struck him down and
overpowered him.

He was put in irons, and found himself in charge of
the most brutal officer in the penal service, — his old
fellow-convict and employer, Isaac Bowman.

VI.

THE BRIBE.

WHEN the party had travelled a dozen miles from
the convict camp, the evening closed, and the sergeant
called a halt. A chain was passed round a tree, and
locked; and to this the manacles of the prisoner were
made fast, leaving him barely the power of lying
down. With a common prisoner this would have been
security enough; but the sergeant meant to leave no
loophole open. He and the private trooper would
keep guard all night; and according to this order, after
supper, the trooper entered on the first four hours'
watch.

The natives and wounded men took their meal and
were stretched on the soft sand beside another fire,
about a hundred paces from the guard and prisoner.

The tired men soon slept, all but the sentry and the
captive. The sergeant lay within arm's length of the
prisoner; and even from deep sleep awoke at the least
movement of the chain.

Toward midnight, the chained man turned his face
toward the sentry, and motioned him to draw near.
The rough, but kind-hearted fellow thought he asked
for water, and softly brought him a pannikin, which he
held to his lips. At the slight motion, the sergeant

awoke, and harshly reprimanded the trooper, posting him at a distance from the fire, with orders not to move till his watch had expired. The sergeant returned to his sleep, and again all was still.

After a time the face of the prisoner was once more raised, and with silent lip but earnest expression he begged the sentry to come to him. But the man would not move. He grew angry at the persistence of the prisoner, who ceased not to look toward him, and who at last even ventured to speak in a low voice. At this, the fearful trooper grew alarmed, and sternly ordered him to rest. The sergeant awoke at the word, and shortly after relieved the trooper, seating himself by the fire to watch the remainder of the night.

When the prisoner saw this, with a look of utter weariness, though not of resignation, he at last closed his eyes and sank to rest. Once having yielded to the fatigue which his strong will had hitherto mastered, he was unconscious. A deep and dreamless sleep fell on him. The sand was soft round his tired limbs, and for two or three hours the bitterness of his captivity was forgotten.

He awoke suddenly, and, as if he had not slept, felt the iron on his wrists, and knew that he was chained to a tree like a wild beast.

The sleep had given him new strength. He raised his head, and met the eyes of the sergeant watching him. The look between them was long and steady.

" Come here," said the prisoner, in a low tone, " I want to speak to you."

Had the gaunt dog beside him spoken, the sergeant could not have been more amazed.

" Come here," repeated Moondyne. " I have something important to say to you."

The sergeant drew his revolver, examined the caps, and then moved toward his prisoner.

"I heard you say you had spent twenty-five years in this colony," said Moondyne, "and that you might as well have remained a convict. Would you go away to another country, and live the rest of your life in wealth and power?"

The sergeant stared at him as if he thought he had gone mad. The prisoner understood the look.

"Listen," he said impressively; "I am not mad. You know there is a reward offered for the discovery of the Vasse Gold Mine. *I can lead you to the spot!*"

There was that in his voice and look that thrilled the sergeant to the marrow. He glanced at the sleeping trooper, and drew closer to the chained man.

"I know where that gold mine lies," said Moondyne, reading the greedy face, "where tons and shiploads of solid gold are waiting to be carried away. If you help me to be free, I will lead you to the mine."

The sergeant looked at him in silence. He arose and walked stealthily toward the natives, who were soundly sleeping. To and fro in the firelight, for nearly an hour, he paced, revolving the startling proposition. At last he approached the chained man.

"I have treated you badly, and you hate me;" he said. "How can I trust you? How can you prove to me that this is true?"

Moondyne met the suspicious eye steadily. "I have no proof," he said; "you must take my word. I tell you the truth. If I do not lead you straight to the mine, I will go back to Fremantle as your prisoner."

Still the sergeant pondered and paced. He was in doubt, and the consequences might be terrible.

"Have you ever known me to lie?" said Moondyne.

The sergeant looked at him, but did not answer.

At length he abruptly asked: "Is it far away?" He was advancing toward a decision.

"We can reach the place in two days, if you give me a horse," said Moondyne.

"You might escape," said the sergeant.

"I will not; but if you doubt me, keep the chain on my wrist till I show you the gold."

"And then?" said the sergeant.

"Then we shall be equals. I will lead you to the mine. You must return, and escape from the country as best you can. Do you agree?"

The sergeant's face was white, as he glanced at the sleeping trooper and then at the prisoner.

"I agree," he said; "lie down, and pretend to sleep."

The sergeant had thought out his plan. He would insure his own safety, no matter how the affair turned. Helping a convict to escape was punished with death by the penal law; but he would put another look on the matter. He cautiously waked the private trooper.

"Take those natives," he said, "all but the mounted tracker, and go on to Bunbury before me. The wounded men must be doctored at once."

Without a word, the disciplined trooper shook the drowsiness from him, saddled his horse, and mounted In half an hour they were gone.

Moondyne Joe and the sergeant listened till the las sound died away. The tracker was curled up again beside the fire.

Sergeant Bowman then unlocked the chain, and the powerful prisoner rose to his feet. In a whisper the sergeant told him he must secure the native before he attempted to take the horse.

Moondyne went softly to the side of the sleeping savage. There was a smile on his face as he knelt down and laid one strong hand on the man's throat, and another on his pistol.

In a few moments it was over. The bushman never even writhed when he saw the stern face above him, and felt that his weapon was gone. Moondyne left him tied hand and foot, and returned to the sergeant, who had the horses ready.

When the convict stood beside the trooper he raised his hand suddenly, and held something toward him — the tracker's pistol, loaded and capped ! He had played and won. His enemy stood defenceless before him — and the terror of death, as he saw the position, was in the blanched face of the sergeant.

" Take this pistol," said Moondyne, quietly. " You may give it to me, if you will, when I have kept my word."

The sergeant took the weapon with a trembling hand, and his evil face had an awed look as he mounted.

" Call the dogs," said Moondyne, " we shall need them to-morrow." In answer to a low whistle the wolf-like things bounded through the bush. The men struck off at a gallop, in the direction of the convicts' camp, the sergeant a little behind, with his pistol ready in the holster.

VII.

THE IRON—STONE MOUNTAINS.

MOONDYNE took a straight line for the Koagulup Swamp, which they " struck " after a couple of hours' ride. They dismounted near the scene of the capture, and Moondyne pulled from some bushes near the edge a short raft of logs bound together with withes of bark. The sergeant hesitated, and looked on suspiciously.

" You must trust me," said Moondyne quietly ; " unless we break the track we shall have that sleuth-dog tracker after us when he gets loose."

The sergeant got on the raft, holding the bridles of the horses. Moondyne, with a pole, pushed from the

bank, and entered the gloomy arches of the wooded
swamp.

It was a weird scene. At noonday the flood was
black as ink and the arches were filled with gloomy
shadows. Overhead the foliage of trees and creepers
was matted into a dense roof, now pierced by a few
thin pencils of moonlight.

Straight toward the centre Moondyne steered, for
several hundred yards, the horses swimming behind.
Then he turned at right angles, and pushed along from
tree to tree in a line with the shore they had left.
After a while the horses found bottom, and waded.

" No more trouble now," said Moondyne. " They 're
on the sand. We must keep along till morning, and
then strike toward the hills."

They went ahead rapidly, thanks to Moondyne's
amazing strength ; and by daylight were a long distance from the point at which they entered. A wide
but shallow river with a bright sand bottom emptied
into the swamp before them, and into this Moondyne
poled the raft and tied it securely to a fallen tree, hidden in sedge grass.

They mounted their horses, and rode up the bed of
the river, which they did not leave till near noontime.
At last, when Moondyne deemed the track thoroughly
broken, he turned toward the higher bank, and struck
into the bush, the land beginning to rise toward the
mountains when they had travelled a few miles.

It was late in the afternoon when they halted for
the day's first meal. Moondyne climbed a mahogany
tree, which he had selected from certain fresh marks on
its bark, and from a hole in the trunk pulled out two
silver-tailed 'possums, as large as rabbits. The sergeant lighted a fire on the loose sand, and piled it high
with dry wood. When the 'possums were ready for
cooking, the sand beneath the fire was heated a foot
deep, and making a hole in this, the game was buried

and the fire continued above. After a time the embers were thrown off and the meat dug out. It looked burnt and black; but when the crust was broken the flesh within was tender and juicy. This, with clear water from the iron-stone hills, made a rare meal for hungry men; after which they continued their travel.

Before nightfall they had entered the first circle of hills at the foot of the mountains. With a springing hope in his heart, Moondyne led the way into the tortuous passes of the hills; and in a valley as silent as the grave, and as lonely, they made their camp for the night.

They were in the saddle before sunrise, and travelling in a strange and wild country, which no white man, except Moondyne, had ever before entered. The scene was amazing to the sergeant, who was used to the endless sameness of the gum forests on the plains of the convict settlement. Here, masses of dark metallic stone were heaped in savage confusion, and around these, like great pale serpents or cables, were twisted the white roots of tuad trees. So wild was the scene with rock and torrent, underbrush and forest, that the sergeant, old bushman as he was, began to feel that it would be dangerous for a man who had not studied the lay of the land, to travel here without a guide. However, he had a deep game to play, for a great stake. He said nothing, but watched Moondyne closely, and observed everything around that might assist his memory by-and-by.

In the afternoon they rode through winding passes in the hills, and toward sunset came on the border of a lake in the basin of the mountains.

"Now," said Moondyne, dismounting by the lakeside, and turning loose his horse to crop the rich grass, "now we may rest. We are inside the guard of the hills."

The sergeant's manner had strangely altered during

the long ride. He was trembling on the verge of a great discovery; but he was, to a certain extent, in the power of Moondyne. He could not help feeling that the man was acting truly to his word; but his own purpose was so dark and deceitful, it was impossible for him to trust another.

The punishment of falsehood is to suspect all truth. The mean of soul cannot conceive nobility. The vicious cannot believe in virtue. The artificial dignity imparted by the sergeant's office had disappeared, in spite of himself; and in its place returned the caitiff aspect that had marked him when he was a convict and a settler. Standing on an equality with Moondyne, their places had changed, and the prisoner was the master.

On the sandy shore of the beautiful lake they found turtles' eggs, and these, with baked bandicoot, made supper and breakfast.

On resuming their ride, next morning, Moondyne said: "To-night we shall reach the gold mine."

The way was no longer broken; they rode in the beds of grassy valleys, walled by precipitous mountains. Palms, bearing large scarlet nuts, brilliant flowers and birds, and trees and shrubs of unnamed species — all these, with delicious streams from the mountains. made a scene of wonderful beauty. The face of Moondyne was lighted up with appreciation; and even the sergeant, coarse, cunning, and brutish, felt its purifying influence.

It was a long day's ride, broken only by a brief halt at noon, when they ate a hearty meal beside a deep river that wound its mysterious way among the hills. Hour after hour passed, and the jaded horses lagged on the way; but still the valleys opened before the riders, and Moondyne advanced as confidently as if the road were familiar.

Toward sunset he rode slowly, and with an air of expectancy. The sun had gone down behind the

mountains, and the narrow valley was deep in shadow.
Before them, standing in the centre of the valley, rose
a tall white tuad tree, within fifty paces of the underwood of the mountain on either side.

When Moondyne, who led the way, had come within a horse's length of the tree, a spear whirred from the
dark wood on the right, across his path, and struck
deep into the tuad tree.   There was not a sound in the
bush to indicate the presence of an enemy.   The
gloom of evening had silenced even the insect life,
and the silence of the valley was profound.   Yet
there was startling evidence of life and hostility in
the whirr of the spear, that had sunk into the tree
before their eyes with such terrific force that it
quivered like a living thing as it stood out from the
tuad.

Moondyne sprang from his horse, and, running to
the tree, laid his hand on the shivered spear, and
shouted a few words in the language of the aborigines.
A cry from the bush answered, and the next moment
a tall savage sprang from the cover and threw himself
with joyful acclamations at the feet of Moondyne.

Tall, lithe, and powerful was the young bushman.
He arose and leant on his handful of slender spears,
speaking rapidly to Moondyne.   Once he glanced at
the sergeant, and, smiling, pointed to the still quivering spear in the tuad.   Then he turned and led them
up the valley, which soon narrowed to the dimensions
of a ravine, like the bed of a torrent, running its perplexed way between overhanging walls of iron-stone.

The sun had gone down, and the gloom of the passage became dark as midnight.   The horses advanced
slowly over the rugged way.   A dozen determined
men could hold such a pass against an army.   Above
their heads the travellers saw a narrow slit of sky,
sprinkled with stars.   The air was damp and chill between the precipitous walls.   The dismal pass was

many miles in length ; but at last the glare of a fire
lit up the rocks ahead.

The young bushman went forward alone, returning
in a few minutes. Then Moondyne and the sergeant,
proceeding with him to the end of the pass, found
themselves in the opening of a small valley or basin.
over which the sky, like a splendid domed roof, was
clearly rounded by the tops of the mountains.

A few paces from the entrance stood a group of
natives, who had started from their rest at the approach
of the party.

VIII.

THE KING OF THE VASSE.

BESIDE the bright fire of mahogany wood, and slowly
advancing to meet the strangers, was a venerable man
— an aborigine, tall, white-haired, and of great dignity.
It was Te-mana-roa (the long-lived), the King of the
Vasse.

Graver than the sedateness of civilization was the
dignified bearing of this powerful and famous barba-
rian. His erect stature was touched by his great age,
which outran, it was said, all the generations then
living. His fame as a ruler was known throughout
the whole Western country, and among the aborigines
even of the far Eastern slope, two thousand miles
away, his existence was vaguely rumored, as in former
times the European people heard reports of a mysterious oriental potentate called Prester John.

Behind the aged king, in the full light of the fire,
stood two young girls, dark and skin-clad like their
elder, but of surpassing symmetry of body and beauty
of feature. They were Koro and Tapairu, the grand-

children of Te-mana-roa. Startled, timid, wondering,
they stood together in the intense light, their soft fur
bokas thrown back, showing to rare effect their
rounded limbs and exquisitely curved bodies.

The old chief welcomed Moondyne with few words,
but with many signs of pleasure and deep respect; but
he looked with severe displeasure at his companion.

A long and earnest conversation followed; while
the cunning eyes of the sergeant, and the inquiring
ones of the young bushman and his sisters followed
every expression of the old chief and Moondyne.

It was evident that Moondyne was telling the reason of the stranger's presence — telling the story just
as it had happened — that there was no other hope
for life — and he had promised to show this man the
gold mine.

Te-mana-roa heard the story with a troubled brow,
and when it had come to 'an end, he bowed his white
head in deep thought. After some moments, he raised
his face, and looked long and severely at the sergeant,
who grew restless under the piercing scrutiny.

Still keeping his eyes on the trooper's face, he said
in his own tongue, half in soliloquy, and half in
query : —

" This man cannot be trusted ? "

Every eye in the group was now centred on the
sergeant's face.

After a pause, Moondyne simply repeated the words
of the chief : —

" He cannot be trusted."

" Had he come blindfolded from the Koagulup," continued the chief, " we might lead him through the
passes in the night, and set him free. He has seen
the hills and noted the sun and stars as he came : he
must not leave this valley."

The old chief uttered the last sentence as one **giving
judgment.**

"Ngaru," he said, still gazing intently on the trooper's face. The young bushman arose from the fire.

"He must not leave the pass, Ngaru."

Without a word the young and powerful bushman took his spears and *wammara*, and disappeared in the mouth of the gloomy pass.

Te-mana-roa then arose slowly, and, lighting a resinous torch, motioned the sergeant to follow him toward a dark entrance in the iron-stone cliff that loomed above them. The sergeant obeyed, followed by Moondyne. The men stooped to enter the face of the cliff, but once inside, the roof rose high, and the way grew spacious.

The walls were black as coal, and dripping with dampness. Not cut by the hands of man, but worn perhaps in ages past by a stream that worked its way, as patient as Fate, through the weaker parts of the rock. The roof soon rose so high that the torchlight was lost in the overhanging gloom. The passage grew wide and wider, until it seemed as if the whole interior of the mountain were hollow. There were no visible walls; but at intervals there came from the darkness above a ghostly white stalactite pillar of vast dimensions, down which in utter silence streamed water that glistened in the torchlight.

A terror crept through the sergeant's heart, that was only strong with evil intent. He glanced suspiciously at Moondyne. But he could not read the faces of the two men beside him. They symbolized something unknown to such as he. On them at that moment lay the great but acceptable burden of manhood — the overmastering but sweet allegiance that a true man owes to the truth.

It does not need culture and fine association to develop in some men this highest quality. Those who live by externals, though steeped in their parrot learning, are not men, but shells of men. When one

turns within his own heart, and finds there the motive
and the master, he approaches nobility. There is
nothing of a man but the word, that is kept or
broken — sacred as life, or unstable as water. By this
we judge each other, in philosophy and practice; and
by this test shall be ruled the ultimate judgment.

Moondyne had solemnly promised to lead to the
mine a man he knew to be a villain. The native chief
examined the bond of his friend, and acknowledged
its force.

The word of the Moondyne must be kept to-night.
To-morrow the fate of the stranger would be decided.

They proceeded far into the interior of the mountain,
until they seemed to stand in the midst of a great
plain, with open sky overhead, though in truth above
them rose a mountain. The light was reflected from
myriad points of spar or crystal, that shone above like
stars in the blackness. The air of the place was
tremulous with a deep, rushing sound, like the sweep
of a river; but the flood was invisible.

At last the old chief, who led the way, stood beside a
stone trough or basin, filled with long pieces of wood
standing on end. To these he applied the torch, and a
flame of resinous brightness swept instantly over the
pile and licked at the darkness above in long, fiery
tongues.

The gloom seemed to struggle with the light, like
opposing spirits, and a minute passed before the eye
took in the surrounding objects.

" Now," said Moondyne to the sergeant, raising his
hand and sweeping it around — " Now, you are within
the GOLD MINE OF THE VASSE."

The stupendous dimensions of the vault or chamber
in which they stood oppressed and terrified the sergeant. Hundreds of feet above his head spread the
shadow of the tremendous roof. Hundreds of feet
from where he stood loomed the awful blackness of the

cyclopean walls. From these he scarce could turn his eyes. Their immensity fascinated and stupefied him. Nor was it strange that such a scene should inspire awe. The vastest work of humanity dwindled into insignificance beside the immeasurable dimensions of this mysterious cavern.

It was long before consciousness of his purpose returned to the sergeant; but at length, withdrawing his eyes from the gloomy stretch of iron-stone that roofed the mine, his glance fell upon the wide floor, and there, on every side, from wall to wall, were heaps and masses of yellow metal — of dust and bars and solid rocks of gold.

IX.

A DARK NIGHT AND DAY.

THE old chief led the way from the gold mine; and the strangely assorted group of five persons sat by the fire while meat was cooked for the travellers.

The youth who had escorted the white men from the outer valley was the grandson of the chief, and brother of the beautiful girls. Savages they were, elder and girls, in the eyes of the sergeant; but there was a thoughtfulness in Te-mana-roa, bred by the trust of treasure and the supreme confidence of his race, that elevated him to an exalted plane of manhood; and the young people had much of the same quiet and dignified bearing.

The revelations of the day had been too powerful for the small brain of the cunning trooper. They came before his memory piecemeal. He longed for an opportunity to think them over, to get them into grasp, and to plan his course of action.

The splendid secret must be his own, and he must

overreach all who would to-morrow put conditions on
his escape. While meditating this, the lovely form
of one of the girls, observed by his evil eye as she bent
over the fire, suggested a scheme, and before the meal
was finished, the sergeant had worked far on the road
of success.

The chief and Moondyne talked long in the native
language. The sisters, wrapped in soft furs, sat and
listened, their large eyes fixed on the face of the Moondyne, their keen senses enjoying a novel pleasure as
they heard their familiar words strangely sounded on
his lips.

To their simple minds the strongly marked white
face must have appeared almost superhuman, known
as it had long been to them by hearsay and the un-
qualified affection of their people.

Their girlhood was on the verge of something fuller;
they felt a new and delicious joy in listening to the
deep musical tones of the Moondyne. They had long
heard how strong and brave he was; they saw that he
was gentle when he spoke to them and the old chief.
When he addressed them, it seemed that the same
thrill of pleasure touched the hearts and lighted the
faces of both sisters.

"One outside, and two here," was the dread burden
of the sergeant's thought. "Two days' ride —but, can
I be sure of the way?"

Again and again his furtive eyes turned on the
ardent faces of the girls.

"Ay, that will do," he thought, "these can be used
to help me out."

The sisters retired to a tent of skins, and, lighting
a fire at the opening to drive off the evil spirit, lay
down to rest. Sleep came slowly to every member of
the party.

The old chief pondered on the presence of the
stranger, who now held the primal secret of the native race

The sergeant revolved his plans, going carefully over every detail of the next day's work, foreseeing and providing for every difficulty with devilish ingenuity.

The sisters lay in dreamy wakefulness, hearing again the deep musical voice, and seeing in the darkness the strange white face of the Moondyne.

Before sleeping, Moondyne walked into the valley, and lifting his face to heaven, in simple and manful directness, thanked God for his deliverance; then, stretching himself beside the fire, he fell into a profound sleep.

In the morning, Moondyne spoke to Koro and Tapairu in their own tongue, which was not guttural on their lips. They told him, with much earnest gesture and flashing of eyes, about the emu's nest in the valley beyond the lake, and other such things as made up their daily life. Their steps were light about the camp that morning.

At an early hour the old man entered the gold mine, and did not return. To look after the horses, Moondyne, with the girls, crossed the valley, and then went up the mountain toward the emu's nest.

The sergeant, with bloodshot eyes from a sleepless night, had hung around the camp all the morning, feeling that, though his presence seemed unheeded, he was in the deepest thought of all.

Whatever his purpose, it was settled now. There was dark meaning in the look that followed Moondyne and the girls till they disappeared on the wooded mountain. When at last they were out of sight and hearing, he arose suddenly, and moved toward the mouth of the mine. At that moment, the young bushman from the outpost emerged from the pass, and walked rapidly to the fire, looking around inquiringly for Moondyne and the girls.

As the sergeant explained in dumb show that they

had gone up the mountain yonder, there rose a gleam of hideous satisfaction in his eyes. The danger he had dreaded most had come to his hand to be destroyed. All through the night he had heard the whirr of a spear from an unseen hand, and he shuddered at the danger of riding through the pass to escape. But there was no other course open. Were he to cross the mountains he knew that without a guide he never could reach the penal colony.

Had the sage Te-mana-roa been present, he would at once have sent the bushman back to his duty. But the youth had drawn his spear from the tuad tree at the outpost, and he proceeded to harden again its injured point in the embers of the fire.

The sergeant, who had carelessly sauntered around the fire till he stood behind the bushman, now took a stride toward him, then suddenly stopped.

Had the native looked around at the moment, he would have sent his spear through the stranger's heart as swiftly as he drove it into the tuad yesterday. There was murder in the sergeant's face as he took the silent stride, and paused, his hand on his pistol.

"Not with this," he muttered, "no noise with him. But this will do."

He stooped for a heavy club, and with a few quick and stealthy paces stood over the bushman. Another instant, and the club descended with crushing violence. Without a sound but the deadly blow, the quivering body fell backward on the assassin's feet.

Rapidly he moved in his terrible work. He crept to the entrance of the mine, and far within saw the old man moving before the flame. Pistol in hand he entered the cavern, from which, before many minutes had passed, he came forth white-faced. As he stepped from the cave, he turned a backward glance of fearful

import. He saw that he had left the light burning
behind him.

Warily scanning the mountain side, he dragged the
body of the youth inside the mouth of the cavern,
then, seating himself by the fire, he examined his pistols, and awaited the return of Moondyne and the
girls.

In the sweet peace of the valley, the livid and
anxious wretch seemed the impersonation of crime.
He had meditated the whole night on his purpose.
All he feared was partial failure. But he had provided for every chance; he had more than half succeeded already. Another hour, and he would be sole
master of the treasure — and, with the sisters in his
power, there was no fear of failure.

It was a terrible hour to wait; but at last he saw
them coming, the lithe figures of the girls winding
among the trees as they crossed the valley.

But they were alone: Moondyne was not with them!

They came with bent faces, as if thinking of pleasant things; but they started with affright, and drew
close together, when they saw the stranger, alone, rise
from the fire and come toward them.

With signs, he asked for Moondyne, and they answered that he had gone across the mountain, and
would return when the sun had gone down.

This was an ominous disappointment; but the sergeant knew that his life would not be worth one day's
purchase with such an enemy behind him. He must
wait.

He returned to the fire, the girls keeping distrust-
fully distant. He feared they might enter the mine,
and too soon discover the dreadful secret; so, getting
between them and the rock, he lay down at the
entrance.

Like startled deer, the girls looked around, instinctively feeling that danger was near. The evil eyes of

the sergeant never left them. He had not foreseen
this chance, and for the moment knew not how to
proceed.

The sisters stood near the fire, alarmed, alert, the
left hand of one in the right of the other. At length
their quick eyes fell upon blood on the sand, and
followed the track till they met again the terrible
face at the mouth of the mine.

And, as they looked, a sight beyond the prostrate
man, coming from the dark entrance, froze their hearts
with terror.

The face of the aged chief, his white hair discolored
with blood, appeared above the dreadful watcher, and
looked out toward the girls. The old man, who had
dragged his wounded body from the cave, rose to his
feet when he saw the sisters, tottered forward with a
cry of warning, and fell across the murderer.

Paralyzed with horror, the sergeant could not move
for some moments. But soon feeling that he was not
attacked, he pushed aside the senseless body, and
sprang to his feet with a terrible malediction. In that
moment of his blind terror, the girls had disappeared.

He ran hither and thither searching for them, but
found no trace of their hiding-place or path of escape.
At length he gave up the search, a shivering dread
growing upon him every instant, and hastened to
catch the horses. He began to realize that his well-
laid plan was a failure.

There was now only one course open. He must
take his chance alone, and ride for his life, neither
resting nor sleeping. The girls would run straight to
Moondyne; and he must act speedily to get beyond
his reach.

In a few minutes the horses were ready, standing at
the entrance of the mine. The sergeant entered, and,
passing the flaming basin, loaded himself with bars
and plates of gold. Again and again he returned, till

the horses were laden with treasure. Then, mounting he called the dogs; but they had gone with Moon-dyne.

Once more the chill of fear struck like an icicle through his heart at his utter loneliness. Leading the spare horse by the bridle, he rode headlong into the ravine and disappeared.

X.

ON THE TRAIL.

IT was evening, and the twilight was gray in the little valley, when Moondyne reached the camp. He was surprised to find the place deserted. He had expected a welcome — had been thinking, perhaps, of the glad faces that would greet him as he approached the fire. But the fire was black, the embers were cold. He looked and saw that there was no light in the gold mine.

A dreadful presentiment grew upon him. A glance for the saddles, and another across the valley, and he knew that the horses were gone. Following the strange action of the dogs, he strode toward the cave, and there, at the entrance, read the terrible story.

The sight struck this strange convict like a physical blow. His limbs failed him, and his body sank till he knelt on the sand at the mouth of the mine. He felt no wrath, but only crushing self-accusation.

" God forgive me!" was the intense cry of heart and brain: " God forgive *me* for this crime!"

The consequence of his fatal selfishness crushed him; and the outstretched arms of the old chief, whose unconsciousness, for he was not dead, was fearfully like death, seemed to call down curses on the destroyer of his people.

The years of his life went miserably down before Moondyne till he grovelled in the desolation of his dismal abasement. A ban had followed him, and blighted all he had touched.

Years were pressed into minutes as he crouched beside the maimed bodies of his friends. The living man lay as motionless as the dead. The strong mind brought up the whole scene for judgment. His inward eye saw the fleeing murderer; but he felt more of pity for the wretch than of vengeance. The entire sensibility of Moondyne was concentrated in the line of his own conscience. Himself accused himself, — and should the criminal condemn another?

When at last he raised his face, with a new thought of duty, the trace of the unutterable hour was graven upon him in deep lines.

Where were the sisters? Had they been sacrificed too? By the moonlight he searched the valley; he entered the cave, and called through all its passages. It was past midnight when he gave up the search and stood alone in the desolate place.

In the loose sand of the valley he scooped a grave, to which he carried the body of the young bushman, and buried it. When this was done he proceeded to perform a like office for Te-mana-roa, but looking toward the cave he was startled at the sight of the sisters, one of whom, Koro, stood as if watching him, while the other, aided by an extremely old woman, was tending on the almost dying chief, whose consciousness was slowly returning.

Benumbed and silent, Moondyne approached the cave. The girl who had watched him shrank back to the others. Tepairu, the younger sister, rose and faced the white man with a threatening aspect. She pointed her finger toward the pass.

"Go!" she said, sternly, in her own tongue.

Moondyne paused and looked at her.

"Begone!" she cried, still pointing; and once again came the words, "begone, *accursed!*"

Remorse had strangled grief in Moondyne's breast, or the agony of the girl, uttered in this terrible re proach, would have almost killed him. *Accursed* she said, and he knew that the word was true.

He turned from the place, not toward the pass, but toward the mountains, and walked from the valley with an aimless purpose, and a heart filled with ashes.

For hours he held steadily on, heedless of direction. He marked no places — had no thoughts — only the one gnawing and consuming presence of the ruin he had wrought.

The dogs followed him, tired and spiritless. The moon sank, and the sun rose, and still the lonely man held his straight and aimless road, — across mountains and through ravines, until at last his consciousness was recalled as he recognized the valley in which he stood as one he had travelled two days before, on the way to the gold mine.

Stretching his exhausted body on a sheltered bank beside a stream, he fell into a deep sleep that lasted many hours.

He awoke with a start, as if a voice had called him. In an instant his brow was set and his mind determined. He glanced at the sun to settle his direction, and then walked slowly across the valley, intently observing the ground. Before he had taken a hundred paces he stopped suddenly, turned at right angles down the valley, and strode on with a purpose, that though rapidly, almost instantaneously formed, had evidently taken full possession of his will.

Sometimes persons of keen sensibility lie down to sleep with a trouble on the mind, and an unsettled purpose, and wake in the night to find the brain clear and the problem solved. From this process of uncon-

scious cerebration Moondyne awoke with a complete
and settled resolution.

There could be no doubt of the determination in his
mind. He had struck the trail of the murderer.

There was no more indirection or hesitation in his
manner. He settled down to the pursuit with a grim
and terrible earnestness. His purpose was clear before
him — to stop the devil he had let loose — to prevent
the escape of the assassin — to save the people who
had trusted and saved him.

He would not turn from this intent though the track
led him to the prison gate of Fremantle ; and even
there, in the face of the guards, he would slay the
wretch before he had betrayed the secret.

Death is on the trail of every man ; but we have
grown used to him, and heed him not. Crime and Sin
are following us — will surely find us out, and some
day will open the cowl and show us the death's-head.
But more terrible than these Fates, because more physically real, is the knowledge ever present that a relent-
less human enemy is on our track.

Through the silent passes of the hills, his heart a
storm of fears and hopes, the sergeant fled toward
security. Every mile added to the light ahead. He
rode wildly and without rest — rode all day and into
the night, and would still have hurried on, but the
horses failed and must have rest.

He fed and watered them, watching with feverish
eyes the renewal of their strength ; and as he watched
them eat, the wretched man fell into a sleep, from
which he started in terror, fearful that the pursuer was
upon him.

Through the day and night, depending on his great
strength, Moondyne followed. While the fugitive
rested, he strode on, and he knew by instinct and
observation that he was gaining in the race.

Every hour the tracks were fresher. On the morn-

ing of the second day, he had found the sand still moist
where the horses had drank from a stream. On the
evening of that day he passed the burning embers of a
fire. The murderer was gaining confidence, and taking
longer rest.

The third day came with a revelation to Moondyne.
The sergeant had lost the way — had turned from the
valley that led toward the Settlement, and had sealed
his doom by choosing one that reached toward the immeasurable deserts of the interior.

The pursuer was not stayed by the discovery. To
the prison or the wilderness, should the track lead, he
would follow.

At first the new direction was pleasant. Dim woods
on either side of a stream, the banks fringed with verdure and pranked with bright flowers. But like the
pleasant ways of life, the tempting valley led to the
desolate plains ; before night had closed, pursuer and
pursued were far from the hills and streams, in the
midst of a treeless sea of sand.

Nothing but fear of death could drive the sergeant
forward. He was bushman enough to know the danger
of being lost on the plains. But he dare not return to
meet him whom he knew was hunting him down.

There was but one chance before him, and this was
to tire out the pursuer — if, as his heart suggested,
there was only one in pursuit — to lead him farther
and farther into the desert, till he fell on the barren
track and died.

It was sore travelling for horse and man under the
blazing sun, with no food nor water save what he
pressed from the pith of the palms, and even these
were growing scarce. The only life on the plains was
the hard and dusty scrub. Every hour brought a more
hopeless and grislier desolation.

How was it with Moondyne ? The strong will still
upheld him. He knew he had gained till they took to

the plains; but he also knew that here the mounted
man had the advantage. Every day the track was less
distinct, and he suffered more and more from thirst.
The palms he passed had been opened by the sergeant,
and he had to leave the trail to find one untouched.

The sun flamed in the bare sky, and the sand was so
hot that the air hung above it in a tremulous haze. In
the woods the dogs had brought him food; but no living thing was to be hunted on the plains. He had
lived two days on the pifh of the palms.

On the third day Moondyne with difficulty found
the sand trail, which had been blown over by the night
breeze. He had slept on the shelterless desert, and
had dreamt of sweet wells of water as the light dew
fell on his parched body.

This day he was quite alone. The dogs, suffering
from thirst, had deserted him in the night.

He began the day with a firm heart but an unsteady
step. There was not a palm in sight. It was hot noon
before he found a small scrub to moisten his throat
and lips.

But to-day, he thought, he must come face to face
with the villain, and would kill him like a wild beast
on the desert; and the thought upheld him.

His head was bare and his body nearly naked.
Another man would have fallen senseless under the
cruel sun; but Moondyne did not even rest, — as the
day passed he did not seem to need rest.

It was strange how pleasant, how like a dream, part
of that day appeared. Sometimes he seemed to be
awake, and to know that he was moving over the sand,
and with a dread purpose; but at these times he knew
that the trail had disappeared — that he was blindly
going forward, lost on the wilderness. Toward evening the cool breeze creeping over the sand dispelled the
dreams and made him mercilessly conscious.

The large red sun was standing on the horizon or

sand, and an awful shadow seemed waiting to fall upon the desert.

When the sun had gone down, and the wanderer looked at the stars, there came to him a new Thought, like a friend, with a grave but not unkind face — a vast and solemn Thought, that held him for a long time with upraised face and hands, as if it had been whispered from the deep quiet sky. Slowly he walked with his new communion, and when he saw before him in the moonlight two palms, he did not rush to cut them open, but stood beside them smiling. Opening one, at length, he took the morsel of pith, and ate, and slept.

How sweet it was to wake up and see the wide sky studded with golden stars — to feel that there were no bonds any more, nor hopes, nor heart-burnings.

The Divine Thought that had come to him the day before was with him still — grave and kindly, and now, they two were so utterly alone, it seemed almost to smile. He raised his body and knelt upon the sand, looking upward, and all things seemed closing quietly in upon him, as if coming to a great rest, and he would have lain down on the sand at peace — but a cry, a human-like cry, startled him into wakefulness, — surely it was a cry!

It was clear and near and full of suffering. Surely, he had heard — he had not dreamt of such a cry. Again — God! how near and how keen it was — from the darkness, — a cry of mortal agony!

With a tottering step Moondyne ran toward the woful sound. He saw by the moonlight a dark object on the sand. The long weak cry hurried him on, till he stood beside the poor throat whence it came, and was smote with pity at the dismal sight.

On the sand lay two horses, chained at the neck, — one dead, the other dying in an agony of thirst and imprisonment. Beside the dead horse, almost buried in the sand, as he had fallen from the saddle, lay a man, seemingly dead, but whose glazing eyes turned with hideous suffering as Moondyne approached. The wretched being was powerless to free himself from the fallen horse ; and upon his body, and all around him, were scattered heavy bars and plates of gold.

Moondyne loosed the chain from the suffering horse, that struggled to its feet, ran forward a few yards, and fell dead on the sand.

The men's eyes met, and the blistered lips of the sergeant — for it was he — moved in piteous appeal. Moondyne paused one stern moment, then turned and ran from the place — ran toward the palm near which he had slept. With hasty hand he tore it open and cut out the pith, and sped back to the sufferer. He knelt down, and squeezed the precious moisture into the mouth of the dying man — the man whom he had followed into the desert to kill like a wild beast.

Till the last drop was gone he pressed the young wood. Then the guilty wretch raised his eyes and looked at Moondyne — the glazed eyes grew bright, and brighter, till a tear rose within them, and rolled down the stained and sin-lined face. The baked lips moved, and the weak hands were raised imploringly. The sergeant fell back dead.

Moondyne knew that his last breath was contrition, and his last dumb cry, " Pardon."

Then, too, the strength faded from the limbs and the light from the eyes of Moondyne — and as he sank to the earth, the great Thought that had come to him filled his heart with peace — and he lay unconscious beside the dead.

The sun rose on the desert, but the sleeper did not move. Before the day was an hour old, other forms rapidly crossed the plain — not wanderers, but fierce, skin-clad men, in search of vengeance.

They flung themselves from their horses when they

reached the scene; and one, throwing himself upon the body of the sergeant, sprang back with a guttural cry of wrath and disappointment, which was echoed by the savage party.

Next moment, one of the natives, stooping to lay his hand on the heart of the Moondyne, uttered an excited call. The spearmen crowded around, and one poured water from a skin on the face and body of the senseless man.

They raised him to the arms of a strong rider, while another took the reins, and the wild party struck off at a full gallop toward the mountains.

When Moondyne returned to consciousness, many days after his rescue, he was free from pursuit, he had cut for ever the bond of the Penal Colony; above him bent the deep eyes and kind faces of the old chief and the sisters, Koro and Tepairu, and around him were the hills that shut in the Valley of the Vasse Gold Mine.

He closed his eyes again and seemed to sleep for a little while. Then he looked up and met the face of Te-mana-roa kindly watching him. " I am free ! " he only said. Then turning to the sisters : " I am not accursed ; " and Koro and Tepairu answered with kind smiles.

BOOK SECOND.

THE SANDALWOOD TRADE.

I.

THE MATE OF THE CANTON.

IT is midwinter, in a little Lancashire village on the coast, not far from Liverpool. One quiet main street, crossed by three or four short side streets, that lead in the summer days into the sweet meadows and orchards. One of these side streets has only three houses on one side, separated by goodly gardens. The house in the centre is the smallest, but it is extremely neat, and the garden fairly glows with color.

This is the home of Mrs. Walmsley, a widow; and the garden is looked after by herself and her daughter Alice, about sixteen years old. The house on the right of Mrs. Walmsley's belongs to Mr. Draper, the richest man in the village, a retired shopkeeper. The house on the left belongs to Captain Sheridan, a bluff old Irishman, retired from the Navy, and now Inspector of Coast Guards, whose family consists of his son and daughter — Will Sheridan, the son, being just twenty years old.

At the gate of Draper's garden, opening on the street, stands a handsome young man in the uniform of the merchant marine. He is Sam Draper, first officer of the *Canton*, arrived a few weeks before from China.

4

"Good-morning, Alice," he says in a cheerful but not a pleasant voice, as Alice Walmsley passes down the road.

Alice stopped and chatted lightly for a minute with her old schoolmate. Draper evidently paid her a compliment, for her cheeks were flushed as she entered her mother's gate, standing near which was young Sheridan, whom she slightly saluted and hurriedly passed, much to his surprise, for their relations were, at least, of the oldest and closest friendship.

"Alice," said Will, in a wondering tone, as the girl passed with her flushed face.

"Well — did you speak?" And she paused and turned her head.

Will Sheridan loved Alice, and she knew it, though no word had been spoken. He had loved her for years in a boy's way, cherishing her memory on his long voyages, for Will, too, was a sailor, as were almost all the young men of the village; but he was soon to leave home for a two years' service on Sam Draper's vessel, and of late his heart had been urging him to speak to Alice.

He was a quiet, thoughtful, manly young fellow, with nothing particular about him, except this strong secret love for the prettiest girl in the village.

"Yes, I spoke," he answered hesitatingly, as if wounded; "but perhaps you haven't time to listen."

"What is it, Will?" she said in a kindlier tone, and smiling, though before she spoke she saw with a side glance that Sam Draper had gone away from the gate.

"O, it isn't anything particular," said Will; "only there's rare skating on the mill-pond, and I was going there this afternoon."

"And —?" queried Alice, archly.

"Yes — I wish you would," said Will, earnestly.

"Well, I think I will," she replied, laughingly, "though you haven't told me yet what I am to do."

"Why, go skating with me," said Will, highly pleased; "Sam Draper and his sisters are going, and there will be a crowd from the village. Shall I come for you at three ?"

"Yes," she replied, "I'll be ready;" and as she turned toward her mother's house, the flush was in her face again.

. Will Sheridan walked lightly on, thinking happy thoughts. Passing Draper's gate, Sam Draper stepped from the shrubbery, whence he had observed the interview. He was a tall, handsome fellow, with fair hair and blue eyes; not the soft blue which usually denotes good nature, but a pale slaty blue that has a hard and shallow look. He had a free-and-easy way with him that made people who met him for the first time think he was cheerful and amiable. But if you observed him closely, you would see, in the midst of a boisterous laugh, that the cold blue eyes were keenly watching you, without a particle of mirth.

There was something never to be forgotten by those who discovered this double expression in Draper's face. He had a habit of waving his arms in a boisterous way, and bending his body, as if to emphasize the heartiness of his laugh or the warmth of his greeting. But while these visible expressions of jollity were in full play, if you caught the cold and calculating look from the blue eyes that were weighing you up while off your guard, you would shudder as if you had looked suddenly into the eyes of a snake.

Draper knew, too, that his face could be read by keen eyes; and he tried to mask even the habit of concealment, until at last his duplicity had become extremely artful and hard to be discovered. But he always knew the people who had caught his eye and read his soul. He never tried his boisterous manner on them again, but treated them gravely and quietly But these were the people he hated.

Seven years before, when he and Will Sheridan were school-boys, Sheridan not only saw through the falsehood of Draper's manner, but exposed it before the whole school. Nearly every boy in the school had had some reason to dislike Draper, but his loud good-natured way had kept them from speaking. But when Will Sheridan publicly pointed out the warm laugh and the cold eye, the friendly word and the cruel act, every one saw it at a glance, and a public opinion against Draper was instantly made among his school-fellows, which no after effort of his could quite remove.

From that day he nourished in his soul a secret desire to do Sheridan some injury that would cut him to the quick.

Not that Draper had no friends — indeed he was always making new friends — and his new friends were always loud in his praise; but when they ceased to be new, somehow, they ceased to admire Sam Draper, and either said they were mistaken in their first impression, or said nothing.

Both young men were sailors. Some years ago, the English merchant service was almost as well ordered and as precise in discipline and promotion as the Royal Navy, and young men of good position entered it as a profession. On his last voyage, Draper had become first mate; and Will Sheridan had lately engaged to take his old place on the *Canton* as second mate.

As Draper stepped from the shrubbery and hailed Will with a cheery word, his hand was outstretched in a most cordial way, and his lips smiled; but his eye was keen and smileless and as cold as ice. He had known for years of Will's affection for Alice Walmsley; and it was commonly said in the village that Alice returned his love.

" Why don't you ask Alice to go skating this afternoon ? " said Draper.

"I have just asked her," said Will, "and she is going."

"Bravo!" said Draper, in a hearty tone, so far as the sound went; "I thought she would like to be asked, when I told her half an hour ago that we were going."

Will Sheridan had some light word on his lip, but he did not speak it; and his smile faded, though without apparent cause, while he looked at Draper's pleasant face.

"She didn't say he had told her," he thought, and somehow the thought troubled him. But he put it away and forgot all about it before the afternoon.

The mill-pond was covered with skaters when Will and Alice arrived. They had often skated together before, and because Alice was timid on the ice, she used to hold Will's hand or take his arm; and now and then, and as often as he could, Will's arm was around her, as he struck out strongly and rapidly.

Unconsciously they had assumed settled relations toward each other,— she resting on him with confidence, and he quite assured of her trust.

To-day there was a disturbing element somewhere. Before they had been ten minutes on the ice, Will noticed that Alice was, for the first time in her life, listening inattentively to his words. And more than once he saw her looking over his shoulder, as if seeking some one in the crowd of skaters. After a while she evidently found whom she had sought, and her face brightened. Will, at the moment, asked her some question, and she did not hear him at first, but made him repeat the word.

With a strange sinking of the heart, he followed the direction of the girl's eyes, and was just in time to see Sam Draper kiss his hand to her — and Alice smiled.

Will Sheridan was a sensitive and proud young fellow, and his quick feelings of honor were wounded by what he perhaps too hastily deemed the deceit of

Alice Walmsley. A change had certainly come in her relation to him, but what right had he to charge her with deceit? He had no claim on her — had never spoken a word of love to her in his life.

The evening had closed when he left her at her mother's gate. They said "Good-night" in a new fashion — the words were as cold as the wind, and the touch of the hands was brief and formal.

After that Will did not ask Alice to walk or skate with him. He called no more at her mother's house as he used to do. He went to none of the usual places of meeting with her. If he had gone, he should have been all the more lonely; for he could not pretend to be pleasantly engaged with others while his heart was full of pain and unrest. But he could not help watching for her from his room window; and surely it were better for his happiness had he overcome this, too.

He saw that where he used to be, there every day was his rival. He heard Draper's loud and happy voice and laughter; and he noticed that Alice was happier and far more boisterous than ever he had known her — and that her happiness and gayety became even louder when she knew he was observing.

But at last came the time of the *Canton's* sailing. On the evening before leaving, Will Sheridan went to Mrs. Walmsley's to say good-by, and as Alice was not there, he remained talking with her mother, with whom he had always been a favorite. After a while he heard the gate swing, and saw Alice approaching the house, and Draper looking after her from the gate.

When Alice entered, he was standing and bidding farewell to her mother, who was weeping quietly.

Alice understood all, and the flush faded from her cheek.

"Good-by, Alice," he said, holding out his hand. "You know I am going away in the morning." He had walked toward the door as he spoke, keeping her hand, and now they stood in the porch.

He saw the tears in her eyes, and his courage gave way, for he had only a boy's heart to bear a man's grief; and he covered his face with his hands and sobbed.

In a few moments he was calm, and he bent over the weeping girl. "Alice!" he whispered, tenderly, and she raised her tear-stained face to his breast. Poor Will, yearning to take her in his arms, remembering what he had seen, only pressed her hands in his, and stooping, kissed her on the forehead again and again. Then he walked, tear-blinded, down the straight path to the gate.

A moment after, he felt a man's hand on his collar, and, turning, met the hard eyes of Draper. Sheridan's face was still quivering with the powerful emotion.

"What do you mean, Draper?" he demanded angrily, dashing the hand aside.

"I mean to let you know," said Draper, contemptuously, weighing the words, "that I saw all your snivelling scene, and that I have seen all your impertinent attentions to that girl."

Will Sheridan controlled himself by a violent effort, because the name of Alice Walmsley was in question.

"That girl, as you impertinently call her," he said, calmly, "is one of my oldest friends. My attentions have never been impertinent to her."

"You lie, you cur!" brutally answered Draper.

Though few words had been spoken, here was the culmination of an enmity that was old and rankling. On both sides there had been repression of feeling; but now the match had touched the powder, and the wrath flamed.

The word had barely passed the insulter's lips, when he reeled and tumbled headlong from Sheridan's terrible blow. As soon as the blow was delivered, Will turned, and walked toward his own home, never even looking behind.

It was half a minute before Draper picked himself from the frozen earth, still dazed with the shock. He showed no desire to follow, or continue the quarrel. With teeth set like a vise, and a livid face, he looked after the strong figure of Will, till he turned into his father's house.

Next day, the young men left the village, and entered on their duty as officers of the *Canton*, which lay in a Liverpool dock. No one knew of their quarrel, as neither had spoken of it, and there had been no witnesses.

The preparations for sea kept them apart for several days. The vessel sailed from Liverpool, and soon cleared the Channel. Two weeks later, when the ship passed on a beautiful night within sight of the Western Islands, the young men came face to face on the poop. Will Sheridan had come on deck to enjoy the delightful scene, not thinking that the first mate was officer of the watch.

" Draper," said Will, in a friendly tone, holding out his hand when they met, " I did not know you were engaged to Miss Walmsley. We should both be sorry for what happened that night."

The eyes of Draper glittered like steel as he answered in a sneering tone, —

" And who told you, sir, that I was engaged ? "

" I judge so from your conduct," said Will.

" You are not a good judge, then," answered Draper.

" Then there's all the less reason for us to quarrel, man. Take back your insulting words, and let me apologize for my violence."

" My insulting words — let me see, what were they ! Ah, yes," — he spoke slowly, as if he meant to wound with the repetition — " I think I said that I had been a witness to your snivelling scene of farewell — and that I was acquainted with your unsought and impertinent attentions to that girl. By the way, I may tell you that she herself made me acquainted with the offensive persistence of her obtuse admirer."

"*She* told you!" said Will, staggered by the word. "She said my love was offensive to her?"

"Ha! no — not love exactly," said the other, with the same biting sneer; "I believe you never gave her a chance to fling that in your teeth."

"Take care, Draper!" said Sheridan.

"Well, let us go on with the insulting words, as you choose to call them. I also said you were a liar, if I remember well; and a cur — did I not?"

"Why do you repeat the foul words, man?" asked Sheridan, indignantly.

"Why? Because I used them after careful choosing — because they are true! Stay!—" he added, raising his voice, and backing to the rail, as he saw Sheridan approaching. "I am the first officer of this ship, and if you dare to raise your hand against me, I will shoot you like a dog. We'll have no mutiny here."

"Mutiny!" cried Sheridan, more astounded and puzzled than angry. "What in heaven's name are you talking about? I want to be calm, Draper, for old time's sake. You call me vile names, and threaten my life, and yet I have given you no earthly cause. What do you mean?"

"I mean, that he who pretends to be my friend, while he ruins my character, is a liar; and that he who tells a slander in secret is a coward."

"Slander your character!" said Sheridan, "I never said an ill word of you — though I have unwillingly become acquainted with some things that I wish I had never known."

The latter part of the sentence was slowly added. Draper winced as if cut with a whip.

"You have made a charge," continued Sheridan,

sternly, "and you must explain it. How have I slan-
dered you?"

Draper hesitated. He hated the man before him,
like a fiend; but he hated still more the subject he
had now to touch.

"You knew about that girl in Calcutta," he said,
now fairly livid with passion; "no one in England
knew it but you."

"Yes," said Sheridan, slowly, "I learned something
about it, against my will."

"Against your will!" sneered the other, "was it
against your will you told the story to — her?"

Draper never repeated Alice's name, as if it were
unpleasant to his tongue.

"I never mentioned your shameful affairs," answered Sheridan, with scorn and indignation; "but
you are justly punished to have thought so."

"You did tell her!" cried Draper, terribly excited;
"you told her about my marriage in Calcutta."

"Your marriage!" and Sheridan stepped back, as
if recoiling from a reptile. Then, after a pause, as if
speaking to a condemned culprit, —

"Your infamy is deeper than I thought. I did not
know till now that your victim in Calcutta was also
your wife."

With lightning rapidity Draper saw the dreadful
confession his error had led him into. He knew that
Sheridan spoke the truth, and he hurriedly attempted
to close the grave he had exposed.

"She is dead," he said, searching Sheridan's face;
"you should have known that, too."

"Dead or alive, God have pity on her!" answered
Sheridan, whose face and voice were filled with revulsion and contempt. "For her sake, I pray that she
may be dead; but I do not believe you. I shall
see that those be warned in time who are still in
danger."

Sheridan deliberately turned on his heel and entered the cabin, while Draper, confounded and dismayed at his self-conviction, leant on the rail looking out at sea, cursing his own stupidity that had betrayed him.

" Who else could have known ? " he muttered ; " and who else could have told her ? But she doesn't wholly believe it — and, when I swore it was false that last evening, I think she believed me. I'll take care, at all events, that he shall have no chance to unsay my word."

For hours the brooding rascal walked the poop-deck, till the watch was changed, when he went below, and tried to sleep.

II.

COUNTERMINING THE MINER.

WILL SHERIDAN's life on the *Canton* was a restless and unhappy one from the night of his altercation with Draper. He was daily associated with a man who had exposed his own villany ; a caitiff so vile, that he had sought, and probably still intended, to blight the life of a girl he had known from childhood

The discipline of the ship required a certain courtesy and respect toward the first officer. This formal recognition Will paid, but nothing more.

A few days after this meeting, Draper made an advance toward intimacy ; but this was repelled with such cold severity as showed him that he had nothing to expect in future from Sheridan's forbearance.

" Do not dare to address me as a friend again," Will said, sternly ; " I shall write to England from the first port, and expose you as the scoundrel you are."

Draper's dry lips — his lips were always dry —

moved as if he were speaking, but no words came. His shallow eyes became wells of hate. He passed by Sheridan without reply, and went to his room.

There are a hundred ways in which the chief officer of a large ship can grind his inferiors; and Sheridan every day felt the subtle malevolence of his enemy. But these persecutions he did not heed. He knew that underneath these symptoms lay a more dangerous rancor that, sooner or later, would try to do him a deadly injury.

What the form of the attack might be, he knew not. But he prepared himself for emergencies. Will Sheridan was not only a brave and straightforward young fellow, but he had a clever head on his shoulders.

"Why should I let this cunning scoundrel injure me?" he asked himself. "His villany is easily seen through, — and I'm going to watch him closely."

He did watch him, and it served him well. Every secret and dangerous move he saw and disarranged. A trumped-up plan of mutiny among the men — which would have excused bloodshed, and the shooting of an officer, perhaps, by accident — he nipped in the bud, and almost exposed the machinations of him who hatched it.

Draper soon understood that he was playing with his master, and changed his method. He began to wait for an opportunity instead of making one.

This will be the case almost invariably; when honest men are fighting cowards and slanderers, the surest way to defeat them is by constant watchfulness. Evil-minded people are generally shallow, and easily countermined. Only, when they are countermined, they should be blown up, and never spared.

The *Canton* touched at Singapore for orders, and was detained a week. Will Sheridan resolved that on the night before she sailed he would leave the ship. Draper seemed to divine his purpose, and watched him like a tiger. But Will's constant attention to duty, and his equable temper, deceived the watcher.

The night before the *Canton* was to sail, Will dropt a bundle into a dingy under the bow, swung himself after it, and went ashore. A close search was made for him next day by the police, headed by Draper, the law in those ports being rigid against deserters. But he could not be found, and the *Canton* sailed without her second officer.

The first thing Will Sheridan did when he knew he was out of danger was to write to Mrs. Walmsley, warning her of Draper's marriage in India. This done, he set about getting some sort of employment.

He was in a strange place, and he knew no business except that of the sea. In a few days he shipped as mate on a bark bound for Western Australia, in the sandalwood trade.

A large and lucrative trade in sandalwood is carried on between China, India, and the Penal Colony. Vast districts in West Australia are covered with this precious wood, which is cut by ticket-of-leave men, and shipped to China and India, where it is used in the burning of incense in the Joss-houses or temples, and in the delicate cabinet and marquetry work which is so plentiful in oriental countries.

This was a life that suited Sheridan's vigorous temperament. He found his occupation pleasant, and would have quite forgotten the enmity of Draper; but he still feared that his influence over Alice Walmsley had not been broken.

He spent a year in the sandalwood trade, and was thinking of taking a trip to England, when he received a package through the post office at Shanghai, containing all his letters, and a brief unfriendly message in Alice Walmsley's handwriting, informing him that she was Captain Draper's wife, and that she scorned the cowardly nature that sought to destroy an honorable man's good name by malicious falsehood.

Will Sheridan was dumbfounded and grieved to the heart. In all he had previously borne, in his efforts to crush out of his heart a hopeless passion almost as strong as his life, he had, he thought, sounded the depths of his love for Alice Walmsley. But now, when he knew her utterly beyond his reach, and saw opening before her a desert life of misery and despair, the pity in his heart almost killed him. He would have given his life then that his enemy might be an honorable man. Her letter did not wound him, because he knew she had been deceived.

At first, he knew not what to do. He feared he had been hasty — he did not actually know that Draper was a villain — his own accusing word was not enough, perhaps, or it might bear an explanation. Should he write to Alice and take back his cruel charges? Or should he remain silent, and let time unravel the trouble?

To do the first would be wrong — to do the second might be wofully unjust. The true course was to find out the truth ; to go to Calcutta and learn for himself : and if he were wrong, to publicly make acknowledgment. If he were right, he could remain silent if it were for the best.

Two months afterward, Will Sheridan returned from Calcutta to Shanghai. He had found out the truth. He proceeded at once to Western Australia to join his ship, and from that time he wrote no more to England. One part of his life, the sweet and tender part, without fault of his, had suffered wofully, and had died before his eyes. It was shrouded in his memory, and buried in his heart. Like a brave man, he would not sit and moan over the loss. He set his face to his duty, hoping and praying that time would take the gnawing pain from his heart.

III.

THE SANDALWOOD AGENCY.

ABOUT a year after his trip to Calcutta, while his
ship lay in Shanghai, Sheridan received an invitation
to dinner from the chief owner, a wealthy and acute
old Scotchman, whose palatial residence and beautiful
grounds overlooked the town. He was surprised at
the courtesy, and showed the invitation to the captain,
a kind old sailor, who had formed an affection for Will
from the first.

"Go, go, my lad," said Captain Mathews. "It's a
piece of luck, no doubt. I've heard that the old man
has a daughter, or a niece, though I believe she's rather
tough; but what's that, when she has a shipload of
money? You're in luck, youngster; of course you'll
go, and in your best rig, too. I'll lend you my old
claw-hammer coat."

"Thank you, Captain," said Will, smiling inwardly,
as his eye took in the short but portly dimensions of
his old friend; "but I think I'll go as a plain sailor,
without any pretence at society dress."

"Well, I don't know but you're right, Sheridan,"
responded the captain; "a sailor's jacket is fit for any
man or any place, lad, when he who wears it loves his
profession, and is worthy of it."

That evening saw Will Sheridan enter Mr. MacKay's
drawing-room, as handsome and gentlemanly a fellow
as ever gave an order through a trumpet.

"Mr. Sheridan," said the kind old merchant, coming
forward to meet him, "you are welcome, for your own
sake, and for that of a dear old friend. You are
not aware, I think, that your father and I were mid-
shipmen together forty years ago."

Will was surprised, but gratified. He had half expected to be patronized, and indeed was more than half prepared to resent such treatment.

Mr. MacKay presented Will to his family — Mrs. MacKay, an invalid, and his step-daughter, Miss Gifford, a handsome, buxom, good-natured maiden lady of a certain age.

They were all very kind, and they treated Will as an old and privileged friend. He forgot all about the patronage, and enjoyed himself immensely. Such an evening of home life, after years of rugged seafaring, was delightfully restful.

At dinner, Mr. MacKay recalled story after story of the time when he and Will's father were careless youngsters on His Majesty's ship *Cumberland*. Will was still more surprised to find that Mr. MacKay had recently been in communication with his father.

"I saw your papers, Mr. Sheridan," explained Mr. MacKay; "and knowing that my old friend was in the Coastguard Service in England, I wrote to him. I found I was right in my conclusion; but I thought I would say nothing about the matter for some time. You will pardon me when I tell you that I have been observing you closely since you entered the service of our Company."

This was the first reference to their relative positions which had been made. Will did not know what to answer.

"You have seen a good deal of our sandalwood trade," said Mr. MacKay, changing the subject; "what do you think of its prospects, Mr. Sheridan?"

This was too extensive a question for Will, and he faltered in his reply. He had, he said, only considered his own duties in the trade, and they offered a limited scope for observation.

The old merchant, however, returned to the point.

"Captain Mathews tells me that you have expressed to him your dissatisfaction at the management of our affairs in Western Australia."

"No, sir," answered Will with a smile, "not with the management, but with the mismanagement."

"Ah, just so," said Mr. MacKay; "we will talk more about this by-and-by."

When the ladies had retired, Mr. MacKay again took up the subject.

"You think our affairs in Australia are mismanaged, then?"

"Well, sir, it appears to me there is no system whatever on the other side, so far as the Company's interests are concerned."

"How is that?" asked the keen business man, opening his eyes. "Does not our agent purchase and ship the sandalwood?"

"Yes, he certainly does, and that's all he does — and that's nothing," said blunt Will, "at least for the Company's benefit."

"Please explain," said Mr. MacKay, nervously.

"Well," said Will, in his earnest way when interested, "as you know, the sandalwood is cut away in the bush, from sixty to a hundred miles from the shipping-station at Bunbury. It is cut by ticket-of-leave men. From them it is bought by speculators, who team it to Bunbury; and from these fellows, who manage to control the wood, your agent buys it at the wharf, paying whatever price is asked."

"You would have him do more?" asked MacKay.

"I would change the whole plan, sir, if it were my concern. First, I would lease all, or as much as I could, of the sandalwood land direct from the Government, then I would set my hired cutters to work, and then carry the wood in my own teams to the wharf. The original cost can be decreased at least fifty per cent. And, besides this, there are other valuable substances, such as gum, tan-bark, and skins, that could be carried and shipped at the same time."

The merchant listened attentively to the broad out-

line of Will's plans, which he spoke about quite freely,
as one outside the matter, but familiar with it.

"Mr. Sheridan," said Mr. MacKay at length, "our
Company has decided to change our agent in Western
Australia, and it gives me great pleasure to offer you
the position.   I will see," he added, interrupting Will's
surprised exclamation, "that you shall have sufficient
power at your disposal to carry out your ideas with
regard to the extension of the trade."

Will hardly heard another word for the rest of the
evening.   His mind scarcely took in the change — from
the poor and unknown sailor, at one step, to a man of
large influence and position, for such would be the
Australian agent of so wealthy a Company.

When he returned to the ship his face flamed with
excitement, as he related the wonderful story to his
old friend Captain Mathews, who became even more
excited than Will — and declared many times over
his glass of " Old Tom," that " they were beginning to
see things right at last," and that " no man could do
land business so well as him who was trained at sea,"
and divers other sentences filled with wisdom drawn
from personal pride and marine philosophy.

IV.

THE TEAMSTERS' TAVERN.

" CURSE that fellow !" hissed Lame Scotty through
his clenched teeth, " I hate him."   The word was emphasized by a blow on the rickety table that made the
glasses jump.

The scene was a public house in the little mahogany
town of Bunbury, Western Australia ; the time, six
months after Will Sheridan had assumed the sandal-

wood agency. The speaker was a ticket-of-leave man, a wiry, red-eyed fellow of middle age, whose face had the cunning ferocity of a ferret. His auditors were a shaggy crowd of woodcutters and ex-convict teamsters, the latter group sitting with him at a long table.

" Don't talk so loud, Scotty," said a rough-looking man of immense stature, with an axe strapped on his back, who leant smoking against the fireplace ; " don't shout so, my friend, or Agent Sheridan will hear it, and kick you out of the team he gave you for charity."

" Kick me out !" retorted Scotty, with an oath ; " he daren't touch me. Curse his charity ; he gave me a team for his own interest."

" Bah !" said the big woodcutter, without moving, " you were always a brag. He gave work and wages to you and a lot of your ugly gang there, for downright charity ; and, like the hounds you always were, you have no thanks in you."

Though the gang so broadly referred to were at the table with Scotty, no one resented the woodcutter's epithet, though dark looks were flung at him.

" This agent has ruined the sandalwood trade," said Scotty, addressing himself to the aroused woodcutters. " Before he came here, a poor man could earn a few pounds ; but now we ain't any better than chain-gang men."

A murmur of approval from the teamsters followed the remark, and Scotty felt that he had struck a popular note. Even one or two of the woodcutters at another table struck the board in approval.

" No, you ain't any better than chain-gang men, that 's true," said the brawny bearer of the axe, still quietly smoking ; " nor you never were. There 's where the whole boiling lot of you ought to be still. *You* talk of ruining poor men," he continued, slightly

shifting his position, so as to face Scotty, "you darned
fox! I know you — and these men know you," pointing
to the group of woodcutters.   'Before this new system
came with this new agent, you and your rats there had
the whole trade in your hands. You bought from the
cutters at your own price, and you paid them in rum.
You cheated the woodcutters and swindled the dealers,
till the wonder was that some day you weren't found
chopped to pieces for your villany."

"That's true as Gospel," said one of the woodcutters
who had lately applauded Scotty.   "You're an infernal
set of wampires, you are!"

Scotty and his ill-looking crew realized that the
woodcutter "had got the drop on them, dead sure."

A stamping and tramping in the outer room or store
suggested new arrivals, as the place was a kind of inn.
All eyes were turned on the door, where entered, one
after another, about a dozen powerful fellows, in the
picturesque garb of stockriders, who noisily but good-
humoredly sat them down to the large central table,
and called for something to eat and drink.

The interrupted discussion was not resumed, but
a whispered and earnest comment on the new-comers
began among Scotty's gang.

"Where do you fellows hail from?" asked the big
woodcutter, after waiting a while, and in a friendly
tone.

"From Dardanup," said one of the stockriders. The
whispering between Scotty and his friends ceased, the
last word passed round being strongly emphasized,
"*Dardanup Irish.*"

There was a colony of Irish settlers at Dardanup, free
men, who had emigrated there forty years before, when
the Western Colony was free from the criminal taint.
The families were all related to each other by inter-
marriage; and the men of the whole settlement, who
had been born and reared in the bush, were famous

throughout the colony for strength, horsemanship, good-fellowship, and hard fighting qualities.

"From Dardanup — eh?" said the big woodcutter, with a mischievous smile at Scotty's group. "Then you be Agent Sheridan's new teamsters, maybe?"

"Ay, we're going to take those teams up to-morrow," said a strong fellow; and then, to call the waiter, he hammered the table with his enormous fist.

"Why," said the woodcutter in his bland way; "it might be as you're the Maguire boys from Dardanup?"

"Only eight Maguires in this crowd," said the table-hammerer, with a pleasant look round the circle.

Scotty and one or two of his friends here gently left their seats, and sauntered toward the door.

"Don't go," said the woodcutter pressingly; "don't be in a hurry, Scotty, man; why it isn't ten minutes ago since you wanted to chaw up that d——d Sheridan and his teamsters."

Scotty scowled at the woodcutter. "A man can come and go as he pleases, can't he?" he growled.

"O, ay; but don't leave the friends as you wanted to meet, just now. Here, you Dardanup fellows, this is your ganger in the teams; this is your 'boss,' as Yankee Sullivan says. This is the fellow that says Agent Sheridan darsn't order him, and that the agent went down on his knees and begged him to drive his black ox team."

"He'll never drive it again," said one of the Dardanup men.

"Why won't he?" demanded one of Scotty's friends.

"Because *I'm* going to drive that team," said the six-foot Australian, wheeling his seat with an ominous velocity.

"Ho, ho! ha, ha!" roared the big woodcutter, enjoying the fallen crest of the braggart; "but you can't have that team, Maguire; Scotty will make ribbons of you."

And the man with the axe heavily stamped on the

floor in his boisterous enjoyment of Scotty's discomfiture.

The Dardanup man rose and walked toward Scotty, who sank back with so sudden a dismay that he stumbled and fell headlong, while a waiter, entering with a tray of plates and glasses, tumbled across the prostrate bully.

At this there was a loud laugh, and the six-footer from Dardanup sat down again. Scotty, too, was wise enough to profit by the hilarity. He picked himself up, laughing with the rest.

"Come," he cried in a jolly tone, but with a humiliated aspect, as if he feared his offer would be refused, "let us have a drink and shake hands, no matter who has the teams."

"Bravo!" cried the Dardanup men, who were just as ready to drink as to fight.

The bottle was passed round, and every man drank with Scotty, except the big woodcutter.

Scotty handed him the bottle and a glass, noticing that he had not tasted.

"No, thank you," said the big man, with a shake of the head, "none of that for me."

A few moments afterwards one of the Dardanup men held up his glass to the big man of the axe. "Drink with me," he said.

"Ay, lad," said the woodcutter, "pass your bottle. I'll drink with you all night."

Scotty pretended not to have noted nor heard; but as soon as he could he escaped from the room with his associates. The Dardanup men ate a mighty supper, and afterwards had a wild time, in which the woodcutter was a partaker.

Powerful and hearty fellows, full of good-nature, but dangerous men to rouse, these young Australians, and their strong blood was excited by the new enterprise they had undertaken.

A combination had been made among the ticket-of-leave teamsters and buyers against the new agent of the sandalwood trade, who had revolutionized the old system. It had come to a serious pass with the business, and Agent Sheridan, knowing that a weak front would invite ruin, had resolved to test the opposition at once, rather than wait for its bursting.

He rode to Dardanup, and called a meeting of the stockriders, who, though every one born in Australia, and bred to the bush from infancy, had a warm feeling for Sheridan, perhaps because of his Irish name. He laid the case before them without hiding the danger.

The ticket-of-leave teamsters were resolved to destroy the sandalwood teams of the company, by rolling great rocks on them as they passed through the Black-wood Gorge.

The Blackwood Gorge was the narrow bed of a stream that wound among the Iron-stone Hills. In the rainy season it was filled with a violent flood ; but for six months of the year its bed was quite dry, and was used as a road to reach the sandalwood districts. For more than thirty miles the patient oxen followed this rugged bridle path ; and for the whole distance the way zigzagged between the feet of precipices and steep mountains.

It would be an easy matter to block up or destroy a slow-moving train in such a gully. And that the discharged ticket-of-leave teamsters had determined on this desperate revenge, the fullest proof was in the hands of Agent Sheridan.

He had considered the matter well, and he was resolved on a plan of action. He told the Dardanup bushmen that he wanted twenty-four men, twelve to act as teamsters, and twelve as a reserve. In a few minutes he had booked the names and settled the conditions with two dozen of the strongest and boldest men in Western Australia.

The meeting in the tavern was the first intimation
the ticket-of-leave men had that their plan had been
discovered.

Next morning, the teams passed peacefully through
the little town, while the discomfited Scotty and his
friends looked on from their skulking-places, and
never stirred a finger.

That evening, in the tavern, Scotty and his men
were moodily drinking, and at another table sat half a
dozen Dardanup stockriders. The woodcutter with the
axe was smoking, as he lounged against the fireplace.

" Why didn't you Dardanup boys go along with the
others ? " he asked the stockriders.

Scotty and his ill-looking group turned their heads
to hear the reply.

" We stayed behind to watch the wind ! " answered
one, with a laugh.

" To watch the wind ? " queried the big woodcutter.

" Ay," said the Dardanup man, very slowly, and
looking squarely at the ticket-of-leave teamsters ; " if
the wind blows a stone as big as a turtle's egg down
the Blackwood Gorge to-morrow, we 'll put a swinging
ornament on every one of those twenty gum trees on
the square. The rope is ready, and some one ought to
pray for fine weather. Just one stone," continued the
giant, who had risen to light his pipe ; and as he
passed he laid a heavy hand on Scotty's shoulder, as if
by chance ; " just one stone, as big as a turtle's egg,
and we begin to reeve that rope."

" Ha, ha ! ho, ho ! " roared the woodcutter, and the
shanty shook with his tremendous merriment. When
his derision had exhausted itself, he sat with the Dardanup men, and drank and sang in great hilarity over
the routing of Scotty's gang.

From that day, the new agent of the sandalwood trade
was treated with marked respect by all classes in
Western Australia. •

V.

IN SEARCH OF HIS SORROW.

NINE years crowded with successful enterprise had made Will Sheridan a strong man in worldly wisdom and wealth. His healthy influence had been felt and acknowledged all over the West Australian Colony. His direct attack on all obstacles never failed, whether the barriers were mountains or men.

He had raised the sandalwood trade into cosmopolitan commerce. In nine years he had made a national industry for the country in which he lived; had grown rich himself, without selfishly seeking it, and in proportion had made millionnaires of the company that employed him.

When men of large intelligence, foresight, and boldness, break into new fields, they may gather gold by the handful. So it was with this energetic worker. His practical mind turned everything into account. He inquired from the natives how they cured the beautiful soft kangaroo skins they wore as *bokas*, and learned that the red gum, tons of which could be gathered in a day, was the most powerful tan in the world.

He at once shipped twenty tons of it to Liverpool as an experiment. The next year he transported two hundred thousand pounds' worth; and five years from that time, Australian red gum was an article of universal trade.

He saw a felled boolah-tree change in the rainy season into a transparent substance like gum arabic; and three years afterwards, West Australia supplied nearly all the white gum in the markets of civilization.

One might conclude that the man who could set
his mind so persistently at work in this energetic
fashion must be thoroughly engaged, and that his rapid
success must have brought with it a rare and solid
satisfaction. Was it so with Agent Sheridan?

Darkest of all mysteries, O secret heart of man,
that even to its owner is unfathomed and occult!
Here worked a brave man from year to year, smiled
on by men and women, transmuting all things to gold;
vigorous, keen, worldly, and gradually becoming phil-
osophic through large estimation of values in men and
things; yet beneath this toiling and practical mind of
the present was a heart that never for one day, through
all these years, ceased bleeding and grieving for a dead
joy of the past.

This was the bitter truth. When riding through
the lonely and beautiful bush, where everything was
rich in color, and all nature was supremely peaceful,
the sleepless under-lying grief would seize on this
strong man's heart and gnaw it till he moaned aloud
and waved his arms, as if to put physically away from
him the felon thought that gripped so cruelly.

While working, there was no time to heed the
pain—no opening for the bitter thought to take shape.
But it was there always — it was alive under the ice —
moving in restless throbs and memories. It stirred at
strange faces, and sometimes it beat wofully at a
familiar sound.

No wonder that the man who carried such a heart
should sooner or later show signs of the hidden sorrow
in his face. It was so with Will Sheridan. His
worldly work and fortune belonged only to the nine
years of his Australian life; but he knew that the
life lying beyond was that which gave him happiness
or misery.

He became a grave man before his time; and one
deep line in his face, that to most people would have

denoted his energy and intensity of will, was truly graven by the unceasing presence of his sorrow.

He had loved Alice Walmsley with that one love which thorough natures only know. It had grown into his young life as firmly as an organic part of his being. When it was torn from him there was left a gaping and bleeding wound. And time had brought him no cure.

In the early days of his Australian career he had received the news of his father's death. His mother and sister had been well provided for. They implored him to come home; but he could not bear to hear of the one being whose memory filled his existence; and so he never wrote to his people. Their letters ceased; and in nearly nine years he had never heard a word from home.

But now, when his present life was to outward appearance all sunshine, and when his future path lay through pleasant ways, the bitter thought in his heart rankled with unutterable suffering. Neither work nor excitement allayed the pang. He shrank from solitude, and he was solitary in crowds. He feared to give rein to grief; yet alone, in the moonlit bush, he often raised his face and hands to heaven, and cried aloud in his grievous pain.

At last the thought came that he must look his misery in the face — that he must put an end to all uncertainty. Answering the unceasing yearning in his breast, he came to a decision.

"I must go home," he said aloud one day, when riding alone in the forest. "I must go home — if only for one day."

VI.

THE DOOR OF THE CELL.

IT was winter again. A sunburnt, foreign-looking man stood on the poop deck of a steamer ploughing with decreased speed past the docks in the long line of Liverpool shipping. The man was young, but, with deep marks of care and experience on his face, looked nearly ten years older than he really was. From the face, it was hard to know what was passing in the heart; but that no common emotion was there might be guessed by the rapid stride and the impatient glance from the steamer's progress to the shore.

It was Will Sheridan; but not the determined, thoughtful Agent Sheridan of the Australian sandal-wood trade. There was no quietness in his soul now, there was no power of thought in his brain; there was nothing there but a burning fever of longing to put his foot on shore; and then to turn his face to the one spot that had such power to draw him from the other side of the world.

As soon as the steamer was moored, heedless of the Babel of voices around him, the stranger passed through the crowd, and entered the streets of Liverpool. But he did not know the joy of an exile returning after a weary absence. He did not feel that he was once more near to those who loved him. It was rather to him as if he neared their graves.

The great city in which he walked was as empty to him as the great ocean he had just left. Unobservant and unsympathetic, looking straight before him, and seeing with the soul's vision the little coast village of his boyhood, he made his way to the railway station, bought a ticket for home, and took his place in the car.

At first, the noise and rush of the train through the

cold evening of a winter day, was a relief to the restless traveller. The activity fell upon his morbid heart
like a cold hand on a feverish forehead. But, as the
sun sank, and the cheerless gray twilight crept round
him, the people who had travelled from the city were
dropped at the quiet country stations, and sped away
to their happy homes.

A man came and lighted a lamp in the carriage,
and all the outer world grew suddenly dark. The
traveller was alone now; and, as the names of the way-
side stations grew more familiar, a stillness fell upon
him, against which he made no struggle.

At last, as once more the train moved to a station,
he arose, walked slowly to the door, and stepped on
the platform. He was at the end of his journey —
he was at home.

At home! He passed through the little station-
house, where the old porter stared at his strange face
and strange clothes, and wondered why he did not ask
the way to the village. On he strode in the moonlight,
glancing at familiar things with every step; for ten
years had brought little change to the quiet place.
There were the lone trees by the roadside, and the
turnpike, and down in the hollow he saw the moon's
face reflected through the ice in the millpond; and
seeing this, he stopped and looked, but not with the
outward eye, and he saw the merry skaters, and Alice's
head was on his shoulder, and her dear voice in his
ear, and all the happy love of his boyhood flooded his
heart, as he bowed his face in his hands and sobbed.

Down the main street of the village he walked,
glancing at the bright windows of the cottage homes,
that looked like smiles on well-known faces. He
passed the post office, the church, and the inn; and a
few steps more brought him to the corner of his own
little street.

The windows of the Drapers' house were lighted, as

if for a feast or merry-making within; but he passed
on rapidly, and stopped before the garden-gate of the
widow's cottage. There, all was dark and silent. He
glanced through the trees at his own old home, which
lay beyond, and saw a light from the kitchen, and the
moonlight shining on the window of his own room.

But here, where he longed for the light, there was
no light. He laid his hand on the gate, and it swung
open before him, for the latch was gone. He passed
through, and saw that the garden-path was rank with
frozen weeds, and the garden was itself a wilderness.
He walked on and stood in the porch, and found a bank
of snow against the bottom of the cottage door, which
the wind had whirled in there, perhaps a week before.

He stood in the cheerless place for a moment, looking into his heart, that was as empty as the cottage
porch, and as cold; and then he turned and walked
down the straight path, with almost the same feeling
that had crushed him so cruelly eleven years before.

He passed on to his own home, which had been
shut out from his heart by the cloud that covered
his way; and a feeling of reproach came upon him, for
his long neglect of those who loved him. Those who
loved him! there was a something warming in his
heart, and rising against the numbness that had stilled
it in the cottage porch. He stood before the door
of his old home, and raised his hand and knocked
twice.

The door opened, and a strange face to William
Sheridan met his look. Choking back a something
in his throat, he said, with an effort:—

"Is this Mrs. Sheridan's house?"

"It was Mrs. Sheridan's house, sir," answered the
man; "but it is my house now. Mrs. Sheridan is
dead."

Another cord snapped, and the stranger in his own
place turned from the door with a moan in his heart

As he turned, a young woman came from within to the porch ; and the man, with a sudden exclamation, stepped after him, and placing his hand on his shoulder, said earnestly, " Be this William Sheridan, that we thought were dead ? " and, looking in his face and recognizing him, he muttered, " Poor lad ! poor lad ! dont 'ee know thy old schoolmate, Tom Bates, and thy own sister Mary ? "

Taking him by the arm, the kind fellow led Sheridan to the door, and said : —

" Wife, here be thy brother Will, safe and sound, and not drownded, as Sam Draper told us he were — and d—n that same Draper for all his evil doin's ! "

Then William Sheridan felt his kind sister's arms on his neck, and the associations of his youth thronged up like old friends to meet him, and with them came the sweet spirit of his boy's love for Alice. They came to his heart like stormers to a city's gate, and, seeing the breach, they entered in, and took possession. For the second time that night, the strong man bowed his head, and sobbed — not for a moment as before, but long and bitterly, for the suppressed feelings were finding a vent at last; the bitterness of his sorrow, so long and closely shut in, was flowing freely.

Brother and sister were alone during this scene; but after a while, Mary's kind-hearted husband entered, a rugged but tender-hearted Lancashire farmer ; and knowing that much was to be said to Will, and that this was the best time to say it, he began at once; but he knew, and Will Sheridan knew, that he began at the farthest point he could from what he would have to say before the end. Will Sheridan's face was turned in the shadow, where neither his sister nor her husband could see it, and so he listened to the story.

" Will," said his brother-in-law, " tha knows 'tis more'n six years since thou went to sea, and that gret changes have come to thee since then ; and tha knows, lad, thou must expect that changes as gret have come to this village. Thy father took sick about a year after thou went, and grieved that he didn't hear from thee. Samuel Draper wrote to his people that thou'd turned out a bad lad, in foreign countries, and had to run away from the ship; and when that news came, it made th' old people sorrowful. Thy father took to his bed in first o' th' winter, and was dead in a few months. Thy mother followed soon, and her last words were a blessing for thee if thou were living. Then Samuel Draper came back from sea, looking fine in his blue uniform; and he said he'd heard thou'd been drownded on a voyage from China. He went to sea again, six months after, and he's never been here since; and 'tis unlikely," Mary's husband said very slowly, "that he ever will come to this village any more."

Tom Bates ceased speaking, as if all were told, and stared straight at the fire; his wife Mary, who was sitting on a low seat near him, drew closer, and laid her cheek against his side, weeping silently; and he put his big hand around her head and caressed it.

Will Sheridan sat motionless for about a minute, and then said, in a hard monotone:—

"What became of Alice Walmsley? Did she—Is she dead, also?"

"Nay, not dead," said his brother-in-law, "but worse than that. *Alice Walmsley is in prison!*"

Will Sheridan raised his head at the word, repeating it to himself in blank amazement and dread. Then he stood up, and faced round to the two people who sat before him, his sister hiding her weeping face against her husband's side, the husband patting her head in a bewildered way, and both looking as if they were the guilty parties who should be in prison instead of Alice.

Had they said that she was dead, or even that she was married, he could have faced the news manfully for he had prepared his heart for it; but now, when he had come home and thought he could bear all, he found that his years of struggle to forget had been in vain, and that a gulf yawned at his feet deeper and wider than that he had striven so long to fill up.

"In the name of God, man, tell me what you mean. Why is Alice Walmsley in prison?"

Poor Tom Bates still stared at the fire, and patted his wife's head; but a moment after Sheridan asked the question, he let his hand close quietly round the brown hair, and raising his eyes to Will's face, said, in a low voice: —

"For murder. For killing her child!"

Will Sheridan looked at him with a pitiful face, and uttered a sound like the baffled cry of a suffering animal that finds the last door of escape shut against it.

His brother-in-law knew that now was the time to tell Will all, while his very soul was numbed by the strength of the first blow.

"They were married in the church, as you know," said Mary's husband, "and they lived together for some time, seeming very happy — though Mary and I said, when it was all over, that from the very day of the wedding there was a shadow on Alice's face, and that she was never seen to smile. Draper was a captain, and his ship was going to India, and Alice wanted very bad to go with him. But he refused her at last so roughly, before her mother, that poor little Allie said no more. Five months after his going, her child was born, and for six months the poor ailing thing looked like her old self, all smiles and kindness and love for the little one. Then, one day, there walked into her house a strange woman, who said that she was Samuel Draper's wife. No one knows what passed between them — they two were alone; but the woman showed the papers that proved what she said. She was a desperate woman, and with no one else in the

6

house, she was like to kill poor Alice with her dreadful words. Alice's heart was changed to stone from that minute. The woman left the village that day, and never was seen here again. But that night the little child was found dead beside the mother — with marks of violence on it. Poor lass! she was charged wi' killing it — she made no defence; she never raised her head nor said a word. She might have told how the thing happened, for we knew — Mary and I knew — that Alice never did that. But she couldn't speak in her own defence — all she wanted was to get out of sight, and hide her poor head. Poor little Allie — poor little Allie! She never raised her hand to hurt her child. It was accident, or it was some one else — but she couldn't or wouldn't speak. She was sent to prison, and her mother died from the blow. God help the poor lass to-night! God help poor little Allie!" And the warm heart overflowed, and husband and wife mingled their tears for the lost one.

"And this was Samuel Draper's work?" asked Sheridan, slowly.

"Ay, damn him for a scoundrel!" said the strong yeoman, starting to his feet, and clenching his fist, the tears on his cheeks, and his voice all broken with emotion. "He may keep away from this village, where the people know him; but there's no rest for him on this earth — no rest for such as he. Mother and child curse him — one from the grave, the other from the prison; and sea or land cannot shut them out from his black heart. Her father was a seaman, too, and he 'll sail wi' him until the villain pays the debt to the last farthing. And Allie's white face will haunt him, even in sleep, with her dead child in her arms. Oh, God help poor Allie to night! God comfort the poor little lassie!"

William Sheridan said no more that night. His sister prepared his own old room for him, and he went to it, but not to sleep. Up and down he walked like a caged animal, moaning now and again, without following the meaning of the words : —

"Why did I come here ? O, why did I come here ?"

He felt that he could not bear this agony much longer — that he must think, and that he must pray. But he could do neither. There was one picture in his mind, in his eye, in his heart, — a crouching figure in a dock, with a brown head sunk on her white hands, — and were he to try to get one more thought into his brain, it would burst and drive him mad.

And how could he pray — how could he kneel, while the miscreant walked the earth who had done all this ? But from this hateful thought he reverted with fresh agony to her blighted heart. Where was she that night ? How could he find her and help her ? · If he could only pray for her, it would keep him from delirium until he saw her.

And he sank on his knees by the bed where he had knelt by his mother's side and learned to pray ; and again the old associations came thronging to his heart, and softened it. The sweet face of his boy's love drew to him slowly from the mist of years ; and gradually forgetting self, and remembering only her great sorrow, he raised up his face in piteous supplication, acknowledging his utter dependence on divine strength, and prayed as he had never prayed before. Such prayers are never offered in vain. A wondrous quiet came to the troubled heart, and remained with it.

When he arose from his knees, he looked upon every familiar object around him with awakened interest, and many things that he had forgotten came back to his memory and affection when he saw them there. Before he lay down to rest, for he felt that he must sleep, he looked through the window at the deserted cottage, and had strength to think of its former inmates.

"God give her peace, and in some way enable me

to bring comfort to her," he said. And when he arose
in the morning this thought was uppermost in his
mind — that he must search for means to bear comfort
to the afflicted heart of Alice Walmsley.

From his sister and her husband he learned that
Alice was confined in Millbank Prison in London, and
he made up his mind to go to London that day. They,
seeing that he was determined on his course, made no
effort to oppose him. He asked them not to mention
his visit to any one in the village, for he did not wish
to be recognized; and so he turned from the kind-
hearted couple, and walked toward the railway station.

Sheridan now remembered that he had brought from
Western Australia some letters of introduction, and
also some official despatches; and he thought it might
be a fortunate circumstance that most of the official
letters were addressed to the Colonial Office and the
Board of Directors of Convict Prisons.

In the Penal Colony of Western Australia, where
there are few free settlers, and an enormous criminal
population, a man of Sheridan's standing and influence
was rarely found; and the Government of the Colony
was desirous of introducing him to the Home Government, knowing that his opinions would be treated with
great consideration. He began to think that these letters might be the means he sought for, and he made up
his mind to deliver them at once.

VII.

MILLBANK.

ARRIVED in London, he proceeded at once to the
Colonial Office, and left his letters for the Secretary,
and with them his address in the metropolis. He went

through the same routine with the despatches for the Prison Directors. Then, though his heart craved instant action, he was forced to exercise his patience, to wait until these high and perhaps heedless officials were pleased to recognize his presence.

The great city was a wonder to him; but in his intense pre-occupation he passed through it as if it had been familiar from childhood. On the day after his arrival, not expecting an answer from the officials, one of whom, the Colonial Secretary, was a Cabinet Minister, he tried to interest himself in the myriad strangenesses of London. He visited Westminster Abbey and the British Museum. But, everywhere, his heart beat the same dolorous key; he saw the white face, the slight crouching figure in the dock, the brown hair bowed in agony and disgrace. On the walls of the great picture-gallery the gilded frames held only this pitiful scene. Among the tombs of the kings in Westminster, he thought of her ruined life and shattered hope, and envied, for her sake, the peace of the sleeping marble knights and ladies.

All day, without rest or food, he wandered aimlessly and wretchedly through the sculptured magnificence of the galleries. When the night closed, he found himself, almost unconscious of how he had come to the place, or who had directed him thither, walking with bared and feverish brow beneath a high and gloomy wall — the massive outer guard of Millbank Prison.

Hour sped after hour, yet round and round the shadowy, silent precipice of wall the afflicted heart wandered with tireless feet. It was woful to think how near she was, and to touch the sullen granite — yet it was a thousand times more endurable than the torture and fear that were born of absence.

Surely, if there be any remote truth in the theory of psychic magnetism, the afflicted soul within those walls must have felt the presence of the loving and suffering heart without, which sent forth unceasingly silent cries of sympathy and comfort. Surely, if communion of living spirits be possible, the dream of the lonely prisoner within must have thrilled with tenderness when his fevered lips were pressed as lovingly to the icy stone of the prison wall, as once they were pressed to her forehead in affectionate farewell.

Back to his hotel, when morning was beginning to break, the lonely watcher went, spiritless and almost despairing. The reaction had begun of his extreme excitement for the past four days. He passed along the lonesome river, that hurried through the city like a thief in the night, flashing under the yellow quay-lights, then diving suddenly beneath dark arches or among slimy keels, like a hunted murderer escaping to the sea. Wild and incoherent fancies flashed through Will's feverish mind. Again and again he was forced to steady himself, by placing his hand on the parapet, or he should have fallen in the street, like a drunken man.

At last he reached his hotel, and flung himself on his bed, prayerless, friendless, and only saved from despair by the thought of an affliction that was deeper than his, which he, as a man and a faithful friend, should be strong to relieve and comfort.

It was past noon when he awoke. The fever had passed, and much of the dejection. While dressing, he was surprised to find his mind actively at work forming plans and surmises for the day's enterprise.

At breakfast, a large official letter was brought him. It was a brief but unofficially-cordial message from the Colonial Secretary, Lord George Somers, appointing an hour — two o'clock on that day — when he should be happy to receive Mr. Sheridan at the Colonial Office.

Under other circumstances such an appointment would have thrown off his balance a man so unused to social or formal ways as this stranger from Australia, whose only previous training had been on a merchant ship. But now, Will Sheridan prepared for the visit without thinking of its details. His mind was fastened on a point beyond this meeting.

Even the formal solemnity of the powdered servant who received him had no disturbing effect. Will Sheridan quite forgot the surroundings, and at length, when ushered into the presence of the Colonial Secretary, his native dignity and intelligence were in full sway, and the impression he made on the observant nobleman was instantaneous and deep.

He was received with more than courtesy. Those letters, Lord Somers said, from Australia, had filled him with interest and desire to see a man who had achieved so much, and who had so rapidly and solidly enriched and benefited the Colony.

The Colonial Secretary was a young man for his high position — certainly not over forty, while he might be still younger. He had a keen eye, a mobile face, that could turn to stony rigidity, but withal a genial and even frank countenance when conversing cordially with this stranger, whom he knew to be influential, and who certainly was highly entertaining.

Will Sheridan was soon talking fluently and well. He knew all about the Penal Colony, the working of the old penal system and the need of a new one, the value of land, the resources of the country, the capabilities for commerce; and all this the Secretary was most anxious to learn.

After a long interview, Sheridan rose to take leave, and the Secretary said he hoped to see a great deal of him before his return to Australia, and told him plainly that the opinions of a settler of wealth and intelligence on colonial matters in Western Australia were just then of special importance to the Government. He also wished it were in his power to give Mr. Sheridan pleasure while he remained in England.

There was only one thought in Sheridan's mind all
this time, and now was the moment to let it work.
He said he desired very much to visit the convict
prisons in England, and compare the home system
with that of the Penal Colony.

The minister was gratified by the request, and,
smiling, asked which prison he would visit first. Will
mentioned Millbank; and the minister with his own
hand wrote a few lines to the governor, and handed
the paper to his visitor.

Will Sheridan took his departure, with a tremulous
hope at his heart, and drove straight to Millbank
Prison.

There is something strange, almost unaccountable,
and yet terrible, in the change that appears in half a
century in the building of prisons. Few people have
thought of this, perhaps; but it contains a suggestion
of a hardening of hearts and a lessening of sentiment.
The old prisons were dark and horrible, even in aspect,;
while the new ones are light and airy. In the latter,
the bar takes the place of a wall — and the bar is often
ornamented with cast-iron flowers and other sightly
but sardonic mockery. Better the old dungeon, with
all its gloom; better for the sake of humanity. The
new prison is a cage — a hideous hive of order and
commonplace severity, where the flooding sunlight is
a derision, and the barred door only a securer means of
confinement. For the sake of sentiment, at least, let
us have the dismal old keep, that proclaims its mission
on its dreadful brow, rather than the grinning bar-
gate that covers its teeth-like rails with vulgar metal
efflorescence.

The great penitentiary of Millbank is, or rather was,
an old-fashioned prison, its vast arched gateway sombre and awful as a tomb. It has disappeared now,
having been pulled down in 1875; but those who
visited it once, or who even passed it,   ver forget

the oppression caused by its grated and frowning portal. In the early part of this century, the Government of Great Britain determined to build an immense
penitentiary, on the plan laid down by Jeremy Bentham in his celebrated "Panopticon, or the Inspection
House." Bentham's scheme proposed a colossal prison, which should contain all England's convicts and dis-
pense entirely with transportation. The Government,
acting on his plan, purchased a large and unhealthy
tract of flat land, lying beside the Thames, and on this
the unique structure was raised. The workmen were
ten years in completing it; but, when it was finished,
Englishmen said that it was the model prison of the
world.

And it certainly was a great improvement on the
older prisons, where those confined were often herded,
many in a room, like cattle — the innocent with the
guilty, the young and pure with the aged and the foul.
In Millbank, every prisoner had his or her own cell —
a room of stone, walls, ceiling and floor, with a large
and heavily-barred window. Each cell was eight feet
square. The prison was built in six vast pentagons
radiating from a central hexagon, from which every
cell was visible.

The entrance to the prison, from the street, was a
wonder of architectural gloom. First, there was a
dark archway of solid masonry, from the roof of which,
about six feet from the portal, sprang a heavy grate or
portcullis, with spear-points apparently ready to fall
and cut the unfortunate off for ever from the world.
Far within the arch appeared a mighty iron gate, pon-
derously barred, with an iron wicket, through which an
armed warder could be seen on sentry within the yard.

These details were not noticed by Will Sheridan as
he entered the echoing archway; but he was chilled,
nevertheless, by the cold shadow of the surroundings.
The warder within came to the wicket, and took the

letter, leaving Will outside. In a few minutes, he found that his introduction was an "open sesame." The governor of Millbank himself, an important gentleman in a black uniform with heavy gold facings, came speedily to the wicket, the ponderous bars were flung back, the awful door rolled aside, and Will Sheridan entered.

The governor was very gracious to his distinguished visitor. On learning his desire to see the arrangements of the prison he himself became the guide.

An hour was spent in the male side of the establishment, which was an age to Will Sheridan. While the governor thought his attention was engaged in observing the features or motions of some caged malefactor, the mind and fancy of the visitor were far otherwise employed. He did not see the wretched, crime-stained countenances in the cells he passed; but in every one he saw the white face, the brown hair, and the crouching figure that filled his mind.

At last the governor asked him to visit the female prison, in which the discipline was necessarily different. They passed through a long passage built in the wall, and entered the corridors of the female prison.

Sheridan's heart beat, and the blood fled from his face, leaving him ghastly pale, as he passed the first iron door. He feared that the governor might notice his agitation; and he wondered how he should learn whether Alice were there or not.

As he walked down the corridor he noticed that on every door was hung a white card, and, approaching, he read the name, crime, and sentence of the prisoner printed thereon. This was a relief to him: as he walked he read the name on every card, and on and on they went, up stairs and down, and round and round the pentagons, until he thought she surely was not in the prison, and the governor concluded that his visitor evidently meant to see all that was to be seen.

When the last corridor on the ground floor was entered, Will read every name on the doors with a despairing persistence, and his heart sank within him as he came to the last.

The governor opened the door at the end of the passage, and they entered a light, short corridor, with large and pleasantly-lighted cells. Here, the governor said, were confined those prisoners, who, by extreme good conduct, had merited less severe treatment than the others.

Will Sheridan's heart leaped within him, for he knew that this was the place he should see her.

On the doors were simply printed the names and sentences of the occupants; and at the fourth door Will stopped, and read the card:—

ALICE WALMSLEY.

LIFE.

Seeing him pause, and intently examine the card, the governor beckoned to the female warder, who was in the passage, to come and open the door.

The woman approached, the key in her hand, and stood aside until the gentlemen withdrew from the door. Will turned and read her intention, and with a shudder he put her back with his hand.

"No, no, not her," he said hurriedly; then recollecting himself: "No, no, the prisoners do not like to be stared at."

Next moment, before he could think of the consequences, he turned again, and speaking rapidly, said, —

" I am wrong. I should like to see — I should like
to see the interior of this cell."

The lock clicked back, the heavy iron door swung
open, and William Sheridan saw Alice Walmsley
before him.

She had been sewing on something coarse and white,
and a heap of the articles lay at her feet. As the
door opened, she stood up from the low seat on which
she had sat in the centre of the stone-floored cell, and,
with her eyes on the ground, awaited the scrutiny of
the visitors, according to prison discipline.

Will Sheridan took in the whole cell at once, although his eyes only rested on her face. She never
looked on him, but stood in perfect calmness, with her
eyes cast down.

She was greatly changed, but so differently changed
to Will's expectations, that he stood amazed, stunned.
He had pictured her fragile, broken, spiritless, wretched.
There she stood before him, grown stronger than when
he had known her, quiet as a statue, with a face not
of happiness, but of intensified peace, and with all
that was beautiful in her as a girl increased a thou-
sand-fold, but subdued by suffering. Her rich brown
hair had formerly been cut close, but now it had
grown so long that it fell to her shoulders. Her face
was colorless for want of open air and sunshine. A
casual observer would have said she was happy.

Something of her peace fell upon William Sheridan
as he looked upon her. Suddenly he was recalled to
consciousness by a simple movement of hers as if
averse to inspection. His heart quickened with fear and
sorrow for his impulsive action in entering the cell, for
now he would give all he possessed that she should
not look upon his face. He turned from her quickly and walked out of the cell, and he did not look
round until he heard the heavy door swing into its
place.

When he had walked so far from the cell that she could not hear his voice, he asked the governor what work these privileged prisoners were engaged in, and was almost startled into an exclamation of astonishment when the governor answered : —

"They are just now engaged on a pleasant task for themselves. They are making their outfit for the Penal Colony."

"Is she — is that prisoner going to the Penal Colony ? " asked Will Sheridan, scarcely able to control his emotion.

"Yes, sir; she and all those in this pentagon will sail for Western Australia in the next convict ship," said the governor. "We shall send three hundred men and fifty women in this lot."

"When does the ship sail ? " asked the visitor, still apparently examining the door-cards.

"On the 10th of April — just three months hence," answered the governor.

With his eyes fixed on a ponderous door, which he did not see, Will Sheridan made a sudden and imperative resolution.

"I shall return to Australia on that convict ship," were the words that no one heard but his own soul.

"I thank you, sir, for your courtesy and attention," he said, next moment, to the governor; "and as I wish to examine more closely the working of your system, I shall probably trouble you again."

The governor assured him that his visits to the prison would be at all times considered as complimentary; and Will Sheridan walked from Millbank with a firmer step and a more restful spirit than he had known for ten years.

VIII.

SIR JOSHUA HOBB'S CONVICT-MILL.

LORD SOMERS, the Colonial Secretary, had evidently conceived a high opinion of Mr. Sheridan from his first brief visit. He soon renewed the acquaintance by requesting another interview. In the course of a few weeks their relations had become almost friendly.

Their conversation was usually about the Australian colonies, on which subject the Secretary found Sheridan to be a perfect encyclopædia. It seemed that every possibility of their condition, latent as well as operative, had come into his practical mind, and had been keenly considered and laid aside.

But Sheridan was a child in London. He was supremely ignorant of everything that this nobleman considered necessary to existence. He knew nothing of British or European politics — did not even know who was Prime Minister. It gratified the genial and intelligent Englishman, on their frequent rides through the city, to impart information and pleasure to his Australian friend.

One day Mr. Sheridan received another large official letter, this time from the Chief Director of Convict Prisons, Sir Joshua Hobb, who, without apologizing for the delayed acknowledgment of Mr. Sheridan's letter, asked him to meet the Board of Directors on the next day at noon, at the Department in Parliament Street.

Sheridan kept the appointment, and became acquainted with the half-dozen men to whose hands Great Britain had intrusted the vast burden of punishing and reforming the criminal class.

Half an hour's conversation, though of a general nature, astonished Will Sheridan, by convincing him of the stupendous conceit and incompetence of these

men. They talked glibly about the weight of a prisoner's loaf, and the best hour to light the cells in the
morning; they had statistics at their finger-ends to
show how much work a convict could perform on a
given number of ounces of meat; but they knew
nothing whatever of the large philosophy of penal
government.

The Chief Director, Sir Joshua Hobb, however, was
an exception, in so far as he had ideas. He was a
tall, gaunt man, of fifty, with an offensive *hauteur*,
which was obviously from habit rather than from
nature. His face said plainly: "I know all — these
gentlemen know nothing — it is not necessary that
they should — *I* am the Convict System." He re-
minded Sheridan of a country pedagogue promoted
to high position for some narrow piece of special
knowledge. He looked superciliously at Sheridan, as
if to ask — "Do you mean to pretend, before me, that
you know anything about prisons?"

"Confound this fellow!" said Sheridan to himself,
five minutes after meeting him; "he deliberately delayed acknowledging my letters, to show his importance."

But Sir Joshua Hobb was an "expert" in penal
systems. He had graduated from a police court, where
he had begun as an attorney; and he was intimately
acquainted with the criminal life of England in its
details. But he had no soul for the awful thought
of whence the dark stream came, nor whither it was
going. He was merely a dried mudbank to keep it
within bounds for a little way.

The admiration of his colleagues was almost rever-
ential. Mr. Sheridan was informed by several of the
Board — in subdued voice, of course, so that the great
reformer should not be put to the blush — of his
wonderful successes in the treatment of criminals.

"They all hate him," said Mr. Pettegrew, one of the

Board, — " I give you my word, sir, that every criminal
in England hates the name of Sir Joshua Hobb. He
has made them feel his power, sir, and they know
him."

"He was knighted by the Queen for his Separate
System," said another Director.

" Is that your present system ? " asked Sheridan.

"No," said the Director. "At present we are on
the other tack."

" The Separate System was a failure, then ? " inquired
Mr. Sheridan.

" Not a failure, sir, but it was abandoned out of
regard to the sentimental reformers.   It increased insanity from 12 to 31 per 1,000.   Sir Joshua himself
was the first to find it out."

" And then you adopted the Public-Works System,
did you not ? " asked Sheridan.

" No, not so soon.   When his Separate System failed,
Sir Joshua introduced the mask — a cloth skull-cap
coming down over the face, with eyelet-holes — to
promote a salutary shame in the prisoners.   He was
made a Knight Commander of the Bath for that
wonderful invention."

" Then that system gave beneficial results?" inquired
Mr. Sheridan.

" Well, there was no doubt of its moral excellence ;
but it increased the insanity from 31 to 39½ per 1,000.
Sir Joshua himself was the first to discover this, also."

" He certainly deserves the name of a discoverer,"
thought Sheridan.   Then aloud, —

" And your present system is his invention, also ? "

" Yes, our present system is wholly his.   We are
just now examining results.   We discover one peculiarity, which Sir Joshua hardly knows how to class
but he says it certainly is a proof of progress."

" May I ask what is this peculiarity ? " inquired Mr
Sheridan.

" That within three years insanity has decreased 2 per cent," answered the Director, " while suicide has increased 17 per 1,000."

" Sir Joshua inclines to the opinion," said another Director, who was listening, " that this fact proves that we are at last getting to bear closely on the criminal principle. The law is touching it — there is no escape — and in despair the baffled criminals give up the fight, and kill themselves."

There was something fearfully repugnant to Sheridan's broad and humane view in all this, and he would gladly have escaped from the place. But the Directors meant to impress him with their ability to manage the entire Penal System, both in Australia and England. To secure this general management, Sir Joshua Hobb had recently introduced a bill to Parliament.

" Have you heard, sir," said Sir Joshua, addressing Sheridan with a patronizing kindness, " of the proposals made to the Government as to penal reform, by Mr. Wyville, of Western Australia ? "

" No," answered Sheridan, smiling at his own ignorance. " I have never even heard of Mr. Wyville."

" Indeed ! " said Sir Joshua, with a stare of rude surprise. " He is the most influential man in the West Australian Penal Colony."

"I never heard his name before," simply answered Will

" He, perhaps, resides in a district far from yours, Mr. Sheridan," said one of the Directors. " Mr. Wyville is a wealthy settler from the Vasse District."

" From the Vasse ?" repeated Sheridan, quite surprised ; " I thought I knew every man, rich and poor, bond and free, in that district. I have lived there many years."

Sheridan saw that his importance was lessened to the Board, but, strange to say, increased to the Chief Director, by his confession of ignorance of Mr. Wyville. However, Sir Joshua continued to speak.

7

"Mr. Wyville wants to introduce the sentimental idea into our penal system, — an absurdity that has never been attempted. There is only one way to blend punishment with reform, sir, — by rigid rules, constant work, low diet, impersonal treatment, — and all this kept up with unflagging regularity for all the years of a prisoner's sentence."

"With educational and religious influences added, of course," suggested Mr. Sheridan.

"No, sir, not of course," said Sir Joshua, in a tone of severe correction; "a chapter of the Bible read by a warder every morning, in a regular way, may do some good; but these influences have been overrated — they are of the sentimental school. The quality that is absent in the criminal class is *order*, sir, *order;* and this can best be supplied by persistent and impersonal regularity of work, meals, exercise, and sleep."

"You subject all prisoners to the same course of treatment?" asked Sheridan.

"Precisely," answered Sir Joshua. "Our system is the measure of normality, sir. We make the entire criminal or abnormal class pass through the same process of elevation, and try to reach one standard."

Mr. Sheridan would have asked what the standard was, and how many had reached it, and what had become of those who had failed to reach it, who had sunk under the Draconian yoke; but he thought it prudent to keep the questions back.

"Suppose a youth commit a first offence," he said, "or a man hitherto respectable and industrious commit a crime in a moment of passion, — will you treat him as if he were a professional criminal?"

"Precisely," repeated the eminent reformer; "our system regards criminality as a mass, and ignores its grades. This is our leading idea, sir — uniformity and justice. The criminal body is diseased — our system is the cure, sir; physician and cure in one."

Accustomed to say the word he meant, Will Sheridan could hardly restrain an indignant comment. "Confound the man," he thought, "he would take a hundred men, with as many diseases, and treat them all for the cholera." He concluded that Sir Joshua would have earned distinction as a torturer as well as a reformer, but he did not say so. As soon as possible he ended the conversation, and withdrew from the presence of the Directors of Prisons.

"Lord help the convicts!" he thought, on his way to the hotel. "No wonder they are eager to be sent to the Penal Colony."

IX.

MR. WYVILLE.

AT the hotel, Sheridan found a note from Lord Somers, requesting him, if disengaged, to call upon him that afternoon. Half an hour later, he and the Colonial Secretary were riding together toward the West End.

"By the way, Mr. Sheridan," said Lord Somers, "there is a gentleman in London I want you to meet, who knows a great deal about the Australian Colonies, and especially about the West. He is our chief adviser on the proposed reform of the Penal System."

"Indeed!" said Sheridan, interested at once. "This is the second time to-day, I surmise, that I have heard of him. Is his name Wyville?"

"Yes; do you know him?"

"No," answered Sheridan; "I have never heard of him. Sir Joshua Hobb does not like his reformatory ideas — which inclines me to think Mr. Wyville must be a superior man."

Lord Somers laughed. "Sir Joshua Hobb is, indeed, a strong counterblast," he said; "by nature, two such men are compelled to antagonize each other."

"You admire Mr. Wyville, my Lord?" asked Sheridan.

"Thoroughly," answered Lord Somers. "He is a most remarkable man — a man of exalted principles and extraordinary power. His information is astonishing — and what he speaks about he knows absolutely. I fancy he has lived a long time in the colonies, for he is enormously wealthy."

"Is he an old man?" asked Sheridan.

"No, I don't think he can be forty — certainly not more — but a person of so much force, and with a manner so impressive, that really one forgets to think of his age. He is altogether a notable man — and I may say, in confidence, that even the Prime Minister has more than once consulted him with advantage on Colonial affairs."

"You interest me exceedingly," said Sheridan. "Such men are not common in Australia."

"We are beginning to think otherwise," laughed the Secretary. "And yet you Australians seem to learn everything without newspapers. I remember, when Mr. Wyville first appeared here, some years ago, he might have dropped from the moon, so oblivious was he of the doings of the European world."

"He must have lived in the bush," said Sheridan, smiling.

"Why, he had never heard of the Crimean War," said the Secretary; "and when I mentioned the Indian Mutiny to him, one day, he gravely stared, and asked, 'What mutiny?' Are you so utterly removed from civiliz — from news, in your bush?"

"Well, Mr. Wyville must certainly have had the minimum of society," responded Will; "we usually get a report, however vague, of what your civilization is doing."

"Shall we call on Mr. Wyville?" asked Lord Somers; "he lives in Grosvenor Street."

"I shall be delighted to meet him," said Sheridan and a few minutes afterward they stopped before a large and handsome mansion.

Mr. Wyville was at home. A colored servant showed the gentlemen into a rich reception-room, in which Sheridan's quick eye noted many Australian features of decoration.

The colored servant seemed a negro of the common African type to the superficial eye of Lord Somers. But there was an air of freedom about him, an uprightness in the setting of his head on the neck and shoulders, the effect being heightened by blue-black hair, that stood straight out like a handsome and very soft brush, which at once attracted the attention of Sheridan.

"Australian!" he thought, half-aloud; "is it possible that a bushman may be trained in this way?"

He smiled at the absurdity of the thought; but was struck once more by the man's air as he turned to the door.

"*Mir-ga-na nago mial Vasse!*" said Sheridan in a low voice — ("*Mir-ga-na,*" a common name among bushmen, "you have known," or "you belong to the Vasse.")

The black man turned as if a shot had struck him, and stared at the gentlemen, not knowing which had spoken.

"*Nago mial wan-gur Vasse!*" repeated Mr. Sheridan.

"*Tdal-lung nago Vasse! Guab-ha-leetch!*" answered the man, the look of amazement slowly changing to one of deep pleasure and curiosity. ("My mouth knows the Vasse! That is good!")

"By Jove!" said a pleasant voice from a window recess in the room; "please ask what was the prince's name in his own country.'

There came from the recess a handsome, well-set
man, who greeted Lord Somers in a familiar manner.

" O, my dear Hamerton," said the Secretary, " I
have great pleasure in making you acquainted with
another Australian gentleman, whom you will find as
interesting as Mr. Wyville."

The gentleman bowed. Sheridan liked him from
the first look. An aristocrat, stamped; with a broad
open forehead, clear, honest eyes, a firm mouth and
jaw, and a manner above trifles, and careless of form.

" Mr. Hamerton is a priest of the new order," said
Lord Somers to Sheridan in mock-earnest; " he is a
journalist and book-maker — hungry for novelty as an
epicure."

The black man had remained in the room, statu-
esque, his eyes fixed on Sheridan's face.

" Mr. Sheridan, will you please ask his royal
name ? " said Hamerton.

" *Wan-gon-di ?* " said Sheridan to the man.

" Ngarra-jil," he answered.

Mr. Sheridan motioned him to go.

" He is Ngarra-jil, a native of the Vasse country,"
said Sheridan.

" Is this really a language, with even an approach to
regular formation, or the local gibberish of incoherent
tribes ? " asked Lord Somers.

" I have not studied its form," answered Mr. Sheridan, " but it certainly is not a mere local dialect. The
same things have the same names all over the continent, with only a slight difference between the Swan
River and Sydney — two thousand miles apart."

" How did you guess this man's particular nativity ? "
asked Hamerton.

" I have lived at the Vasse many years," said Sheridan, " and have grown familiar with the people. I
believe the Vasse natives are the most superior tribe
in Australia."

"You are right, sir," said a deep voice behind them; "the Vasse people are the parent stock of Australia."

"Mr. Wyville!" said both Lord Somers and Hamerton, with sudden gravity and respect.

Sheridan turned, and met the eyes of him who had spoken — deep, searching eyes that held him strongly for a moment, then passed quietly to another direction.

Never, among all the men he had known, had Sheridan seen such a man as this. The head, with all its features, the eye, the voice, the whole body, were cast in one mould of superb massiveness and beauty. There was no point of difference or weakness. Among a million, this man would not have merely claimed superiority, but would have unconsciously walked through the opening crowd to the front place, and have taken it without a word. Before him now stood three men least likely of any in London to be easily impressed — a young and brilliant statesman, a cynical and able novelist, and a bold and independent worker; and each of these felt the same strange presence of a power and a principle to be respected.

Nature, circumstances, and cultivation had evidently united to create in this man a majestic individuality. He did not pose or pretend, but spoke straight the thing he meant to say; yet every movement and word suggested a reserve of strength that had almost a mysterious calmness and beauty.

He was dressed in such a way that one would say he never could be dressed otherwise. Dress was forgotten in the man. But he wore a short walking or shooting coat, of strong dark cloth. The strength and roughness of the cloth were seen, rather than the style, for it seemed appropriate that so strangely powerful a figure should be strongly clad.

His face was bronzed to the darkness of a Greek's. His voice, as he spoke on entering the room, came easily from his lips, yet with a deep resonance that was pleasant to hear, suggesting a possible tenderness or terror that would shake the soul. It was a voice in absolutely perfect accord with the striking face and physique.

"Mr. Sheridan," he said, holding out his hand, which the other took with a feeling of rare pleasure, "we should not need a formal introduction. We are both from a far country, where formality is unknown; and I have been quite intimate with your plans and progress there for several years."

Sheridan could hardly stammer a reply, he was so profoundly astonished. He could only recall the wild nature of West Australian life, and wonder how it could have contained or developed this important man.

"You have studied with some effect," continued Mr. Wyville with a smile, "to have learned the language and discovered the superiority of the Vasse tribe."

"My life for nine years has been passed among them," answered Sheridan; "but the possibility of training them to European manners I should not have thought possible."

"Oh, civilization is only skin deep," said Mr. Wyville, pleasantly. "The gamut of social law is not very extensive; and a little skill, practised with kindness and attention, will soon enable one to run over all the keys."

"You really think it possible, Mr. Wyville," asked Lord Somers, "to transform the average savage into an obedient footman?"

"Yes, my Lord, I know it is possible — and I have seen stranger things accomplished with little difficulty. Refinement and gracious intercourse, even according to civilized rule, are quite in keeping with the natural character. We assume that to be savage which is contrary to our habit; but　　　no proof of inferiority.

Degraded civilization is brutal, indeed; but the natural or savage life is not."

"Then," said Mr. Hamerton, "why can't we put all our savages in Australia through your civilizing process, and do away with savagery at one stroke?"

"Why not begin at home?" quietly asked Mr. Wyville.

"Ah, just so; I hadn't thought of that!" and Hamerton lapsed into listening, with a shrug.

"Have you actually civilized your savage servant?" asked Lord Somers.

"I don't think I quite know your meaning, my Lord," answered Mr. Wyville. "All my people are Australians, taken from the bush. I am well served, and honestly; and I have no gossips in my household, for no one in Europe can speak to my people — except Mr. Sheridan here," he added smiling.

"But how have you changed the nature of the bushmen?" asked Lord Somers, very much interested.

"I haven't changed it; my men are bushmen still. I have attempted no change whatever, — and that is the secret of my success. It is true, I have asked Ngarra-jil and the others to wrap some warm cloth round their bodies while we live in this cold climate; to open the door when the bell rings; and to drive slowly and carefully in the streets. This was learned easily in a week or two. The bushmen are natural horsemen, trained to riding through close woods. We have no collisions with other carriages, I assure you. Then, again, my men, being savages, never lie and never steal."

"But is not this actual civilization?" asked Lord Somers.

"I really don't know," said Mr. Wyville.

"Ha, ha!" chuckled Hamerton. "I really think it is!"

"Yes, you may laugh, Hamerton; but this is very

interesting," said Lord Somers. "Have your men re-
tained any of their savage ways, Mr. Wyville?"

"I think they have kept all their natural customs,
which people in England call savage ways. They eat
and sleep in their own fashion — I do not see any
reason for imposing my way upon them, if they prefer
theirs. Mine is in itself no better, except as it pleases
me. They even keep their familiar implements, if
they please."

"What, for instance?" asked Lord Somers.

Mr. Wyville touched a bell. Ngarra-jil appeared at
the door.

"*Yanga dan-na wommera,*" said Mr. Wyville.

The Australian disappeared, and in a few moments
returned to the door, holding three or four long and
slender spears in one hand, and the *wommera* or throwing stick in the other.

Lord Somers and Mr. Hamerton examined the
weapons with great interest, vainly trying to draw a
word from the observant Australian; while Mr. Wyville
took Mr. Sheridan aside, and conversed with him for
several minutes.

On taking their leave, Mr. Wyville gave Sheridan a
cordial invitation to come and see him soon, as he had
much to say to him.

"You will find me at home almost always," he said.

"And if Mr. Wyville is absent, you will certainly
find Mr. Hamerton," said Lord Somers, jestingly.

Before they parted, Lord Somers informed Mr. Sheridan that Hamerton was a wealthy gentleman, who
had refused to adopt his hereditary title, and who had
also decided to earn his own livelihood, making a
yearly division of the profits of his estate among his
farmers and tenants. This had earned him quite
another kind of title amongst the upper classes; but he
had gone on working in his own way, and had already
won for himself an honorable name as an author.

" Hamerton is a Republican now," said Lord Somers,
after a pause ; " he was a Socialist in the University."

Mr. Sheridan remarked that he seemed quite to
agree with Mr. Wyville's opinions.

" Yes," the Secretary said, " he has been much attracted to this remarkable man — more so than to any
one he has ever known." Lord Somers also mentioned
that the Government was about to introduce a sweeping reform of the entire Penal System, at home and
abroad, and that the assistance of Mr. Wyville had
been deemed of the utmost importance.

" He has already reformed our system at the Andaman Islands, the Penal Colony for India," said the
Secretary ; " but the Australian colonies offer a profound problem. If possible, we are bound, he says, to
use the convicts not merely as slaves, preparing the
way for civilized life, but to transform them gradually
into a healthy basis of population."

" It certainly is a wide field, and a grand undertak-
ing," responded Sheridan, " and it is terribly needed.
But Mr. Wyville is an uncommon mind. I trust his
views will be largely heeded by the Government."

" He has the matter in his own ·hands," said the
Secretary, confidentially and earnestly ; " the Prime
Minister has asked him to draft the entire bill."

X.

THE UPAS-TREE.

IN a few days, as soon as he could do so without
apparent haste, Will Sheridan visited Millbank again,
and was escorted by a warder to the governor's office,
where he was graciously received by that dignitary.
Very soon, Sheridan adroitly turned the conversation

on the transport service, and the class of prisoners to
be transported in the next ship. The governor, who
was a portly old army major, was willing enough to
talk on this subject.

" The Government has no special ships for transport," said the governor; " we charter a large merchant
vessel, and fit her up for the voyage. The *Houguemont*,
which will sail in April, is now lying at Portland, under preparation."

" The convicts to be transported you select from
those who are best conducted, do you not ?" asked
Sheridan.

" No," said the governor, " only the women. These
are the healthiest and best among their class ; because
they are soon released in Australia, and get married to
liberated men, or go to service in settlers' houses. But
the men who go to Australia are the opposite — they
are the worst criminals in Great Britain. They are
first selected for their sentence ; men imprisoned for
life, or for twenty years, are sure to go. Next we take
them for re-conviction; we want to send away as many
professional criminals as possible. Then we make up
the number with strong young fellows, who have never
been in prison before, but who are able to do a good
deal of hard work."

" I presume the Australian authorities soon give this
last class their liberty, and encourage them to become
settlers ?" said Sheridan inquiringly.

" Quite the contrary," answered the governor, very
gravely, as if he, subordinate though he was, could see
the wrong of the system. "These men, who should
be punished lightest, have the heaviest burden in Australia. The professionals escape hard tasks, by knowing how; but these poor fellows, being strong, and
ignorant of the rules, are pushed into the quarry gangs.
The chain-gang of Fremantle, of which you have
heard, is filled with these men. Very rarely, indeed,

does a really dangerous criminal get heavy punishment in prison. As a rule, the worst characters outside are the best in prison."

"It is a bad system," said Sheridan. "Does Mr. Wyville's plan propose a reform ?"

"Mr. Wyville," said the old governor, walking toward the door, which he closed, then, sinking his voice almost to a whisper, "Mr. Wyville is a man and a Christian, sir. I have heard him say that the true penal law should be filled with the spirit of Christ, and that our present code had none of it. He is going to change the whole machinery. He knows more about humanity and reform than a regiment of your K. C. B.'s."

The bluff old major mopped his face with his large handkerchief. He was excited.

"Pardon me, Mr. Sheridan," he continued, "I speak too quickly against my superiors, perhaps. But I don't do it often; and I think you Australian gentlemen may have a good deal of influence in making the new law."

"You know Mr. Wyville intimately, Major ?" asked Sheridan.

"I have known him for five years, sir," answered the governor; "since first he visited this prison with an order from Lord Palmerston. He has done more good to convicts in that time than all the men in Britain — I 'm free to say that," added the major emphatically. "Four years ago, I called his attention to an extraordinary case among our female convicts — the very prisoner you saw the other day. She had never prayed, and had hardly spoken a word for five years after she came here. Mr. Wyville took an interest in her, and he has changed the whole manner of her life."

"By what means ?" asked Sheridan, profoundly interested.

"Means ?" repeated the governor, again resorting to

his sail-like handkerchief; " it was done in his own
way — unlike any other man's way. That poor girl's
life was saved from insanity and despair, by what do
you think ? by a poor little flower — a little common
flower he went and pulled in my garden, down there."

Sheridan was about to hear the story of this strange
event, when a low knock came to the door. The governor opened it, and there entered and stood near the
threshold two ladies, dressed in black, with snowy
head-dresses. They were Sisters of Mercy, who attended the female school and hospital. They had
come for their ward keys, without which it was impossible to pass through the pentagons, each ward or
passage ending with a door.

The governor treated the ladies with respect and
courtesy. He handed them their keys with a knightly
bow, and, as they retired, he bowed again, and waited
until they had reached the end of the passage before
he closed the door. Sheridan, who was a Catholic, was
gratified and much surprised at seeing all this.

The governor turned to him with a radiant face.
" God bless them ! " he said, earnestly ; " they may believe in the Pope of Rome, but it doesn't prevent them
spending their lives for the love of God."

" Are they constant attendants in the prison ? " asked
Sheridan.

" Yes ; they might as well be penal convicts, for all
they see of the outside world. It was through these
ladies, and the little flower I spoke of, that Mr. Wyville
did so much for the poor girl. I 'll tell you that story
some day, Mr. Sheridan, if you care to hear it. Just
now I have to make my rounds of inspection. Will
you join me ? "

" With pleasure," said Sheridan ; and they passed
into one of the male pentagons.

It was a monotonous and unpleasant routine, this
visiting of the wards. Will Sheridan was glad when

they entered the female pentagon, after half an hour's rapid walking. When at last they came to the short ward in which Alice was confined, Sheridan's heart was beating rapidly.

The door of Number Four was open, and one of the nuns was standing in the cell beside Alice, who sat with her work in her lap. Will Sheridan heard the low sound of her voice, as she spoke to her visitor, and it thrilled him like a strain of exquisite music. In after years, he never forgot the subtile pleasure and pain he experienced at the sound of her soft voice in that brief sentence.

The governor stood at the doorway, and greeted Sister Cecilia respectfully, then passed on. Will Sheridan had only for one instant rested his eyes on Alice; out he went away happy, his heart filled with gratitude. The old governor wondered at the earnest warmth of his manner as he thanked him and took his leave.

When Will Sheridan emerged from Millbank Prison, he seemed impatient, and yet pleased. He hailed a cab, and drove straight to Mr. Wyville's. He was drawn there by a deep, pleasurable feeling of mingled respect, gratitude, and expectation. He felt unaccountably light-hearted and joyous. He had no actual thoughts, but only happy perceptions. The world was changed. He did not know in what the change consisted; but he certainly was a different man from the unhappy stranger who had wandered round Millbank a few weeks before.

He sprang from the cab in Grosvenor Square, thinking he would quiet his excitement by walking the remainder of the way. As he turned into Grosvenor Street, his eye was attracted by a low and elegant brougham, driven by a colored coachman, who wore a peculiar oriental dress. This driver had caught Sheridan's eye at first, and he was rather surprised when he recognized Mr. Wyville's Australian servant, Ngarra-jil.

In the carriage sat two young girls of extraordinary beauty and similarity of face and age. They were dark-skinned rather than "colored," with intensely-black hair and flashing eyes. Their faces were of a splendid, rich bronze, warmer than the Moorish brown of Spain, and darker than the red bronze of Syria. They were wrapped in soft furs, their faces only visible. They might have been twins; they were certainly sisters. They were talking and smiling as they spoke, as the brougham slowly passed Sheridan, and drew up at Mr. Wyville's door.

The ladies sprang lightly to the sidewalk, having thrown off their heavier wraps in the carriage. Their dress beneath was still of rich furs, of two or three colors. They walked lightly to the door, which was held open by a black servant, and entered the house.

The incident surprised Sheridan; but he was little given to curiosity. "Those ladies," he thought, "are certainly Australian natives, and yet it seems absurd to believe it. But then, it is no stranger than everything connected with this remarkable man."

At Mr. Wyville's he found Lord Somers, who had brought a copy of Sir Joshua Hobb's new Prison Bill, and Mr. Hamerton. The greeting of all was pleasant, but Sheridan was specially pleased with the almost silent cordiality of Mr. Wyville.

They had been conversing on criminal matters; and the conversation was renewed.

"Mr. Wyville," said the Secretary, "I wish to ask you a question I have put to many philanthropists, with varying results: Have you ever sought, or rather have you ever found the roots of the criminal upas-tree?"

Mr. Wyville had stood facing the window; he turned toward the Secretary, and his impressive face was in shade, as he answered, in a low tone. —

"Yes, my Lord, I have sought for it, and I have found it."

"Then why not announce the discovery ? Why not lay the axe to the root of this tree of evil, and let the world, or at least England, be freed from the criminal incubus ?"

The question was earnestly put, and Hamerton and Sheridan, with deep interest, watched the face of Mr. Wyville till the answer came.

"Because, my Lord, the tree of evil is a banian — its roots drop from above ; its blood is not drawn directly from the soil, but pours from the heart of the main stem, which you think healthy. Its diseased branches ramify through the admirable limbs, and cannot be separated with a knife."

"You are allegorical, Mr. Wyville, but I presume that you mean — "

"That the criminal principle is rooted in the heart of society, underlies the throne — or let me say, that the throne cannot escape injury if the axe be laid to its base," said Mr. Wyville, speaking slowly.

The nobleman glanced nervously at Hamerton, who was smiling broadly, as if intensely pleased.

The Secretary could not give up the point just then, having reached dangerous ground. And as Wyville remained silent, he was forced to continue.

"My dear Mr. Wyville," he said jocosely, "you speak to-day almost like a French Republican, and I fear Mr. Sheridan will conceive a violent prejudice against you. You mean, of course, that the law dare not attempt to suddenly suppress all crime for fear of exciting revolution ?"

"No, my Lord, that was not my meaning," said Mr. Wyville.

"Well, then, I give it up," said the pleasant nobleman, laughing, and turning to Hamerton to change the conversation.

8

"Don't you think, Mr. Hamerton, that with all the public and private money spent in charity and religious work in England, the existence of a great criminal class is a vastly difficult problem, and a monstrous popular ingratitude?"

"I agree as to the problem," answered Hamerton, becoming grave; "but I do not quite see the ingratitude. But may I ask Mr. Wyville to read us the riddle of his allegory, or to continue it further?"

"Pray do, sir," said the Secretary, seeing no escape.

"My Lord," said Mr. Wyville, slightly smiling, but yet very earnest in look, "my views are personal, as my researches have been. I have drawn no political dissatisfaction from foreign schools. I have merely sought among the poor and the tempted for the dangerous and the lawless; and I have found them, and lived among them, and have investigated the causes of their state. I have followed the main root of the criminal plant till I found it disappear beneath the throne; and its lateral issues run through and under the titled and hereditary circles that ring the monarch."

Mr. Hamerton opened his eyes and locked his hands tightly, as he looked at the speaker; Lord Somers seemed puzzled, and rather dismayed; while Sheridan enjoyed the conversation keenly.

"Do the roots spring from the throne and the aristocracy, or enter their crevices from the outside?" asked Hamerton.

"They are born of aristocracy," answered Wyville, impressively. "They spring from the rotting luxuries that fall from the tables of kings and earls and hereditary gentry. They creep from the palaces, where custom and care are too strong for them, and they crawl to the cabins and seize on the hearts of the poor for their prey. The seed of crime is in the flower of aristocracy."

"You speak in paradoxes now, sir," said Lord Somers, interested in spite of himself.

"I take aristocracy as the efflorescence of the social and political evil," said Mr. Wyville, now deeply moved by his theme. "It presupposes the morality of hereditary classes. Men would not, in a justly ordered state, be born either to luxury, poverty, disease, or crime. I do not know where or how mankind began to do the social sum wrong; but I do know, for I see, that the result is appalling, — that millions have evil for a heritage, as truly as you, my Lord, have your entailed estate."

"But how can this be changed or bettered, my dear Mr. Wyville, except by the spread of charity and religion among the wealthy?" asked the peer.

"Ah, pardon me; I consider these things from another standpoint. Charity among the rich simply means the propriety of the poor being miserable, — that poverty is unfortunate, but not wrong. But God never meant to send the majority of mankind into existence to exercise the charity and religion of the minority. He sent them all into the world to be happy and virtuous, if not equal; and men have generated their evils by their own blind and selfish rules."

"Surely, Mr. Wyville," interrupted Hamerton, "you do not believe in the American absurdity that men are born equal?"

"I do not think the Americans mean that in your sense," answered Wyville. "I do believe that every generation of men should have a fair start, and let the best lives win."

"But it never can be done," said Lord Somers.

"It has never been tried, I think, except by fanatics or philanthropic charity-mongers, who have done more harm than good. The good shall not come from the stooping of the rich, but from the raising of the poor; and the poor had better remain poor for another cycle than be raised by charity, and so pauperized and degraded."

"How would you begin the improvement, had you absolute power?" asked Mr. Hamerton.

Mr. Wyville checked himself with an effort, as he was about to speak.

"You have led me to utter latent thoughts rather than opinions," he said, smiling, and looking toward the nobleman. "I fear my upas roots have led me out of bounds."

Mr. Hamerton seemed annoyed at the check, and strode across the room impatiently.

"Confound it, Somers," he cried, "throw off your official airs, and take an interest in principles, as you used to. Mr. Wyville, I beg of you to continue; you should not only talk freely here, but I wish to Heaven you could preach these things in Westminster Abbey."

"Let me recall the question of this excitable person, Mr. Wyville," said his lordship; "he asked how you would begin the reform of society, had you absolute power?"

"By burning the law-books."

"Splendid!" cried Hamerton.

"And then?" asked Lord Somers.

"By burning the title-deeds."

"Magnificent!" ejaculated Hamerton.

"Could society exist without law?" asked the nobleman.

"Not just yet; but it could have a better existence with better laws. At present the laws of civilization, especially of England, are based on and framed by property — a depraved and unjust foundation. Human law should be founded on God's law and human right, and not on the narrow interests of land and gold."

"What do you propose to effect by such law?" asked Lord Somers.

"To raise all men above insecurity, which is the hot-bed of lawlessness," answered Mr. Wyville.

"But by what means can law make poor men rich?" asked the nobleman.

"By allowing no one to hold unproductive land while a single man is hungry. By encouraging small farmers, till every acre of land in England is teeming with food."

"But men do not live by bread alone. Englishmen cannot all be farmers. What then?"

"By developing a system of technical education, that would enable the town and city populations to manufacture to advantage the produce of the fields and mines."

"Admirable!" cried Hamerton.

"But this is revolution," said the nobleman.

"I know not what it may be called, my Lord," responded Mr. Wyville impressively; "but it is lawful and right. This can all be achieved by legal reform — ay, even under present laws."

"Let me not misunderstand you, Mr. Wyville," said the nobleman seriously. "Would you propose that the estates of wealthy men be wrested from them by law?"

"Not without compensation, my Lord; and not at all unless they refused to cultivate the soil or to pay the heavy tax necessary to insure cultivation. I would do no wrong to make a right. No inherited nor purchased land should be taken for the benefit of the people without giving a fair recompense to the aristocrat."

"Well, and having done all this, where should we be?" asked Lord Somers.

"At the starting-point," answered Mr. Wyville, with a sad smile; "only at the starting-point. At present, the level of society is insecurity, poverty, misery, from which spring fear, ignorance, disease, and crime.

Under a better system, the lowest point would be at least sufficiency, enough for all the human beings in the country; and this, in time, would eradicate much of the evil, perhaps most of it."

"Do you think, if there were enough for all, there would not still be some who would steal?" asked Hamerton.

"For a time there would be," answered Wyville, gravely; "perhaps for a thousand years or more we should have remnants of common crime. Men have been thousands of years learning to steal, and cringe, and lie; at least give them one thousand to unlearn."

"But if it take so long," said Lord Somers, laughing, "we may as well go on as we are."

"Not so, my Lord," answered Wyville, and as he spoke, his face was lighted with an exaltation of spirit that made it marvellously beautiful and powerful; "no man who sees the truth, however distant, can conscientiously go on as if it were not there. Thousands of years are vast periods; but the love of human liberty and happiness shall reach out and cling to the eternal. Let every man who believes, faithfully do his share, sow the seed that he has received, and in God's time the glorious harvest will come of a pure and truthful people, whose aristocrats shall be elevated by intelligence and virtue, and the love of humanity, and not by accident of birth and superiority in vice and pride."

The three who heard were deeply moved by the earnestness of the speaker, whose whole being seemed filled with the splendid prophecy. Lord Somers was the first to speak, returning to the subject of the Penal Reform Bill.

"And yet, Mr. Wyville, with all your enthusiasm for social reform, you have given us a bill which is filled with practical attention to existing institutions."

"Ah, it is too soon to begin; and the beginning will not be at that point," said Mr. Wyville. "The real evil is outside the prison, and at present our legal morality calls it good. Until society is changed by the new common sense of abstract justice, we must temporize with our criminal codes."

There was a pause; no one seemed willing to break the floating possibilities of the future.

"You are going to Australia with the next convict ship, are you not?" Mr. Hamerton at length asked Mr. Wyville.

"Yes; I wish to see the machinery of the new system put in motion. Besides, I have personal matters to attend to in the Colony."

Sheridan had started so sudden at the question, that now all three turned their eyes on him.

"I have thought," he said, looking at Lord Somers, "that I also should like to return to Australia on that ship."

"Would you not prefer to go in my yacht, Mr. Sheridan?" asked Mr. Wyville. "She will sail for Australia about the same time, and you shall command her for the voyage."

"I should prefer the ship," said Sheridan. Then thinking he had rudely refused, he added: "I desire very keenly to have this experience."

"You shall have your wish, sir," said the Secretary "and I envy you the companionship of your voyage."

BOOK THIRD.

ALICE WALMSLEY.

I.

MISERERE !

O, SPIRITS of Unrest and Pain, that grieve for the sorrow dealt out to weak humanity, sweep from my heart the dull veil of individuality, and let my being vibrate with the profound pulsation of those who mourn in the depths. Spirits of Sorrow and Sympathy, twin sisters of the twilight, touch the trembling chords that sound the symphony of wrong, and desolation, and despair.

Almighty God, in Thy wisdom, and surely also in Thy love, Thou layest Thine awful finger on a poor human soul, and it is withered in Thy sight even to agony and death. Thy ways, far-seeing, our eyes may not discover. In those supreme moments of trial, when that which we see is black as night, teach us to trust in Thy guidance, give us light to deny the fearful temptation of Chance, and faith to believe that all who labor and are heavy laden may bring their heavy burden trustingly to Thee !

With a prayer, we enter the cell of Alice Walmsley — a cell where no prayer had been uttered, woful to say, for the first five years of her life therein. We look upon the calm white face and the downcast eyes, that during the hopeless period had never been raised to Heaven — except once, and then only in defiance and imprecation.

God's hand had caught her up from the happy plain, to fling her into the darkest furrows of affliction ; and from these depths the stricken soul had upbraided the judge and rebelled against the sentence.

Alice Walmsley had been born with a heart all kindness and sympathy. From her very infancy she had loved intensely the kindly, the unselfish, and the beautiful. She had lived through her girlhood as happy, healthy, and pure as the primroses beneath her mother's hedgerows. She had approached womanhood as a silver stream ripples to the sea, yearning for its greatness and its troubles and its joys — hurrying from the calm delights of the meadow banks to the mighty main of strength, and saltness, and sweetness.

The moment of communion was reached at last, when her girlish life plunged with delicious expectation into the deep — and in one hideous instant she knew that for ever she had parted from the pure and beautiful, and was buried in an ocean of corruption and disappointment, rolled over by waves of unimaginable and inevitable suffering and wrong.

From the first deep plunge, stifled, agonized, appalled, she rose to the surface, only to behold the land receding from her view — the sweet fields of her innocent and joyous girlhood fading in the distance.

She raised her eyes, and saw the heaven calm and beautiful above her, sprinkled with gem-like stars — and she cried, she screamed to God for help in her helplessness. The answer did not come — the lips of God were dumb — it seemed as if He did not heed nor see the ruin of one puny human life. The sky was as beautiful and serene as before, and the stars were as bright.

Then, from the crest of the wave, as she felt herself slipping back into the dreadful depths again, and for

ever, she raised her face to heaven, and shrieked reproach and disbelief and execration !

On the very day of her marriage, before the solemn
words of the ceremony had left her memory, she had
looked for one dread moment beneath the mask of him
who had won her love and trust — some old letters of
her husband relating to Will Sheridan had fallen into
her hands — and she shrank within herself, affrighted
at the knowledge of deceit and habitual falsehood that
the glimpse had brought her. It was her first grief and
secret, and she hid it in her soul for months before
she dared look upon it again.

But a single grief, even though a heavy one, could
not crush the light out of so joyous and faithful a heart.
She still possessed the woman's angelic gifts of hope
and faith. She had, too, the woman's blessed quality
of mercy. She forgave — trusting that her forgiveness
would bring a change. She prayed, and waited, and
hoped — in secret confidence with her own heart.
Another influence would be added to hers ere long.
When she gave his child into his arms, and joined its
supplication to hers, she believed, nay, she knew, that
her happiness would be returned to her.

But before that day came, she was left alone. Her
husband, from the hour she had given herself into his
power, had followed one careless, selfish, and cynical
course. She would not, could not believe that this was
his natural life, but only a temporary mood.

When first he spoke of going to sea again, on a long
voyage, she was pleased, and thought gladly of the
change for her, who had never seen the great world.
When he coldly said that she was to remain, she became
alarmed, — she could not be left alone, — she implored,
she prayed to go with him.

Then came the sneer, the brutal refusal, the master's
command, the indelible insult of expressed weariness
and dislike. She held her peace.

When the day came, he would have left her, for years of absence, without a kiss; but the poor soul, hungering and waiting for a loving word or look, unable to believe her great affection powerless to win a return, could not bear this blighting memory. She clung to him, sobbing her full heart on his breast; she kissed him and prayed for him, with her hands on his shoulders, and her streaming eyes on his; she blamed herself, and told him she would be happy till he returned, — the thought of her coming joy would bless her life, and bless and preserve him on the sea. With such words, she let him go.

Firmly and faithfully the loving heart kept this last promise. Months passed, and her lonely home grew very dear to her. Her young heart refused to remember the pain of the past, and would recall day after day, untiringly, the few poor pleasures of her wedded life. She would not allow herself to think how much even of these pleasures was due to others than her husband — to her mother and her old friends.

But all her sorrow died, and her doubt and fear fled away on the day when she took to her yearning breast the sweet baby that was hers and his. God's eye seemed too full of love that day. The harvest of her young life was the bursting of a flower of exquisite joy. Her baby was a prayer — God had come near to her, and had sent her an angelic present. Her life for many days was a ceaseless crooning melody of soft happiness, mingled with prayers for her husband absent on the sea.

Then came the lightning, and blasted her fabric of joy, and shrivelled her future life into hopelessness before her face. One moment it rose fair and sightly and splendid; the next, it was scattered at her scorched feet, a pile of blackened and pitiful ruin. O, day of sorrow, would it had been of death !

It was a bright and happy morning, and she sat in her pleasant little room, with the baby in her arms.

She had been dreaming awake. She was full of peace and thankfulness for her exceeding joy.

Suddenly, a shadow fell upon her — some one had entered the room. She looked up, and met a terrible face — a woman's face, glaring at her and at her child. She could not scream — she was paralyzed with terror. The face was crowded with passion — every dreadful line seemed to possess a voice of wrath and hatred.

Alice had no power to defend herself; but she folded her baby closer to her breast, and looked straight at the dreadful face.

"You think you are his wife!" cried the woman, with a laugh of hideous derision. "You think he loves you! You lie! You lie! He is my husband! He never was yours! He is mine, mine! And he lied to you!"

More was said by the woman — much more; but it all resolved itself into this in Alice's confused memory. Papers the stranger produced, and held before Alice's eyes. She read the written words — they were transferred to her brain in letters of fire. Nearer and nearer came the dreadful woman, and more threatening the insults she hissed into Alice's face. She laid her hand on the baby's shoulder, and crushed it, cursing it.

Still Alice could not scream. Her heart gave irregular throbs — her brain was beginning to reel. Nearer, still nearer, the hateful face — the words struck her in the eyes like missiles — they sprang like knives at her heart — her body grew weak — the baby fell from her breast and lay upon her knees —— O God! the silent agony — the terrible stranger had seized the child — the mother's senses failed — the sunlight grew dark — the sufferer fell unconscious at her enemy's feet.

When she raised her head, after hours of a merciful blank, she was alone, — her baby lay dead before her, — and the love and trust of her life lay stark and strangled by its side.

What more ? Nay, there was no more to be borne.
The worst had come. The flaming rocket had spent
its last spark in the dark sky — the useless stick was
falling to the earth to be forgotten for ever.

Friends ? What had they to say ? Kindness was
dead. Shame had no existence. Sorrow, disgrace, infamy, what had she to do with these ? But they had
taken her, had seized her as their prey, and she would
make no resistance.

With bonds of faith and love and trust and hope,
Alice Walmsley's life had been firmly bound to all that
was good and happy. The destroyer's knife had sev-
ered all these at one merciless sweep; and the separated and desolated heart sank like lead into the abyss
of despair.

Then followed a blank — intermixed with turmoil
of formal evidence and legal speeches, and voices of
clinging friends, who implored her to speak and clear
herself of the dreadful charge. At this word, her mind
cleared — she looked at and understood her position —
and she refused to speak — she would not plead " not
guilty " when charged with killing her own child.
Her mother, broken with years and with this affliction,
tottered from the rails of the dock, against which she
had leant, and sank heart-broken on the floor of the
court. She was carried to the open air by weeping
strangers, — carried past Alice, who never looked upon
her dear face again.

Still she stood silent, tearless, but conscious of every
act and relation. Anguish had changed her in one
day from a girl into a strong, self-reliant woman. To
her own soul she said : " My life is in ruin — nothing
can now increase the burden. If I speak, another
will stand here — another who has been wronged as I
have been. She was wretched before she became
guilty. Let me undergo — let me never see the face
of one who knew me, to remind me of the past. Be-

tween freedom and memory, and imprisonment and forgetfulness — I choose the latter."

These thoughts never became words in Alice's mind; but this was the mental process which resulted in her silence in the dock. The trial was short — she was found guilty. Then came the solitude and silence of the great prison.

Four white walls, a stone floor, a black iron door, a heavily barred window, through which she looked up at the moon and stars at night — and, enclosed within these walls, a young and beautiful girl, a tender heart that had never throbbed with a lawless desire, a conscience so sensitive, and a mind so pure that angels might have communed with her.

Shall not this prisoner find peace in solitude, and golden sermons in the waves of pain?

She had been one day and night in Millbank. The severe matron or warder of the pentagon opened her cell-door in the morning, and handed her two books, a Bible and prayer-book.

The window of the cell, outside the bars, was open. Without a word to the warder, the prisoner threw the books out of the open window.

" They are not true; I shall pray no more," she said, not fiercely, but firmly, as they fell into the yard within the pentagon.

She was reported to the authorities. They sent the Bible-reader to pray with her, in the cell, according to the rule laid down for the convict prisons; but she remained silent. They punished her, — for the dreadful word " Murder " was printed on her door-card; they shut her up in a dark cell for days and weeks, till her eyes dilated and her body shrank under the meagre food. Remember, a few weeks before, she was a simple, God-fearing country-girl. Neither prayer nor punishment could bring her into relenting, but only deepened the earnestness of her daily answer: —

" I shall pray no more."

Her case was brought before the Chief Director, Sir Joshua Hobb. This disciplinarian visited her dark cell, and, with a harsh " Ho, there ! " flashed a brilliant lamp on the entombed wretch. She sat on a low seat in the centre of the dark cell, her face bowed into her hands, perhaps to shut out the painfully sudden glare.

" She won't pray, eh ? " said the great reformer, looking at the slight figure that did not move. " We 'll see." He evidently took a special interest in this case.

An hour later, the prisoner was taken from her cell, and dragged or pushed by two strong female warders till she stood in an arched passage beneath the prison. Her clothing was rudely torn from her shoulders to the waist; her wrists were strapped to staples in the wall ; and, before her weakened and benumbed brain had realized the unspeakable outrage, the lash had swept her delicate flesh into livid stripes.

Then, for one weak moment, her womanhood conquered, and she shrieked, as if in supplication, the name of Him she had so bitterly refused to worship.

But the scream of her affliction was not a prayer, — it was the awful utterance of a parting spirit, the cry of a wrecked and tortured soul, an imprecation born of such agony as was only utterable in a curse. May God pity and blot out the sin !

They carried her senseless body to the hospital, where unconsciousness befriended her for many weeks. A brain-fever racked her; she lived the terrors of the past every hour; a weaker body would have sunk under the strain; but her time had not yet come.

The fever left her at last, — her consciousness returned; the austere, philanthropic women and hackneyed preachers labored by her bedside in rigid charity and sonorous prayer, during which her eyes remained closed and her lips motionless.

As her strength returned, she moved about the

ward, feeling a pleasant relief when she could do a
kindness to another inmate weaker than herself. She
would warm the drinks, smooth the pillows, or carefully give the medicines as prescribed, to her unfortunate sisters. And all this she performed silently.
She never smiled, and no one but her own heart knew
that her labor for others gave her comfort.

When her health was quite restored, she had become
valuable to the physicians and warders. She was
asked to remain in the hospital rather than to go back
and work in the cells.

She chose the hospital, and entered at once on her
regular duties as a nurse.

Why did she choose the busy hospital, instead of
the solitary cell? Because she was still a woman.
Trust in God had been taken from her; but she remained unselfish, or, rather, her life had assumed an
exalted selfishness, possible only to highly organized
natures. Though God was deaf, she could not believe
that good was dead, for she still felt sympathy for her
fellow-sufferers. God had made the world, but had
forgotten it, and the spirit of evil had taken His place.

"They say you don't believe in religion?" said a
dying woman to her one day; "then maybe you don't
believe that God has punished me like this for my
evil ways?"

Alice Walmsley looked at the unfortunate — then
searched her own heart before answering. Her affliction was her own; God had deserted her — had He
also deserted this poor wretch?

"God has not punished you," she answered; "you
have brought on your own punishment."

"Then God will give me my child in the other
world?" cried the woman with pitiful earnestness; "O,
say He will, and I shall die happy!"

Alice did not answer; but the iron of the question
pierced her soul. There lived beneath all the burden

of her suffering a love that thrilled her day and night, a yearning that never slept, a memory and pity of unspeakable tenderness for her dead child. It was grief in love and love in grief. She had tried to reason it away, but in vain. God, who had tortured her, or allowed her torture, had seized her babe for ransom. While she was wronged before Him, He held a hostage for her silence.

How should she answer this dying woman's question?

She walked from the ward straight to the matron's office, and asked to be sent to the cells — she could work no more in the hospital.

Expostulation, argument, threats, had no effect on her determination. Her resolution troubled every one in the hospital, for her services were highly prized. But she had settled the question. The mind may delay in solving a problem, but the soul's solution is instantaneous and unalterable. She was sent to the cell.

II.

A FLOWER IN THE CELL.

FIVE years of silent imprisonment had passed over Alice Walmsley — years of daily and hourly change and excitement for the outer world. Five years in solitary confinement are only one day, one day of dreary monotony repeated one thousand eight hundred and twenty-five times.

Take a starving beggar from the street, and seat him at your table, and tell him that he shall have food and money if he will turn his plate face downward, and return it face upward, one thousand eight hundred and twenty-five times — and the hungry wretch will drop from exhaustion before half the turnings are

done, and will run from your house with curses. The
solitary prisoner turns the same number of days with
harrowing weariness a thousand times multiplied in
five years. The days and nights of those years had
passed like a black and white vibration over Alice
Walmsley's life. They had brought little change to
the outward eye; and the inward change was only a
settlement of the elements of doubt and disbelief and
despair into a solid deposit in her heart.

No friends had visited her. When her mother died,
there was left no living relative. She had no love nor
attraction beyond her cell — beyond her own soul.
Every tie worth keeping had then been torn asunder.
Some lesser bonds she since had unloosed herself.
Why should any happy thing be united to one so for-
lorn and wretched ?

For God's pleasure she was undergoing this torture
— so they told her. She had neither sinned nor rebelled. She had been given life, and she had grown
to love it — but when the summer of her life had
come, she was drenched with affliction and wrong,
which she had not earned, of the cause of which she
was as innocent as her babe, murdered before her
eyes. Her heart, hope, love, trust, had been flung down
and trampled in the dust.

The alms of prayer that were doled out by the nasal
Scripture-readers had long since been carried past her
door. They regarded her as hopelessly lost. She never
spoke her dissent; but they could see that she did not
hear them, that she did not believe them. So they
left her to herself.

One day, a man sat in the governor's office with a
large book before him, in which he had been carefully
reading a page on which the governor, standing beside
him, had placed his index-finger.

"It is a remarkable case," said the governor; "and
she certainly is not insane."

"She was not a criminal by association ?" asked the visitor, closing the book. He was a powerfully built, dark-faced man, with a foreign air, and a deep voice. The studied respect of the governor proved him to be a person of importance. It was Mr. Wyville, who had recently arrived in London, and who was visiting the prisons, with authority from the Ministry itself.

"No," said the governor; "she was a village-girl, wife of a sea-captain. Here, at page 42, we find the police reports — see, only one short entry. The police didn't know her."

"She has never defended herself, nor reproached others ?" asked Mr. Wyville.

"Never," answered the governor. "She has never spoken about herself."

"It is very strange, and very sad," said Mr. Wyville to the governor. And to himself he murmured, "She must have suffered fearful wrong."

Soon after, in company with the governor, he passed along the corridor, and stopped at Alice Walmsley's cell. The warder opened the door. Mr. Wyville did not look at the prisoner, but walked across the cell, as if observing the window bars, upon which he laid his hand.

"The iron is covered with rust," he said to the governor. "The windows of this range certainly need repainting."

Then, apparently looking around in the same practical way, Mr. Wyville remained, perhaps, a minute in the cell. He had scarcely turned his eyes on the prisoner; yet the mute intensity of her face had sunk into his heart.

"She has been terribly wronged," he repeated to himself, as he left the prison. "God help her! she is very young to be so calm."

When Mr. Wyville emerged from the prison arch, he walked rapidly along the river toward Westminster. He was in deep thought. He proceeded a little dis-

tance, then stopped, and looked down on the turbid
stream, as if undecided. This was unlike the usual
calm deliberateness of his conduct. He was evidently
perplexed and troubled. After pausing a while, he
looked at his watch, and then retraced his steps, passed
Millbank, and walked on in the direction of Chelsea.

It was an old habit of his to solve difficult questions
as he walked; and he selected a quiet suburb, with
streets leading into the country roads.

In the streets, there was nothing very noticeable
about the man, except his athletic stride and deeply
bronzed face. He might be classed by the passing
observer as a naval officer who had served many years
in Southern latitudes, or as a foreign captain. His
dress had something of the sailor about its style and
cloth. But it is the inner man who interests us : let
us follow the burden of his thought.

"Remorse does not end in this calmness, unless the
prisoner be insane. Her mind is clear; she is not
melancholy; she is self-possessed and firm. Her
health has not suffered. Yet, she has abandoned belief in man's truth and God's mercy. She does not
claim that she is innocent; she makes no defence and
no charge; she accepts her punishment without a com-
plaint. These are not the symptoms of remorse or
guilt. She has abandoned prayer; she deliberately
shuts out the past and the future. Yet she is in all
other respects obedient, industrious, and kind. There
is only one explanation of these contradictions — she
is innocent, and she has suffered terrible wrong."

Mr. Wyville did not return to his house till late in
the evening. He had walked for hours; and, as he
went, he had unravelled, with infinite patience, the
psychological net-work that had troubled him. He
had come to a decision.

Two days after his visit to the prison, Alice Walmsley sat in her cell, sewing tirelessly. The morning had

opened like all the other mornings of her imprisonment; there was nothing new, nothing to suggest a new train of thought.

Some one who walked along the corridor about ten o'clock had seemed to hesitate a moment at her cell, and then had passed on. The governor, she thought, who had glanced through the watch-grate.

In the wall of every cell there was a minute hole, about two inches square on the exterior, cut in the solid stone. The opening, which grew wide towards the interior of the cell, was in the shape of a wedge. A warder outside could see a large part of the cell, while the prisoner could only see the eye of the warder. As the officers wore woollen slippers, they could observe the prisoners without being heard or seen.

At this opening, Alice Walmsley thought, the governor had stopped as he passed, and had looked into her cell. It was not unusual.

A few minutes later she paused in her work, almost impatiently, and tried to put away from her an unwelcome thought. After a short pause she renewed her sewing, working rapidly for a few minutes; and then she laid the coarse cloth aside, and buried her face in her hands.

She was thinking of her old life, of her old self; she had tried to escape from it, but could not. For years she had separated the past and the present until she had actually come to think of herself as two beings — one, who had been happy, and who was dead — the other, living, but separated from all the world — alone, with neither memories nor hopes, neither past nor future.

Yet to-day, without apparent cause, the two selves had drawn together — the happy Alice had come beseechingly to the unhappy one.

For an hour she remained motionless, her face bowed in her hands. Then she raised her head, but she did not renew her work. She stood up, and walked across the cell, and re-crossed it, in the rapid way of restless prisoners; but on the second passage, she stood still, with a bewildered air. Her eye had caught a gleam of bright color in the opening of the watch-grate. There was a flower in her cell!

She trembled as she reached her hand to take it. She did not try to recover her dispassionate calmness. She took it in her hand, and raised it to her lips slowly, and kissed it. It was a sweet rosebud, with two young leaves. She had not seen a flower nor heard a bird sing since she left her own little garden.

This tender thing had stolen inside her guard. Its sweet fragrance, before she knew of its presence, had carried her mind back to the happy days of her girl-hood. She kept the flower to her lips, kissing it. She fed her wistful eyes on its beauty. She had been so long without emotion, she had so carefully repressed the first promptings of imagination, that her heart had become thirsty unto death for some lovely or lovable thing. This sweet young flower took for her all forms of beauty. As she gazed on it, her soul drank in its delicious breath, like a soft and sensuous music; its perfect coloring filled her with still another delight; its youth, its form, its promise, the rich green of the two leaves, its exquisite complete-ness, made a very symphony for the desolate heart.

Two hours passed, and still she fondled the precious gift. She had not once thought of how the flower had come into her cell.

"You are pleased at last, Number Four," said a female warder, who had been looking into Alice's cell.

Number Four raised her eyes from the flower, and looked silently her answer. For the first time in five years, the warder saw that her eyes were flooded with tears.

She did not sew any more that day, — and, strange

to say, the officers took no heed of her idleness. There was a change in her face, a look of unrest, of strangeness, of timidity.

When first she looked upon the flower, a well had burst up in her heart, and she could not stop its flood. In one hour it had swept away all her barriers, had swamped her repression, had driven out the hopeless and defiant second self, and had carried into her cell the wronged, unhappy, but human and loving heart of the true Alice Walmsley.

She was herself. She feared to think it, — but she knew it must be so. When the warder spoke to her now, she shrank from the tone. Yesterday, it would have passed her like the harsh wind, unheeded.

That night, unlike all the nights of her imprisonment, she did not lie down and sleep as soon as the lights were extinguished. With the little flower in her hand, she sat on her low bedside in the still darkness, feeling through all her nature the returning rush of her young life's sympathy with the world.

The touch of the rosebud in her hand thrilled her with tenderness. She made no attempt to shut out the crowding memories. They flooded her heart, and she drank them in as a parched field drinks the drenching rain.

Toward midnight the moon rose above the city, silver-white in a black-blue sky, lovelier than ever she had seen it, Alice thought, as she looked through the bars of her window. She stood upon her low bed, opened the window, and looked up. At that moment her heart was touched with a loving thought of her dead mother. Her arms rested on the window-ledge, and her hands were raised before her, holding between them the little flower, as she might have held a peace-offering to a king.

Softly as the manna falls upon the desert, or the dew upon the wild flower, descended on the afflicted

heart the grace of God's love and mercy. The Eye
that looked from above on that white face upturned
amid the gloom of the prison, beheld the eyes brimmed
with tears, the lips quivering with profound emotion,
and the whole face radiant with faith and sorrow and
prayer.

"O, thank God!" she whispered, her weeping eyes
resting on the beautiful deep sky; "thank God for
this little flower! O, mother, hear me in heaven, and
pray for me, that God may forgive me for doubting
and denying His love!"

With streaming eyes she sank upon her knees by
the bedside, and poured her full heart in passionate
prayer. And, as she prayed, kneeling on the stones
of her cell, with bowed head, the beautiful moon had
risen high in the vault of night, and its radiance
flooded the cell, as if God's blessing were made manifest
in the lovely light, that was only broken by the dark
reflection of the window bars, falling upon the mourner
in the form of a cross. It was long past midnight
when she lay down to rest.

But next day Alice began her monotonous toil as
on all previous days. She was restless, unhappy; her
face was stained with weeping in the long vigil of the
night. But her heart had changed with the brief rest
she had taken. She began her day without prayer.
Her mind had moved too long in one deep groove to
allow its direction to be changed without laborious effort.

The little flower that had touched her heart so deeply
the day before lay upon the low shelf of her cell.
Alice took it up with a movement of the lips that
would have been a sad smile but for the emptiness of
her poor heart. "It grew in its garden, and loved its
sweet life," she thought; "and when the sun was
brightest, the selfish hand approached and tore it
from its stem, to throw it next day into the street,
perhaps."

Then flashed, for the first time, into her mind the question — Who had placed the flower in her cell? Had she been unjust — and had the hand that pulled this flower been moved by kindness, and kindness to her?

The thought troubled her, and she became timid and impressionable again. Who had brought her this flower? Whoever had done so was a friend, and pitied her. Else why — but perhaps every prisoner in the ward had also received a flower. Her heart closed, and her lips became firm at the thought.

A few moments later, she pulled the signal-wire of her cell, which moved a red board outside the door, so that it stood at right angles from the wall. This brought the warder, to know what was wanted. The door was opened, and the warder, a woman with a severe face but a kind eye, stood in the entrance. Alice had the flower in her hand.

" Have all the prisoners received flowers like this ? " she inquired, with a steady voice.

" No," said the warder.

In five years, this was the first question Number Four had ever asked.

" Why was this given to me ? " she asked, her voice losing its firmness, and her eyes filling with tears.

" I don't know," said the warder.

This was true : the hand that had dropped the flower into the watch-grate had done so unseen. The warder only knew that orders had been received from the governor that Number Four was not to be disturbed, nor the flower taken away.

The door closed again, and Alice raised the flower to her lips and kissed it. Some one had pitied her, had thought of her. She was not alone in the world. This reflection she could not drive away. She sat down to her work; but she could not see the cloth — her eyes were blurred with tears, her hands trembled. At last she rose, and pressed her open hands to her streaming eyes, and then sank on her knees beside her bed, and sobbed convulsively.

How long she remained so she did not know, but she felt a hand laid softly on her head, and heard her name called in a low voice, —

"Alice!"

A woman had entered the cell, and was kneeling beside her.

Alice raised her head, and let her eyes rest on a face as beautiful as an angel's, a face as white as if it were a prisoner's, but calm and sweet and sympathetic in every feature; and round the lovely face Alice saw a strange, white band, that made it look like a face in a picture.

It was a Sister of Mercy she had seen before when she worked in the hospital; she remembered she had seen her once sit up all night bathing the brow of a sick girl, dying of fever. This thought came clearly to her mind as she looked at Sister Cecilia's face, and saw the unselfishness and devotion of her life in her pure look.

"Alice," said Sister Cecilia, "why do you grieve so deeply? tell me why you are so unhappy — tell me, dear, and I will try to make you happier, or I will grieve with you."

Alice felt her whole self-command deserting her, and her heart melting at the kindness of the voice and words.

"Turn to me, and trust me, dear," said Sister Cecilia; "tell me why you weep so bitterly. I know you are innocent of crime, Alice; I never believed you guilty. And now, I have come to bring you comfort."

Sister Cecilia had put one arm around Alice, and, as she spoke, with the other hand she raised the tearful face and kissed it. Then the flood-gates of Alice's affliction burst, and she wept as if her heart were breaking.

Sister Cecilia waited till the storm of sorrow had exhausted itself, only murmuring little soothing words all the time, and patting the sufferer's hand and cheek softly.

"Now, dear," she said at length, "as we are kneeling, let us pray for a little strength and grace, and then you shall tell me why you grieve."

Sister Cecilia, taking Alice's hands between her own, raised them a little, and then she raised her eyes, with a sweet smile on her face, as if she were carrying a lost soul to the angels, and in a voice as simple as a child's, and as trustful, said the Lord's Prayer, Alice repeating the words after her.

Never before had the meaning of the wonderful prayer of prayers entered Alice's soul. Every sentence was full of warmth and comfort and strength. The words that sank deepest were these, — she repeated them afterwards with the same mysterious effect, — "*Thy will be done on earth, as it is in heaven.*" She did not know why these words were the best, but they were.

"Now, Alice," said Sister Cecilia, rising cheerfully, when the prayer was done, "we are going to bathe our faces, and go on with our sewing, and have a long talk."

Alice obeyed, or rather she followed the example. Sister Cecilia's unaffected manner had won her so completely that she felt a return of her girlish companionship. All other teachers of religion whom Alice had seen in the prison had come to her with unsympathetic formality and professional airs of sanctity, which repelled her.

Half an hour later, Alice was quietly sewing, while Sister Cecilia sat on the pallet and talked, and drew Alice into a chat. She made no reference to the grief of the morning. The cases in the hospital, the penitence of poor sick prisoners, the impenitence of others,

the gratitude and the selfishness and the many other
phases of character that came under her daily observation — these were the topics of the little Sister's conversation.

"Why, I might as well be a prisoner, too," she said,
smiling, and making Alice smile; "I have been in the
hospital seven years. I was there two years before
you came. You see, I am as white as a prisoner."

"Yes," said Alice, looking sadly at her; "it is not
right. Why do you not grieve as they do?"

"Why?" answered Sister Cecilia, gayly, "because
I am not a criminal, perhaps. I am like you, Alice;
I have less reason to grieve than the other poor
things."

Alice had never seen it in this light before, and she
could not help smiling at the philosophy of the little
Sister. But she was affected by it very deeply.

"If you had remained in the hospital, Alice," said
the nun, "you would have been as much a Sister of
Mercy as I am. Do you know, I was very sorry when
you left the hospital."

Every word she said, somehow, touched Alice in a
tender place. Was the wise little nun choosing her
words? At any rate, it was well and kindly done.

When she kissed Alice, and pulled the signal-wire
to go out, her smile filled the cell and Alice's heart
with brightness. She promised to come and see her
every day till the ship sailed; and then they would be
together all the day.

"Are you going to Australia?" asked Alice, in
amazement.

"Certainly," said Sister Cecilia, with a smile of
mock surprise. "Why, those poor children couldn't
get along without me — fifty of them. Now, I'm
very glad I shall have you to help me, Alice. We'll
have plenty to do, never fear."

She was leaving the cell — the warder had opened

the door — when Alice timidly touched her dress, and drew her aside, out of the warder's sight.

"I am not a Catholic," said Alice, in a tremulous whisper.

"No matter, child," said the little nun, taking her face between her hands and kissing her eyes; "you are a woman. Good-by, till to-morrow; and say your prayers, like my own good girl."

Alice stood gazing at the spot where she had stood, long after the door had closed. Then she turned and looked through the window at the bright sky, with her hands clasped at full length before her. As she looked, a sparrow perched on her window-sill, and she smiled, almost laughed at the little cautious fellow. She took some crumbs from her shelf and threw them to him; and as she did so she thought that she might have done it every day for five years had she been as happy as she was then.

III.

FOLLOWING A DARK SPIRIT.

ABOUT a week after the incident of the flower, Mr. Wyville, accompanied by his black servant, Ngarra-jil, left London on the Northern train. The black man was clad from throat to feet in a wrap or mantle of thick cloth, though the summer day was bland and warm. He settled silently into a corner of the railway carriage, watching his master with a keen and constant look. Mr. Wyville, sitting beside the window, seemed to observe the richly cultivated fields and picturesque villages through which the mail train flew without pausing; but in truth he neither saw nor thought of outward things.

There is a power in some minds of utterly shutting
out externals — of withdrawing the common functions
from the organs of sense to assist the concentration of
the introverted mind. At such a time, the open eye is
blind, it has become a mere lens, reflecting but not
perceiving; the tympanum of the ear vibrates to the
outward wave, but has ceased to translate its message
to the brain. The soul within has separated itself
from the moving world, and has retired to its cell like
an anchorite, taking with it some high subject for con ·
templation, or some profound problem for solution.

From this closet of the soul emerge the lightning
thoughts that startle, elevate, and deify mankind,
sweeping away old systems like an overflow of the
ocean. Within this cell the Christ-mind reflected for
thirty-three years, before the Word was uttered. Within
this cell the soul of Dante penetrated the horrescent
gloom of the infernal spheres, and beheld the radiant
form of Beatrice.   Within this cell the spirit that was
Shakespeare bisected the human heart, and read every
impulse of its mysterious network. Here, the blind
Milton forgot the earth, and lived an awful æon beyond the worlds, amid the warring thoughts of God.

Great and sombre was the Thought which lay within
the cell of this traveller's soul, to be investigated and
solved.   Villages, and fields, and streams passed the
outward eye, that was, for the time, the window of a
closed and darkened room.

As the pale corpse lies upon the dissecting table,
before the solitary midnight student, so lay upon the
table within this man's soul, a living body for dissec-
tion — the hideous body of Crime. For years it had
lain there, and the brooding soul had often withdrawn
from the outer world to contemplate its repulsive and
mysterious aspect. The knife was in the hand of the
student, but he knew not where to begin the incision.
The hideous thing to be examined was inorganic as a

whole, and yet every atom of its intertexture was a
perfect organ.

To his unceasing vision, the miscreated form became luminous and transparent; and he saw that,
throughout its entire being, beat one maleficent pulsation, accordant with the rhythm of some unseen and
intermittent sea. He saw that the parts and the
whole were one, yet many — that every atom had
within itself the seminal part and the latent pulse of
the ocean of Sin.

For years he had looked upon this fearful body,
wonderful, observant, speculative. For years, when
the contemplation had ceased, he had knelt beside the
evil thing and prayed for light and knowledge.

Day and night were as an outward breath to the
soul of the thinker. The light faded and the darkness
fell, but he knew it not. His whole being was turned
within, and he would have groaned with sorrow at
what he saw, were it not for an adamantine faith in
God, love, and justice, that bridged the gulf of doubt
with a splendid arch.

It was midnight when the train arrived in Liverpool.
The black man, Ngarra-jil, who had watched so long
and tirelessly the marvellous face of his master, rose
from his corner, purposely arousing Mr. Wyville's
attention. He smiled kindly at Ngarra-jil, and spoke
to him in his own language, continuing to do so as
they were driven through the streets to a hotel.

Something of unusual importance had brought Mr.
Wyville from London. That night, though the fatigue
of the journey would have overpowered an ordinary
man, he did not retire to rest till early morning, and
then he slept scarcely three hours. In the forenoon
of that day, leaving Ngarra-jil at the hotel, he took a
further journey, to the little village of Walton-le-Dale,
— the native village of Alice Walmsley.

It was clear that Mr. Wyville had come to Lanca-

shire on some purpose connected with this unhappy
girl, for his first visit, having inquired at the inn, was
to the quiet street where stood her old home. He
walked up the weed-grown pathway to the deserted
house, and finding the outer door of the porch unlocked,
as it had been left five years before, he entered, and
sat there on the decaying bench for a short time. Then
he retraced his steps, and inquired his way to the
police station.

The solitary policeman of Walton-le-Dale was just
at that time occupied in painting a water-barrel, which
stood on its donkey-cart in the street.

There was only one well of sweet water in Walton,
the village lying on very low land ; and the villagers
paid each week a halfpenny a family to their policeman, in return for which he left in their houses every
day two large pails of water.

Officer Lodge, they called him ; and though he was
a modest and unassuming old fellow, he made a point
of being deaf to any remark or request that was not
prefaced by this title. He resented even " Mr." Lodge ;
but he was excited to an indignant glance at the
offensive familiarity of plain " Lodge."

He was a small old man, of a gentle and feminine
disposition ; but he had "served his time " on a man-
of-war, and had been pensioned for some active service
in certain vague Chinese bombardments. It was
queerly inconsistent to hear the old fellow relate wild
stories of carnage, with a woman's voice and a timid
maiden air.

As Mr. Wyville approached Officer Lodge, that
guardian of the peace was laboriously trying to turn
the barrel in its bed so that he might paint the under-
side. The weight was too great for the old man, and
he was puzzled. He stood looking at the ponderous
cask with a divided mind.

" Raise it on its end," said Mr. Wyville, who had

reached the spot unseen by the aquarian policeman.

Officer Lodge looked at him in distrust, fearing
sarcasm in the remark; but he met the grave impressive look, and was mollified. Besides, the advice
struck him as being practical. Without a word, he
easily heaved the cask into an upright position, and
found that he could paint its whole circumference.
This put him in good humor.

"If that were my barrel, I should paint the hoops
red instead of green," said Mr. Wyville.

"Why?" asked Officer Lodge, dipping his brush in
the green paint.

"Because red lead preserves iron, while the verdi-
gris used to color green paint corrodes it."

Officer Lodge wiped his brush on the rim of the
paint-pot, and looked at Mr. Wyville timidly, but
pleasantly.

"You know things, you do," he said. "But suppose
you hadn't no red paint?"

"I should paint the whole barrel white — white
lead preserves iron — and then give the hoops a smart
coat of black. That would make a handsome barrel."

"I should think so! By jewkins! wouldn't it so?"
said Officer Lodge.

Mr. Wyville stood on the road talking with the old
man, until that personage had quite decided to paint
the barrel white.

"Now, my friend," said Mr. Wyville, "could you
direct me to the office of the police inspector of this
village?"

Officer Lodge was rather taken aback. He was in
his shirt-sleeves, like a common laborer, and here was
a gentleman, evidently a foreigner, in search of the
police inspector; he was gratified at the important
title. He took his coat from the cart, and slipped it
on, obtruding its brass buttons on the stranger.

"There ain't exac'ly a hinspector in Walton," he said, with an air of careless pomp; "but I'm the police, at your service, sir."

"I am very glad," said Mr. Wyville, gravely; "I wish to make some inquiries about a case of murder that occurred in this village some years ago. Can you assist me?"

"There was only one such a case, sir," said Officer Lodge, the kindliness of his feminine heart speaking in his saddened tone; "I know all about it. It was me as arrested her; and it was unwilling work on my side. But a hofficer must do his duty, sir."

"Can we not sit down somewhere, and talk it over?" asked Mr. Wyville.

"At the hinn, sir, certingly," replied Officer Lodge "and a good glass a' hale you can 'ave, too, sir."

They were soon seated in a quiet little room, and each had his "glass a' hale" before him.

Officer Lodge told the story like a man who had often told it before: all the angles were rounded, and the dramatic points were brought out with melodramatic emphasis. Mr. Wyville let him run on till he had no more to say.

"And this strange woman, who came to the village on the morning of the murder," he said, when he had heard all; "this woman who was Draper's first wife— has she ever been heard of since?"

"O, Harriet Draper, bless you, yessir," said Officer Lodge; "she comes back periodical, and gets into quod — parding me, sir, I mean into jail."

"What does she do?" asked Mr. Wyville.

"Well, she's a bad 'un. We don't know where she comes from, nor where she goes to. She drinks 'eavy, and then she goes down there near Draper's 'ouse, and the other 'ouse, 'an she kicks up a muss of crying and shouting. She does it periodical; and we has to lock her up."

" When was she here last ? " asked Mr. Wyville.

Officer Lodge pulled out a leather-covered pass-book, and examined it.

" She 's out of her reg'lar horder, this time," he said, " she 'aven't been 'ere for a year. But I heerd of her later than that in the penitentiary at Liverpool."

Mr. Wyville asked no more questions. He wrote an address on a card, and handed it to Officer Lodge.

" If this woman return here," he said, " or if you find out where she is, write to that address, and you shall be well rewarded."

" Head Office of Police, Scotland Yard, London," read Officer Lodge from the card. " Yessir, I 'll do it. O, no, none of that," he said, firmly, putting back some offering in Mr. Wyville's hand ; " I 'm in your debt, sir ; I was a'most going to make a fool of myself with that bar' l. I 'm obliged to you, sir ; and I 'll do this all the better for remembering of your kindness."

Mr. Wyville took a friendly leave of good-natured Officer Lodge, and returned to Liverpool by the next train. Arrived there, he did not proceed straight to his hotel, but drove to the city penitentiary, where he repeated his inquiries about Harriet Draper ; but he only learned that she had been discharged eight months before.

Neither police nor prison-books could give him further information. Disappointed and saddened, next day he returned to London.

IV.

MR. HAGGETT.

SISTER CECILIA visited Alice Walmsley every day
for several weeks, until the happy change in the
latter's life had grown out of its strangeness. Their
intercourse had become a close and silent communion.

For the first month or so, the kind and wise little
nun had conversed on anything that chanced for a
topic; but afterwards they developed the silent system
— and it was the better of the two.

Sister Cecilia used to enter with a cheery smile,
which Alice returned. Then Sister Cecilia would
throw crumbs on the sill for the sparrows, Alice watching her, still smiling. Then the little Sister would
seat herself on the pallet, and take out her rosary, and
smilingly shake her finger at Alice, as if to say: —

"Now, Alice, be a good girl, and don't disturb me."

And Alice, made happy by the sweet companionship, would settle to her sewing, hearing the birds
twitter and chirp, and seeing the golden sunlight pour
through the bars into her cell.

Sister Cecilia had a great many prayers to say every
day, and she made a rule of saying the whole of them
in Alice's cell.

The change in Alice's life became known to all the
officials in the prison, and a general interest was
awakened in the visits of the good Sister to her cell.
From the governor down to the lowest female warder,
the incident was a source of pleasure and a subject of
every-day comment.

But there was one official who beheld all this with
displeasure and daily increasing distrust. This was
Mr. Haggett, the Scripture-reader of the prison.

Into the hands of Mr. Haggett had been given the

spiritual welfare of all the convicts in Millbank, of every creed — Christian, Turk, and Jew.

It was a heavy responsibility; but Mr. Haggett felt himself equal to the task. It would be wrong to lay blame for the choice of such a teacher on any particular creed. He had been selected and appointed by Sir Joshua Hobb, whose special views of religious influence he was to carry out. Mr. Haggett was a tall man, with a highly respectable air. He had side-whiskers, brushed outward till they stood from his lank cheeks like paint-brushes; and he wore a long square-cut brown coat. He had an air of formal superiority. His voice was cavernous and sonorous. If he only said "Good-morning," he said it with a patronizing smile, as if conscious of a superior moral nature, and his voice sounded solemnly deep.

One would have known him in the street as a man of immense religious weight and godly assumption, by the very compression of his lips. These were his strong features, even more forcible than the rigid respectability of his whiskers, or the grave sanctity of his voice. His lips were not exactly coarse or thick; they were large, even to bagginess. His mouth was wide, and his teeth were long; but there was enough lip to cover up the whole, and still more — enough left to fold afterwards into consciously pious lines around the mouth.

When Mr. Haggett was praying, he closed his eyes, and in a solemnly-sonorous key began a personal interview with the Almighty. While he was informing God, with many deep "Thou knowests," his lips were in full play; every reef was shaken out, so to speak. But when Mr. Haggett was instructing a prisoner, he moved only the smallest portion of labial tissue that could serve to impress the unfortunate with his own unworthiness and Mr. Haggett's exalted virtue and importance.

Mr. Haggett visited the cells for four hours every day, taking regular rounds, and prayed with and instructed the prisoners. He never sympathized with them, nor pretended to, and, of course, he never had their confidence — except the sham confidence and contrition of some second-timers, who wanted a recommendation for a pardon.

There was another official who made regular rounds, with about the same intervals of time as Mr. Haggett. This was the searcher and fumigator — a warder who searched the cells for concealed implements, and fumigated with some chemical the crevices and joints, to keep them wholesomely clean. When a prisoner had a visit from the searcher and fumigator, he knew that Mr. Haggett would be around soon.

The sense of duty in the two officials was very much alike under the surface; and it would have saved expense and time had Mr. Haggett carried, besides his Bible, the little bellows and probe of the fumigator — if he had been, in fact, the searcher and fumigator of both cells and souls.

Mr. Haggett had observed, with horror, the visits of the Popish nun to the cell of a prisoner whom he knew to be a Protestant. Though he never had had anything to say to Number Four, and never had prayed with her for five years, he now deemed her one of those specially confided to his care. He was shocked to the centre when first he saw the white-capped nun sitting in the cell, with a rosary in her hands.

Mr. Haggett would have complained at once, but he did not like the governor. He had been insulted, he felt he had, by the governor, who never met him but he asked the same impertinent question: "Well, Mr. Haggett, got your regular commission in the ministry yet?"

Mr. Haggett was in hopes of becoming, some day, a regular minister of the Established Church. He was "studying for it," he said ; and his long experience in the prison would tell in his favor. But the years had flown, and he had not secured the reverend title he so ardently coveted. The Lords Bishops were not favorably impressed by Mr. Haggett's acquirements or qualities.

The daily presence of the nun in one of his cells goaded him to desperation. He stopped one day at the door of Number Four, and, in his deepest chest-tones, with a smile that drew heavily on the labial reefs, addressed the Sister : —

"Is this prisoner a Rom — ah — one of your per-suasion, madam ? "

"No, sir," said the little Sister, with a kind smile at Alice ; "I wish she were."

"Hah ! — Why, madam, do you visit a prisoner who is not of your persuasion ? "

"Because no one else visited her," said Sister Ce-cilia, looking at Mr. Haggett with rather a startled air , "and she needed some one."

"Madam, I wish to pray with this prisoner this morning, and ah — ah — I will thank you to leave this cell."

The work dropped from Alice's hands, and a wild look came into her eyes. First, she stared at Mr. Haggett, as if she did not understand. From his un-inviting face, now flushed somewhat, and working as if the godly man were in a passion, she turned, with a mute appeal, to Sister Cecilia.

The nun had risen, startled, but not confused, at the unexpected harshness of the tone, rather than the words. She realized at once that Mr. Haggett, who had never before addressed her, nor noticed her presence, had power to expel her from Alice's cell, and forbid her entrance in future.

She determined on the moment to make an effort for Alice's sake.

" This prisoner is to be my hospital assistant on the convict ship," said Sister Cecilia to Mr. Haggett.

" Madam!" said Mr. Haggett, harshly, and there was a movement of his foot as if he would have stamped his order ; " I wish to pray with this prisoner !"

He motioned commandingly with his hand, ordering the nun from the cell.

Sister Cecilia took a step toward the door, rather alarmed at the man's violence, but filled with keen sorrow for poor Alice.

The rude finger of the angry Scripture-reader still pointed from the cell. Sister Cecilia had taken one step outward, when Alice Walmsley darted past her, and stood facing Mr. Haggett, her left hand reached behind her with spread fingers, as if forbidding the nun to depart.

" Begone !" she cried to Haggett; " how dare you come here ? I do not want your prayers."

Mr. Haggett grew livid with passion at this insult from a prisoner. He had, perhaps, cherished a secret dislike of Alice for her old rebellion against his influence. He glared at her a moment in silent fury, while his great lips curved into their tightest reefs, showing the full line of his long teeth.

But he did not answer her. He looked over her, into the cell, where Sister Cecilia stood affrighted. He reached his long arm toward her, and still commanded her from the cell, with a hand trembling with wrath. He would settle with the recalcitrant convict when this strange ally and witness had departed.

" Come out !" motioned the lips of the wrathful Scripture-reader, while his long finger crooked, as if it were a hook to drag her forth.

At this moment, a key rattled in the door at the end of the corridor, and there entered the passage Sir Joshua Hobb, Mr. Wyville, and the governor, followed by the two warders of the pentagon. The gentlemen were evidently on a tour of inspection. When they had come to the cell of Number Four, they stood in astonishment at the scene.

Alice Walmsley, hitherto so submissive and silent, was aroused into feverish excitement. She stood facing Mr. Haggett, and, as the others approached, she turned to them wildly.

"How dare this man interfere with me?" she cried. "I will not allow him to come near me. I will not have his prayers!"

"Be calm, child!" said Mr. Wyville, whom she had never before seen. His impressive and kind face and tone instantly affected the prisoner. Her hands fell to her sides.

"Lock that cell!" said Sir Joshua Hobb, in a hard, quick voice. "This prisoner must be brought to her senses."

Alice was again defiant in an instant.

"Tell this man to begone!" she excitedly demanded.

"Come out!" hissed Mr. Haggett, grimly stretching his neck toward Sister Cecilia, and still bending his lean finger like a hook.

"She shall not go out!" cried Alice, in a frenzy.

It seemed to her as if they were tearing something dearer than life from her. She dashed the hooked hand of the Bible-reader aside, bruising it against the iron door.

"Warders?" shouted Sir Joshua Hobb, "take this woman to the refractory cells. She shall remain in the dark till she obeys the rules. Take her away!"

The warders approached Alice, who now stood in the door-way. She had turned her agonized face as she felt Sister Cecilia's hand laid upon her shoulder, and her breast heaved convulsively.

As the warders seized her arms, she started with pitiful alarm, and shuddered.

"Stop!" cried a deep voice, resonant with command. Mr. Wyville had spoken.

"Release the prisoner!"

Every eye was turned on him. Even Alice's excitement was subdued by the power of the strange interruption. The Scripture-reader was the first to come to words. He addressed the governor.

"Who is this, who countermands the order of the Chief Director?"

Before the governor could answer, Sir Joshua Hobb spoke.

"This is insolence, sir! My order shall be obeyed."

"It shall not!" said Mr. Wyville, calmly, and walking to the cell door.

"By what authority do you dare interfere?" demanded Sir Joshua Hobb.

"By this!" said Mr. Wyville, handing him a paper.

The enraged Chief Director took the document, and glanced at the signature.

"Bah!" he shouted. "This Ministry is dead. This is waste paper. Out of the way, sir!"

"Stay!" said Mr. Wyville, taking from his breast a small case, from which he drew a folded paper, like a piece of vellum, which he handed to the governor of the prison.

"This, then, is my authority!"

The prompt old major took the paper, read it, and then, still holding it before him, raised his hat as if in military salute.

"Your authority is the first, sir," he said, decisively and respectfully, to Mr. Wyville.

"I demand to see that paper!" cried the Chief Director.

The governor handed it to him, and he read it through, his rage rapidly changing into a stare of blank amazement and dismay.

"I beg you to forgive me, sir," he said at length, in a low tone. "It would have been for the benefit of discipline, however, had I known of this before."

"That is true, sir," answered Mr. Wyville, "and had there been time for explanation you should have known my right before I had used it."

"You have shaken my official authority, sir," said Sir Joshua, still expostulatory.

"I am very sorry," answered Mr. Wyville; "but another moment's delay and this prisoner might have been driven to madness. Authority must not forget humanity."

"Authority is paramount, sir," humbly responded Sir Joshua, handing the potent paper to Mr. Wyville; "allow me to take my leave."

The humiliated Chief Director walked quickly from the corridor.

Mr. Wyville turned to the cell, and met the brimming eyes of the prisoner, the eloquent gratitude of the look touching him to the heart. He smiled with ineffable kindness, and with an almost imperceptible motion of the hand requested Sister Cecilia to remain and give comfort.

Mr. Haggett still remained in the entry, hungrily watching the cell. Mr. Wyville passed in front of the door, and turning, looked straight in his face. The discomfited Scripture-reader started as if he had received an electric shock. He was dismayed at the power of this strange man.

"You have passed this door with your prayers for five years, sir," said Mr. Wyville; "you will please to continue your inattention."

"The prisoner is not a Roman —" Haggett began, with shaken tones.

The hand of the soldierly old governor fell sharply, twice, on his shoulder. He looked round. The governor's finger was pointed straight down the passage, and his eye sternly ordered Mr. Haggett in the same direction. He hitched the sacred volume under his arm, and without a sound followed the footsteps of Sir Joshua.

His eager eyes had been denied a sight of the mysterious document; but his heart, or other organs, infallibly told him that he and his chief were routed beyond hope of recovery.

V.

TWO HEADS AGAINST ONE.

SIR JOSHUA HOBB sat in his Department Office in Parliament Street, with every sign of perplexity and rage in his face and attitude. His contest of authority with the unknown and mysterious man had fairly crushed him. In the face of the officials whom he had trained to regard his word as the utterance of Power itself, never to be questioned nor disobeyed, he had been challenged, commanded, degraded. It was a bitter draught; and what if he had only taken the first sickening mouthful?

He was interrupted in his morose reflections by the entrance of Mr. Haggett, whose air was almost as dejected as his superior's.

Haggett stood silently at the door, looking at the great man, somewhat as a spaniel might look at its master. The spare curtain of his lips was folded into leathery wrinkles round his capacious mouth.

" Haggett," said Sir Joshua, turning wearily to the fire, " who the devil is this man?"

" He's a rich Australian — " began Haggett, in a confidential voice.

" Ass!" said the Chief Director, without looking at him.

Mr. Haggett, returning not even a glance of resentment, accepted the correction, and remained silent.

" Haggett," said Sir Joshua, after a pause, during

which he had stared into the fire, "when does the convict ship sail?"

"In two weeks, sir."

"I want you to go to West Australia on that ship, Haggett."

"I, Sir Joshua? Leave London — I shall be ordained this year — I shall —"

"Pshaw! I want you, man. No one else will do. You can attend to private matters on your return. I shall personally assist you with my influence."

"Well, Sir Joshua?"

"No one else can do it, Haggett."

"What is to be done, sir?"

"I want to know all that is to be known in Western Australia about this Wyville."

"Do you suspect anything, sir?" asked Mr. Haggett.

"No; I have no reason either for suspicion or belief. I know absolutely nothing about the man, nor can I find any one who does."

"And yet that commission —"

"Yes — that was a disappointment. In one or two cases I have heard of the same high influence, given in the same secret manner."

"Were the other holders mysterious, too?" asked Haggett, reflectively, folding and unfolding his facial hangings.

"They were all cases in which philanthropists might meet with opposition from officials; and this strange but unquestionable power was given as a kind of private commission."

"It strikes down all the rules, and —"

"Yes, yes," interrupted Sir Joshua, striking the coal with the tongs; "but there it is. It must be acknowledged without question."

"Have you no clew to the reason for which this special authority was given to him?" asked Haggett.

"I have not thought of it; but I am not surprised.

This man, as you know, has reformed the Indian **Penal**
System at the Andaman Islands, expending immense
sums of his own money to carry out the change.
Afterward, he was received by the French Emperor as
an authority on the treatment of crime, and had much
to do with their new transportation scheme. A man
with this record, accepted by the Prime Minister, was
just the person to be specially commissioned by the
Queen."

"He is young to be so very wealthy," mused
Haggett.

"Yes; that is mysterious — no one knows the source
of his wealth. This is your mission — find out all
about him, and report to me by mail within six
months."

"Then I am really to go to Australia?" said Haggett, with a doleful aspect.

"Yes, Haggett; there's no other way. Inquiry into
mysterious men's lives is always worth the trouble.
You may learn nothing, but — it had better be done."

"Well, Sir Joshua, I want a favor from you in
return."

"What is it? You shall have it, if it lie in my
power."

"Send that prisoner, Number Four, on the ship; but
countermand the order for the Papist nun."

"You want the nun to remain?"

"Yes, sir; they ought to be separated. This Wyville
takes a great interest in Number Four. It was he that
sent the nun to her."

"Certainly, Haggett; it shall be done. Stay, let me
write the order now."

"Thank you, Sir Joshua," said Haggett, rubbing his
hands.

"There; take that to the governor of Millbank.
Number Four shall be sent with the first batch to the
ship The nun is to remain."

Mr. Haggett departed, and as he walked down Parliament Street, glancing furtively around to see that he was unobserved, he smiled to the uttermost reef.

VI.

FEMALE TRANSPORTS.

THE morning arrived for the convict ship to sail, and the last chains of male prisoners were mustered in the prison yard of Millbank, ready to be marched to the train, for embarkation on the convict ship at Portland.

In one of the pentagonal yards stood the female prisoners, fifty in number. They whispered covertly to each other, enjoying for the first time for years the words that were not orders, and the faces that were not cold.

" What is your name ? "

" How long have you served ? "

" What nice hair you have."

" Will they cut off our hair again in Australia ? "

" Were you lagged before ? "

" That one there, with the red mark on her cheek, was sentenced to be hung."

" This is my second time."

These were the words that might be heard in the ranks — short sentences, full of direct meaning, such as are always spoken when formality is absent, and curiosity is excited.

The male chains having been inspected by the governor, who was accompanied by Mr. Wyville, had marched from the prison to the railway station.

Four great wagons or tumbrils rolled into the yard, to carry away the female convicts. Before they entered the wagons, the governor addressed the women, telling them that their good conduct in prison had earned this change; that their life in the new country to which they were going would be one of opportunity; that their past was all behind them, and a fair field before them to work out honest and happy lives.

Many of the prisoners sobbed bitterly as the kind governor spoke. Hope, indeed, was bright before them but they were parting from all that they had ever loved; they would never more see the face of father or mother, brother or sister; they would never more see an English field or an English flower. Their lives had been shattered and shameful; but the moment of parting from every association of youth was the more embittered, perhaps, by the thought of their unworthiness.

When the governor had spoken, they entered the tumbrils, and the guards fell in. The old governor raised his hat. He was deeply affected at the scene, common though it must have been to him.

"Good-by, and God bless you all in your new life!" he said.

The driver of the front tumbril looked round, to see that all was ready before starting his horses.

"Wait," said a tall man, who was rapidly and eagerly scanning the faces of the women, as he passed from wagon to wagon; "there's a mistake here."

"What is the matter there?" shouted the governor.

"There is one prisoner absent, sir," said the tall man, who was Mr. Haggett; "one prisoner absent who was ordered for this ship."

"What prisoner?" asked the governor.

"Number Four."

"Start up your horses," shouted the governor; and the first tumbril lumbered out of the yard.

The governor was looking at Mr. Haggett, who stood beside the last wagon, his face a study of rage and disappointment.

"That prisoner was specially ordered for this ship," he repeated. "Sir Joshua Hobb wrote the order with his own hand."

"He has countermanded it," said the governor, curtly.

"When?" asked Haggett.

"Two hours ago," said the governor. "The prisoner will remain in Millbank."

Mr. Haggett looked his baffled malevolence at the governor, who paid no heed to the glance. Mr. Wyville stood close to him; but Haggett never met his eye during the scene. As he departed, however, in passing him, he raised his eyes for an instant to Mr. Wyville's face and said, —

"I am going to West Australia. I shall soon return."

Mr. Wyville's face might have been of marble, so absolutely unconscious did he seem of the presence or words of Haggett.

The tumbrils rolled from the yard with their strange freight, and Mr. Haggett strode from the prison. He stood on the poop of the transport as she sailed from Portland that afternoon.

More than once that day did Haggett's words repeat themselves like a threat in Mr. Wyville's mind; and when all was silent in sleeping London that night, he arose from the study-table at which he wrote, and paced the room in sombre thought. His mind was reasoning with itself, and at last the happier side conquered. He stopped his tireless walk, and smiled; but it was a sad smile.

"Poor children!" he murmured; "what would become of them here? I must instruct Tepairu, and — and then," he said, looking reverently upward through the night, "Thy will be done."

11

VII.

AFTER NINE YEARS.

So the state of Alice Walmsley was not changed by the zeal of Mr. Haggett; indeed no change had resulted from it except the increased hatred of the Chief Director for Mr. Wyville, and the sleuth-dog errand on which Haggett had sailed for Australia.

Alice did not know nor think of the causes that had kept her from transportation. One day she was quietly informed by the warder that the ship had sailed. She hardly knew whether to be glad or sorry, for her own sake; but of late she had not been quite alone in the world. Her eyes filled with tears, and she clasped her hands before her.

"You are sorry, Number Four," said the warder.

"She was so good — she made me so happy," answered Alice, with streaming eyes.

"Who?"

"Sister Cecilia."

"She has not gone," said the warder, smiling; "see, she is coming here. Good day, Sister; somebody was crying for you."

The joy of Alice was unbounded, as she held the serge dress of Sister Cecilia, and looked in her kind and pleasant face. The change in Alice's character was more marked in this scene than in any circumstance since the gleam of the flower had caught her eye in the cell. The strong will seemed to have departed; the self-reliance, born of wrong and anguish, had disappeared; she was a simple and impulsive girl again.

Between the innocent happiness of her young life and the fresh tenderness now springing in her heart, there lay an awful gulf of sorrow and despair. But she was on the high bank — she looked across the gloom and saw the sunny fields beyond, and, as she looked, the far shore drew nearer to her, and the dismal strait between grew narrower.

" Alice," said Sister Cecilia, gravely, when the happy greeting was over, " it is now time that something were done for your release."

The light faded from Alice's face, and after a long look, full of sadness, at the Sister, she bent her face into her hands, remaining silent.

" Would you not like to be free, Alice ? "

" I am happy here — I do not think of it — why do you ask me ? " she said, wistfully.

" Because it is not right that an innocent person should remain here. Tell me the whole sad story, child, and let me see what can be done."

" O, Sister Cecilia, I cannot — I cannot ! " sobbed Alice. " O, do not ask me — do not make me think of my sweet little baby — I cannot think of it dead — indeed, I cannot speak of that ! "

" Alice," said the nun, " your baby is with God, saved from the stains and sorrows of life. This woman," and the voice of Sister Cecilia grew almost severe, " this terrible woman — I have heard that she is a bad and wretched woman, Alice — deserves nothing from you but justice. God demands justice to ourselves as well as to others."

" I cannot accuse her," answered Alice, in a low voice, gradually returning to its old firmness. " She has suffered more than I — God pardon her ! And I know that she suffered first."

" Well, poor child," said the nun, deeply affected, " we must ask for a pardon, then, for you."

Alice rose from her low seat, and stood before the window, looking upward, with her hands clasped before her — an attitude grown familiar to her of late.

" My dead mother knows I am innocent of crime,'

she said slowly, as if speaking to her own heart; "no one else knows it, though some may believe it. I cannot be pardoned for a crime I have not committed. That were to accept the crime. I shall not accuse her, though my own word should set me free. Do not ask me to speak of it any more, Sister Cecilia. I shall remain here — and I shall be happier here."

Sister Cecilia dropped the subject, and never returned to it again. From that day she treated Alice Walmsley in another manner than of old. She spoke with her of all the crosses that came in her path, either to herself or others. By this means the latent sympathies of Alice were touched and exercised. She entered with interest into every story of the sorrow or suffering of the unfortunate, related to her by the kind little Sister.

In this communion, which, if not happy, was at least peaceful, the months grew into years, and the years followed each other, until four summers more had passed through Alice's cell.

During those years, she had developed her true nature, saddened though it was by her surroundings. It seemed that her youth had been too thoughtless, too unstable, too happy, even to indicate her future. That bright girlhood was the rich, fallow ground. The five dark years of her agony and unbelief were the season of ploughing and harrowing the fertile soil and sowing the fruitful seed. The four years of succeeding peace were the springtime and the early summer of her full life, during which the strong shoots grew forward toward the harvest of ripe womanhood.

Toward the end of these four years a word of change came to her cell — she was once more selected among the fifty female prisoners to be sent on the annual convict ship to Western Australia.

It was during the preparation for this voyage that Will Sheridan returned, a rich man, to find the shattered pieces of his love and happiness. It was during, one of these quiet days within Alice's cell that he without, had wandered through London, a heart-stricken man, vainly seeking for interest in the picture-galleries and churches. It was during one of these peaceful nights within the cell that he, without, led by the magnetism of strong love, found himself beneath the gloomy walls of Millbank, round which he wandered through the night, and which he could not leave until he had pressed his feverish lips against the icy stone of the prison.

On the day when Will Sheridan at last stood before the door of Alice Walmsley's cell, and read her beloved name on the card, she sat within, patiently sewing the coarse cloth of her transport dress. When the door opened, and his yearning sight was blessed with that which it had longed for, she stood before him, calm, and white, and beautiful, with downcast eyes, according to her own modesty and the prison discipline.

When he passed her door a few weeks later, and saw within the sweet-faced Sister Cecilia, and heard, after so many years, the voice of her he loved, in one short sentence, which sent him away very happy, she dreamt not that a loving heart had drunk up her words as a parched field drinks the refreshing rain.

So strong and so futile are the outreachings of the soul. They must be mutual, or they are impotent and vain. Reciprocal, they draw together through the density of a planet. Single, the one reaches for the other weakly, as a shadow touches the precipice, hopelessly as death.

That which we desire, we may feel; but that which we neither know nor think, might just as well be nonexistent.

BOOK FOURTH.

THE CONVICT SHIP.

I.

THE PARLIAMENTARY COMMITTEE.

"MR. SHERIDAN is to go before the Committee to-day, is he not?" asked Lord Somers, the Colonial Secretary, as he sat writing in Mr. Wyville's study, with Sheridan reading the *Times* by the window, and Hamerton lounging in an easy-chair.

"What Committee?" asked Hamerton, heedlessly.

"The Committee appointed to hear Sir Joshua Hobb's argument against our Penal Bill," said the Secretary, as he continued to write.

"Does Sheridan know anything about prisons?" drawled Hamerton.

"He knows something about Australia, and the men we send there," said the Secretary.

"Well — Hobb doesn't. Hobb is a humbug. What does he want?"

"To control the Australian Penal System from Parliament Street, and, instead of Mr. Wyville's humane bill, to apply his own system to the Penal Colony."

"What do you think of that, Mr. Sheridan?" asked Hamerton, without raising his head from the cushion.

"That it would be folly before Mr. Wyville's bill was drawn, — and criminal afterward."

"Bravo!" said Hamerton, sitting straight. "Bravo,

Australia! Go before the Committee, by all means ; and talk just in that tone. When do they sit ? "

"In an hour," said Lord Somers. " We are only waiting for Mr. Wyville, and then we go to the House."

" May I go ? " asked Hamerton.

" Certainly," said the Secretary. " You may get a chapter for a novel, or a leader for the *Telegraph*."

Mr. Wyville soon after entered, and the merits of the opposing bills were freely discussed for a quarter of an hour. At length, Lord Somers said it was time to start, and they proceeded on foot toward the Parliament House, Lord Somers and Hamerton leading, and Mr. Wyville and Sheridan following.

On the way, Mr. Wyville led his companion to speak of the sandalwood trade, and seemed to be much interested in its details. At one point he interrupted Sheridan, who was describing the precipitous outer ridge of the Iron-stone Hills.

" Your teams have to follow the winding foot of this precipice for many miles, have they not ? " he asked.

" For thirty-two miles," answered Sheridan.

" Which, of course, adds much to the expense of shipping the sandalwood ? "

" Adds very seriously, indeed, for the best sandalwood lies back within the bend ; so that our teams, having turned the farther flank of the hills, must return and proceed nearly thirty miles back toward the shore."

" Suppose it were possible to throw a chain-slide from the brow of the Blackwood Head, near Bunbury, to a point on the plain — what would that save ? "

" Just fifty miles of teaming," answered Sheridan, looking at Wyville in surprise. " But such a chain could never be forged."

" The Americans have made slides for wood nearly as long," said Mr. Wyville.

"Five ships could not carry enough chain from England for such a slide."

"Forge it on the spot," said Mr. Wyville. "The very hills can be smelted into metal. I have had this in mind for some years, Mr. Sheridan, and I mean to attempt the work when we return. It will employ all the idle men in the colony."

Sheridan was surprised beyond words to find Mr. Wyville so familiar with the very scenes of his own labor. He hardly knew what to say about Wyville's personal interest in a district which the Sandalwood Company had marked off and claimed as their property, by right of possession, though they had neglected Sheridan's advice to buy or lease the land from the Government.

The conversation ceased as they entered the House of Commons, and proceeded to the committee room, where sat Sir Joshua Hobb at a table, turning over a pile of documents, and beside him, pen in hand, Mr. Haggett, who took in a reef of lip as Mr. Wyville and Sheridan entered.

Since Haggett's return from Australia, three years before, he had adopted a peculiar manner toward Mr. Wyville. He treated him with respect, perhaps because he feared him; but when he could observe him without himself being seen, he never tired of looking at him, as if he were intently solving a problem, and hoped to read its deepest meaning in some possible expression of Mr. Wyville's face.

On the large table lay a map of the Penal Colony of Western Australia.

The Committee consisted of five average M. P.'s, three country gentlemen, who had not the remotest knowledge of penal systems, nor of any other than systems of drainage; and two lawyers, who asked all the questions, and pretended to understand the whole subject.

The Committee treated Sir Joshua Hobb, K. C. B., as a most distinguished personage, whose every word possessed particular gravity and value. He delivered a set speech against lenience to prisoners, and made a deep impression on the Committee. He was about to sit down, when Mr. Haggett laid a folded paper beside his hand. Sir Joshua glanced at the document, and resumed, in a convincing tone : —

"Here, gentlemen," he said, touching the paper repeatedly with his finger, " here is an instance of the sentimental method, and its effect on a desperate criminal — and all those who are sent to Australia are desperate. Twenty years ago, a young man was convicted at York Assizes, for poaching. It was during a time of business depression; the capitalists and employers had closed their works, and locked out their hands. Nothing else could be done — men cannot risk their money when markets are falling. During this time, the deer in Lord Scarborough's park had been killed by the score, and a close watch was set. This man was caught in the night, carrying a deer on his shoulders from the park. He made a violent resistance, striking one of the keepers a terrible blow that felled him to the earth, senseless. The poacher was overpowered, however, and sent to prison until the Assizes. At his trial he pleaded defiantly that he had a right to the deer — that thousands were starving to death — men, women, and children — in the streets of the town ; and that God had given no man the right to herd hundreds of useless deer while human beings were dying of hunger. The ignorant and dangerous people who heard him cheered wildly in the court at this lawless speech. Gentlemen, this poacher was a desperate radical, a Chartist, no doubt, who ought to have been severely treated. But the judge looked leniently on the case, because it was proved that the poacher's own mother and sisters were starving. The prisoner

got off with one month's imprisonment. What was
the result of this mildness? At the very next Assizes
the same judge tried the same prisoner for a similar
crime, and the audacious villain made the same defence. 'If it were a light crime six months ago,' he
said to the mistaken judge, 'it is no heavier now, for
the cause remains.' Well, he was sentenced to ten
years' penal servitude, and was transported to Western
Australia. After serving some years there, the lenient
system again came in, and he was hired out to a settler,
a respectable man, though an ex-convict. Three months
afterwards, the violent Chartist attempted to murder
his employer, and then escaped into the bush. He
was captured, but escaped again, and was again re-cap-
tured by the very man he had tried to murder. Mark
the dreadful ending, gentlemen, to this series of mistaken lenities to a criminal. On their way to the
prison, the absconder broke his manacles, seized a
pistol from a native policeman, murdered his brave
captor, and escaped again to the bush."

"God bless me! what a shocking story!" said one
of the Committee.

"Was the fellow captured again?" asked one of the
lawyers.

"No," said Sir Joshua; "he escaped to the swamps.
But there is a rumor among the convicts that he is
still alive. Is there not, Mr. Haggett?"

Mr. Haggett bent his head in assent. Then he
rubbed his forehead and eyes, as if relieved of a strain.
He had been watching the face of Mr. Wyville with
painful eagerness as Sir Joshua spoke; but in that im-
passive visage no line of meaning to Haggett's eyes
could be traced.

Sir Joshua sat down, confident that he could depend
on the Committee for a report in his favor.

"Is there actual evidence that this convict of whom
you spoke murdered his captor?"

Mr. Wyville addressed Sir Joshua Hobb, standing at the end of the long green table. There was nothing in the words, but every one in the room felt a thrill at the deep sound of the resonant voice.

The Committee, who had not looked at Mr. Wyville before, stared at him now in undisguised surprise. He was strangely powerful as he stood there alone, looking calmly at Sir Joshua for an answer.

"Evidence? Certainly, there is evidence. The brave settler who captured the malefactor disappeared; and the bushman from whom the convict seized the pistol saw him point it at the head of his captor. Is not that evidence enough?"

"Not for a court of justice," quietly answered Mr. Wyville.

"Sir," said Sir Joshua Hobb, superciliously, "it may not appeal to sentimental judgments; but it carries conviction to reasonable minds."

"It should not — for it is not true!" said Mr. Wyville, his tone somewhat deepened with earnestness.

Sir Joshua Hobb started angrily to his feet. He glared at Mr. Wyville.

"Do you know it to be false?" he sternly asked.

"Yes!"

"How do you know?"

"I, myself, saw the death of this man that you say was murdered."

"You saw his death!" said in one breath Sir Joshua and the Committee.

"Yes. He accepted a bribe from the man he had captured, and released him. I saw this settler afterwards die of thirst on the plains — I came upon him by accident — he died before my eyes, alone — and he was not murdered."

Sir Joshua Hobb sat down, and twisted nervously on his seat. Mr. Haggett looked frightened, as if he had introduced an unfortunate subject for his master's use. He wrote on a slip of paper, and handed it to Sir Joshua, who read, and then turned to Mr. Wyville.

" What was the name of the man you saw die ? " he asked.

" Isaac Bowman," answered Mr. Wyville.

Both Sir Joshua and Mr. Haggett settled down in their seats, having no more to say or suggest.

" You have lived a long time in Western Australia, Mr. Wyville ? " asked one of the lawyers of the Committee, after a surprised pause.

" Many years."

" You are the owner of property in the Colony ? "

" Yes."

Sir Joshua Hobb pricked up his ears, and turned sharply on his chair, with an insolent stare.

" Where does your property lie ? " he asked.

" In the Vasse District," answered Mr. Wyville.

" Here is a map of Western Australia," said Sir Joshua Hobb, with an overbearing air; " will you be kind enough to point out to the Committee the location of your possessions ? "

There was obviously so malevolent a meaning in Sir Joshua Hobb's request, that the whole Committee and the gentlemen present stood up to watch the map, expecting Mr. Wyville to approach. But he did not move.

" My boundaries are easily traced," he said, from his place at the end of the table; " the northern and southern limits are the 33d and 34th parallels of latitude, and the eastern and western boundaries are the 115th and 116th of longitude."

One of the Committee followed with his finger the amazing outline, after Mr. Wyville had spoken. There was deep silence for a time, followed by long breaths of surprise.

"All the land within those lines is your — estate?" diffidently asked one of the country gentlemen.

Mr. Wyville gravely bowed.

"Estate!" said one of the lawyers in a low tone, when he had summed up the extent in square miles; "it is a Principality!"

"From whom did you purchase this land?" asked Sir Joshua, but in an altered tone.

"From the Queen!" said Mr. Wyville, without moving a muscle of his impressive face.

"Directly from Her Majesty?"

"I received my deeds through the Colonial Office," answered Mr. Wyville, with a quiet motion of the hand toward Lord Somers.

The Colonial Secretary, seeing the eyes of all present turned upon him, bowed to the Committee in corroboration.

"The deeds of Mr. Wyville's estate, outlined as he has stated, passed through the Colonial Office, directly from her Majesty the Queen," said Lord Somers, in a formal manner.

The Committee sat silent for several moments, evidently dazed at the unexpected issue of their investigations. Mr. Wyville was the first to speak.

"I ask to have those prison records corrected, and at once, Sir Joshua Hobb," he said slowly. "It must not stand that the convict of whom you spoke was a murderer."

"By all means. Have the records corrected immediately," said the Committee, who began to look askance at Sir Joshua Hobb.

Mr. Wyville then addressed the Committee, in favor of the new and humane penal bill. Whether it was his arguments, or the remembrance of his princely estate that worked in his favor, certain it was that when he had concluded the Committee was unanimously in his favor.

"Mr. Wyville," said the chairman, before they adjourned, we are of one mind — that the Bill reported by the Government should be adopted by the House; and we shall so report. Good-day, gentlemen."

Sir Joshua Hobb rapidly withdrew, coldly bowing. He was closely followed by Haggett.

Lord Somers, Hamerton, and Mr. Wyville were speaking together, while Sheridan, who was attentively studying the map, suddenly startled the others by an excited exclamation.

"Hello!" said Hamerton, "has Sir Joshua dropped a hornet for you, too?"

"Mr. Wyville, this is terrible!" cried Sheridan, strangely moved. "Those lines of your property cover every acre of our sandalwood land!"

"Ah — ha!" ejaculated Hamerton.

"I thought this land was ours," continued Sheridan, in great distress of mind. "How long has it been yours?"

"Ten years," said Mr. Wyville.

Sheridan sank nerveless into a seat. The strong frame that could brave and bear the severest strains of labor and care, was subdued in one instant by this overwhelming discovery.

He had been cutting sandalwood for nine years on this man's land. Every farthing he had made for his company and himself belonged in common honesty to another!

Mr. Wyville, who was not surprised, but had evidently expected this moment, walked over to Sheridan, and laid a strong hand on his shoulder, expressing more kindness and affection in the manly force and silence of the act than could possibly have been spoken in words. Sheridan felt the impulse precisely as it was meant.

"The land was yours," Mr. Wyville said after a pause; "for I had made no claim. I knew of your work, and I gave you no warning. According to the law of the Colony, and of higher law, you have acted right."

Sheridan's face brightened. To him personally his success had brought little to covet; but he was sensitive to the core at the thought of trouble and great loss to the Company, caused under his supervision.

"We return to Australia together, Mr. Sheridan," said Wyville, holding out his hand; "and I think, somehow, we shall neither of us leave it again. The vigor of your past life shall be as nothing to that which the future shall evoke. Shall we not work together?"

Swift tears of pleasure rushed to Sheridan's eyes at the earnest and unexpected words; and the look that passed between the two men as they clasped hands was of brief but beautiful intensity.

"Well, Hamerton?" asked Lord Somers, smiling, as if astonished beyond further speech.

"Well? What of it? I suppose you call this strange," said Hamerton.

"You don't?" asked the Secretary.

"No, I don't," said Hamerton, rising from his chair. "I call it utter commonplace — for these Australians — the most prosaic set of events I have yet seen them indulge in. I begin to realize the meaning of the Antipodes: their common ways are our extraordinary ones — and they don't seem to have any uncommon ones."

II.

HARRIET DRAPER.

FOUR years had passed since Mr. Wyville's visit to Walton-le-Dale; and he had heard no word of the woman he had then sought

During this time the case of Alice Walmsley had grown to be a subject of rare interest to this student of humanity. Scarcely a day had passed in all that time that he had not devoted some moments to thinking on the innocent prisoner, and devising some allowable means of affording her comfort and pleasure.

Perhaps the secret of his special observance of this case arose from the fact that beneath the self-imposed suffering he beheld the golden idea. To him this peaceful and silent adherence to a principle was a source of constant interest.

In all those years, Alice Walmsley had never heard his name, and had only once seen his interference. The memory of the strong dark face that had then interposed to save her, and the look of kind compassion, were treasured in her heart; but she knew no more than this. Sister Cecilia, perhaps, would have told her who this powerful man was; but she shrank from asking, and she never asked.

About a week after the event in the Committee Room, Mr. Wyville, sitting with Sheridan and Hamerton in his study, received a letter, brought from Scotland Yard by a policeman.

As usual with the group, when not conversing, Sheridan read, and Hamerton lounged.

Mr. Wyville started from his seat with an exclamation, when he had read the letter. He rarely betrayed even the slightest excitement; and Mr. Hamerton would not have been more surprised had a bomb exploded under the table than he was to see Mr. Wyville thrown off his balance so unexpectedly and completely. Hamerton, however, had too profound a respect for his friend to speak his astonishment.

"Thanks, kind and simple heart!" exclaimed Mr. Wyville, holding the letter before him. "You have been faithful to your word for four years; and you shall rejoice for it all your life!"

Then, recollecting himself, he smiled in his grave way and said, —

"I have received long-expected news. I have found something I sought. To-night, I must leave London for a few days; so I must say good-by, now."

"Are you leaving England, too?" asked Hamerton.

"No; I go only to Lancashire — to a little village called Walton-le-Dale." He turned to his desk, and was busily arranging his papers.

"Why, what's the matter, Sheridan? You are growing nervous of late."

"The name of the village took me by surprise, that is all," said Will. He was going on to say that Walton was his native village; but the entrance of Lord Somers temporarily changed the subject. Before it could be resumed, Mr. Wyville had said "Good-by," and the gentlemen took their leave.

The letter which Mr. Wyville had received ran as follows: —

"Sir, — The woman Harriet Draper, as was Samuel Draper's wife before he married Alice Walmsley, has been arrested for a dedly assawlt on Draper's sister and is at this present riteing in the lock-up of Walton-le-Dale. — Your umbel servant,
"Benjamin Lodge, *Police Officer.*"

Accompanied by his black servant, Mr. Wyville left London that evening; and on the forenoon of the next day he stepped from the train at Walton-le-Dale, and walked toward the police-station or lock-up.

It was a small stone building, containing four rooms, two of which were Officer Lodge's quarters; the third a court-room, with a dock or bar, and a raised desk and seat for the magistrate; and behind this, and opening from it, a strong room, with barred windows, used as the lock-up.

Mr. Wyville pushed the outer door, and stepped at once into the court-room, which was empty. He was about to withdraw, when a door on the left opened, and Officer Lodge, quite unchanged in four years, greeted Mr. Wyville, as if he had seen him only yesterday.

"She was out of horder bad, this time, sir; but I knew she'd turn up some time."

"Many thanks, my friend," said Mr. Wyville; "I had almost concluded you had forgotten."

Officer Lodge was a little hurt at this expression of doubt; but he was quite too mild of temper for resentment.

"Where is the woman?" asked Mr. Wyville.

Officer Lodge pointed to the heavy door of the lock-up, with a grim shake of the head. He sank his voice to a whisper.

"She's a bad 'un, she is — worse and worse hevery time. But now she's done for."

"Done for?"

"Ay, she'll go, this time, sir. Seven year at the least. She nearly killed a woman, and she would have killed her altogether if she'd had her way a minute longer."

"Tell me the facts," said Mr. Wyville.

"Well, sir, she were down near Draper's 'ouse all one day, last week, and she hacted queer. They came for me and told me, and I looked after her all the hafternoon. But she were doing no harm to nobody. She only sat on the roadside, looking at Draper's 'ouse. Toward evening she went into Mrs. Walmsley's old 'ouse, wich is hopen, and she stayed there an hour. Draper's sister, who was too curious, maybe, went up to the 'ouse, to see what she were doing; and then it began. I heerd two voices, one a' screaming and the tother swearing, and when I ran to the spot, I sees Harriet assaulting the woman, choking her and beating her head against the stones. If I had been half a minute later, there would have been murder."

"Does the prisoner speak to any one?" asked Mr.
Wyville.

"No; there's no one to speak to her but me; and
she never hopens her lips to me."

"Can I see her, and speak with her?"

"Yessir," said Officer Lodge; "but be careful —
she's not safe."

Officer Lodge carefully locked the outer door, and
then approached the lock-up. He knocked on the
door heavily with the key, as if to rouse the prisoner.
No sound came from within. He turned the key in
the lock, and opened the door.

Mr. Wyville entered the lock-up, which was a room
about twelve feet square, with one window. A wooden
bench ran round three sides of the room, and in the
farther corner, upon the bench, was something like a
heap of clothes.

It was the prisoner, who sat upon the bench, her
back to the wall, her knees drawn up, and her face
sunk upon them. A tattered shawl covered her, so that
she presented the appearance of a heap of wretched
clothes.

She did not move as the door opened, nor for a
minute afterwards. But as some one had entered, and
the door had not been closed, she became aware of the
intrusion. She raised her head, and looked around
on the floor, slowly, till her glance fell on Mr. Wyville's feet. Then she raised her eyes, till they rested
on his face.

She seemed to have been in a sort of daze or waking
dream. She did not take her eyes away, but looked at
the strange face before her as if she were not yet
awake.

She was a woful wreck of womanhood. Her eyes
had cavernous circles around them, and her cheeks were
sunken, as if with consuming disease. Her hair, un-
kempt, was covered with the old shawl, but its

straggling locks fell across her forehead. As she looked
at Mr. Wyville, some remnant of womanly feeling
stirred within her, and she raised a wasted hand and
pressed backward the tangled hair from each side of
her face.

Wretched as she was, and lost, there was something
beneath all the stains that spoke of a face once comely
and soft and lovable.

" Harriet Draper ! " said Mr. Wyville, with unusual
emotion in his deep voice, and speaking in a subdued
tone.

She moved uneasily at the name, and her large eyes
grew fearfully bright.

" Harriet Draper, I have been searching for you
many years. May God pardon the man whose crime
sent you here ! "

" Ach ! " gasped the woman, suddenly burying her
face again, as if she had been stabbed in the breast.
Then she started, and sprang to the floor, and put her
hands on her eyes.

" O God ! what did he say ? " she hoarsely whispered,
as if speaking to herself; " O God ! God ! to pardon
him, and not me ! "

She took away her hands, and looked severely for a
moment at Mr. Wyville. He met her gaze with a
severity greater than her own.

" Yes ; God pardon him, for through him you have
been made guilty," he said.

" Who are you ? " she cried, becoming excited
" Who are you that pretend to know me ? No man
made me commit crime. You lie ! you lie ! you don't
know me — you don't know him ! "

Her voice became high with excitement, and her
eyes blazed, as with frenzy.

" Harriet Draper, I know you and I know him —
your guilty husband. I have searched for you for
years, to ask you to lighten your soul of one grievous

crime. Before long, you will need repentance ; for your health is broken, and you cannot die with this terrible burden on your conscience."

" What — what are you talking about ? " she cried, still fiercely, but in a lower tone. " What have I done ? "

" You have committed murder ! "

She looked at him without a word, and increased the pitiful fixity of her gaze by raising her hands to press her temples, as if to keep down pain.

" You murdered Alice Walmsley's child ! "

Her eyes closed, and she grasped at her breast with both hands, and tottered backward, sinking on the bench with a long moan.

" You killed the child, and you saw the innocent mother dragged to prison for your crime. You have remained silent for nine years, and destroyed your own life, while she has borne your punishment. You shall now confess, and save her who has suffered so much to save you."

" Ha ! ha ! ha ! ha ! " screamed the woman, in a laugh so sudden and hellish, that Mr. Wyville stepped back appalled. He had expected a different result. Again and again the horrid laugh rang through the place, till it had exhausted the strength of the ferocious and most miserable being who uttered it, and she sank heavily on the bench.

" Save *her* ! " she cried at length, clenching her hands, and shaking them over her head. " Ha ! ha ! save *her* ! Save the false woman that sent me here ! Never ! I hate her ! She brought her suffering on herself by stealing my husband — he was only a fool in her hands ! "

She rocked herself to and fro for a time, and then cried wildly, —

" Why should I forgive her ? Why should I save her ? Am I to bear all the misery she made ? He was my husband, and he loved me, till she made him false !"

Here she became wildly excited, almost screaming her words.

"If she were free to-day, she would seek him out, and go back to him. Why should I save her to do that? Begone! I will not! I know nothing about her. I would rather die than speak a word to save her!"

A fit of coughing, that almost convulsed the miserable frame, now seized the woman; and when it had passed she sank back against the wall, exhausted.

Mr. Wyville remained silent; he feared that more excitement might affect her reason, or her life. He looked down upon the unfortunate being with profound pity. He had expected a depraved and selfish nature, shrinking from confession through selfish fear. He saw, instead, a woman's heart, criminal through its own love and truth, and cruelly unjust through jealousy of its rival.

Darkest and saddest of human sights — the good tortured from its straight course until it actually had become evil; the angelic quality in a heart warped by deceit and wrong until it had become the fiendish part.

"O, man, man!" murmured Mr. Wyville, as he looked upon the wreck, but only saw the evil-doer beyond her, "your sin is deeper than the sea. Not here, not here must I seek to right the wrong."

He walked from the place with bowed head. Officer Lodge, without speaking, locked the door, and followed him. Mr. Wyville sat down in the court-room, and after a long pause, said to Officer Lodge, —

"Has this man, Draper, ever been here — since the crime was committed?"

"No, sir, he hasn't never been seen; but they say as he has been here; that he came in the night to his own folks once. He can't never live in Walton, sir."

" Has he been outlawed ? "

" No, sir, there was no one to go again' him. The law let him pass ; but the people couldn't stomach him — though they never thought he was as bad as this."

" You have heard, then, what I have said to this woman ? It will do no good to speak about it. She has made no confession — nor will she confess till the hand of death is upon her. When is she to be tried for this last offence ? "

" In two weeks, sir; and she 'll get at least seven years."

" Well, my kind friend, remember she has been cruelly wronged ; and so long as she is in your charge, treat her with mercy. She is not the author of her crime and wretchedness."

Officer Lodge promised to be kind, though his heart overflowed when he thought of poor Alice Walmsley and her great wrong. He also promised to send by mail to Mr. Wyville a report of Harriet Draper's sentence.

Mr. Wyville thanked him, but offered no reward.

" I shall see you again before long," he said, as he left the little court-room. His journey to London that night was mainly consumed in reflection on the tangled web of crime and injustice in which he had become so deeply interested.

Two days later, Mr. Wyville sat in the office of the governor of Millbank, relating to him the story of Harriet Draper and Alice Walmsley.

" Good heavens ! " cried the kind old governor ; " the case must be brought at once before the Directors."

" No," said Mr. Wyville, " not yet — and not at any time before them. Release cannot right the wrong of this injured woman. She must be cleared by the confession of the criminal — and then we shall send her case to the Queen."

"Well," said the governor, " but how are you to get the confession?"

" This woman, Harriet Draper, will come to Millbank within two weeks. If she does not confess before the convict ship sails, she must be sent to Western Australia next month."

"We never send convicts in their first year," said the governor.

" She must go, " said Mr. Wyville, warmly; "break your rule for the sake of justice."

" I 'll break it for your sake, Mr. Wyville," said the governor. " I shall put her name on the roll."

" And she must be kept aloof from the others. Can this be done?"

" Yes; we can enter her on the hospital list, and send her before the others to the ship. She will be confined on board in the hospital."

Mr. Wyville held out his hand to the governor.

" I thank you sincerely," he said; " I am deeply interested in this case."

When he had gone, the bluff old major walked up and down his office, and mopped his head with his big handkerchief.

" It 's like good health and a good conscience to come near that man," he said to himself. " How strange it is that he should have such deadly enemies!"

III.

A CAPTAIN FOR THE HOUGUEMONT.

IN Mr. Wyville's house, in the library or study, sat Mr. Hamerton. He had been writing for hours. On the table beside him lay a heap of documents, with large red seals, like title-deeds; and in another heap lay a number of letters, addressed and stamped.

Mr. Wyville entered, and they talked for some min-
ates in a serious vein. It was evident that Mr. Hamerton was engaged in some more important business
than usual, and that he had advised with Mr. Wyville
during its progress.

Lord Somers called, as usual, on his way to the
Department; and shortly afterward Sheridan arrived.
Mr. Hamerton continued to write, and a cursory conversation began, the gentlemen glancing at the morning
papers.

An exclamation from Lord Somers broke the commonplace.

"Hello! What the deuce! Why, Hamerton, this
must be your place. Are you going to sell Broadwood?"

"Yes," said Hamerton, and he went on with his
writing.

"The whole estate and manor house?" asked the
peer, in plain astonishment.

"The whole thing," said Hamerton, in the same
prosaic tone.

Will Sheridan took the paper, and read the adver-
tisement: Magnificent and historic demesne and manor
house of Broadwood — 400 acres of rich land — entire
village of Broadwood — valuable church living — an-
tique furniture, pictures, armor, etc., — in a word, the
entire surroundings of an English aristocrat of the first
standing, advertised in the daily papers to be sold by
auction, not as a whole, but in lots.

"What do you mean by that?" asked Lord Somers;
"why not sell the right to one purchaser?"

"Because he couldn't buy it," answered the stolid
Hamerton, who was in a mood for apothegms.

"What! you want too much money for it?"

"No, I do not."

"Come, come, Hamerton — this is unkind. Your
place is close to mine, and I am naturally interested,
independent of my sincere interest in your affairs."

"Well, you spoke of buying the *right*. Now, Somers, no one man could buy or hold the right to so much land as Broadwood, in this populous and poverty-stricken country — yes, poverty-stricken — there are only a few rich people. Eighty out of every hundred are miserably poor. The best a rich man could do would be to buy the title-deeds; but the abstract right of ownership would remain with the farmers who tilled the land."

"I don't understand you," said Lord Somers.

"I propose to sell the deeds to the men who already hold the land by right."

"You will break up Broadwood, and sell it to your farmers ?"

"I will."

Lord Somers was seriously affected by this extraordinary announcement; but he knew Hamerton too well to remonstrate or argue.

Mr. Wyville, looking across his paper, observed both speakers, and listened to the conversation, evidently pleased.

"You will be no nearer to your republican idea when this is done," said Lord Somers, at length; "you will have sold the land; but the money it brings has not been earned by you."

"Quite true," answered Hamerton.

"Why keep it, then ?"

"I shall not keep it."

"Why, Hamerton — what do you mean ? What will you do with it ?"

"I shall invest it in schools and a library for the people of that section 'for ever,' as the lawyers say. Mr. Wyville and I have been looking at the matter, and we think this money will establish a school with three technical branches — chemistry, engineering, and agriculture.

"And you ? will you teach in the schools for a living?"

"Oh no; I am going to Australia"

"To Australia!" said Lord Somers and Sheridan in a breath. Then Sheridan asked,—

"Are you going to settle there?"

"Yes; I am tired of Europe. I shall never return here."

"I am glad," cried Sheridan, starting up and seizing Hamerton's hand. "Australia is going to send out the largest-hearted men that ever owned the earth. You will be at home there. You will breathe freely in its splendid air. Oh, I am proud to see such men turn by nature to the magnificent South!"

Mr. Wyville had approached the table with a look of intense pleasure. He laid his hand almost caressingly on Will Sheridan's shoulder. As they were placed, these three men — Wyville, Sheridan, and Hamerton — they formed a remarkable group.

"You are dangerous company," said Lord Somers, looking at them with admiration. "You almost tempt me to follow you, or go with you, to Australia. When do you sail?"

"Mr. Sheridan and I will sail on the convict ship in three weeks," said Mr. Wyville. "Mr. Hamerton will take my steam-yacht, and follow when he has settled his plans — perhaps a week later."

"I am dumbfounded," said Lord Somers. "I cannot speak on this new thing. I only foresee that I shall be very lonely, indeed, in London when you have gone."

After some further conversation on this point, Mr. Wyville changed the subject.

"You have engaged a captain for the convict ship?" he said to Lord Somers.

"Yes; Captain Rogers, late of the P. & O. Company's service."

"You were not aware that I wished to engage him for my yacht?" said Wyville.

"No; I should be sorry to take him from you. But his articles are signed now, and good commanders for such a service are not easily found."

"If I find you a suitable captain, and guarantee his command, will you oblige me by cancelling Captain Rogers's commission?"

"Certainly — if you give him, instead, the command of your steamer."

"Thank you; that is my intention."

"But have you found another captain for the convict ship?" asked Lord Somers.

"Yes — I have been looking into the matter with the view of saving you further trouble. I have settled on a man who is classed as a first-rate master-mariner and commander, and who is now in London, disengaged."

"I shall make a note of it," said Lord Somers, taking out his pocket-book. "What is his name?"

"Draper," said Mr. Wyville; "Captain Samuel Draper."

"That will do," said the Secretary. "I shall have new articles made out. Will you see to it that he is engaged at once, and sent to the ship at Portland?"

"Certainly. I shall attend to it to-day."

Mr. Hamerton and Sheridan, who had been talking together, at the other end of the room, now approached, and the conversation became general. Soon after, Lord Somers said "Good-morning," and proceeded to his Department.

IV.

CAPTAIN SAMUEL DRAPER.

IN the inner office of Lloyd's great shipping agency, in London, on the day following Mr. Wyville's conversation with Lord Somers, the former gentleman sat, while one of the clerks in the office brought him books and documents.

"This completes Captain Draper's record," said the clerk, handing a paper to Mr. Wyville. "It is from his last ship."

"Thanks. Now, can you give me his address in London?"

"Yes; No. 37 Horton Street, East."

Mr. Wyville left the office, and the clerk collected his papers, from which the visitor had taken notes.

Mr. Wyville hailed a cab, and said to the driver, "Horton Street." It was a long way off, and during the slow progress through the crowded streets, Mr. Wyville examined his notes, and arranged them carefully in a certain order. At last the cab stopped.

"What number?" asked the driver.

"I shall get out here," said Mr. Wyville. "But you may wait for me — say half an hour."

He walked down the quiet little street, with its uniform brick houses, green blinds, and white curtains. It was a street of comfortable residences of small business men and well-to-do mechanics. Number 37 was in no way different from the neighboring houses.

Mr. Wyville rang the bell, and an old lady, with glasses pushed up to her forehead, and a piece of sewing in her hand, opened the door, and looked inquiringly at the caller.

"Does Captain Draper live here?" he asked.

"Yes, sir; but he is out at present," said the intelligent old lady.

"I am sorry; I will call again," said Mr. Wyville, turning to go.

"He will be in soon," said the old lady; "he comes in to dinner always."

"Then I shall wait, if you please," said Mr. Wyville, and he entered the house, and sat down in a comfortable little parlor, while the old woman, drawing down her glasses, went on with her sewing.

"Captain Draper is my grand-nephew," said she, after a silent interval.

"Indeed!" said Mr. Wyville. "Then you will be pleased to know that I come to offer him a good command."

"Oh, I am delighted!" said the old lady; "he is so good, so conscientious. I always said as Samuel would come to something 'igh. He has been waiting for a ship for nearly a year. I know he doesn't please his owners, because he is too conscientious."

"You will also be pleased to hear, madam, that his owners this time will be quite conscientious, too."

"I am so delighted!" said Captain Draper's grand-aunt.

At this moment, the outer door opened, and immediately after Captain Draper entered the room. It was rather a chilly day, and he had buttoned his coat close up to his throat. He was not a robust figure — rather slim, and bent forward. The past ten years had laid a strong hand on him. The charm of his younger manhood, the boisterous laugh and hearty manner of waving his hand, was much lessened; but the cold watchfulness of his prominent blue eyes was proportionately increased.

He had a long and narrow face, thin jaws, covered with faded side-whiskers, worn rather long. His upper lip and chin were shaven, showing his wide mouth. His lips were dry, as of old, but now they were bluer, and more offensively cracked. On the whole, he was a decent-looking man in outward appearance; as he walked rapidly through the streets, with shoulders bent forward, one would say he was a consumptive hurrying home. But there was a compression of the mouth, accompanied with a quick watchfulness of eye, and an ugly sneer in the muscles of the nose, that would make his face detestable to any one who had the power of rapidly perceiving character.

Mr. Wyville read the face as easily as if it were a printed page.

" Captain Draper, I presume ? "

" That is my name," said the other, with a wide and unmeaning smile of the cracked lips, in which the rest of the face took no part.

" I have come from the Treasury, to offer you command of a vessel in the service of the Government."

" Ah — that's good. In what branch of the service, may I ask ? "

" Transport," said Mr. Wyville.

" Troops, I suppose ? " said Draper, still smiling.

" No; convicts."

Captain Draper placed a chair so as to see Mr. Wyville's face in the light. As he took his seat he had ceased to smile.

" Ah ! — convicts. Where are they going ? "

" Western Australia."

Captain Draper remained silent so long that Mr. Wyville spoke again.

" You are willing to take such a vessel, are you not ? "

" Well, I want a ship — but these convict ships I don't like ; I don't want to —— Are they male convicts ? " he asked, interrupting himself.

" Yes, mainly; there will be three hundred men, and only fifty female convicts on board."

" Fifty." Draper stood up and walked across the room to the mantel-piece. He leant his elbow on it for a time ; then he took up a little glass ornament in an absent-minded and nervous way.

Mr. Wyville sat silently watching him. As Draper raised the piece of glass, his hand trembled and his face worked. He dropped the glass to the floor, and it was shattered to pieces. This recalled him. He smiled at first, then he laughed aloud, his eyes watching Mr. Wyville.

"Well—I don't want that ship," he said; "I don't like convicts."

"I am sorry," said Mr. Wyville, rising; "you were highly recommended, Captain Draper; and as the duty is considered onerous, the voyage will be quite remunerative for the commander."

Draper's cupidity was excited, and he seemed to hesitate.

"Do you know anything about these convicts?" he asked.

"Yes; what do you wish to know?"

"How long have they been in prison?"

"On an average, about three years."

"Three years; did you ever know any to be sent after nine or ten years?"

"No; not one such case has occurred for the past twenty years. It would be very unusual."

"Yes; well, you know, I don't care about them—but I have a curiosity. I suppose they're all right—all about three years, eh?"

"That will be the average, certainly."

"Well, I think I'll take the ship. Where does she lie, and when is she to sail?"

Mr. Wyville gave him all the particulars; and when his questions ceased Mr. Wyville drew out a set of articles to be signed.

"You came prepared, eh?" said Draper.

"Yes;" said Mr. Wyville, gravely reading over the form. "We were anxious to secure your services, and I thought it just as well to save time. Please sign your name here—and here. Thank you. Now I shall say good-day, Captain Draper."

"The ship is ready, you say?" said Draper, following him to the door; "then I am expected to take command at once, I suppose?"

"No; not until the day of sailing. Your officers will see to the preparations for sailing. At two o'clock, P. M., on the 10th, you will take command, and sail."

"Well," said Draper; and as he looked after the strong figure of Wyville, he muttered to himself: "Well — just as well; they only average three years. But I'd rather go on board at once, and see them before we sail."

V.

KOBO AND TEPAIRU.

"Now," said Mr. Wyville, communing with himself, as he walked from Draper's house, and entered his cab at the end of Horton Street, "the elements are moving. May good influences direct them."

At his own house, he dismissed the cab, and, entering, with unusual gravity greeted Mr. Hamerton, who was awaiting him.

"You said in your note that you had an important business communication to make to me," said Hamerton, without appearing to notice Wyville's mental disturbance.

Mr. Wyville did not answer, but paced the room to and fro slowly, sunk in deep thought, his arms crossed on his breast.

"These results may follow," he said at length, evidently thinking aloud; "but there is need of an intelligence to make them inevitable. Mr. Hamerton," he said, stopping before his friend, and fixing his eyes upon him, "I have a trust to offer you that involves a heavy responsibility. Will you undertake it, for my sake, and, in case of what may come, carry out my desire to the letter?"

"If it lie in my power, I will. If it lie beyond me, I will do my best to the end," answered Hamerton.

"Yes, I am sure of it. I am very grateful." Mr. Wyville took his hand, and pressed it warmly, with still the same grave look. He then went to a small but massive iron safe in the room, opened it, and from a drawer took two large sealed packets.

"Here," he said, "are two envelopes that contain all my wishes and all my power. They are mine, so long as I am alive, with freedom to control my actions. Please remember well my words. In case of my death or disappearance, or — other event to impede my action for those who depend on me, these packets belong to you, to open, and read."

"Have you written full instructions therein which I am to follow?" asked Hamerton.

"No; I will not instruct you, because I trust you as I would my own soul. You will understand, when you have read; and you will act for the best. Do you promise me this?"

"I do, most solemnly; but, Mr. Wyville, suppose I should be unable — suppose I should die before your trust were carried out — is there any one else to whom I may transfer the duty?"

"Yes; to Sheridan."

Mr. Wyville locked the safe, and handed the key to Hamerton.

"I shall send the safe to the yacht before we sail," he said. "Now let us inform the children."

Mr. Wyville struck a bell, and Ngarra-jil silently entered. A word in his own language from his master sent him out as quickly. In a few minutes, Mr. Wyville and Mr. Hamerton went upstairs and entered a large and richly draped room, in which the entire furniture consisted of low and soft divans, lounges, cushions, and furs, the effect of which was very extraordinary, but very beautiful. The room seemed to have no occupant, as the gentlemen walked its length toward a deep bay-window.

" We — are — here ! " said a low voice, in distinctly measured syllables, as a diffident child might slowly strike three notes of an air, and then there were two laughs, as clear and joyous as the sound of silver bells, and the light sound of hand-clapping.

The gentlemen, smiling, turned to the draped recess, and there, half shaded by the curtains, peeped the dark, laughing faces of the Australian sisters, Koro and Tepairu, the grandchildren of Te-mana-roa, the King of the Vasse.

That Mr. Hamerton had become familiar to the girls was evident from their natural and unrestrained conduct.

A residence of several years in a northern climate had arrested in the sisters the immature development so common in warm countries. They had matured slowly ; and while preserving all that was charming and natural of their woodland graces, the restraint of another and a gentler mode of life covered them like a delicate robe. They were so outlandish and beautiful, in their strange and beautiful room, that they might be mistaken for rare bronzes, were it not for their flashing eyes and curving lips.

As they sat in the curtained recess, greeting the gentlemen with a joyous laugh, there entered the room a very old Australian woman, followed by two young men, bearing trays with several dishes. These were set down on a low square divan. The old woman removed the covers, and with quick, short words directed the black men to place cushions around the divan.

The sisters, Koro and Tepairu, came from their seclusion, speaking in their own rapid tongue both to the old woman and to Mr. Wyville. They took each a corner of the divan, seating themselves on the cushions placed on the floor, Mr. Wyville and Hamerton taking the opposite corners.

The food, to which each helped himself, was a savory meal of boiled rice, yams, and rich stews, of which the Australians are very fond; and, following these dishes, a varied supply of delicious fruit, among which were mangoes, guavas, and the ambrosial mungyte or honey-stalk of Western Australia.

The conversation during the meal was wholly in the language of the sisters, so that Mr. Hamerton remained silent. Koro and Tepairu had evidently been studying English; but they could by no means converse in the strange tongue.

As if instinctively aware that something unforeseen was about to happen, Tepairu, the younger but braver of the sisters, had asked Mr. Wyville to speak.

"You are soon to leave this cold country," he said, in their tongue, looking from sister to sister; "and return to your own beautiful Vasse."

The girls answered, as if they were a single thing of nature, by a silent and inquiring look. It was hard to read either pleasure or pain in their faces, or anything but surprise; yet a close observer would have discerned a subtending line akin to doubt or fear.

"Are you not glad?" asked Mr. Wyville, with a smile of astonishment at their silence.

"Yes," they softly answered, in one breath, after a pause, but not joyously. "Yes; we shall see the good Te-mana-roa, and we shall find the emu's nests on the mountain. We are very glad."

The old woman, who had remained in the room, chuckled audibly, and, when the others looked round at her, laughed outright in uncontrollable joy at the thought of returning to her beloved life of freedom in the forest. More rapidly than a skilled musician could evoke notes, she ran from treble to bass in voluble gratitude and benediction. Then she slid off to carry the joyous word to the other dusky members of this extraordinary household.

"You will be happy in your old home in the yacht,"
continued Mr. Wyville; "and this friend, my brother
and yours, will take you in his care till we see Te
mana-roa and the Vasse."

As Mr. Wyville spoke, the hidden fear became plain
in Tepairu's face. She looked only at Mr. Wyville, her
large deer-like eyes slowly filling with tears. Her
sister, too, was distressed, but in a lesser degree; and her
eyes, instead of being fixed on Mr. Wyville, passed on
to Hamerton, and rested.

"You are not coming with us to the Vasse?" at
length said Tepairu, in a slow, monotonous voice.
"You will remain here."

"No; I, too, shall go, and even before you. But
we voyage on different ships."

"Why does not your brother and ours go on the
other ship, and let you come with us?"

Mr. Wyville looked troubled at the reception of his
news by the sisters. As Tepairu spoke, in the last
question, his face became exceedingly grave, as if he
could never again smile. The sisters saw the shadow,
and were troubled also. Mr. Wyville, without looking
at them, spoke:—

"Children, you should trust that I will do what
is best; and I know the world better than you. Tepairu, I am acting wisely. Koro, I am sure of your
confidence, at least."

Before the words had died, Koro, with swimming
eyes, had risen and taken Mr. Wyville's hand, which
she kissed, and placed upon her head. The act was
full of affection and faith.

Tepairu, on whom the reproof had fallen like a
blow, sat just as before, only the light had faded from
her eyes, and her bosom heaved visibly. Her sister
went and sat beside her, throwing her arms round
her, as to give comfort. Tepairu allowed the embrace,
but did not move a muscle of face or body.

Mr. Wyville rose and walked to the window, glanced
out for a moment, then, turning, looked at the sisters.
He approached and laid his hand with inexpressible
gentleness on Tepairu's head, as he had done on
Koro's.   The proud but sensitive nature yielded at the
touch, and with one quick look of sorrow and appeal,
she buried her face in her sister's bosom, and sobbed
unrestrainedly.

The old woman, who had re-entered, began an excited
and guttural remonstrance against this unreasoning
grief.   Mr. Wyville chose this moment to depart.   He
knew that the brief season of cloud would soon pass,
and let the sun shine again; that the reflection following petulance is often the purer for the previous
error.

VI.

THE CHILD'S GRAVE.

THE *Houguemont*, chartered by the Government to
carry the convicts to Western Australia, lay in Portland Roads.   She rode within the dark shadow of the
gloomy cliff, upon which is built one of the greatest
of the English imperial prisons.   She was a large,
old-fashioned merchant ship, of two thousand tons
burden, a slow sailer, but a strong and roomy vessel.

She was fitted in the usual way of convict ships.
Her main deck and her lower deck were divided into
separate compartments, the dividing walls below being
heavy and strong bulkheads, while those on deck were
wooden barriers about nine feet high, with side doors,
for the passage of the sailors while working the ship.
At each of these doors, during the entire voyage,
stood two soldiers, with fixed bayonets on their loaded
rifles.

The hatch coverings opening to the lower deck, where the convicts were confined, were removed; and around each hatchway, reaching from the upper deck, or roof of the convict's room, to the lower deck or floor, was one immense grating, formed of strong iron bars. This arrangement gave plenty of air and a good deal of light, the only obstruction being the bars.

Seen from below, on the convicts' deck, every hatchway stood in the centre of the ship like a great iron cage, with a door by which the warders entered, and a ladder to reach the upper deck.

The convicts below never tired of looking upward through the bars, though they could see nothing above but the swaying ropes and sails, and at night the beautiful sky and the stars.

In the forward and smallest compartment of the ship between decks lived the crew, who went up and down by their own hatchway. In the next, and largest compartment lived the male convicts, three hundred in number. The central compartment was the hospital; and next to this the compartment for the female convicts. The after compartment between-decks was occupied by the sixty soldiers who kept guard on the ship.

The main or upper deck was divided as follows: the after part, under the poop deck, was occupied by the staterooms for officers and passengers, and the richly furnished cabin dining-room. Forward of this, beginning at the front of the poop, was a division of the deck to which the female convicts were allowed at certain hours of the day. The next section was the deck where the male convicts were allowed to exercise, one hundred at a time, throughout the day.

The fore part of the main-deck, running out to the bowsprit like a Λ, was roofed in, the angular section taking in the bowsprit. The front of this section, running across the deck, was composed of enormous bars, thicker than a man's arm, like those around the hatches, and within these bars, in sight of the male convicts on deck, were confined the malefactors or rule-breakers.

This triangular section was the punishment cell of the ship. It was entered by a ponderous door, composed of bars also. Its two rear walls were the acute angle of the ship's bulwarks; its front was the row of bars running from side to side of the vessel, and facing aft on the main deck.

The evil-doers confined here for punishment had neither bed nor seat; they sat upon the deck, and worked at heavy tasks of oakum picking. They could not shirk, for a warder kept sentry outside the cage.

As these refractory ones looked through-their bars at the deck, they saw, strapped to the foremast, a black gaff or spar with iron rings, which, when the spar was lowered horizontally, corresponded to rings screwed into the deck.

This was the triangle, where the unruly convicts were triced up and flogged every morning.

Above this triangle, tied around the foremast, was a new and very fine hempen rope, leading away to the end of the foreyard. This was the ultimate appeal, the law's last terrible engine, — the halter which swung mutineers and murderers out over the hissing sea to eternity.

The *Houguemont* had taken on board her terrible cargo. From early dawn the chains had been marching down the steep hill from Portland Prison, and passing on tugs to her deck, where the convict officers unlocked their chains, called their rolls, and sent them below to their berths.

Last of all, the female convicts had come, fifty in number, in five chains.

As they stood huddled on the deck of the transport, answering to their numbers, there were hysterical sounds and wild eyes among them. At last, their chains were unlocked, and the female warders handed to each the number of her berth, and sent her below.

Toward the end of one of the chains stood a prisoner
with a white face and a strangely calm air. She did
not stare around in the dazed way of her unfortunate
sisters ; but remained on the spot where they bade her
stand, motionless. She only turned her head once,
with a smile of silent comfort to some unhappy one
near her who had made the hysterical sound.

When the key came to her link of the chain and
unlocked it, and she stood unshackled, another warder
thrust into her hand a card, and pushed her toward the
hatch. She tottered beneath the rough and needless
force, and would have fallen down the open hatchway,
had she not caught at a swinging rope, and saved
herself. As she recovered, she gave a kind of pitiful
short cry or moan, and looked round bewildered, the
tears springing to her eyes. The rough and busy
warder again approached her, and she shrank aside
in terror.

At this moment she felt a soft hand take her own,
and hold it tightly. The touch restored her confidence.
She turned and met the sweet face and kindly smile of
Sister Cecilia. The warder at the same moment respectfully saluted the nun.

"This is my hospital assistant, warder," said Sister
Cecilia, still holding Alice's hand. "She is to be allowed to go to my room."

"All right, ma'am," said the warder, who, in reality,
was not harsh, but only rude and hurried in manner ;
"pass on, Number Four. Here !" she shouted to the
next on the chain, "take this card — and down you go,
quick !"

And as Alice stood aside with a great sense of relief
and thankfulness, and with swimming eyes, the warder whispered to Sister Cecilia : "I'm glad she's not
going among 'em — we're all glad on it."

Sister Cecilia, holding Alice's hand, led her along a
narrow boarded way, at the end of which was a door

opening into a pleasant room, one side of which was covered with a large medicine-case, and off which lay two bright little sleeping-rooms. When the door was closed, Sister Cecilia took Alice's white face between her hands with hearty force, and kissed her.

"Thank God, my child!" she cried, "you are safe at last!"

Alice could not speak; but she controlled herself, and kept from sobbing. She looked around wonderingly.

"This is my room, Alice," said Sister Cecilia; "my room and yours. This narrow passage is for us alone. It leads straight to the female compartment and the hospital; and no one can come here but you and I — not a soul, for the next four months. Just think of that, child! Look out that pretty little window, and say 'good-by' to gloomy old England and her prisons. We'll be all alone till we arrive in Australia — except when we are attending the sick."

Alice Walmsley did not answer in words — her heart overflowed, and the kind little nun led her into the pleasanter sleeping-room of the two, and left her, saying that this was her own room for the voyage.

When she had gone, Alice sank on her knees with such a flood of feeling as seemed to melt her very heart. With eyes drowned in tears she raised her hands toward the frowning cliffs of Portland, while her quivering lips moved in yearning words.

She was saying farewell, not to England, but to that which was greater to her than England — to the little spot of earth where lay the body of her dead child.

O, true heart of motherhood, that never changes, never forgets, never loses the sound of the maternal music, once the immortal key has been struck.

"Good-by, my darling! O, if I had only one single withered blade of grass to cherish!" cried the poor mother; and as she spoke she saw clearly in her mind's eye the little neglected and forgotten grave. "Good-by, my darling, — for ever — for ever!"

She buried her face in the bed, and wept bitterly and long. Sister Cecilia came twice to the room softly, and looked in at the mourner, but did not disturb her. The second time she came, Alice was weeping, with bowed head.

Sister Cecilia leant over her, and placed beside her hand a little box, covered with white paper, on which lay a sealed letter. Having done so, the Sister laid her hand caressingly on Alice's head, and withdrew quietly.

It was many minutes before Alice raised her tear-stained face. As she did so, she laid her hand on the little box, and saw the letter. She did not heed it at first, thinking it was Sister Cecilia's. But another instant, and she had read her own name — "Alice Walmsley" — written on the letter, and in a hand that was strangely familiar. The written name itself was not more familiar than the handwriting.

Something thrilled her as she took the little box in her hand, and opened it. She found within a piece of soft mould, in which some sweet young grass was growing, and on one side a fresh wild flower, that must have been pulled that day.

As she looked, with blurred sight, the meaning of the blessed gift poured into her heart like balm, and her thought rose up to heaven in an ecstasy of gratitude.

She did not need to look at the letter; she divined its contents. But at length she took it, and broke the seal, and read the few words it contained : —

"Dear Alice, — The grass and flowers were growing this morning on your baby's grave. The wild flowers have covered it for years. I have arranged that it shall never be neglected nor disturbed.   Yours faithfully,
"WILLIAM SHERIDAN."

An hour later, Sister Cecilia entered the outer room, purposely making a noise to distract Alice's reverie. But she had to come at last and touch her arm, and take the box and the letter from her hands, before Alice realized the revelation that had come to her. She did not see it even then as a whole ; but piece by piece in her mind the incredible happiness dawned upon her, that she actually had with her the precious grass, with young life in it, fresh from her darling's grave.

And later on, slowly, but by sure degrees, entered another thought, that rested like a holy thing beside this pure affection.

The last words of the letter repeated themselves like a strain of distant music in her ears: " Yours faithfully — yours faithfully," — and though the sense that was touched had in it a tone of pain and reproach that smote her, it roused her from further dwelling on her own unhappiness.

VII.

THE SAILING OF THE HOUGUEMONT.

THE last convict had been sent below. The barred doors in the railed hatchways were locked. The hundreds of cooped criminals mingled with each other freely for the first time in many years. The sentries had been posted at the hatches and passages on deck. The sailors had shaken out the sails. The capstan had been worked until every spare link of cable was up.

The *Houguemont* was ready for sea. She only awaited the coming of her commander.

Mr. Wyville walked to and fro on the poop deck, casting now and again a searching glance at the pier and the steep cliff road. At length his pace became less regular, and his usually imperturbable face betrayed impatience. It was two hours past the time when the captain had engaged to be on board.

As Mr. Wyville stood looking landward, with a darkened brow, the chief warder in command of the prison officers, rapidly approached him, with an excited air, and saluted in military fashion.

"Well, Mr. Gray," said Mr. Wyville, turning, "what is it?"

"One man missing, sir! not on board — he must have slipped overboard from the soldiers, and attempted to swim ashore."

"When did he come on board?"

"With the last chain, sir."

"Then he must be in the water still. He would strike for the mainland, not for the island."

As he spoke, a soldier who had run up the rigging shouted that there was a hamper or basket floating a short distance astern of the ship.

Mr. Wyville asked one of the ship's officers for a glass, which he levelled at the floating basket. He saw that it moved obliquely toward the shore of the mainland, though a strong tide was setting in the contrary direction, toward the island. He lowered the glass with a saddened air.

"Poor fellow!" he murmured, shutting the glass, irresolutely. He knew that the absconder, finding the floating hamper, had placed it over his head in order to escape the eyes of the guards. As he laid down the telescope, a rifle shot rang from the maintop, and the water leaped in a jet of spray within a foot of the basket. Next instant, came two reports, the basket was knocked on its side, and all on the deck of the convict ship plainly saw a man swimming in the sea. One of the bullets had struck him, evidently, for he shouted, and dashed about wildly.

All this had happened in a few seconds. The shots had followed each other as rapidly as file-firing. At the second shot, Mr. Wyville looked at the soldiers with a face aflame with indignation. As the third shot rang out, he shouted to the soldiers; but his voice was drowned in the report.

Next moment, he saw the levelled rifle of another soldier, and heard the officer directing his aim. Without a word, Mr. Wyville seized the long and heavy marine telescope, which he had laid on the rack, and, balancing himself on the poop for an instant, he hurled the glass like a missile from a catapult right into the group of soldiers on the top.

The missile struck lengthwise against the rifleman, and knocked him toward the mast, his weapon going off harmlessly in the air. Consternation seized the others, and the young officer began an indignant and loud demand as to who had dared assault his men.

"Come down, sir," said Mr. Wyville, sternly, "and receive your orders before you act."

The subaltern came down, and joined Mr. Wyville on the poop, saluting him as he approached.

"I was not aware, sir," he said, "that I was to wait for orders in cases of mutiny or escape."

"This man could be overtaken," said Mr. Wyville; "your guards allowed him to escape; and you have no right to kill him for escaping, if the law had no right to kill him for his crime."

As he spoke, he brought the glass to bear on the unfortunate wretch in the water, to whom a boat was now sweeping with swift stroke.

"My God! he said, putting down the glass, and turning from the officer; "the man is drowned!"

The struggling swimmer, spent with previous exertions, had been struck by a bullet in the shoulder; and though the wound was not mortal, it rapidly spent his remaining strength. Before the boat had reached him the poor fellow had thrown up his arms and sunk. His body was found and taken to the ship.

During this scene, Captain Draper had come on deck, unobserved. He had passed quite close to Mr. Wyville as he spoke severely to the military officer. A few minutes later, when Mr. Wyville stood alone, the captain approached him.

"Am I supposed to command this ship, or to take orders also?" he asked, not offensively, but with his usual hybrid smile.

Mr. Wyville remained silent a moment, as if undecided. The recent shocking event had somewhat changed his plans.

"You command the ship, sir," he said, slowly, and fixing his eyes on Captain Draper's face, "under me. So long as your duty is done, no interference will be possible. It may be well to understand now, however, that there is a higher authority than yours on board."

Captain Draper bowed; then turning to his chief officer, who had heard the conversation, he gave orders for sailing.

VIII.

FACE TO FACE.

THE convict ship, with all sail set, before a strong quarter-breeze, ploughed heavily round the South of England, and then spread her arms like a sea-spirit as she swept majestically toward the deep southern seas.

No need to moralize afresh on the weird contrast between the tall ship, nobly and beautifully breasting the waves, and the hideous secret she bears within, —

"Who, as she smiles in the silvery light,
Spreading her wings on the bosom of night,

Alone on the deep, as the moon in the sky,
A phantom of beauty, could deem with a sigh,
That so lovely a thing is the mansion of sin,
And that souls that are smitten lie bursting within!
Who, as he watches her silently gliding,
Remembers that wave after wave is dividing
Bosoms that sorrow and guilt could not sever,
Hearts that are broken and parted for ever ?
Or deems that he watches, afloat on the wave,
The death-bed of hope, or the young spirit's grave?"

The first few days of the voyage are inexpressibly
horrible. The hundreds of pent-up wretches are unused to the darkness of the ship, strange to their
crowded quarters and to each other, depressed in
spirits at their endless separation from home, sickened
to death with the merciless pitch and roll of the vessel, alarmed at the dreadful thunder of the waves
against their prison walls, and fearful of sudden engulf-
ment, with the hatches barred. The scene is too hideous
for a picture — too dreadful to be described in words.

Only those who have stood within the bars, and
heard the din of devils and the appalling sounds of
despair, blended in a diapason that made every hatch-
mouth a vent of hell, can imagine the horrors of the
hold of a convict ship.

About a week out from England, the *Houguemont*
went bowling down the Atlantic, and across the Bay
of Biscay. The night was cold and dark, and the
strong breeze held the ship steady, with every sail
drawing.

Mr. Wyville and Sheridan, the latter of whom had
come on deck for the first time since the vessel sailed,
in warm great-coats, walked the lee side of the poop ;
while the captain, also heavily wrapped, paced the
weather side, glancing now and again at the sails, and
taking an occasional look at the course.

"You have got over your sea-sickness ? " asked Mr.
Wyville.

Sheridan laughed.

"You forget that I am a sailor, Mr. Wyville," he said. "I had another reason for keeping my room."

Will Sheridan, for months past, had often been on the point of telling Mr. Wyville the whole story of his life, his love for Alice Walmsley, and her terrible suffering for another's crime; but the moment still had gone by, and he had never broached the subject. He longed to speak his warm gratitude to the wise friend who had preserved Alice's reason and life in Millbank.

Mr. Wyville never dreamt that Sheridan and Alice Walmsley had known each other. He did not know that on the deck at that moment stood Sheridan's deadliest enemy, within five yards of the man he hated, and who mortally hated him.

"I will tell him all now," were the words in Sheridan's mind; and he turned to Mr. Wyville, and took hold of his arm. They paused in their walk, and stood at the foot of the mizzen-mast.

At that moment, the captain went toward the wheel, and bent his head to look at the compass. The strong binnacle-light fell full upon his face, just as Will Sheridan stopped and laid his hand on Mr Wyville's arm.

The face in the binnacle glare was straight before Sheridan. His eyes were arrested by it as by a spectre; his hand closed like a vise on the arm of his friend.

"God Almighty!" The words rushed from his heart in a hissing whisper.

Mr. Wyville was astounded, but he could not even surmise the cause of Sheridan's tremendous excitement. He had seen the face of the captain as it remained for a moment in the strong light; but he did not connect this with his friend's emotion. He waited for Sheridan to speak.

Instead of speaking, Sheridan watched the dark

14

figure of the captain as he passed from the wheel to
the weather side of the poop, and paced slowly up and
down. Then he drew a deep breath, tremulous with
aroused passion.

"Who is that man?" he asked, in a low voice, after
a long look.

"That is the captain," answered Mr. Wyville. "Let
me introduce you. Captain Draper!"

The captain walked toward them. Sheridan remained just as he had been standing.

"Captain Draper, let me introduce — "

"Stay!" said Sheridan, laying his hand on Mr.
Wyville's breast, "one moment."

He strode to the binnacle, seized the lamp, and returned with it in his hand. When he was within two
feet of Draper, he threw the light full on his own
face, sternly turned toward his enemy.

"Now!" he said, "now, introduce me!"

The sight of the terrible face struck Draper like a
physical blow. His breath came in a short gasp, and
he staggered back till he leaned against the mast. He
never said a word.

Sheridan turned the glare of the lamp upon him for
an instant, then snatched it rapidly away from the repulsive sight. At that moment, with the veil of darkness suddenly torn back, Draper's face was ghastly, and
his attitude full of terror.

Will Sheridan replaced the lamp in the binnacle,
and walked straight to his own room.

Mr. Wyville was profoundly astonished and puzzled
at this scene. He remained on deck for an hour or
more after Sheridan's abrupt departure; but he did
not speak to Captain Draper, who paced his side of
the poop in gloomy silence.

It was an hour of fearful torture to Draper, for, like
most scoundrels who are cowards, he suffered over and
over again the agonies of shame and exposure which

he knew he had earned. But, like this class, too, he always planned his conduct, even his words, beforehand. As soon as the appalling interview had passed, and he found himself personally unmolested, his adroit and subtle mind began weaving the warp and woof of a devil's plot that should make him the winner in this contest now begun.

He looked at Wyville, who stood gazing out on the sea, and asked himself, "Does he know?" And he speedily ran over the signs, and concluded that Mr. Wyville knew nothing of his relations to Sheridan. He remembered that Wyville had called him to be introduced to Sheridan, and he had noticed the surprised exclamation with which Wyville had observed Sheridan's extraordinary conduct.

The midnight eight bells sounded, and the mate came to relieve the captain from his watch; but Draper said he could not sleep, and would remain on deck an hour longer.

In that hour, he was alone on the poop; Mr. Wyville had gone below. Draper, looking down through the glass roof of the dining-room, saw that a bright light was burning in Sheridan's room. As he looked at the light, secretly and alone, a desperate hatred burned in his heart like poison. The years of his guilt were melted down into that one hour, and they took the form of a blighting curse. Could malediction have murdered Sheridan, he would have been withered to death by the baneful light of Draper's eyes.

But the hatred of a man so naturally evil as Draper is apt to turn into practical injury. The coward who hates is never at rest; he will either malign his enemy with foul words in secret, or he will dig a pit for his feet. It is only manly men who can hate and hold their tongues.

As Draper paced the deck, towards the end of the hour, his tread actually became stealthy and fearful,

as if he dreaded lest the nature of his thoughts might
be read in the sound of his steps. Slowly and carefully
he turned the circumstances over in his mind. Wyville
certainly did not know of his relations with Sheridan.
Sheridan himself had evidently been surprised at the
meeting. Only one knew: none else had any interest
in knowing. That one must be silenced, or — he,
Draper, must face disgrace. Once before, Sheridan
had eluded his design; but this time — and, as he concluded his walk and plot together, he glared at the
light in Will Sheridan's room, like a serpent in the
outer darkness, — this time there would be no mistake or hesitation on his part.

IX.

HOW A PRISONER MIGHT BREAK A BAR.

THE days slipped into weeks as the *Houguemont*
sailed southward down the great commercial highway
of the Atlantic. The mild airs of the warmer latitudes surprised and delighted those who had only
known the moist climate of Britain. As the vessel
sailed close to the island of Pico, one of the Azores,
the deck was crowded with gazers on the unknown
land.

It was the forenoon of a lovely day. The sun shone
with radiant splendor on the soaring peak and purple
cliffs of Pico. The island seemed to most of those
on the ship like some legendary land of fairy lore.
They had never seen any country but England, and
they had never before heard even the name of this
important-looking place.

On the bow of the convict ship, standing on the
raised deck, which was the roof of the punishment-
cell or compartment, stood three men, looking up at

Pico. These three, from the day of the ship's sailing, had been drawn together by inherent attraction; and now, among all the queer new friendships of the voyage, there was none stronger than theirs. And yet they were very dissimilar, inwardly and outwardly.

One was a tall man, solemn-faced and severe, dressed in sombre garments; the next was a small man, mild of face and manner, clad in old-fashioned sailor's blue; the third was a very black man, whose hair stood upright on his head when he removed his immense fur cap, and whose body from throat to feet was clothed in furs.

Strange it was, that this seemingly discordant trio, Mr. Haggett, Officer Lodge, and Ngarra-jil, had developed a mutual attraction, each for the other; and, after a few weeks at sea, had spent almost their whole waking time in each other's company.

They did not converse much, if any. Ben Lodge did not quite understand Mr. Haggett's solemn scriptural illustrations and heavy comments; Mr. Haggett did not pay much heed to Ben Lodge's dreadful tale of carnage in the Chinese bombardment; and neither of them understood Ngarra-jil, nor did he comprehend a word they said.

Yet they passed day after day in each other's company, leaning over the vessel's side or sitting on the sunny forecastle.

The presence of Officer Lodge on board needs explanation. Two days before the convict ship sailed, Mr. Wyville walked into the lock-up at Walton-le-Dale, followed by Ngarra-jil.

Officer Lodge met him with a mild, every-day air, and, pointing with a backward motion of the hand toward the cell, informed him that it was "hempty."

"Have you any relatives or others depending on you?" asked Mr. Wyville, falling into the matter-of-fact simplicity of the little policeman.

"No, sir; no one as can't get along without me. I 've lived here alone for fifteen year. I don't know a man, though, in Walton to take my place. There's a deal of trust in this hoffice, sir; a deal of trust."

"What property do you own here?" asked Mr. Wyville.

"The donkey and water-cart is mine, though the village gave 'em to me. That's all the property."

"I need a careful man to oversee a settlement," said Mr. Wyville. "But he will have to go to Australia. He will be comfortably placed, much more so than you are here; and his engagement will be permanent. I came to offer the place to you — can you come?"

"Yessir," said Officer Lodge, as quietly as if he were asked to walk down the street. "Do you want me to start now."

"It is now noon; I will return to London on the two o'clock train. Meanwhile, I will walk through the village." Turning to Ngarra-jil, Mr. Wyville said in his own language, "You can remain here."

Mr. Wyville walked straight to the old home of Alice Walmsley, and lingered a long time in and around the deserted and decaying cottage. There was a warm feeling in his heart, a new and happy growth which was thrilled and strengthened as his eye fell on objects that might once have been familiar to Alice Walmsley.

As he left the place, to return for Officer Lodge, it seemed as dear to him as if he had known and loved it all his life. He turned toward it, as he walked down the road, and there was a quiet gladness in his face.

"She will leave it all behind," he murmured. "There shall be no picture of its wretchedness in her memory."

He passed to the court-house. Officer Lodge and Ngarra-jil were sitting in the office, silently looking at each other. At first, Officer Lodge had spoken to his companion; but Ngarra-jil had answered only by a gruff and unintelligible monosyllable. They then had subsided into perfect silence.

"Are you ready?" asked Mr. Wyville.

"Yessir."

"Come."

They went to the railway station, and took their seats for London. Officer Lodge and Ngarra-jil sat opposite each other, and continued their acquaintance in the same silent fashion which had marked its beginning in the station-house.

On board the convict ship, they had attracted the lonely Mr. Haggett, who, in a patronizing manner at first, joined their company.

As these three stood near the bow of the *Hougue-mont*, looking up at the purple cliffs of lofty Pico, there rose an extraordinary commotion on the deck, among the convicts.

That morning, two men, the worst and most disorderly characters in the ship, had been locked up in the punishment-crib. They had first been sentenced to work at oakum-picking; but they sat within the bars idle, staring out at the crowd of convicts on deck, and singing and shouting. For this they had been again reported, and the officers had now come to take them out for further punishment.

The officers stood waiting for him who had the key of the barred door; and he was searching vainly in his pockets. After a while, it was evident that the key had been mislaid or lost. The officers could not open the barred door.

The two culprits within were the first to understand this, and they set up a howl of derision. They danced about in their den, cursing the officers and snapping their fingers at them through the bars.

At length a dreadful idea struck one of the desperate wretches. His eye had fallen on the heap of

loosely-picked oakum inside the bars.   With a yell he
seized an armful of the inflammable material and
threw it far within the cage, against a heap of tarred
rope ready for picking.

The officers stood outside, watching the fellow's
action with alarm.   When he had gathered all the
oakum into a pile, he drew from his pocket a lucifer
match, and flourished it before the officers' eyes with
a grin of triumph and devilish meaning.   His brutal
associate within the bars, upon whom the meaning of
the preparations broke suddenly at sight of the match,
gave a wild shout of delight and defiance.

"Damn you!" he cried, shaking his fist at the
powerless warders, "you can't help yourselves.   We'll
set fire to the ship before your eyes!"

The dreadful threat struck terror into the convicts
on deck, who began to huddle together like sheep.

The officers looked into each other's pale faces, dumb
and helpless.   One of them caught hold of the massive
bars of the door, and shook them with all his force.
He might as well have tried to shake down the
mast.

Yelling with delight at their power, the two mis-
creants within piled up the pyre.   Then, he who held
the match selected a dry place on deck to strike it.
He bent down on his knees, and covered his action
from the eyes of the officers.

In another instant he sprang to his feet, holding a
blazing rope of loosely-twisted oakum.   With a laugh
that rang through the ship, he applied the torch to the
pile of oakum, and the yellow flame licked up the
ready material with fearful rapidity.

At sight of the flame, a cry of alarm rose from the
huddled convicts, drowning the reports of the officers'
pistols, who were shooting down the incendiaries.

It was too late.   Had they used their pistols before
the match was struck, they would have acted in time.

To slaughter the wretches now was to insure the continuation of the fire. Were the prisoners let alone, they might have become terrified at their own danger, and have quenched the blaze before it had seized the ship.

One of the officers placed the muzzle of his pistol to the ponderous lock of the cage, and fired. The bullet destroyed the lock, but did not force it. At that moment, with a cry of success, an officer dashed through the crowd and seized the lock. He had found the key !

But it would not turn in the shattered wards. The bullet had wedged everything together, and the bolt had become a rivet.

By this time the flames had swept over the pile of tarred rope, and had fastened on the beams overhead. The pitch bubbled up between the seams of the deck, and dense volumes of smoke poured through the bars.

The alarm had spread to the convicts below, and an awful sound of affright arose from the hundreds of horrified hearts.

The officers dashed wildly to and fro. Some of the ship's crew had begun to work with axes on the roof of the cage, which was a heavily-timbered deck. The fire began to roar with the dreadful sound that denotes the untamable power of approaching conflagration.

At this moment, Mr. Wyville came forward, and with one glance took in the whole scene. Every one gave way for him as he strode to the cage. The convicts prayed him, "save us!" the ultimate appeal of terror-stricken men.

He stood an instant looking at the fire — saw the mortal danger. In ten minutes more, no earthly power could subdue the flames.

"Shall we open the hatches, and let the convicts come on deck?" asked the pallid chief warder, the key in his hand.

"No!" shouted Wyville with such sudden force that the man staggered back in dismay.

Mr. Wyville looked at the lock, and saw its condition. He shook the bars with amazing force.

A gust of flame and smoke now rushed through the bars, and drove every one back, even Mr. Wyville. He rushed forward again; then turned to the officers, who had retreated to the foremast, and called them to him. Not one moved — they were cowed.

Another instant, and a tall man pushed through the crowd, and stood beside Wyville. It was Mr. Haggett. Their eyes met for one instant. They understood one another.

"What do you want?" asked Haggett, in a low, steady voice.

"The silk curtains from the dining-room — quick!" answered Mr. Wyville in the same tone.

Next moment, Haggett was clearing a lane for himself through and over the crowd. He disappeared toward the cabin. They knew he would return, and they kept the way open for him. In half a minute he flew back, in each hand a long red silken curtain, torn from the cabin windows.

Mr. Wyville stood waiting for him, holding in his hand a heavy iron belaying-pin, which he had taken from the rail. He took one of the curtains, twisted it into a rope, and pushed one end through the bars. This end he brought out four bars off, and around these four bars he wound both curtains, one after the other.

When the curtains were entirely wound in this way, he inserted the heavy iron rod between the folds, at the two central bars, and began to turn it end over end like a lever. The first turn made the silken rope rigid; the second strained it; the third called out all the muscular power of the man. But there was nothing gained.

Mr. Wyville turned, and looked toward Haggett who approached. Both men seized the iron lever, and pulled it down with all their force.

"This is a convict's trick," said Haggett, as they paused for breath.

Mr. Wyville made no reply; but continued the tremendous leverage. There was a cry from the convicts: they saw the massive bars yielding — the two outer bars bending toward the centre under the terrific strain.

Once again the upper end of the lever was seized by both men, and with a united effort of strength pulled and pressed down. The next turn was easily made: the mighty bars had bent like lead in the centre and then broken, leaving two gaps wide enough to allow the entrance of a man.

When this was done, Mr. Wyville and Mr. Haggett fell back, while the officers and sailors dashed into the burning cage, smothering the flames with wet sails, beneath which they trampled out the fire.

The vessel was saved, and not one minute could have been spared. In the wild uproar that followed, each one giving vent to the pent-up excitement of the moment, Mr. Wyville, turning in the crowd, met the eyes of Haggett, earnestly fixed on his face. He had often observed his watchfulness before; but there was another meaning in his eyes to-day.

Without a word, Mr. Wyville put out his hand, which Haggett grimly seized.

"Thank you," said Mr. Wyville.

"That's not right," said Haggett; "you have saved all our lives."

Mr. Wyville negatively shook his head, with his usual grave smile, and was about to pass on. Mr. Haggett slowly let go his hand, still looking at him with the same strange expression. They had parted a few paces, when Haggett strode after Mr. Wyville with a

new impulse, seized his hand once more in a grip of
iron, and met his eye with a face working in strong
emotion, every possible reef in his immense lips quivering with suppressed feeling.

" Forgive me ! " he said ; and without another word
he dropped Mr. Wyville's hand, turned, and strode off
to his room by the other side of the ship.

That night, when the excitement had died, and the
usual quiet had been restored, Mr. Wyville and Sheridan walked the poop for hours. Mr. Wyville made
no mention of Haggett's strange conduct.

Toward midnight they went to their rooms. The
extraordinary events of the day had kept them from
talking about Captain Draper, though the subject had
been for days uppermost in both minds.

When Mr. Wyville entered his room, his eyes fell
on a letter, fixed endwise on his table to attract his
attention. It was addressed to him. He opened it,
and took out a photograph — the portrait of a convict
in chains. There was no other enclosure.

On the back of it were written these words, in Mr.
Haggett's handwriting, dated four years before : —

"This is the only photograph of the man known as MOONDYNE.
It was taken in Western Australia, just before his latest escape
from Fremantle Prison.   All other photographs of this prisoner
have unaccountably disappeared from the prison books."

Mr. Wyville gazed a long time at the strange present.
Then he laid it on the table, locked his door, and
walked meditatively to and fro his narrow room. At
times he would stop and take the picture from the
table, look at it with deep attention, while his lips
moved as if he were addressing it.

At last he took the portrait, tore it to pieces, and,
opening the window of his room, threw the pieces
into the sea.

X.

DEAD-SEA FRUIT.

FROM the moment that Will Sheridan had recognized Draper in the captain of the *Houguemont*, his mind was filled with an acute fear that Alice Walmsley might suddenly come face to face with the wretch who had blighted her existence. Such a meeting might be fatal — it certainly would be grievous.

It was the sudden touch of this fear that made Sheridan walk so quickly to his room on the night of the recognition. It came like a flash; and he deemed it best to consider his course of action calmly.

Sailor as he was, he knew that the commander of a ship usually had absolute power over all on board. He had observed, however, that Mr. Wyville, on one or two occasions, had assumed an authority in certain matters relating to the prisoners. This gave him comfort. In case Draper recognized Alice Walmsley on the ship, that instant, Sheridan resolved, he would make known the whole terrible story to Mr. Wyville, and avert intended evil, if possible by fear, if necessary by force.

Meanwhile, Sheridan saw Sister Cecilia, who knew that he was an old friend of the innocent and much-wronged girl, and requested her to keep Alice at all times off the main deck. He gave no reason for the request.

"But, Mr. Sheridan," said the nun, thinking of Alice's health, "she must come into the open air some time."

"It were better not — better not," answered Sheridan, in a troubled mind; "it were better that she should remain all day in the hospital."

"In the hospital!" repeated the wise little nun,

with a pitying smile. She evidently saw, more clearly
than any one on board, the strange complications
around her. The hearts of at least four of the prin-
cipal actors in the sorrowful drama were open to her
eyes; she saw the relations of Sheridan, Alice, the
miserable Harriet Draper, and her guilty husband.

But even Sister Cecilia, wise as she was, did not
know that there was a fifth heart deeply concerned in
the play. As she repeated Sheridan's words, her pitying smile died away into lines of sorrow, seeing how
blindly he would turn Alice's steps from one danger to
a deeper one. She recalled, too, at the word, the
supreme desolation and misery of that one who now
spent her days in the hospital.

"Do not fear, Mr. Sheridan," she said, as she went
on her way of mercy; "Alice will be safe. She will
remain in my hospital."

Taking this as an agreement with his request, Mr.
Sheridan resolved that his conduct toward the captain
should be absolutely reserved, until the vessel reached
port. Then, what to do was beset with difficulties.
That dire punishment should overtake the villain was
clear; but what if his public arraignment would disturb the peace of Alice, whose slowly-healing wounds
would thus be torn open?

Instead of coming to a decision, Sheridan resolved
that on the first opportunity he would lay the whole
matter before Mr. Wyville, and follow his advice.

Soon after entering the tropics, the *Houguemont*
had caught the trade winds, and sailed swiftly down
the level seas. Her tall masts dwindled pigmy-like as
she passed beneath the awful shadow of Teneriffe.
Her sky-sails cut a line on the cliff a finger's breadth
from the sea; while above her towered into the air the
twelve thousand feet of tremendous pinnacle. She
coasted the great Northwestern bulge of Africa; and
here, for the first time since leaving England, her speed

was checked, the trade winds faded and died, the sea lost its ripples, but kept its waves, that rose and fell slowly, with long, monotonous rolls, like an ocean of molten glass. The sails of the *Houguemont* slapped backward and forward, the ropes hung useless, the pennant clung down the mast. The convict ship was becalmed, off the coast of Africa, seven degrees above the Line.

The faces of the ship's officers grew serious when the wind died. They did not welcome a calm in such a latitude, and at that season. The heat was intense and continuous, scarcely lowering by ten degrees at night.

"I wish we were five degrees to the westward," said Sheridan to Mr. Wyville, his old marine lore recurring to him; "I hate this Gulf of Guinea."

"Why?" asked Mr. Wyville, standing in shade of a sail, while the young military officer sat beside Sheridan on the rail.

"I hate it first for its sharks; you can't dip your hand in this water, for a thousand miles South and East, without having it snapped off. I hate it for its low coast, where so many splendid ships have sailed straight to destruction. I hate it for its siroccos, whirlwinds, and, above all, I hate it for its fevers. I don't think there's anything good about the coast of Guinea."

"That is a bad showing, certainly," said the military officer.

"Yes; and it's quite true," continued Sheridan. "No one can say a good word about this coast."

"Not so fast, not so fast," said Mr. Wyville, smiling at Sheridan's earnestness. "On this very coast, within two hundred miles of us, is being solved one of the most interesting political problems in human history. Yonder lies a settlement with a national story unequalled for dignity and pathos."

Sheridan and the young soldier looked up, astonished.

"What is it ?" asked Sheridan.

"The Republic of Liberia," said Mr. Wyville.

Sheridan looked at the soldier, who, at the same moment, looked at him. They both smiled broadly, confessing their ignorance.

"I was too busy with sandalwood — " began Sheridan.

"And I with tactics," said the soldier. " But what is this Republic, sir ? "

"A new country, honestly acquired," said Mr. Wyville; "the only country on earth not torn by force from its rightful owners. A country where slaves have peacefully founded a nation of elevated freedom ; where black men have faced God in manly dignity, and declared their right to wipe out the scriptural curse ; whose citizenship is an honor to the holder, and whose citizens are an honor to mankind."

"Who are the citizens ?" asked the surprised officer.

"Slaves from America !" said Wyville with an earnestness that made them forget the heat; " men who bear on their bodies the marks of the lash, and on their minds the rust of accursed laws ; men who might be pardoned for hating their kind. God bless them !" and, as he spoke, he looked away in the direction of the land ; "the kindest and most amiable race on earth. They have carried with them from the great Republic of the West only that which was good — its first principles. Its unrepublican practices they have left behind."

"Will they not become corrupt ? " asked Sheridan.

" When ? "

"When they become rich," said the officer innocently.

"It is to be feared," answered Mr. Wyville. "But they have one safeguard."

"What is that ? "

"Their climate is deadly to white men," said Mr. Wyville.

The appearance of Captain Draper, coming from his stateroom, interrupted the conversation. The young officer stopped to chat with him, while Mr. Wyville and Sheridan walked to the other side of the poop.

"There are two powers of government represented on this ship," said Sheridan, determined to bring the conversation to the point he wished to speak about; "which is in command — the civil or military? The captain of the vessel or the military officer?"

"Neither."

"I do not understand."

"When convicts sail from England, they are assumed to be at once in the Penal Colony. As soon as the convict ship leaves land, she becomes subject to the penal law of Western Australia."

"Who administers the law on board?"

"The representative of the Comptroller-General of Convicts, the actual authority over the criminals in Western Australia."

"Then we have a representative of the Comptroller-General on board?"

"No."

"Pardon me, Mr. Wyville; you speak riddles to-day. You said a moment ago that every convict ship had such a representative."

"Yes; unless it have the Comptroller himself."

"Then we have — Are you the Comptroller-General?"

"Yes. The office was vacant, and at the request of the Prime Minister I accepted a temporary appointment. I am glad it was offered; for it will enable me to see our new law fairly started."

The evening had closed in as they conversed, and now the shade became somewhat tolerable. Mr. Wyville and Sheridan had drawn their deck chairs toward the wheel-house.

"I am glad there is a power on board above that of

15

the scoundrel who commands the ship," said Sheridan, sternly, after a long pause. Then he continued rapidly: "Mr. Wyville, I have feared every day that I should have to strangle the wretch. I should have told you before; but something always prevented. By some strange fatality there is on board this ship a woman whom I have loved all my life, and who has been mortally wronged by this man. I have come on this ship only to protect her."

Sheridan's lowered voice was husky with deep emotion. Having said so much he remained silent.

Mr. Wyville had been looking out on the glassy and slow roll of the waves. As Sheridan spoke, his lips and mouth closed with a gradual compression, and a light almost of alarm came into his eyes. He was thinking of Alice Walmsley.

"You have loved her all your life," he repeated slowly, still looking at the sea.

"Since I was a boy — and she loved me once."

Mr. Wyville was about to speak; but it seemed as if he changed his mind. Still his lips moved, but he said nothing.

"Who is she, and where?" he said after a pause, and in his usual calm voice.

"She is a prisoner," answered Sheridan; "and she is confined in the hospital."

"In the hospital!" cried Wyville, starting to his feet, with almost a cry of joy; then, seeing Sheridan's face, he controlled himself.

"That unhappy one!"

"Yes," said Sheridan, sadly, thinking that so he described Alice Walmsley.

"God help you, my friend! yours is a terrible grief."

"I have feared that he would see her, or that she might see him."

"Fear no more," said Wyville, tenderly; "I have taken measures to prevent such a meeting."

"You knew, then?" asked Sheridan, surprised.

"1 knew his guilt — but not your sorrow. I knew that he and she were on this ship. It was I who brought him here; and I had beforehand secured her confinement during the voyage in the hospital."

Sheridan was surprised at this, having so lately spoken to Sister Cecilia on the subject. But he set it down to the customary thoughtfulness of Mr. Wyville.

"I cannot speak my gratitude to you," continued Sheridan; "your visit to her prison awakened in her the life that wrong and grief had crushed. I know the whole story, and I have longed to speak my gratitude."

Mr. Wyville deemed that Sheridan referred to his visit to Harriet Draper in Walton-le-Dale. But how could Sheridan have discovered it? He had certainly never communicated with Harriet Draper.

"How did you learn of my visit to her?" asked Mr. Wyville.

"From the governor of Millbank."

"Ah — yes; I told him."

Sheridan felt a great relief from this confidence. He asked Mr. Wyville's advice as to his conduct toward Draper during the voyage; and was glad to find that it coincided with his own view; to treat him with cold neutrality until the *Houguemont* had landed her passengers and had ceased to be a government ship.

When Sheridan had gone to his room, Mr. Wyville remained on deck alone. His heart was strangely happy that night, though he was oppressed by the grief of his friend. For one moment he had feared that the next would crush to death something that had grown within him like a new and sweeter life. As he recalled the scene, his heart stood still with the fear, even in fantasy.

"Thank God!" he murmured, as he watched the moon rise, red and large, on the sultry horizon. "One blow has been spared!"

XI.

THE FEVER.

MR. HAGGETT at first had found himself a lonely man on the convict ship. His position was anomalous. He was neither a minister nor a prison officer. Had he been the former, the ship's officers and the military officers would have taken him into their mess; had he been the latter, the convict officials would have been his companions. But he was only a hired drudge, a non-professional. He was called simply "the Scripture-reader."

So he was thrown for companionship on the two other lonely passengers, Ben Lodge and Ngarra-jil, who were glad of his company, and entirely ignorant of his position.

Mr. Haggett's nature was by no means a bad one; indeed, in other circumstances it would have been an admirable one. He was simply one of those persons who make up the million, who are common vessels to hold that which is put into them. He was a queer mixture of zeal and conceit. His mind had two keys, as a sparrow has only two notes, and these were earnestness and vanity.

Had he been trained as a mechanic, he would have patiently mastered his trade, never improving on what he had been taught; and he would have been vain of his skill, and faithful to it.

To give such a man a field of metaphysical labor, to put into his callow hands the absolute spiritual control of hundreds of lives in need of wise spiritual guidance, was an experiment far more injurious to poor Haggett than to the convicts. It is so always. A priest's vestments are too great for small natures, which they injure, if they do not destroy.

He became puffed up with an absurd wind of conceit, that almost amounted to real character; while the convicts, heedless before, only confirmed their opinion that Christianity was a wordy and stiff profession rather than a true saving principle.

When Mr. Wyville humiliated Haggett in Millbank, the blow appeared terrible; but in truth it only struck Haggett where he was puffed. As a man might cut a balloon with a sharp sword, Mr Wyville's interference and authority had gashed the swelling vanity of the Scripture-reader.

From that day, though he afterwards set out to do Sir Joshua Hobb's dirty work, Mr. Haggett had changed — he was gradually returning to his real nature, which was, as it ought to be, humble, diffident, and commonplace.

"This is a good man," something within him kept saying of Mr. Wyville; "why are you his enemy?" And the answer came, and repeated itself: "Because you are Sir Joshua Hobb's tool."

These thoughts floated through Haggett's mind on his first visit to Australia; and that they had an effect on his conduct was certain. Vague hints and doubts and clews, which Sir Joshua would have been eager to seize, Haggett indeed had found, but had kept to himself.

Since the *Houguemont* sailed he had been especially disturbed in mind. When the incident of the fire came, and he spoke his mind to Mr. Wyville in the hurried words, "Forgive me!" it was not a sudden thought. But it was overwhelming. As a dam may tremble for years, especially in time of storm, and go down at last with a rush, so the last barrier of Haggett's vanity broke that day, and left the reservoir of his conceit dry and unsightly to himself.

A man suffers deeply who has to turn an inward eye on such a scene. But an honest man, helped by humility, will do it, and survive; and at bottom Haggett was honest and humble.

He did not appear on deck for days after the fire; and when he did come out, he spent his time in strange fashion. He would hang around the passage to Sister Cecilia's quarters for hours; and when the little nun was on her way to the female convicts, the ungainly Scripture-reader would start from some unexpected angle, and watch for an opportunity to offer some service.

This continued for weeks, until at last Sister Cecilia noticed the attention. She quietly bowed her head one day in thanks for some slight favor; and for the rest of the day Mr. Haggett's face was lined with good humor and gratification.

When the ship was becalmed in the tropics, the suffering of the imprisoned wretches in the steaming and crowded hold was piteous to see. They were so packed that free movement was impossible. The best thing to do was to sit each on his or her berth, and suffer in patience.

The air was stifling and oppressive. There was no draught through the barred hatches. The deck above them was blazing hot. The pitch dropped from the seams, and burned their flesh as it fell.

There was only one word spoken or thought — one yearning idea present in every mind — water, cool water to slake the parching thirst.

Two pints of water a day were served out to each convict — a quart of half-putrid and blood-warm liquid. It was a woful sight to see the thirsty souls devour this allowance as soon as their hot hands seized the vessel.

Day in and day out, the terrible calm held the ship, and the consuming heat sapped the lives of the pent-up convicts. They suffered in strange patience. The hold was silent all day. They made no complaints. When the officers passed among them, and spoke to them, they smiled and sat still on their berths.

Only once, there was a sound of discontent: when the order was given that the daily allowance of water be reduced to one pint.

Among the officers of the ship, there was silence also. They knew they were in a latitude where calms lasted for long periods. They flushed the decks with water constantly, to try and keep them cool, for the sake of the prisoners below.

"We shall need fresh water in a week," said Captain Draper to Mr. Wyville one day; "the tanks are low already, and evaporation rapidly increases."

Mr. Wyville did not answer, except with an inclination of the head. Words were useless.

"Where is the nearest land?" he asked Sheridan that afternoon, as they paced the poop.

"The island of Principe is about 200 miles to the South," said Sheridan. "There is good water there."

The thought in Mr. Wyville's mind never came to words. As Sheridan spoke, he stopped suddenly, looking away to the North, and pointing his hand with an eager face. A dark line, very faint, was moving on the face of the glassy ocean.

"Thank heaven!" he said, "yonder comes the breeze."

In half an hour it fanned their faces, but so gently that still the sails hung useless, and the pennant only stirred an inch from the mast. But it was a breath — it was a drink. When the night fell, the breeze strengthened, and the ship moved.

There was no sleep on board that night. The hearts of all were filled with deep relief and gratitude. The

breeze held for four days, growing steadier as they
sailed.   On the evening of the fourth day, a man aloft
cried out, " Land ho ! "

They had sighted Principe. From deck, the land
was not seen for an hour later; and the *Houguemont*
stood off and on till morning, when boats would be
sent ashore for water.

At the first flush of dawn the ship was steered toward the island.   A fog lay close to the water, and
the eager eyes of the voyagers only saw a line of
wooded mountain, the base and summit of which were
rolled in mist.

The *Houguemont* sailed into the fog-bank; and before those on board had time to realize the change, her
foresails caught the sunshine, and she swung to within
a land-locked harbor as beautiful as a dream of para-
dise.

The water broke against the wooded shores all round
the lovely haven.   The hills were covered with trees
to the top, and the cocoa palms crowded their lower
slopes to the very shore.   At the end of the harbor
stood the little town of St. Antonio.

The *Houguemont* came to anchor, and boats were
sent ashore to fill the water-casks.   The swift, clear
streams were seen running into the beautiful basin of
the port.

While this work was going on, a sail-boat put off
from the town, and held toward the vessel.   There
were three men in it, and as they came within hail of
ship, keeping to leeward, they ran up a yellow flag.

" My God ! " said Sheridan, who had been watching
the boat; " they have the fever ! "

" Get out as fast as you can," cried a man in the
boat.   " And be sure you allow no one from shore
near the ship.   We have the plague in St. Antonio."

Without another word, the boat's course was changed,
and she returned to the town.   The crew of the *Hou-*

guemont needed no incentive to work. By ten o'clock that night, the casks were filled and the ship was under sail.

" A fortunate escape ! " said the medical officer to Sheridan, who did not answer, but looked at the pennant. The wind had changed, and was blowing directly from St. Antonio.

Next morning the beautiful island was out of sight. The convicts got plenty of water that day, and their hearts were glad. Toward evening, one of the warders went to the doctor's room, and said there was a prisoner very ill, who complained of nausea and pains in the head and shoulders. The doctor's face grew pale at the word ; but he turned away from the warder.

"Take that man on deck at once," he said, quietly, "and place him in the punishment division forward."

The warder went to carry out the order. The doctor hurriedly consulted a book, then left his room and walked forward.

The sick prisoner was there before him. The doctor examined him, quietly ordered his treatment, and retired. He joined Mr. Wyville on the poop.

" We have the fever on board," he said in a low voice. " A man has been attacked by the worst symptoms."

An hour later, two more convicts complained of sickness. They were taken from the hold, and placed in the cell forward.

Next day it was known throughout the ship that the fever, which the sailors and convicts called " the black vomit," was on board; and before nightfall thirty prisoners were seized.

The sick were taken away from the hold at first ; but this separation had soon to be abandoned. There was no room for them apart. The hospital was full. Those who took the fever had to lie side by side with their terror-stricken fellows.

Like an angel of comfort, Sister Cecilia tended on the sufferers. Following her steps, and quietly obeying her word, went Mr. Haggett. In the female compartment, where twelve prisoners lay with the fever, Alice Walmsley moved ceaselessly in the work of mercy.

On the third day, the chief officer of the ship said to Mr. Wyville, —

"Captain Draper has the fever."

The doctor, shortly after, came from the captain's room, and reported that Draper had, indeed, been seized, but with symptoms of less virulence than the others.

"Who will attend on Captain Draper?" asked the doctor. "He will be unconscious in another hour, and will need care."

"I will attend him," said Mr. Wyville, after a pause; "write your directions, doctor, and I will stay beside him to-night."

XII.

HUSBAND AND WIFE.

HIDEOUS incidents filled the days and nights as the convict ship sailed southward with her burden of disease and death. The mortality among the convicts was frightful. Weakened and depressed by the long drought, the continuous heat, and the poisonous atmosphere, they succumbed to the fever in its first stages.

The dead were laid in a row on the port side, as they were carried from the hold. Relays of sailors worked at the shrouding and burial. The bodies were wrapped in sail-cloth, with a cannon-ball tied at the feet. As each corpse was hastily shrouded, it was passed forward, and the ghastly roll was committed to the deep.

There was no time for ceremony; but Mr. Haggett, as often as he could be spared from the hold, stood beside the opening in the rail, where the bodies were launched, and followed each dull plunge with a word of prayer.

"Mr. Sheridan," said Mr. Wyville, as he came from Captain Draper's room on the first night of his illness, " will you take command of the ship until the captain's recovery ?"

Sheridan assented; and Mr. Wyville, calling the ship's officers to the poop, instructed them to obey Captain Sheridan as the commander of the vessel.

As soon as Sheridan took command, he spread every inch of canvas the ship could carry, and held her before the wind.

"We shall shake off this fever when we clear the Southern tropics," he said to Mr. Wyville. "The cold wind round the Cape will kill it in an hour."

Captain Draper lay in his stateroom, half comatose, muttering incoherent words in the low delirium of the fever. By his side sat Mr. Wyville, giving him now and again the medicines prescribed.

The sick man's face was a ghastly sight. The offensiveness of the protruding eyes and cracked lips was hideously exaggerated. And as he lay smouldering in the slow fire of the sickness, he muttered things even more repulsive than his physical appearance.

The female hospital of the ship was filled with sufferers — indeed the entire hold of the vessel was at once a hospital and charnel-house. There were no regular attendants among the male convicts; those who had not been attacked waited on those who had, till their own turn came.

In the female compartment, which was separated from the regular hospital, Alice Walmsley had entire charge. Her healthy life enabled her to bear an extraordinary strain; day and night she was ministering to the stricken, and they blessed her with words and looks as she passed from sufferer to sufferer. The door leading thence to the hospital Sister Cecilia kept locked, and she herself carried the key.

Sister Cecilia stood one day within the hospital, at the door of a small room. Kneeling before her, on the floor, with streaming eyes and upraised hands, as if praying for a life, was a woman, in the gray dress of a convict.

" O, for God's sake let me tend them ! O, don't deny me — let me go and wait on the poor sufferers. My heart is breaking when I think that I might be doing some good. Don't refuse — O, don't refuse me. I feel that God would pardon me if I could work out my life caring for others."

It was Harriet Draper who supplicated the nun, and who had besought her for days with the same ceaseless cry. Sister Cecilia would gladly have allowed her to work for the sick, but she feared that Alice would see her. She had been compelled for days to refuse the heartrending petition.

"You shall have your wish," said the nun, this day, with a kind look at Harriet, "but not in the hospital."

"Anywhere, anywhere !" cried Harriet, rising, with a wistful face; "only let me tend some one who is sick. I want to do some good."

"Harriet," said Sister Cecilia, "you have told me your unhappy story, and I am sure you wish to be a good woman — "

"I do — God knows I do !" interrupted the unfortunate one.

"As you hope to be forgiven, you must forgive — you must forgive even your husband."

Poor Harriet covered her face in her hands, and

made no answer, only moved her head from side to side, as if in pain.

"Harriet, if your husband were on board this ship, sick and dying of the fever, would you not tend him and forgive him before he died?"

Wild-eyed, the woman stared at Sister Cecilia, as if she had not understood the question.

"He is on board — he is dying of the fever — will you not take care of him?"

"Oh-oh!" wailed Harriet, in a long cry, sinking on her knees and clasping Sister Cecilia's dress. "He would drive me away — he would not let me stay there — he does not love me!"

"But you love him — you will tend him, and you will forgive him. Will you not?"

"Yes, I will — I will wait on him day and night, and he shall recover with my nursing."

She dried her weeping eyes, to show the Sister her immediate readiness and calmness.

"Take me to him," she said, with only quivering lips; "let me begin now."

"Come, then," said Sister Cecilia; and she led Harriet Draper to the hatch, and aft to the captain's quarters.

Mr. Wyville rose as Sister Cecilia entered, followed by Harriet. As he did so, the sick man moved, and muttered something, with upraised feeble arm.

With a low sob or cry, Harriet darted past Sister Cecilia, and sank beside the bed. She took the upraised arm and drew it to her breast, and covered the feverish hand with tearful kisses. At the touch, the sick man ceased to wander, and turning his head, seemed to fall at once into a peaceful sleep.

Harriet, seeing this, after her first emotion, turned to Mr. Wyville and Sister Cecilia with a smile of joy, and, still holding her husband's arm to her breast, pointed to his restful sleep. They smiled at her in return, though their eyes were brimming with tears.

Sister Cecilia instructed her as to the attendance, and then withdrew, leaving the guilty and unconscious husband in his wife's care. There was joy at least in one heart on board that night. From her low seat beside the bed, Harriet Draper watched his face, murmuring soft and endearing words, and obeying the doctor's instructions to the letter and second.

"He will recover, and he will know me," she whispered to her heart; "I shall win back his love by being faithful and forgiving."

The climax of the fever would not come till the sixth day; and during these days Harriet watched her husband with scarcely an hour's rest. Every hour that passed added to his chance of recovery, as the ship was sailing swiftly toward the cooler latitudes.

One day, while Harriet sat beside the bed, holding the feeble hand, as she loved to do, there came a lucid interval to her husband. She had been murmuring soft words as she kissed his hand, when, looking at his face, she met his eyes fixed upon her. For a moment there came a light of recognition and dismay in his look; but before she could speak his name, or recall his memory, the light faded, and he reverted to a state of sluggish delirium.

For the first time since she came to his side, a chill of fear pierced Harriet's heart. For one instant she knew he had seen her. But there was no love in the look of recognition. What if the same cold stare should return on his recovery, and continue?

"God will not let it be!" whispered her heart "When he recovers, he will surely love me as of old!"

XIII

WOMAN'S LOVE AND HATRED.

On the later days of Captain Draper's illness he moaned and tumbled restlessly. One of the worst symptoms of the fever was its persistent hold on the brain. The sick man raved constantly, carried on excited conversations, gave orders to the sailors, and, in the midst of these wanderings, again and again reverted to one dark subject that seemed to haunt his inflamed mind.

He lived over and over again, day after day, terrible scenes, that had surely been rehearsed in his mind before the sickness. In his fantasy he was standing by the rail of the ship, while a boat was slowly lowered, in which sat Sheridan. As the boat swung over the raging sea, suspended by a rope at bow and stern, the bow rope parted, the boat fell perpendicularly, and Sheridan was flung into the ocean, and drowned.

During this series of mental pictures, the action of the raving man plainly showed that his hand had cut the rope; and his exultation at the completion of the murder was horrible to see. He would turn his face to the partition, away from the light, and chuckle with a vile sound, rubbing his hands in devilish delight.

One day Mr. Wyville sat beside the bed, intending to relieve the tireless Harriet for a few hours. But Harriet still lingered in the room.

Draper had gone once more through the hideous pantomime, accompanying every act with words expressing the baleful intention. Mr. Wyville sat regarding him with compressed lips. When the horrible culmination had come, and the wretch chuckled over his success, Mr. Wyville looked up and met Harriet's fearful gaze.

"Curse him!" whispered Draper, "he was always in my way. I meant it always — but this was the best plan. Ha! ha! better than pistol or poison — accident — ha! ha! drowned by accident!"

"Do you know of whom he speaks?" asked Mr. Wyville of Harriet.

"A man named Sheridan," she answered; "he talks of him a great deal."

"A man named Sheridan!" repeated Mr. Wyville to himself. "She speaks as if she did not know him."

He sat silent for a time, his eyes fixed on the guilty man before him, who was unconsciously laying bare the foul secrets of his heart. At last he turned to Harriet and said, —

"Do you not know this man named Sheridan?"

"No."

The answer surprised him, and he became silent again. Presently he sent Harriet to her rest.

"I do not see the end," he wearily murmured, when he was alone with the sick man; "but I forebode darkly. Providence has kept this miscreant from a deeper crime than he has yet committed. Heaven grant that he has also been preserved for repentance and atonement!"

Mr. Wyville had resolved to be at Draper's side when the hour of sanity returned, and to keep his unfortunate wife out of sight until he had prepared him for her presence.

It was midnight when that moment arrived. Draper had slept soundly for several hours. Mr. Wyville first knew that he had returned to consciousness by the movement of his hands. Presently he spoke, in a feeble voice.

"I have been sick, haven't I? How many days?"

"Six days."

"Are we still becalmed?"

"No; we are in the Southern trades."

Draper said no more. He moved his head from side to side, trying to look around the room. Mr. Wyville remained still and silent.

"Have you been here with me?" he asked at length. "You couldn't have been here all the time."

"Not all the time."

"I suppose I spoke aloud, and — and — raved about people?"

Mr. Wyville looked suddenly at him, and caught the reptilian eye that watched the effect of the question. He was impelled to speak sooner than he had intended, by the cunning of the fellow.

"Yes," he said, keeping his powerful look on Draper's face, as if he addressed his inner soul as well as outward sense; "you have told the whole villanous purpose of your heart. If you recover, you may thank God for striking you with sickness to keep you from murder and the murderer's doom. Had you carried out your design, nothing could have saved you; for there are others here who knew your history and your motive."

Draper did not answer, but lay like a scotched snake, perfectly still, hardly breathing, but watching Mr. Wyville with a cold eye.

"Do you know who has nursed you through your sickness?"

Draper moved his head negatively.

"Would you like to know?"

He only looked more keenly at Mr. Wyville, but there was a light of alarm in the look.

"You have been cared for by one whom you have blighted — who owed you nothing but curses. Day and night she has been with you — and she has saved your life."

Still Draper did not move or speak, but only looked.

16

"You know of whom I speak," said Mr. Wyville "are you ready now to meet your unhappy wife, and to ask her forgiveness ?"

He had risen as he spoke — Draper's eyes followed his face. The strength of manhood, even of facial deceit, having been drained by the fever, there was nothing left of Draper's real self but his wily nature.

As Mr. Wyville rose, the door opened slowly, and Harriet entered, advanced a few steps, and stood still in fear. She looked at her husband's face; for one instant his cold eye glanced from Mr. Wyville and took her in, then returned to its former direction.

Harriet's heart seemed to stop beating. A cold and despairing numbness began to creep over her. She foresaw the nature of the meeting — she knew now what would be her reception. Her limbs slowly failed her, and she sank on the floor, not heavily, but hopelessly and dumb. Mr. Wyville, hearing the slight sound, turned, and read the story of despair like an open page. With a rush of indignation in his blood, almost amounting to wrath, he regarded Draper.

"Remember," he said sternly, "your guilt is known. You still have one chance to escape the punishment you deserve. It lies in her hands."

He turned from the bed, and left the room. Draper lay motionless for several minutes, knowing that his victim and wife was grovelling in the room, waiting for his word.

"Come here," he said at length, in a voice all the colder for its weakness.

Harriet crept to the bed, and laid her head near his hand. But he did not touch her.

"I want to see you," he said.

The poor woman raised her miserable face until their eyes met. Hers were streaming with bitter tears. His were as cold and dry as a snake's. She would have cried out his name ; but the freezing glitter of his eyes

shivered her impulse, and fixed her in terrified fasci-
nation.

" You and he !" he said slowly, as if thinking aloud.
" And after all, you would have been left. And so,
I'm in your power at last ? "

It was appalling to see the lips and wasted lower
face of the man twist into a smile, while the serpent
glance above was intensified.

Poor Harriet sank down slowly, the slow shudder
creeping over her once more. Her blood had ceased
to course in her veins at the cruel reception. She had
no thoughts : she only felt there was no hope for
her.

The first love of some women is mysteriously tena-
cious. It ceases to be a passion, and becomes a principle of life. It is never destroyed until life ceases.
It may change into a torture — it may become excited
like white-hot iron, burning the heart it binds ; or it
may take on a lesser fire, and change into red hatred ;
but it never grows cold — it never loses its power to
command at a thrill the deepest motives of her
nature.

Through all phases but one had passed the love of
Harriet Draper. She knew that her husband was a
villain ; that her hideous degradation had come from
his hand ; that he hated her now and would be rid of
her ; and the knowledge had only changed her love to
a torture, without killing it.

But the change from white heat to fierce red is not
infinite. It is a transition rapidly made. At the
white heat, the woman's love burns herself; at the red,
it burns the man she loves. A woman's hatred is only
her love on fire.

" I didn't think it was you," said Draper, making no
pretence to deceive her; "I thought *you* were dead
years ago."

Something stirred in Harriet's heart. at the emphasis — something like a grain of resentment. She had forgotten self; she now thought of herself, and of what she had gone through for this man's sake.

"How did you come here?" he asked. "Did — *he* bring you here? O, curse you, you 've got me in the trap. Well! we 'll see."

"I have made no trap," said Harriet; "no one brought me here but myself and — you. I am a prisoner."

Draper was evidently surprised at this news; but it only momentarily checked his rancor.

"I suppose you robbed some one, or mur — ?" As he spoke, Harriet struggled to her knees with a pitiful gulping sound, and clutched at the bedclothes, trying to gain her feet. Draper looked at her a moment and then continued slowly, —

"I suppose you robbed some one, or *murdered* —"

With a spring like a tiger, and a terrible low cry, Harriet was on her feet, the coverlet in her clenched hands, her flaming eyes on her husband's face.

"Dare!" she hissed, "and I will tear the tongue from your cruel mouth!"

For half a minute the two regarded each other. In that half minute, the white heat of Harriet's love became red. Hitherto, she had hated the one for whom Draper had deserted her, and had hated herself. Now, for the first time, she hated him.

"Villain! monster!" she cried, throwing the coverlet from her with fierce revulsion; "you speak of murder to the murderess you made! O, God, God! is there no lightning to strike this man dead! Murder I have done in madness" — She paused, with upraised hands, as if she saw a vision — "O, merciful God! that innocent one!"

Harriet staggered across the room at the first dreadful thought of the bitter suffering endured by another for her crime. She had partially repented, it is true; but, secretly, she knew that she had never pitied her rival. Now, she could have suddenly died with grief for her wrong.

Harriet did not know that a strong hand upheld her as she fell, and supported her from the room. She recovered in the open air, and looked about her as if awakening from a terrible dream. Sister Cecilia came and led her back to her old solitary quarters in the hospital.

Mr. Wyville and the doctor stood beside Draper's bed. He had swooned.

" Is he dead ? "

" No," said the doctor; " he has come out of the fever quite strong. He will recover, unless something unforeseen interfere. He is out of danger."

XIV.

THE DARKNESS OF DESOLATION.

THE recovery of Captain Draper was regarded as a good omen by the sailors and convicts; and with a return of confidence to them the fever daily declined.

The average of recoveries grew larger, and there were few new seizures.

From the day of his interview with Harriet, Draper saw her no more. Neither did he see Mr. Wyville. The steward alone attended him. He was forced to ponder on the future, and every new possibility was harder to accept than the last. During those days of convalescence, his coward soul preyed upon by his villanous imagination, Draper suffered almost the torments of the damned.

When the heartbroken Harriet recovered from the excitement of the dreadful interview, her soul had only one feeling — remorse. As one dying of thirst might sit down on the burning sand, and commune with the devouring fire in the body, so this unhappy one sat upon her pallet in the hospital room, and communed for hours with the newly-lighted consuming fire in her soul.

At last Mr. Wyville entered the hospital, with the physician. He approached Harriet, and spoke in a low tone, such as he had used when addressing her once before.

" Do you remember me ? "

She looked at him in surprise, at first; but, as she continued to gaze, there rose in her mind a recollection that brought the blood strongly from her heart. She clasped her hands beseechingly.

" I thought I had dreamt it in the cell — I did not know that it was real. O, sir, did you not come to me and speak blessed words of comfort ? Did you not say that he was guilty of part of my crime ? "

" Yes ; it was I who visited you in Walton-le-Dale. I come now to say the same words — to ask you to save the innocent one who has borne your penalty."

" Thank Heaven, it is not too late ! This moment let me do what is to be done. O, sir, I know now the whole of my crime — I never saw it till this day. I never pitied her nor thought of her ; but now, when I could ask for even God's pardon, I dare not ask for hers."

Seeing Harriet in this repentant mind, Mr. Wyville lost no time in having her confession formally taken down and witnessed. This done, he spoke comforting words to Harriet, who, indeed, was relieved by the confession, and felt happier than she had been for years. Assembling the officers of the Convict Service in the cabin, immediately afterward, Mr. Wyville took his first step as Comptroller-General, by announcing that Alice Walmsey was no longer a prisoner, that her innocence had been fully established by the confession or the real criminal, and that henceforth she was to be treated respectfully as a passenger.

When this news was given to Sister Cecilia, she almost lost her placid self-control in an outburst of happiness. But she controlled herself, and only wept for very gladness. Then she started up, and almost ran toward her secluded room, to break the tidings to Alice.

Alice was sewing when Sister Cecilia entered. She had acquired a habit of sewing during her long solitary confinement, and now she was happiest while working at a long seam. She smiled pleasantly as Sister Cecilia entered.

The kind little nun almost regretted that she bore news that would break the calm stream of Alice's life. She was happy as she was: would she be happier under better circumstances? would the awakened memories counterbalance or sink the benefit.

"Good news, Alice!"

Alice looked up from her sewing inquiringly.

"Is the fever over at last?" she asked.

"Better than that, my child," said Sister Cecilia, sitting down beside her, and putting an arm around her with tender affection. "I have special good news, that will gladden every kind heart on the ship. One of our prisoners, who has been in prison a long time, has been proved innocent, and has been made free by order of the Comptroller-General!"

As Sister Cecilia spoke, she still embraced Alice, and looked down at her face. But there was no perceptible change, except a slight contraction of the brow-muscles denoting awakened interest.

"And she, who was a poor prisoner an hour ago, is now a respected passenger on the Queen's ship!" continued Sister Cecilia, lightly; but in truth she was alarmed at Alice's calmness.

"It is a woman, then?" said Alice.

"Yes, dear; a woman who has been nine years in prison, suffering for another's crime. And that other has confessed — Alice! Alice!" cried Sister Cecilia, dismayed at the effect of her words. But Alice did not hear; she had slipped from her seat, pale as marble, fainting: and were it not for the supporting arms of the nun she would have fallen headlong to the floor.

Sister Cecilia did not alarm any one; she was experienced in emotional climaxes. She did the few things proper for the moment, then quietly awaited Alice's recovery.

In a few minutes the pale face was raised, and the mild eyes sought Sister Cecilia as if they asked a heartrending question. The little Sister did not understand the appeal; so she only encouraged Alice by a kind word to regain strength.

"And *she!*" whispered Alice, with quivering lips, now speaking what she had looked; "where is she — the forsaken one?"

"She is on board, my child; she is a prisoner, and a most unhappy one. She has no hope but the peace of atonement. God send her comfort!"

"Amen! Amen!" cried Alice, laying her head on the Sister's arm, and sobbing without restraint.

XV.

THE NEW PENAL LAW.

THERE being no female passengers in the cabin of the *Houguemont*, it was decided that Alice Walmsley should remain in her room with Sister Cecilia till the end of the voyage. The only change made was in her dress, and this, by some strange foresight on the part

of the little Sister, as it seemed, was quite extensively
and fittingly provided for.

Alice selected the quietest possible dress, and when
she stood arrayed in it, after so many weary years in
prison gray, she could not help glancing at her face in
the glass, and blushing as she looked; and at this very
pretty and womanly moment, Sister Cecilia came upon
her and gave a pleasant little laugh. Upon this, Alice
blushed deeper, and turned her confused face away,
while Sister Cecilia reached after it, and drawing it to
the light kissed her affectionately.

"Why, Alice," she said, with a provoking smile,
"you are quite a beauty."

Unquestionably, even a few days without the burden
of bondage had worked wonders in Alice's life. She
was no longer moody; she instantly and naturally
began to take fresh interest in everything she saw and
heard around her.

The ship cleared the Tropics and raced down towards the Cape in the vigorous Southern trades. The
blustering winds and the rough sea brought refresh-
ment even to the feeble, and to Alice renewed strength.
Her face lost the pallor of confinement, and her step
became elastic. The years of her imprisonment had
kept dormant the energies that waste with exertion.
She began to feel as youthful and as cheerful as when
she was a girl.

One day she was standing beside her open window,
looking out on the sea, when she plainly heard above
her, on the poop deck, a voice that held her rooted to
the spot.

"I cannot foresee the result" — she heard these
words — "but I shall go on to the end. I have loved
her dearly always; and I shall, at least, prove it to
her before the dream is dispelled."

Alice held herself to the window, not meaning to
listen to the words so much as to obey the strong

prompting of her heart to hear the honest ring of the
voice.

It was Will Sheridan who spoke — he stood on the
poop with Mr. Wyville — and Alice knew the voice.
After so many years, it came to her like a message
from her girlhood, and bridged over the chasm in her
life.

No other words reached her; but the conversation
continued for a long time; and still she stood beside
the window, her cheek laid on her hands, while she
allowed the familiar tones to transport her back to
happy scenes.

Sister Cecilia found her so, and playfully coaxed
her to tell her thoughts; but Alice's diffidence was so
evident that the little nun sat down and laughed
heartily.

The voyage round the Cape had no special interest;
and a few weeks later the officers began their preparations for disembarkation. The air grew balmy once
more, and the sky cloudless.

"We are just three hundred miles from the mouth
of the Swan River," said Sheridan one day to Mr. Wyville, when he had taken his observations. "Have
you ever landed at Fremantle?"

"Yes, once — many years ago," said Mr. Wyville,
and he crossed the deck to observe something in the
sea.

Throughout the voyage, neither Sheridan nor Wyville had seen Alice Walmsley. Each in his own mind
deemed it best to leave her undisturbed with Sister
Cecilia. Mr. Wyville was still impressed with the
conviction of Sheridan's unhappy and hopeless affection for Harriet; but he was much perplexed by her
forgetfulness of his name. However, when they reached
Australia, one day ashore would clear up matters without the pain of preliminary explanation.

Day after day, in the mild Southern air, the ship

glided slowly on, and still the watchers on the crowded deck saw no sign of land. From morning light they leant on the rail, looking away over the smooth sea to where the air was yellow with heat above the unseen continent. There was a warmth and pleasure in the promise it gave.

The straining eyes were saved the long pain of watching the indistinct line. The shore of Western Australia is quite low, and the first sign of land are tall mahogany trees in the bush. The ship passed this first sight-line early in the night; and next morning, when the convicts were allowed on deck, they saw, only a few miles distant, the white sand and dark woods of their land of bondage and promise.

The sea was as smooth as a lake, and the light air impelled the ship slowly. At noon they passed within a stone's throw of the island of Rottenest, and every eye witnessed the strange sight of gangs of naked black men working like beavers in the sand, the island being used as a place of punishment for refractory natives.

An hour later, the ship had approached within a mile of the pier at Fremantle. The surrounding sea and land were very strange and beautiful. The green shoal-water, the soft air, with a yellowish warmth, the pure white sand of the beach, and the dark green of the unbroken forest beyond, made a scene almost like fairyland.

But there was a stern reminder of reality in the little town of Fremantle that lay between the forest and the sea. It was built of wooden houses, running down a gentle hill; and in the centre of the houses, spread out like a gigantic star-fish, was a vast stone prison.

There was a moment of bustle and noise on the deck, through which rang the clear commanding voice of Sheridan, and next moment the anchor plunged into the sea and the cable roared through the hawse-hole.

Every soul on board took a long breath of relief at the end of the voyage.

A tug was seen coming from the wharf, the deck of which was crowded. At its mast-head floated the governor's flag. On the deck was the governor of the Colony with his staff, and a host of convict officers from the prison.

The tug steamed alongside, and the governor came on board the convict ship. He wore a blue tunic, with epaulettes like a naval officer, white trousers, and a cocked hat. He greeted Mr. Wyville with official welcome on account of his position, and warmly expressed his admiration of his philanthropy.

"I understand you bring us a new penal system," said the governor. "I hope it is a stronger one than that we have."

"It certainly is stronger," said Mr. Wyville, "for it is milder and juster."

"Well, well," said the governor, who was a testy old general, "I hope you won't spoil them. They need a stiff hand. Now, I suppose you want those warders from the prison to get your crowd into order for landing. Shall I order them on board?"

Mr. Wyville had been looking down on the tug, observing the officers, who were a rough crew, each one carrying a heavy cane or whip, as well as a pistol in the belt, and a sword. He turned with a grave face to the governor.

"Your Excellency, I am sure, will see the wisdom of beginning with our new code at once. We have here the best opportunity to emphasize its first principles. Shall I proceed?"

"By all means, sir; you have absolute control of your department. I shall watch your method with interest."

At his order, the warders boarded the ship, formed in line, and saluted. Mr. Wyville descended from the poop, and carefully inspected them as they stood in rank.

"Go to the steward," he said to the chief warder, as he came to the end of the line, "and get from him a large basket."

The man was astonished, but he promptly obeyed. In a minute he returned with a capacious hamper.

"Begin on the right," said Mr. Wyville, in curt tones, "and place in that hamper your pistols, swords, canes, and whips."

The warders scarcely believed their ears; but they obeyed.

"Now listen!" said Mr. Wyville, and his voice thrilled the warders with its depth and earnestness. "I am going to read for you the new law of this colony, of which you are the officers. Its first word is, that if any of you strike or maltreat a prisoner, you shall be arrested, discharged, and imprisoned."

The warders fairly gasped with astonishment. The old governor, who had listened attentively at first, opened his eyes wide, then nodded his head in decided approval.

Mr. Wyville read the heads of the new law, emphasizing the mild points. As he proceeded, the faces of the warders lost all expression but one of blank amazement. The entire meaning of the law was that convicts were expected to rise from bad to good, rather than descend from bad to worse. In other words, it was a law meant for reformation, not for vengeance.

In passing along the line, Mr. Wyville's eye rested on a silver medal worn by one of the warders. He looked at it keenly.

"What is that medal for?" he asked.

"For the mutiny of two years ago," said the chief warder; "this officer killed three mutineers."

"Take that medal off," said Mr. Wyville to the

warder, "and never put it on again. We are to have
no more mutiny."

The warders were then dismissed from the rank, and
instructed to go below and get the convicts in order
for disembarkation. As they departed, Mr. Wyville
gave them one word more.

"Remember, you are dealing with *men*, not with
brutes — with men who have rights and the protection
of law."

When they had disappeared into the hold, the old
governor shook Mr. Wyville warmly by the hand.

"By the lord Harry, sir, this is excellent," he said,
heartily. "This d—d colony has been a menagerie
long enough. If you succeed with your system, we'll
make it a civilized country at last."

XVI.

A PRISONER AT LARGE.

THE disembarkation of the convicts was a novel
scene to them, and to the officers directing their
movements. The absence of shouting and violence
made it quite unprecedented to the warders. The convicts reached the wharf on barges, and marched in
single file up the little street leading to the great gate
of the prison of Fremantle.

Inside the gate, in the centre of an immense yard or
walled sand-plain, the governor and comptroller-general
stood; and as the long line of convicts filed by, each
saluted in military fashion, and passed on to the
prison.

It was late in the afternoon when the last convict
passed. The governor was about to leave the ground,
when his attention was called to one more stranger

from the ship, who approached. It was Captain Draper. He walked slowly, as if still feeble from his illness; but he was carefully dressed, and was really much more vigorous than he pretended. He raised his hat to the governor as he approached, and received a curt return of the salute, followed by a cold stare. The governor had looked into Captain Draper's case that forenoon.

"Shall I retain the crew, your Excellency?" said Draper, with an obsequious smile; "or is the ship to go out of commission for the present?"

"I don't know, sir," said the stiff old governor, not hiding his dislike and contempt; "and I don't care, sir. The ship belongs to the convict department." He turned on his heel as he spoke.

"Captain Draper," said Mr. Wyville, in an official tone, "you are relieved of your command. The ship goes out of commission."

Draper's face was a study of disappointment at the news.

"The crew will remain — " he began.

"The crew will be taken to Adelaide on my yacht, which will arrive this week."

"Shall I have quarters on board?" asked Draper, with an alarmed look.

"No, sir," said Mr. Wyville shortly. "You must seek some other means of transport."

"But," said Draper, imploringly, "there are no ships in the colony, nor are any expected. I shall have to remain here."

"True," said the governor, who enjoyed the scene. "There will be no visitors here for twelve months to come, nor any means of leaving."

Draper looked from one to the other of the men before him; but he drew no gleam of satisfaction from their faces. He began to feel a sinking of the heart, such as all cowards feel in the presence of danger. He instinctively knew that his cunning had been over-reached, and was useless. He knew not where to look for the hand that had played against him; but through every nerve the knowledge rushed on him that he had been overmastered by a superior intelligence — that he was beaten, discovered, and impotent.

This knowledge came suddenly, but it came overwhelmingly. At one glance he saw that he had been led into a trap, and that the door had just closed. He turned to Mr. Wyville, crestfallen.

"If you refuse to let me go on the steamer, I might as well be a prisoner here."

"Precisely," said Mr. Wyville.

"Except that you will be a prisoner at large," said the governor. "There is a saying in this colony," he added laughingly to Mr. Wyville, "that there are only two classes here — the people who are in prison, and the people who ought to be. Come, now, the horses are waiting; we have a ride of ten miles to Perth before we get dinner."

The governor, Mr. Wyville, and the gentlemen of the staff moved off, leaving Captain Draper alone in the centre of the prison yard. He regarded them with baleful eyes till they went through the gate and disappeared. Then he followed, emerged from the gate, and was directed by one of the prison guard to an inn or public house for ticket-of-leave men, where he took up his residence.

BOOK FIFTH.

THE VALLEY OF THE VASSE.

I.

THE little town of Fremantle, with its imposing centre, the great stone prison, is built on the shore, within the angle formed by the broad Swan River as it flows calmly into the calm sea. At its mouth, the Swan is about two miles wide. The water is shallow, and as clear as crystal, showing, from the high banks, the brown stones and the patches of white sand on the bottom. The only ripple ever seen on its face, except in the rainy season, is the graceful curve that follows the stately motion of the black swans, which have made the beautiful river their home, and have given it its name.

One mile above the mouth of the river, where the gloomy cliff hangs over the stream, are situated the terrible stone-quarries of Fremantle, where the chain-gang works. Many a time, from the edge of the over-hanging cliff, a dark mass had been seen to plunge into the river, which is very deep at this point. After this, there was one link missing in the chains at night, and there was little stir made and few questions asked. Not one swimmer in a thousand could cross a mile of water with fifty pounds of iron chained to his ankles.

For ten miles above Fremantle, the Swan winds in

17

and out among the low hills and the wooded valleys.
Its course is like a dream of peace. There is never a
stone in its bed great enough to break the surface into
a whirl or ripple. Its water turns no busy wheels.
Along its banks are seen no thriving homesteads.
Here and there, in the shallows, a black man, with
upraised spear, stands still as an ebony statue, while
his wives and children sit upon the shaded rocks on
the shore, and silently watch his skilful fishing. Presently, without a quiver of warning, the statue moves
its arm, the long spear is driven under water like a
flash, and is raised to bear ashore its prize of a wide-
backed plaice. Along the wooded banks, the kangaroo
nibbles the fresh grass, and the bright-skinned carpet-
snake dives into the pleasant water, that has become
almost his second home.

On a lovely bend of the river, ten miles from its
mouth, stands the little city of Perth, the capital of
the Penal Colony, and the residence of the governor.
It is a petty town to-day, of four or five thousand
people; it was much smaller at the date of our story.
The main building, as in all West Australian towns, is
the prison; the second is the official residence, a very
spacious and sightly mansion.

Just outside the town, on a slope of exquisite lawn,
running down to the river, stood a long, low building,
within a high enclosure. This was the Convent of the
Sisters of Mercy, where the children of the colony were
educated.

In the porch of the convent one evening, some two
weeks after the arrival of the *Houguemont*, sat Alice
Walmsley, Sister Cecilia, and two growing girls from
the convent school.

" Yes," said Alice, in answer to some remark of the
nun, " this is, indeed, a scene of utter rest. But," she
added, sadly, " it is not so for most of those who see
what we see. There is no rest for — "

"The wicked, Alice," said one of the school-girls, the daughter of a free settler. "Neither should there be. Why do you always pity the convicts so? One would think you ought to hate them."

The other girl stood beside Alice's chair, touching her soft hair with her hand in a caressing manner.

"Alice couldn't hate even the convicts," she said, bending to smile in Alice's face.

It was evident that the loving nature was fully alive, and sending out already its tendrils to draw toward it everything within its reach. Sister Cecilia smiled kindly as she heard the girls, and saw their expressions of love for Alice. She, however, changed the subject.

"Mr. Wyville's yacht, with Mr. Hamerton and Mr. Sheridan, will return from Adelaide next week," she said to Alice. "Here is the report in the *Fremantle Herald.*"

Alice turned her head as if interested in the news. Sister Cecilia continued reading.

"And then they will start for Mr. Wyville's home in the Vasse."

Alice silently sank back in her chair. Her eyes slowly withdrew from the newspaper in her friend's hand, and settled far away on the other side of the Swan, in a waking dream — and a dream that was not content. A few moments later she rose, and said she would walk home early that evening.

"You like your new home and friends?" said Sister Cecilia, not trying to detain her, though the girls did. "I thought it would be pleasanter and more natural to you than our monotonous convent life."

"They are very kind," said Alice; "and I love to work in the dairy and among the children. It reminds me of my own dear old home in England."

She said the words without pain, though her eyes filled with tears.

" My good Alice ! " said Sister Cecilia, taking her
face between her hands in the old way; " I am so
happy to hear you say that.   Come, girls, let us walk
to Mr. Little's farm with Alice."

With characteristic wisdom and kindness, Sister
Cecilia had obtained for Alice, shortly after their arrival, a home in a rich settler's family.   Her mind, so
recently freed from the enforced vacancy, became instantly filled with new interests, and her life at once
took root in the new country.

When she had been settled so for about a fortnight,
and was becoming accustomed to the new routine, she
received a letter from Will Sheridan.   She knew it
was from him ; but she did not open it among the
children.   When her duties for the day were done, she
walked down toward the convent, which was only half
a mile away ; but when she came to the tall rocks beside the river, where she was utterly alone, she opened
and read her letter.

It was a simple and direct note, saying " Good-by
for a time," that he was going to Adelaide to leave the
crew of the convict ship there ; but he should call on
her, " for the old time's sake," when he returned.

Alice read the letter many times, and between each
reading her eyes rested on the placid river.   Once before, she had been haunted with the last words of his
letter, " Yours faithfully ; " and now she repeated and
repeated the one sentence that was not prosaic — " I
will come for the old time's sake."

A few weeks later she received a letter from him,
written in Adelaide, telling her of the voyage, and
stating the time of their probable return to Fremantle.
Alice could not help the recurring thought that he was
thinking of her.

One day, at dinner, Mr. Little spoke to her about the
voyage.

" You brought us back a man we wanted in this

colony, Miss Walmsley," he said; "the man who has
made the country worth living in."

"Mr. Wyville — yes," said Alice confidently; "he
could ill be spared from any country."

"No, I don't mean Wyville; I mean Mr. Sheridan
— Agent Sheridan, we call him."

"Yes, sir," said Alice, her eyes lowered to the table.

"He's the cleverest man that ever came to this
colony," said the well-meaning farmer; "I hope he'll
get married and settle down here for life."

"O, Sam, who could he marry in the West? There
is no one here," said the farmer's wife.

"Nonsense," said Mr. Little; "there's the gov-
ernor's daughter for one, and there are plenty more.
And don't you know, the governor is going to give
Mr. Sheridan a grand dinner, in the name of the
Colony, when he comes back from Adelaide?"

Throughout the dinner Alice was particularly atten-
tive to the children, and did not eat much herself.

"Mr. Wyville is coming here to-morrow," said Mr.
Little, presently. "He wants to buy that meadow below the convent, to put up another school. He's a
good man that, too, Miss Walmsley; but the other
man knows the needs of this colony, and has taught
them to us."

"Mr. Wyville is a man whose whole life seems given
to benefit others," said Alice, quite heartily; and she
joined the conversation in his praise, telling many incidents of his care for the prisoners on the journey.

But, though Farmer Little again and again returned
to the praise of Sheridan, who was his man of men,
Alice sat silent at these times, and earnestly attended
to the wants of the children.

II.

SOONER OR LATER, A MAN MUST FACE HIS SINS.

THE inn where Draper had taken up his residence, known as "The Red Hand," was one of the common taverns of the country, the customers of which were almost entirely of the bond class, ticket-of-leave men, working as teamsters or wood-cutters, with a slight sprinkling of the lowest type of free settler. The main purpose of every man who frequented the place was to drink strong liquor, mostly gin and brandy. The house existed only for this, though its sign ran: "Good Victuals and Drink for Man and Beast." But whatever food was eaten or sleep taken there was simply a means toward longer and deeper drinking.

Champagne, too, was by no means unknown. Indeed, it was known to have been swilled from stable buckets, free to all comers to the house. This was when a crowd of sandalwood-cutters or mahogany sawyers had come in from the bush to draw their money for a year, or perhaps two or three years' work. These rough fellows, released from the loneliness of the forest, their pockets crammed with money, ran riot in their rude but generous prodigality.

There was no other way to have a wild time. In a free country, men who have honest money and want to spend it may do as they please. But, in Western Australia, the free-handed, and, for the time, wealthy ticket-of-leave man, can only drink and treat with drink, taking care that neither he nor his companions are noisy or violent or otherwise ostentatious. The first sign of disturbance is terribly checked by the police.

Draper's introduction to this strange company was most favorable to him. He was known to be the captain of the convict ship; and every frequenter of "The

Red Hand" was ready to treat him with respect. This is one of the unexpected purities of convict life: it never loses its respect for honor and honesty.

But Draper had no power to keep this respect. In the first place, he did not believe in its existence — he was too shallow and mean of nature to think that these rugged fellows were other than vicious rascals all through, who sneered at morality. He felt a sense of relief as soon as he found himself among them, as if he had at last escaped from the necessity of keeping up a pretence of honesty or any other virtue.

Acting under this conviction, Draper let loose his real nature in the convicts' tavern. He did not drink very deeply, because he was not able; but he talked endlessly. He joined group after group of carousing wood-cutters, keeping up a stream of ribaldry and depravity, until, after a few days' experience, the roughest convicts in the place looked at him with disappointment and aversion.

Then a rumor crept to the inn, a story that was left behind by the sailors of the *Houguemont*, of Harriet's confession on board ship, exposing the heartless villany of Draper. When this news became current at the inn, the ticket-of-leave men regarded Draper with stern faces, and no man spoke to him or drank with him.

One evening he approached a group of familiar loungers, making some ingratiatory remark. No one answered, but all conversation ceased, the men sitting in grim silence over their glasses.

"Why, mates, you're Quakers," said Draper, rallying them.

"We're no mates of yours," growled a big fellow with a mahogany face.

"And we don't want to be," said a slighter and younger man, with pronounced emphasis.

"Why, what's the matter?" asked Draper, in a surprised and injured tone. "Have I done anything to offend you fellows?　Have I unconsciously **said** somethingto hurt your feelings by alluding to your——"

"Shut up, you miserable rat," cried one of the convicts, starting to his feet indignantly; "you couldn't hurt our feelings by any of your sneaking allusions. We're not afraid to hear nor say what *we* are; but we have just found out what you are, and we want you never to speak to us again.　Do you understand?　We are men, though we are convicts, and we only want to talk to men; but you are a cowardly hound."

Draper's jaw had fallen as he listened; but he backed from the table, and gained confidence as he remembered that these men were wholly at the mercy of the police, and would not dare go any further.

"You are an insolent jail-bird," he said to the speaker; "I'll see to you within an hour."

At this, one of the men who sat at the end of the table nearest Draper leant toward him, and taking his glass from the table, cast its contents into his face.

"Get out!" he said; and without noticing him further, the ticket-of-leave men resumed their conviviality.

Burning with wrath, Draper left the tavern, and walked rapidly down the street toward the police station.　As he left the inn, a tall man, who had sat at a side table unnoticed, rose and followed him.　Half way down the street he overtook him.

"Hello, Preacher!" said Draper, giving a sideglance of dislike at the man, and increasing his speed to pass him.　But Mr. Haggett, for it was he, easily kept by his shoulder, and evidently meant to stay there.

"Hello, Pilferer!" retorted Haggett, with a movement of the lip that was expressive and astonishing.

Draper slackened his pace at once, but he did not stop.　He glanced furtively at Haggett, wondering

what he meant. Haggett ploughed along, but said no
more.

" What title was that you gave me ? " asked Draper,
plucking up courage as he thought of the friendlessness
of the timid Scripture-reader.

" You addressed me by my past profession," answered
Haggett, looking straight ahead, " and I called you by
your present one."

" What do you mean, you miserable —"

Mr. Haggett's bony hand on Draper's collar closed
the query with a grip of prodigious power and sugges-
tiveness. Haggett then let him go, making no further
reference to the interrupted offence.

" You 're going to report those men at the tavern,
are you ? " asked Haggett.

" I am — the scoundrels. I 'll teach them to respect
a free man."

" Why are they not free men ? "

" Why ? Because they're convicted robbers and
murderers, and —"

" Yes ; because they were found out. Well, I 'll go
with you to the station, and have another thief discovered."

" What do you mean ? " asked Draper, standing on
the road ; " is that a threat ? "

" I mean that those men in the tavern are drinking
wine stolen from the *Houguemont*, and sold to
the inn-keeper by — the person who had charge of
it."

Draper's dry lips came together and opened again,
several times, but he did not speak. He was suffering
agonies in this series of defeats and exposures. He
shuddered again at the terrible thought that some
unseen and powerful hand was playing against him.

" Mr. — Reader," he said at last, holding out his
hand with a sickly smile, " have I offended you or
injured you ? "

Haggett looked at the proffered hand until it fell back to Draper's side.

"Yes," he answered, "a person like you offends and injures all decent people."

Without a pretence of resentment, the crestfallen Draper retraced his steps towards the tavern. Mr. Haggett stood and watched him. On his way, Draper resolved to leave Fremantle that evening, and ride to Perth, where he would live much more quietly than he had done here. He saw the mistake he had made, and he would not repeat it.

He quietly asked the landlord for his bill, and gave directions for his trunks to be forwarded next day. He asked if he could have a horse that night.

"Certainly," said the landlord, an ex-convict himself; "but you must show me your pass."

"What pass? I'm a free man."

"O, I'm not supposed to know what you are," said the landlord; "only I'm not allowed to let horses to strangers without seeing their passes."

"Who grants these passes?"

"The Comptroller-General, and he is at Perth. But he'll be here in a day or two."

Draper cursed between his teeth as he turned away.

A short man, in a blue coat with brass buttons, who had heard this conversation, addressed him as he passed the bar.

"There ain't no fear of your getting lost, Captain Draper. They take better care of a man here than we used to in Walton-le-Dale."

Draper stared at the speaker as if he saw an apparition. There, before him, with a smile that had no kindness for him, was Officer Lodge, who had known him since boyhood. His amazement was complete · he had not seen Ben Lodge on the voyage, the latter having quietly avoided his eye.

"Why, old friend," he said, holding out his hand with a joyful lower-face, "what brings you here?"

Instead of taking his hand, Ben Lodge took his "glass a' hale" from the counter, and looked steadily at Draper.

"That's the foulest hand that ever belonged tc Walton," said the old man.

Draper was about to pass on, with a "pshaw," when Ben Lodge stopped him with a word.

"Maybe you wouldn't want to go to Perth so bad if you knew who was there."

"Who is there?"

"Alice Walmsley — free and happy, thank Heaven; Do you want to see her?"

Draper stepped close to the old man with a deadly scowl.

"Be careful," he hissed, stealing his hand toward Ben's throat, "or ——"

A long black hand seized Draper's fingers as they moved in their stealthy threat, and twisted them almost from the sockets; and, standing at his shoulder, Draper found a naked bushman, holding a spear. It was Ngarra-jil, whom he did not recognize in his native costume, which, by the way, at first, too, had greatly shocked and disappointed Officer Lodge and Mr. Haggett.

"There's some one else from Walton will be in Perth by-and-by," continued Ben Lodge, with a smile at Draper's discomfiture; "and, let me tell you beforehand, Samuel Draper, if *he* lays eyes on you in that 'ere town, you'll be sorry you didn't die of the black womit."

Without a look to either side Draper strode from the tavern, and walked toward a hill within the town, which he climbed. He sat him down on the summit, amid the rough and dry salt-grass. He was shaken to the place where his soul might have been. He felt that he could not move tongue nor hand without discovery. The cunning that had become almost intellectual from long use was worthless as chaff. His life recoiled on him like a hissing snake, and bit him horribly. Before his death, he was being judged and put in hell.

He sat hidden in the salt-grass, among the vermin of the hill, until the night had long fallen. The stars had come out in beautiful clearness; but he did not see them. He only saw the flame of the sins that had found him out, as they burned in their places along his baleful career. When the sea-wind came in, damp and heavy, and made him cough, for his chest was weak, he rose and crept down toward the tavern, to spend the remaining hours of the night on his bed of torture.

III.

WALKING IN THE SHADOW.

THERE was nothing apparent in the possibilities of Alice Walmsley's new life to disturb the calm flow of her returning happiness. Even her wise and watchful friend, Sister Cecilia, smiled hopefully as she ventured to glance into the future.

But when the sky was clearest, the cloud came up on the horizon, though at first it was "no larger than a man's hand."

The visits of Mr. Wyville to Farmer Little's pleasant house were frequent and continuous. Mr. Little's colonial title was Farmer; but he was a gentleman of taste, and had a demesne and residence as extensive as an English duke. He was hospitable, as all rich Australians are; and he was proud to entertain so distinguished a man as Mr. Wyville.

Gravely and quietly, from his first visit, Mr. Wyville

had devoted his attention to Alice Walmsley, and in such a manner that his purpose should not be misunderstood by Mr. Little or his wife. Indeed, it was quite plain to them long before it was dreamt of by Alice herself. From the first, she had been treated as a friend by these estimable people; but after a while she began to observe something in their manner that puzzled her. They were no less kind than formerly|; but they grew a little strange, as if they had not quite understood her position at first.

Alice could discover no reason for any change; so she went on quietly from day to day. Mr. Wyville always drew her into conversation when he came there; and with him she found herself as invariably talking on subjects which no one else touched, and which she understood perfectly. It seemed as if he held a key to her mind, and instinctively knew the lines of reflection she had followed during her years of intense solitude. Alice herself would have forgotten these reflections had they not been brought to her recollection. Now, they recurred to her pleasantly, there are so few persons who have any stock of individual thought to draw upon.

She took a ready and deep interest in every plan of Mr. Wyville for the benefit of the convicts; and he, seeing this, made his purposes, even for many years ahead, known to her, and advised with her often on changes that might here and there be made.

One evening, just at twilight, when the ladies of the family were sitting under the wide verandah, looking down on the darkened river, Mrs. Little pleasantly but slyly said something that made Alice's cheeks flame. Alice raised her face with a pained and reproachful look.

"There now, Alice," said the lady, coming to her with a kind caress; "you mustn't think it strange. We can't help seeing it, you know."

"What do you see?" asked Alice in bewilderment.

"Mr. Wyville's devotion, dear. We are all delighted to think of your marriage with so good and eminent a man."

Alice sank back in her chair, utterly nerveless. It was so dark they did not see her sudden paleness. She held the arms of her chair with each hand, and was silent for so long a time that Mrs. Little feared she had wounded her.

"Forgive me if I have pained you, Alice," she said kindly.

"O, no, no!" said Alice, with quivering lips; "I thank you with all my heart. I did not know — I did not think — "

She did not finish the sentence. Mrs. Little, seeing that her rallying had had quite another effect from that intended, came to Alice's aid by a sudden exclamation about the beauty of the rising moon. This was successful; for ten minutes every eye was turned on the lovely crescent that rose, as bright as burnished silver, above the dark line of forest. In the midst of this admiration, Alice slipped away from the happy group, and spent the evening alone in her own room.

A few days later, she sat in the arbor of the convent garden, while Sister Cecilia watered her flower-beds. Sitting so, her mind went reaching back after one memorable incident in her life. And by some chance, the already-vibrating chord was touched at that moment by the little nun.

"Here is my first rose-bud, Alice," she said, coming into the arbor; "see how pretty those two young leaves are."

Alice's eyes were suffused with tears as she bent her head over the lovely bud. It appealed to her now, in the midst of her happiness, with unspeakable tenderness of recollection. She held it to her lips, almost prayerful, so moved that she could not speak

"Only think," continued Sister Cecilia, "for nine months to come we shall never want for roses and buds. Ah me! I think we value them less for their plenty. It's a good thing to visit the prison now and again, isn't it, Alice? We love rose-buds all the better for remembering the weeds."

Alice raised her head, and looked her eloquent assent at Sister Cecilia.

"I love all the world better for the sweet rose-bud you gave me in prison," she said.

Sister Cecilia seemed puzzled for a moment, and then she smiled as if she recalled something.

"It was not I who gave you that rose-bud, Alice."

Alice's face became blank with disappointment: her hands sank on her knees.

"O, do not say that it was left there by accident or by careless hands. I cannot think of that. I have drawn so much comfort from the belief that your kind heart had read my unhappiness, and had discovered such a sweet means of sending comfort. Do not break down my fancies now. If you did not give it me, you prompted the act? You knew of it, Sister, surely you did?"

"No. I did not know of it until it was done. I should never have thought of it. It was thought of by one whose whole life seems devoted to others and to the Divine Master. Do not fear that careless hands put the flower in your cell, Alice. It was placed there by Mr. Wyville."

"By Mr. Wyville!"

"Yes, dear; it was Mr. Wyville's own plan to win you back to the beautiful world. I thought you knew it all the time."

"It was nearly five years ago; how could Mr. Wyville have known?" There was a new earnestness in Alice's face as she spoke.

"He had learned your history in Millbank from the

governor and the books; and he became deeply interested. It was he who first said you were innocent, long before he proved it; and it was he who first asked me to visit you in your cell."

Alice did not speak; but she listened with a look almost of sadness, yet with close interest.

" He was your friend, Alice, when you had no other friend in the world," continued Sister Cecilia, not looking at Alice's face, or she would have hesitated; " for four years he watched your case, until at last he found her whose punishment you had borne so long."

" Where did he find her ?" Alice asked, after a pause.

" He found her in the jail of your native village, Walton-le-Dale."

" Walton-le-Dale !" repeated Alice in surprise; " he took much trouble, then, to prove that I was innocent."

" Yes; and he did it all alone."

" Mr. Sheridan, perhaps, could have assisted him. He was born in Walton," said Alice, in a very low voice.

" Yes, Mr. Sheridan told me so when he gave me the package for you at Portland; but he was here in Australia all the years Mr. Wyville was searching for poor wretched Harriet. But come now, Alice, we will leave that gloomy old time behind us in England. Let us always keep it there, as our Australian day looks backward and sees the English night."

Soon after, Alice started to return to her home. She lingered a long time by the placid river, the particulars she had heard recurring to her and much disturbing her peace. In the midst of her reflections she heard her name called, and looking toward the road, saw Mr. Wyville. She did not move, and he approached.

" I have come to seek you," he said, "and to prepare you to meet an old friend."

She looked at him in surprise, without speaking.

"Mr. Sheridan has just returned from Adelaide," he said; "and you were the first person he asked for. I was not aware that you knew him."

There was no tone in his voice that betrayed disquiet or anxiety. He was even more cheerful than usual.

"I am glad you know Mr. Sheridan," he continued; "he is a fine fellow; and I fear he has been very unhappy."

"He has been very busy," she said, looking down at the river; "men have a great deal to distract them from unhappiness."

"See that jagged rock beneath the water," he said, pointing to a stone, the raised point of which broke the calm surface of the river. "Some poet likens a man's sorrow to such a stone. When the flood comes, the sweeping rush of enterprise or duty, it is buried; but in the calm season, it will rise again to cut the surface, like an ancient pain."

Alice followed the simile with eye and mind.

"I did not think you read poetry," she said with a smile, as she rose from her seat on the rocks.

"I have not read much," he said — and his face was flushed in the setting sun — "until very recently."

As they walked together toward the house, Alice returned to the subject first in her mind. With a gravely quiet voice she said, —

"Mr. Sheridan's unhappiness is old, then?"

"Yes; it began years ago, when he was little more than a boy."

Alice was silent. She walked slowly beside Mr. Wyville for a dozen steps. Then she stopped as if unable to proceed, and laying her hand on a low branch beside the path, turned to him.

"Mr. Wyville," she said, "has Mr. Sheridan told you the cause of his unhappiness?"

"He has," he replied, astonished at the abrupt ques-

18

tion; "it is most unfortunate, and utterly hopeless. Time alone can heal the deep wound. He has told me that you knew him years ago: you probably know the sad story."

"I do not know it," she said, supporting herself by the branch.

"He loved a woman with a man's love while yet a boy," he said; "and he saw her lured from him by a villain, who blighted her life into hopeless ruin."

"Does he love her still?" asked Alice, her face turned to the darkened bush.

"He pities her; for she is wretched and — guilty."

At the word, Alice let go the branch and stood straight in the road.

"Guilty!" she said in a strange voice.

"Miss Walmsley, I am deeply grieved at having introduced this subject. But I thought you knew — Mr. Sheridan, I thought, intimated as much. The woman he loved is the unhappy one for whom you suffered. Her husband is still alive, and in this country. I brought him here, to give him, when she is released, a chance of atonement."

A light burst on Alice's mind as Mr. Wyville spoke, and she with difficulty kept from sinking. She reached for the low branch again; but she did not find it in the dark. To preserve her control, she walked on toward the house, though her steps were hurried and irregular.

Mr. Wyville, thinking that her emotion was caused by painful recollections, accompanied her without a word. He was profoundly sorry that he had given her pain. Alice knew, as well as if he had spoken his thought, what was passing in his mind.

As one travelling in the dark will see a whole valley in one flash of lightning, Alice had seen the error under which Mr. Wyville labored, and all its causes, in that one moment of illumination. Then, too, she read his heart, filled with deep feeling, and unconscious of the gulf before it; and the knowledge flooded her with sorrow.

At the door of the house, Mrs. Little met them with an air of bustle.

" Why, Alice ! " she exclaimed, " two gentlemen coming to dinner, and one of them an old friend, and you loitering by the river like a school-girl. Mr. Wyville, I believe you kept Alice till she has barely time to put a ribbon in her hair."

Mr. Wyville, with some easy turn of the subject, covered Alice's disquiet, and then took his leave, going to Perth, to return later with Sheridan and Hamerton.

" Dear Mrs. Little," said Alice, when his horse's hoofs sounded on the road, " you must not ask me to dine with you to-night. Let me go to the children."

There was something in her voice and face that touched the kind matron, and she at once assented, only saying she was sorry for Alice's sake.

" But you will see Mr. Sheridan ? " she said. " Mr. Little says he was very particular in asking for you."

" I will see him to-morrow," said Alice; " indeed, I am not able to see any one to-night."

An hour later, when the guests arrived, Alice sat in her unlighted room, and heard their voices ; and one voice, that she remembered as from ·yesterday, mentioned her name, and then remained silent.

IV.

THE MEETING.

WITH the first warm flush of morning, Alice was away on her favorite lonely walk by the river. The

day opened, like almost all days in Western Australia,
with a glorious richness of light, color, and life. The
grand shadowy stretches in the bush were neither
silent nor humid, as in tropical countries. Every inch
of ground sent up its jet of color, exquisite though
scentless; and all the earth hummed with insect life,
while the trees flashed with the splendid colors of
countless bright-necked birds.

Alice breathed in the wondrous beauty of her surroundings. Her heart, so long unresponsive, had burst
into full harmony with the generous nature of the
Australian bush.

Down by the river, where the spreading mahogany
trees reached far over the water, she loved to walk in
the early morning and at the close of the day. Thither
she went this morning; and an hour later some one
followed her steps, directed where to find her by Mrs.
Little.

That morning, as she left the house, Mrs. Little had
told her that Mr. Sheridan was to call early, and had
asked to see her.

" I shall be home very soon," Alice said, as she went
out.

But she did not return soon; and when Mr. Sheridan called, much earlier than he was expected, Mrs.
Little told him where Miss Walmsley usually spent her
mornings, and he, leaving his horse in the stable,
walked down through the bush toward the river.

The shadows and the flowers and the bright-winged
birds were as beautiful as an hour before, but Will
Sheridan, though he loved nature, saw none of them.
He walked rapidly at first, then he slackened his pace,
and broke off a branch here and there as he passed,
and threw it away again. When he came to the river,
and stood and looked this way and that for Alice, all
the determination with which he had set out had
disappeared.

But Alice was not in sight. He walked along by the river bank, and in a few minutes he saw her coming toward him beneath the trees.

He stood still, and waited for her. She walked rapidly. When within ten yards of where he stood, she turned from the river, to cross the bush toward the house. She had not seen him, and in a minute she would be out of sight. Sheridan took a few paces toward her and stopped.

"Alice," he said aloud.

She turned and saw him standing, with an eager face, his hands reached out toward her. Every premeditated word was forgotten. She gave one look at the face, so little changed, — she felt the deep emotion in voice and act and feature, and her heart responded impulsively and imperatively. She only spoke one word.

"Will!"

He came forward, his eyes on hers, and the eyes of both were brimming. Without a word they met. Alice put out both her hands, and he took them, and held them, and after a while he raised them one after the other to his lips, and kissed them. Then they turned toward the house and walked on together in silence. Their hearts were too full for words. They understood without speech. Their sympathy was so deep and unutterable that it verged on to the bounds of pain.

On the verandah, Alice turned to him with the same full look she had given him at first, only it was clear as a morning sky, and with it she gave him her hand. Sheridan looked into the cloudless depths of her eyes, as if searching for the word that only reached his senses through the warm pressure of her hand.

It was a silent meeting and parting, but it was completely eloquent and decisive. They had said all that each longed for, in the exquisite language of the soul. As Sheridan was departing, he turned once more to Alice.

"I shall come here this evening."

She only smiled, and he went away with a satisfied heart.

On that morning, Mr. Wyville had started early for Fremantle, his mind revolving two important steps which he meant to take that day. Since the arrival of the ship he had been disquieted by the presence of Draper in the colony. He questioned his own wisdom in bringing him there, or in keeping him there when he might have let him go.

But, in his wide experience of men, and of criminals, Mr. Wyville had never met one who was wholly bad ; he had discovered, under the most unsightly and inharmonious natures, some secret chord that, when once struck, brought the heart up to the full tone of human kindness. This chord he had sought for in Draper. He had hoped that in the day of humiliation his heart would return to her he had so cruelly wronged.

There was only one step more to be taken — to release Harriet, and, if she would, let her seek her husband and appeal once more to his humanity.

On this day, Mr. Wyville intended to issue a pardon to Harriet Draper. The Government had awarded to Alice Walmsley, as some form of recompense for her unjust suffering, a considerable sum of money ; and this money Mr. Wyville held, at Alice's request, for the benefit of Harriet.

Arrived at Fremantle, he proceeded to the prison, and signed the official papers necessary for the release. The money was made payable to Harriet at the Bank of Fremantle. He did not see her himself, but he took means of letting her know the residence of her husband ; and he also provided that Draper should be informed of her release.

He watched her from his office window as she was led to the prison gate. And as she took the pardon in her hand, and turned toward the outer world in a bewildered way, the utter misery and loneliness of the woman smote Mr. Wyville's heart.

"God help her!" he murmured; "she has no place to go but to him."

This done, Mr. Wyville set his mind toward Perth, where, on his return that day, he was to enter on another act of even deeper personal importance. Somehow, his heart was heavy as he walked from the prison, thinking of the next few hours. He had been more deeply impressed than he thought, perhaps, by the wretched fate of the poor woman he had just released.

At the stable where his horses were put up, he found Officer Lodge, who, with Ngarra-jil, he sent on to Perth in a light carriage before him. He followed on horseback. As he rode through the town, he passed the bank. In the portico sat a woman on a bench, with her head bent low on her hands. He was startled by the attitude; it recalled to his mind the figure of the unhappy Harriet, as he had seen her in the lock-up of Walton-le-Dale.

Something induced him to look at the woman a second time. As he did so, she raised her face, and smiled at a man who came quickly out of the Bank, pressing something like a heavy pocket-book into his breast. The woman was Harriet; and the man was Draper, who had just drawn her money from the Bank.

Mr. Wyville was in no mood to ride swiftly, so he let his horse choose its own pace. When about half way to Perth, however, he broke into a canter, and arrived shortly after the trap containing Ben Lodge and his native servant.

Mr. Wyville had not occupied the official residence of the Comptroller-General; but had kept his quarters at the hotel, a very comfortable establishment. As he dismounted in the yard, Ben Lodge held his horse, and seemed in garrulous humor.

"Mr. Sheridan were here, sir," said Ben. "and he

asked after you. He said he were going to Mr. Little's
to-night, and he hoped to see you there."

Mr. Wyville nodded to Ben, and was going toward
the house; but Officer Lodge looked at him with a
knowing look in his simple face, as if enjoying some
secret pleasure.

"He's found her at last, sir," he said.

Mr. Wyville could only smile at the remark, which
he did not at all comprehend.

"He were always fond of her. I've known him
since he were a boy."

Still Mr. Wyville did not speak; but he seemed interested, and he ceased to smile. Old Ben saw that he
might continue.

"I thought at one time that they'd be married. It's
years ago; but I see them as plain as if it were yesterday. He were a handsome fellow when he came
home from sea — just like his father, old Captain
Sheridan — I knew him well, too, — and just to
think!"

Here old Ben stopped, and led the horse toward the
stable, satisfied with his own eloquence. Mr. Wyville
stood just where he had dismounted. He looked after
Ben Lodge, then walked toward the hotel; but he
changed his mind, and returned, and entered the stable,
where Ben was unsaddling the horse.

"Was Mr. Sheridan alone when he started for Mr.
Little's?" he asked.

"Yessir, he were alone." Then Ben added with a
repetition of the knowing look: "Happen, he don't
want no company, sir; he never did when he were a
boy, when *she* was 'round."

Mr. Wyville looked at Ben Lodge in such a way
that the old man would have been frightened had he
raised his head. There was a sternness of brow rarely
seen on the calm, strong face; and there was a light
almost of terror in the eye.

"He were very fond of Alice, sure-ly," said the old fellow, as he went on with his work; "and I do believe he's just as fond of her to-day."

"Do you tell me," said Mr. Wyville, slowly, "that Mr. Sheridan knew Miss Walmsley, very intimately, in Walton-le-Dale, years ago?"

"O, yessir; they was very hintimate, no doubt; and they were going to be married, folk said, when that precious rascal Draper hinterfered. They say in Walton to this day that he turned her head by lies against the man she loved."

Ben Lodge carried the saddle to another part of the yard. Had he looked round he would have seen Mr. Wyville leaning against the stall, his face changed by mental suffering almost past recognition. In a minute, when the old man returned, Mr. Wyville passed him in silence, and entered the hotel.

The door of his room was locked for hours that day, and he sat beside his desk, sometimes with his head erect, and a blank suffering look in his eyes, and sometimes with his face buried in his hands. The agony through which his soul was passing was almost mortal. The powerful nature was ploughed to its depths. He saw the truth before him, as hard and palpable as a granite rock. He saw his own blind error. His heart, breaking from his will, tried to travel again the paths of sweet delusion which had brought so great and new a joy to his soul. But the strong will resisted, wrestled, refused to listen to the heart's cry of pain — and, in the end, conquered.

But the man had suffered wofully in the struggle. The lines on his bronzed face were manifestly deeper, and the lips were firmer set, as, toward evening, he rose from his seat and looked outward and upward at the beautiful deep sky. His lips moved as he looked repeating the bitter words that were becoming sweet to his heart—"Thy will be done!"

Two hours later, when the glory of the sunset had departed, and the white moon was reflected in the mirror-like Swan, Will Sheridan and Alice stood beside the river. With one hand he held one of hers, and the other arm was around her. He was looking down into her eyes, that were as deep and calm as the river.

"It has been so always, dear," he said tenderly. "I have never lost my love for one day."

She only pressed closer to him, still looking up, but the tears filled her eyes.

"My sorrow, then, was not equal to yours," she said.

"Darling, speak no more of sorrow," he answered: "it shall be the background of our happiness, making every line the clearer. I only wish to know that you love me as I love you."

Their lips met in a kiss of inexpressible sweetness and unity — in a joy so perfect that the past trembled out of sight and disappeared for ever.

While yet they stood beside the river, they heard a footstep near them. Alice started with alarm, and drew closer to her protector. Next moment, Mr. Wyville stood beside them, his face strangely lighted up by the moonlight. He was silent a moment. Then Sheridan, in his happiness, stretched out his hand as to a close friend, and the other took it. A moment after, he took Alice's hand, and stood holding both.

"God send happiness to you!" he said, his voice very low and deeply earnest. "Your past sorrow will bring a golden harvest. Believe me, I am very happy in your happiness."

They did not answer in words ; but the truth of his friendship was clearer to their hearts than the bright moon to their eyes. He joined the hands he held, and without speaking further, left them together by the river.

V.

MR. WYVILLE FACES A STORM.

In the peaceful water of Fremantle harbor, Mr. Wyville's yacht had lain at anchor for several months. On her return from Adelaide with Mr. Sheridan, she had taken on board a cargo, contained in large cases and swathings, which had arrived from Europe some time before. She also took on board many persons of both sexes, mostly mechanics and laborers, with their families ; and among the crowd, but with airs of trust and supervision, as caretakers or stewards, were Mr. Haggett and Officer Lodge. Their friend Ngarra-jil had come on board to bid them good-by, and as he strode about the deck, naked, except his fur boka, hanging from the shoulder, and carrying two long spears in his hand, he seemed a strange acquaintance for two persons so prosaic as Mr. Haggett and Ben Lodge.

This thought, indeed, occurred to both of them with renewed strength that day ; and it was emphasized by the remark of one of the mechanics, —

"That black fellow seems to know you putty well ;" addressed to Ben Lodge.

"Yes," said Ben, with hesitation, and a glance or doubt at Ngarra-jil; "we knew him in England. He were dressed fine there."

"Well," said the good-natured mechanic, "he's the same man still as he war theer. 'Tisn't clothes as we ought to vally in our friends."

This remark brightened Officer Lodge's face, and his hesitating manner toward his wild friend vanished. When the anchor was weighed, and the last visitor had jumped on the barges to go ashore, there were no warmer farewells spoken than those of Mr. Haggett and Ben Lodge to Ngarra-jil.

That evening, at Mr. Little's pleasant dinner-table, Mrs. Little spoke to Mr. Wyville about the destination of the passengers.

"They are going to settle in the Vasse district," he said; "they have purchased homesteads there."

"You have built extensively on your own land there, I believe," said Mr. Little.

A shadow, scarcely perceptible, flitted over Mr. Wyville's face; but his voice had its accustomed tone as he answered.

"Yes; I have worked out an old fancy as to the site and plan of a dwelling-house. But the building was not for myself. Mr. Sheridan has bought the place from me."

"Bless me!" said Mrs. Little, in a disappointed tone; "after sending scores of workmen and gardeners from Europe, and spending four years and heaps of money to make a lovely place, to go and sell it all, just when it was finished! I'm sure Mr. Sheridan might go and make some other place beautiful. It really is too provoking."

"Mrs. Little," said Hamerton, adroitly taking the good lady's attention from a subject which she was in danger of pursuing, "will you not direct me to some rare spot that is capable of beauty and hungry for improvement? I, too, am hunting for a home."

The lure was quite successful. Mrs. Little ran over in her mind all the pretty places she knew in the Colony, and instructed Mr. Hamerton with much particularity and patience.

The further conversation of the evening touched no matter of importance to the persons present.

After some weeks the steamer returned to Fremantle, and lay at anchor for several months, except some pleasure-trips round the adjacent coast, arranged by Mrs. Little, and taking in many of the ladies of the Colony.

Mr. Wyville was engaged every day in directing the operation of the new and humane law he had brought to the Colony. At first, it seemed as if it must end in failure. Its worst enemies were those it proposed to serve. The convicts, as soon as they found the old rigor relaxed, and a word take the place of a blow; when they saw offences that used to earn five years in chains, punished by five minutes of reproach from a superintendent, or at worst, by a red stripe on the sleeve, — when first they saw this, they took advantage of it, and shamefully abused their new privileges.

Among the officials of the convict service were many who watched this result with satisfied eyes, — croakers, who always predict defeat, and a few envious and disappointed ones, who had lost some selfish chance by the change.

At last, it came to such a condition, — the reports from the outlying districts were so alarming, and the croakers and mischief-makers became so bold in their criticism, — that even the warmest friends of the new system held their breath in fear of something disastrous.

But through the gloom, there was one steadfast and reliant heart and hand. He who had planned the system had faith in it. He knew what its foundations were. When even the brave quailed, he still smiled; and though his face grew thin with anxious application, there was never a quiver of weakness or hesitation in it.

His near friends watched him with tender, sometimes with terrified interest. But, as the storm thickened, they spoke to him less and less of the danger, until at last they ceased to speak at all. They only looked on him with respect and love, and did his few behests without a word.

Mr. Wyville knew that he was trying no experiment, though he was doing what had never been done before. It was not experimental, because it was demonstrable. He had not based his system on theory or whim, but on the radical principles of humanity; and he was sure of the result. All he wanted was time, to let the seething settle. Those who doubted, were doubting something as inexorably true as a mathematical axiom. His ship was in the midst of a cyclone; but the hand on the tiller was as true as the very compass itself, for it obeyed as rigidly a natural law.

One flash of passion only did the tempest strike from him. On the great parade-ground of the prison at Fremantle, one day, a thousand convicts stood in line, charged with grossly breaking the new law. On their flank was unlimbered a battery of artillery; and in their rear was a line of soldiers with fixed bayonets and loaded rifles. Scattered in front were the convict officers, and in the centre of the line, within hearing of the convicts, the malcontents had gathered, and were openly denouncing the law as a failure, and declaring that the Colony was in danger. Among them, loud in his dissent, stood an officer with a broad gold band on his cap, — the deputy superintendent of the prison.

Mr. Wyville had ridden hard from Perth, whence he had been summoned by a courier with a highly-colored report. His face was deeply-lined and care-worn, for he had scarcely slept an hour a day for weeks. But he knew that the turning-point had come. Six months of the new system had passed. During that time there had only been a moral restraint on the convicts, — henceforth, there would be a personal and selfish one.

From this day the convicts would begin to receive reward for good conduct, as well as reproach for bad.

A hundred yards behind Mr. Wyville, rode silently the two men who loved him best, — Hamerton and Sheridan. They had seen him start, had questioned the courier, and discovered the cause. Thrusting their revolvers into their holsters, they had followed him in silence.

Mr. Wyville checked his steaming horse as he drew near the prison. He rode up to the gate, and entered the yard calmly, but with such a bearing, even imparted to the horse, as made every man feel that he was full of power.

As he approached, there was deep silence for half a minute. Then, his ear caught the sound of a murmur in the central group of officers. He reined his horse stiffly, and regarded them with flaming eyes.

There was no sound for a moment; then there was a whisper; and then the deputy with the gold band walked to the front, and, without salute or preface, spoke:—

"The warders cannot control the men by your new rules. The Colony is in a state of mutiny."

There ran a sound, like a terrible growl, along the line of a thousand convicts.

Mr. Wyville dismounted. His horse stood unattended. Sheridan and Hamerton closed up, their hands quietly on their holster-pipes.

It was a moment of awful responsibility; the lives of thousands were in the balance. One weak or false step, and the yell of blind revolt would split the air, to be followed by the crash of artillery, and the shrieks of a wild tumult.

Two revolts stood in Mr. Wyville's presence — the warders' and the convicts'. Toward which side lay the dangerous step?

There was no indecision — not a moment of delay in his action. With a few rapid strides he was close to the mutinous deputy, had plucked the conspicuous cap from his head, rent off its broad gold band, flung it on the earth, and put his foot on it. The next instant his hand had torn the insignia of rank from his collar, unbuckled his belt, and thrown his sword on the ground. Then, with a voice that rang like a trumpet through the prison yard, he called to the military officer for a file of men, with irons.

The leader of the warders had never moved — but he had grown pale. He had expected a parley, at least, perhaps, a surrender of the Comptroller's plan. But he was dealing with one who was more than a man, who was at that moment an embodied principle.

In a few moments the degraded and dumfounded deputy was in irons, with a soldier at each shoulder.

"Take him to the cells!" said Mr. Wyville. His stern order reached every ear in the yard. Then he addressed the military commander.

" Limber up those guns, and march your riflemen to their quarters !"

In two minutes there was not a soldier nor a gun in sight.

" The warders will bring their prisoners into square, to listen to the first half-yearly report of the Penal Law."

Rapidly and silently, with faces of uncertainty, the movement was performed, and the thousand convicts stood in solid mass before the austere Comptroller-General, who had mounted his horse, and looked down on them, holding in his hand the report. There was a profound silence.

Mr. Wyville read from the paper, in a rapid but clear voice the names of twelve men, and ordered them to step to the front, if present. Seven men walked from the convict square, and stood before him; the other five were on the road-parties throughout the Colony. Mr. Wyville addressed the seven.

" Men, by your good conduct as recorded under the old law, and your attention to the rules of the present penal code, you have become entitled to a remission of the unexpired term of your sentences. To-day's misconduct shall not stop your reward. You are free. Guard, allow those men to pass through the gate!"

The seven men, wide-eyed, unable to realize the news, almost tottered toward the barrier. The eyes of their fellows in the square followed them in a daze till they disappeared through the outer gate.

There was a sound from the square, like a deep breath, followed by a slight shuffling of feet. Then again there was absolute stillness, every eye intently fixed on the face of the Comptroller-General.

Again he read a list of names, and a number of men came quickly to the front and stood in line. The new law had awarded to these a certain considerable remission, which sounded to their ears like the very promise of freedom.

Still the lists were read, and still the remissions were conferred. When the report was ended, seven men had been released, and sixty-seven out of the thousand present, all of whom had that morning threatened mutiny, had received rewards striking away years of their punishment.

"Men! we have heard the last sound of mutiny in the Colony."

Mr. Wyville's voice thrilled the convicts like deep-sounded music: they looked at him with awe-struck faces. Every heart was filled with the conviction that he was their friend; that it was well to listen to him and obey him.

"From this day, every man is earning his freedom, and an interest in this Colony. Your rights are written down, and you shall know them. You must regard the rights of others as yours shall be regarded. This law trusts to your manhood, and offers you a reward for your labor; let every man be heedful that it is not disgraced nor weakened by unmanly conduct. See to it, each for himself, and each helping his fellow, that

19

you return as speedily as you may to the freedom and independence which this Colony offers you."

Turning to the warders, he gave a brief order to march the men to their work; and, turning his horse, rode slowly from the prison.

From that hour, as sometimes a tempest dies after one tremendous blast, the uproar against the new law was silent. As swiftly as couriers could carry the news, the scene in the prison yard was described to every road-party in the Colony.

Among the warders, opposition disappeared the moment the gold band of the deputy's cap was seen under the Comptroller's foot. Among the convicts, disorder hid its wild head as soon as they realized that the blind system of work without reward had been replaced by one that made every day count for a hope not only of liberty, but independence.

In a word, from that day the Colony ceased to be stagnant, and began to progress.

VI.

THE VALLEY OF THE VASSE.

THERE was a large and pleasant party on the deck of Mr. Wyville's steamer as she slowly swung from her moorings and headed seaward through the islands of Fremantle Harbor. It was evidently more than a coast excursion, for the vessel had been weeks in preparation, and the passengers had made arrangements for a long absence.

Beneath the poop awning, waving their handkerchiefs to friends on shore, stood Mrs. Little and several other ladies. Standing with them, but waving no adieu, was Alice Walmsley; and quietly sitting near her, enjoying the excitement and pleasure of the others, was Sister Cecilia.

There were many gentlemen on board, too, including the stiff old governor of the Colony, and several of his staff. Mr. Wyville stood with the governor, pointing out, as they passed, something of interest on the native prison-isle of Rottenest; Mr. Hamerton lounged on the forecastle, smoking, and with him the artillery officer of Fremantle; while Mr. Sheridan leant over the rail, watching the sea, but often raising his head and looking sternwards, seeking the eyes that invariably turned, as if by instinct, to meet his glance.

It was a party of pleasure and inspection, going to the Vasse, to visit the new settlement purchased from Mr. Wyville by Mr. Sheridan. They proposed to steam slowly along the coast, and reach their destination in two days.

The excursion was a relief to Mr. Wyville, after the severe strain he had borne for months. From the day of the threatened mutiny, which he had quelled by the report, the new law had become an assured success, and the congratulations and thanks of the whole Colony had poured in on the Comptroller-General.

It appeared to those who knew him best, that, during the period of trial, he had withdrawn more and more from social life, and had increased his silence and reserve. This change was ascribed to the anxiety he felt for the reform of the penal law. In his conversation, too, even Hamerton admitted that he had become almost irritable on personal or local topics, and was only willing to converse on abstract or speculative ideas.

"'The individual withers, and the world is more and more,'" quoted Hamerton one day, as the subject of Mr. Wyville's reserve was quietly discussed on the poop. "I don't know what he will do for a cause, now that his penal law has succeeded."

" He will turn his attention to politics, I think," said one of the gentlemen of the staff; " every patriotic man has a field there."

There was a pause, as if all were considering the proposition. At length Hamerton spoke.

" Can you call Mr. Wyville a patriot ?"

" Every Englishman is a patriot," answered the first speaker; " of course he is one."

Again there was a lapse; and again Hamerton was the first to speak.

" I don't like the word — applied to him. I don't think it fits, somehow."

" Surely, it is a noble word, only to be given to a noble character," said one of the ladies.

" Well," drawled Hamerton, assenting, but still dissatisfied.

" Mr. Wyville has the two highest characteristics of an Englishman," said the old governor, sententiously.

" Which are ?" queried Hamerton.

" Patriotism, and love of Law."

There was an expression of approval from almost every one but Hamerton, who still grumbled. The governor was highly pleased with himself for his prompt reply.

" Are these not the noblest principles for an Englishman, or any man ?" he asked exultingly.

" Let us leave it to Mr. Wyville himself," said Hamerton; " here he comes."

" We have been discussing public virtues," said the governor to Mr. Wyville, who now joined the group; " and we appeal to you for a decision. Are not Patriotism and love of Law two great English virtues ?"

" English virtues — yes, I think so;" and Mr. Wyville smiled as he gave the answer.

" But are they virtues in the abstract ?" asked Hamerton.

" No; I think not — I am sure they are not."

There was a movement of surprise in the company. The answer, given in a grave voice, was utterly unexpected. The old governor coughed once or twice, as if preparing to make a reply; but he did not.

"Patriotism not a virtue!" at length exclaimed one of the ladies. "Pray, Mr. Wyville, what is it, then?"

Mr. Wyville paused a moment, then told a story.

"There were ten families living on a beautiful island, and owning the whole of it. They might have lived together in fraternal peace and love; but each family preferred to keep to themselves, neither feeling pride nor pleasure in the good of their neighbors, nor caring about the general welfare of the whole number. They watched their own interest with greedy care; and when they were strong enough they robbed their fellows, and boasted of the deed. Every person of each family was proud of its doings, though many of these were disgraceful. The spirit which filled these people was, I think, patriotism — on a small scale."

"Good!" said Hamerton, looking at the governor; "I thought that word didn't fit, somehow."

"Well, if patriotism is to be condemned, shall we not still reverence Law?" asked some one. "Have you another allegory, Mr. Wyville?"

Again he thought a moment, before his reply came.

"There was a lake, from which two streams flowed to the sea. One river wound itself around the feet of the hills, taking a long course, but watering the fields as it ran, and smiling back at the sun. Its flood was filled with darting fish, and its banks fringed with rich grass and bright flowers. The other stream ran into a great earthen pipe, and rolled along in the dark. It reached the sea first, but it had no fish in its water, except blind ones, and no flowers on its banks. This stream had run so long in the tunnel without its own will that it preferred this way to the winding course of its natural bed; and at last it boasted of its rever-

ence for the earthen pipe that held it together and
guided its blind way."

"The earthen pipe is Law, I suppose," said Mr.
Little, "that men come in time to love."

Mr. Wyville, who had smiled at the ladies all
through his allegory, did not answer.

"But do you apply the allegory to all law?" asked
a gentleman of the staff.

"To all law not founded on God's abstract justice,
which provides for man's right to the planet. Sooner
or later, human laws, from the least act to the greatest,
shall be brought into harmony with this."

"Will you give us substitutes for those poor virtues that you have pushed out? What shall we have
instead?"

"Mankind and Liberty — instead of Patriotism and
Law. Surely, the exchange is generously in our favor."

Then followed a general discussion, in which every-
one had a hasty word. Mr. Wyville said no more; but
drew off the governor and Hamerton to his cabin to
settle some geographical inaccuracy in a chart of the
coast.

So the hours passed on the steamer, as she slowly
rounded headlands and cut across bays. The air was
laden with the breath of the interminable forest. On
shore, when the great fires swept over miles of sandalwood and jamwood bush, the heavy perfume from the
burning timber lingered on the calm air, and extended
far over land and sea.

On the afternoon of the second day, they saw before
them the mountains of the Vasse, running sheer down
to the sea, in two parallel ridges about six miles apart.

The land between these high ridges was cut off, some
four or five miles back, by a line of mountain which
joined the ridges, thus forming the valley which Mr.
Sheridan had bought from Mr. Wyville.

As the steamer drew close to the land, the valley assumed the perfect shape of a horse-shoe. From the sea, at a distance, it seemed a retreat of delicious coolness and verdure. The mountains were wooded high up their sides, and the tops were so steep they seemed to overhang the valley. Two broad and bright shallow streams, which tumbled from the hills at the head of the valley, wound through the rich plain and calmly merged in the ocean.

Exclamations of wonder and delight were on every lip as the surpassing beauties of the scene came one after another into view.

The end of the ridge on the southern side ran far into the sea; and here, under Mr. Wyville's directions years before, a strong mahogany pier had been erected, which made a safe landing-place for even great ships. A railed platform ran round the foot of the hills, and brought the passengers to a road shaded by majestic trees that swept toward the farther end of the valley.

Awaiting their arrival, were easy open carriages, evidently of European build, in which the astonished party seated themselves. The drivers were some black, some white, but they were all at home in their places.

The scene was like a field from fairy-land. No eye accustomed only to Northern vegetation and climate can conceive unaided the glory of a well-watered Australian vale. The carriages rolled under trees of splendid fern from fifteen to twenty feet in height; the earth was variegated with rich color in flower and herbage; spreading palms of every variety filled the eye with beauty of form; the green and crimson and yellow parrots and paroquets rose in flocks as the carriages passed; and high over all the beauteous life of the underwood rose the grand mahogany and tuad and gum trees of the forest.

They passed cottages bowered in flowers, and ringed

by tall hedgerows composed wholly of gorgeous gera-
niums.   The strangers who looked on these changing
revelations of loveliness sat silent, and almost tearful.
Even those long accustomed to Australian scenery were
amazed at the beauty of the valley.

Mr. Wyville and Mr. Sheridan had ridden rapidly
on before the others, and stood uncovered and host-like
on the verandah of the house where the drive ended.

Alice Walmsley sat in the foremost carriage, and
was the first to alight, with Sheridan's hand holding
hers.   Their eyes met as she stepped to his side.   His
lips formed one short word, of which only her eye and
ear were conscious, —

"Home!"

Exclamations of wonder came from all the party at
the peerless beauty of their surroundings.   The house
was wholly built of bright red mahogany beams, perfectly fitted, with rich wood-carving of sandalwood and
jamwood on angle, cornice, and capital.   It was very
low, only one story high for the most part, though
there were a number of sleeping-rooms raised to a
second story.   From the verandah looking seaward,
every part of the wooded valley was visible, and the
winding silver of the rivers glanced deliciously through
the trees.   Beyond, lay the level blue water of the
Indian Ocean, stretching away to the cream-colored
horizon.

The house within doors was a wonder of richness,
taste, and comfort.   Everything was of wood, highly
finished with polish and carving, and the colors were
combined of various woods.   Soft rugs from India and
Persia lay on halls and rooms.   Books, pictures, stat-
uary, rare bric-à-brac, everything that vast wealth and
cultivated taste could command or desire, was to be
found in this splendid residence.

Almost in silence, the strangers passed through the
countless rooms, each differing from the others, and

each complete. Mr. Wyville led the larger party or guests through the place. He had not before seen it himself, but he was wholly familiar with the plans, which, indeed, were largely his own.

"But it will have an owner now," he said, "who will better enjoy its restfulness, and take closer interest in its people."

"But you should rest, too, Mr. Wyville," said Mrs. Little; "the Colony is now settled with your excellent law."

"There is much to be done yet," he said, shaking his head, with the old grave smile. "I have not even time to wait one day."

There was a general look of astonishment.

"Why, Mr. Wyville, surely you will not leave this lovely place — "

"I must leave to-night," he said; "I am very sorry, but it is imperative."

Then, not waiting for further comment, he took them out to the stables and village-like out-houses. There was no regular garden: the valley itself was garden and farm and forest in one.

Alice Walmsley had lingered behind the others, in a quiet and dim little room, looking away out to sea. Contentment filled her soul like low music. She wished to be alone. She had sat only a few minutes when she heard a step beside her. She did not look up; she knew whose hand was round her cheek, and standing over her. They did not say a word; but remained still for a long, long time. Then he bent over her, turning her face to his. She raised her arms, and he took her to his breast and lips in the fulness of happiness and love.

When they left the dim little room, which was ever after to be the dearest to them in their rich home, they saw the sombre robes of Sister Cecilia as she sat alone on the verandah.

"Where shall the school be, Sister?" asked Sheridan; "have you selected your site?"

"She shall build it on the choicest spot that can be found," said Alice, seating herself beside Sister Cecilia.

"Dictation already!" laughed Sheridan, at which Alice blushed, and sent him away.

Toward evening, there stood on the verandah, having quietly withdrawn from the guests, Mr. Wyville, Sheridan, and Hamerton. Mr. Wyville meant quietly to leave, without disturbing the party.

"I am sorry beyond expression," said Sheridan, holding his hand; "your presence was our chief pleasure. Can you not even stay with us to-night?"

"It is impossible!" answered Mr. Wyville, with a look of affectionate response; "the work yet before me will not bear delay. Good-bye. God bless you — and yours!"

He walked rapidly away, his horse having been led by Ben Lodge before him to the entrance.

"Good-bye, Sheridan!" said Hamerton, suddenly seizing his friend's hand, "I'm going, too."

"What? You —"

"Stop! Don't try to prevent me. I can't let him go alone. Go in to your people, and say nothing till to-morrow. Good-bye, my dear fellow!"

That night the steamer returned to Fremantle, having on board Mr. Wyville and Hamerton.

VII.

THE CONVICT'S PASS.

ON Mr. Wyville's return from the Vasse, he set himself with tireless will to the complete organization of the Penal Law. Not content with writing copious rules for the guidance of warders, he proposed to visit all the districts in the Colony, and personally instruct the chief officers of depots, from whom the system would pass directly to their subordinates.

For many days Mr. Hamerton saw little of him, and the time was heavy on his hands. He intended to purchase land in the Colony, and bring some of his old farmers from England to settle on it.

One day, he went to the prison at Fremantle, and waited for Mr. Wyville in his office. As he sat there, by a window that looked over a wide stretch of sandy scrub, he noticed that though the sky was clear and the heat intense, a heavy cloud like dense vapor hung over all the lowland. He remembered that for a few days past he had observed the smoky sultriness of the atmosphere, but had concluded that it was the natural oppression of the season.

"That vapor looks like smoke," he said to the convict clerk in the office ; "what is it ?"

"It is smoke, sir," said the man. "This is the year for the bush-fires."

Just then Mr. Wyville entered, and their meeting was cordial. Mr. Wyville, who looked tired, said he had only an hour's writing to do, after which he would ride to Perth. He asked Hamerton to wait, and handed him some late English papers to pass the time.

Hamerton soon tired of his reading, and having laid aside the paper, his eyes rested on Mr. Wyville, who was intently occupied, bending over his desk. Hamerton almost started with surprise at the change he observed in his appearance — a change that was not easily apparent when the face was animated in conversation. When they sailed from England, Mr. Wyville's hair was as black as a raven ; but now, even across the room, Hamerton could see that it was streaked with white. The features, too, had grown thin, like those of a person who had suffered in sickness.

But, when the hour had passed, and he raised his head and looked smilingly at Hamerton, it was the same striking face, and the same grand presence as of old. Still, Hamerton could not forget the change he had observed.

"Come," he said, unable to conceal an unusual affectionate earnestness, "let us ride to Perth, and rest there — you need rest."

"Why, I never felt better," answered Mr. Wyville, lightly; "and rest is rust to me. I never rest unless I am ill."

"You will soon be ill if this continue."

"Do you think so?" and as he asked the question, Hamerton saw a strange light in his eye.

"Yes, I think you have overtaxed yourself lately. You are in danger of breaking down — so you ought to rest."

Hamerton was puzzled to see him shake his head sadly.

"No, no, I am too strong to break down. Death passes some people, you know; and I am one of the — fortunate."

Hamerton did not like the tone nor the mood. He had never seen him so before. He determined to hurry their departure. He walked out of the office and waited in the prison yard. Mr. Wyville joined him in a few moments.

"I thought this smoke was only a sultry air," Hamerton said; "where does it come from?"

"I think it comes from Bunbury district; a native runner from there says the bush is burning for a hundred miles in that direction."

"Are lives lost in these fires? A hundred miles of flame is hard to picture in the mind."

"Yes, some unlucky travellers and wood-cutters are surrounded at times; and the destruction of lower life, birds, animals, and reptiles, is beyond computation."

"Does not the fire leave a desert behind?"

"For a season only; but it also leaves the earth clear for a new growth. The roots are not destroyed; and when the rain comes they burst forth with increased beauty for the fertilizing passage of the flame."

By this time they were riding slowly toward Perth. The road was shaded with tall mahoganies, and the coolness was refreshing. Hamerton seized the opportunity of bringing up a subject that lay upon his mind.

"You gave me, sir," he said, "some documents in London which you wished me to keep until our arrival here. Shall I not return them to-morrow?"

Mr. Wyville rode on without answering. He had heard; but the question had come unexpectedly. Hamerton remained silent until he spoke.

"Do not return them yet," he said at length; "when we get back from our ride to the Vasse, then give them to me."

"When shall we start?"

"In ten days. By that time my work will be fairly done; and the rest you spoke of may not come amiss."

"Shall we ride to Sheridan's settlement?"

"O no; we go inland, to the head of the mountain range. Those papers, by the way, in case anything should happen to me — the sickness you fear, for instance — belong to one whom we may see before our return. In such a case, on breaking the outer envelope, you would find his name. But I may say now else you might be surprised hereafter, that he is a native bushman."

"A native! Would he understand?"

"Yes; he would understand perfectly. He is my heir — heirs generally understand."

He was smiling as he spoke, evidently enjoying Hamerton's astonishment.

"Seriously, the package you hold contains my will. It is registered in London, and it bequeaths a certain section of land in the Vasse Mountains to the native chief Te-mana-roa, and his heirs for ever, as the lawyers say. We may see the chief on our ride."

"Then why not give him the package?"

"Because he is a bushman, and might be wronged. With two influential persons, like you and Sheridan, to support his title, there would be no question raised. You see I compel you to be my executor."

"Is he not the grandfather of Koro, of whom she often spoke to me."

"Yes," said Mr. Wyville, smiling, "and also of Tepairu. This property will descend to them."

"Are they with the chief now?"

"No; by this time they have reached Mr. Sheridan's happy valley, where it is probable they will remain. You see, it is possible to step from the bush into civilization; but it is not quite so pleasant to step back into the bush — especially for girls. Ngarra-jil, you observed, had no second thought on the subject; he was a spearman again the moment he landed."

The ride to Perth was pleasantly passed in conversation; and, on their arrival, they ordered dinner to be served on the cool verandah.

While waiting there, a rough-looking man approached and touched his hat to Mr. Wyville.

"Be ycu the Comptroller-General?" he asked.

"Yes."

"Well, sir, here, you see my ticket, and here's my full discharge. I want to leave the colony; and I want a pass to King George's Sound, where I can find a ship going to Melbourne."

Mr. Wyville examined the papers; they were all right. The man had a right to the pass. He rose to enter the hotel to write it, holding the documents in his hand.

"You're not going to keep them papers, sir, be you?" asked the man, in evident alarm.

"No," said Mr. Wyville, looking closely at him; "but if I give you a pass you do not need them."

"Well, I'd rather keep them, sir; I'd rather keep them, even if I don't get the pass."

"Well, you shall have them," said Mr. Wyville, rather surprised at the fellow's manner. He entered the hotel and wrote the pass.

But, as the hand wrote, the mind turned over the man's words, dwelling on his last expression, that he would rather have his ticket-of-leave than take a pass from the colony without it; yet, in any other country, it was a proof of shame, not a safeguard. The man did not look stupid, though his words were so. As Mr. Wyville finished writing, he raised his head and saw Ngarra-jil watching him as usual. He raised his finger slightly — Ngarra-jil was beside him.

A few words in the native tongue, spoken in a low tone, sent Ngarra-jil back to his bench, where he sat like an ebony figure till he saw Mr. Wyville return to the verandah. He then rose and went out by another door.

Mr. Wyville called the ex-convict toward him till he stood in the strong lamplight. He spoke a few words to him, and gave him his papers and the pass. The man clumsily thanked him and went off.

"That's an ugly customer," said Hamerton. "I suppose you know it from his papers. He was strangely restless while you were writing his pass."

Mr. Wyville did not answer, but he took hold of Hamerton's arm, and pointed to a corner of the street where at the moment the man was passing under a lamp, walking hurriedly. Following him closely and silently strode a tall native with a spear.

"Ngarra-jil?" said Hamerton.

Mr. Wyville smiled and nodded.

" I thought it just as well to know where the man passed the night," he said.

A few minutes later, Ngarra-jil came to the verandah, and spoke in his own language to Mr. Wyville, who was much disturbed by the message. He wrote a letter, and sent it instantly to the post-office.

" The callous wretch!" he said, unusually moved. He had just learned that the man had gone straight to Draper, by whom he had been hired to get the pass. Draper's purpose was plain. He intended to leave the Colony, and desert again his most unfortunate wife, with whose money he could return comfortably to England.

" What will you do with the miscreant ?" asked Hamerton.

" Nothing, but take the pass from him."

" But he is a free man. Can you interfere with his movements ? "

" No man is allowed to desert his wife, stealing her property. He can have a pass by asking ; but he dare not come here for it. And yet, I fear to keep him; he may do worse yet. If no change for the better appear, I shall hasten his departure, and alone, on our return from the Vasse."

VIII.

THE BUSH-FIRE.

IT was the afternoon of a day of oppressive heat on which Mr. Wyville and Hamerton started from Perth to ride to the mountains of the Vasse. They were lightly equipped, carrying with them the few necessaries for the primitive life of the bush.

For weeks before. the air had been filled with an irritating smoke, that clung to the earth all day, and was blown far inland by the sea-breeze at night.

As the horsemen were leaving Perth, they met a travel-stained police trooper, carrying the mail from the southern districts. He recognized the Comptroller-General, and saluted respectfully as he passed.

"Where is the fire, trooper?" asked Mr. Wyville.

"In the Bunbury district, sir, and moving toward the Vasse Road. It has burnt on the plains inside the sea-hills for three weeks, and in a day or two will reach the heavy bush on the uplands."

They rode at a steady and rapid pace, conversing little, like men bent on a long and tedious journey. The evening closed on them when they were crossing the Darling Range. From the desolate mountain-road, as they descended, they saw the sun standing, large and red, on the horizon. Before them, at the foot of the range, stretched a waste of white sand, far as the eye could reach, over which their road lay.

The setting of the sun on such a scene has an awfulness hard to be described. The whiteness of the sand seems to increase until it becomes ghastly, while every low ridge casts a black shadow. During this time of twilight the sand-plain has a weirdly sombre aspect. When the night comes in its black shroud or silvery moonlight, the supernatural effect is dispelled.

As the travellers rode down toward the plain, impressed by this ghostly hour, Mr. Wyville called Hamerton's attention to two dark objects moving on the sand at a distance.

Hamerton unslung his field-glass, and looked at the objects.

"A man and a woman," he said; "they are going ahead, and the woman carries a load like the natives."

Soon after, the sun went down beyond the desert, and the plain was dark. The horsemen spurred on, oppressed by the level monotony before them. They

20

had forgotten the travellers who were crossing the weary waste on foot.

Suddenly Hamerton's horse swerved, and a voice in the darkness ahead shouted something. It was a command from the man on foot, addressed to the woman, who, in her weariness and with her burden, had not been able to keep pace with him, and had fallen behind.

"Come along, curse you! or I'll be all night on this plain."

The speaker had not seen nor heard the horsemen, whose advance was hidden by the night and the soft sand. They rode close behind the woman, and heard her labored breathing as she increased her speed.

A sense of acute sorrow struck at once the hearts of the riders. They had recognized the voice as that of Draper — they knew that the miserable being who followed him and received his curses was his wife.

They rode silently behind her, and halted noiselessly as she came up with her husband. He growled at her again as she approached.

"I am very tired, Samuel," they heard her say in a low, uncomplaining voice; "and I fear I'm not as strong as I thought I was."

She stood a moment as she spoke, as if relieved by the moment's breathing-space.

"Look here," he said in a hard voice, meant to convey the brutal threat to her soul; "if you can't keep up, you can stay behind. I'll stop no more for you; so you can come or stay. Do you hear?"

"O, Samuel, you wouldn't leave me in this terrible place alone! Have pity on me, and speak kindly to to me, and I will keep up — indeed, I'll not delay you any more to-night."

"Have pity on you!" he hissed between his teeth; "you brought me to this, and I'm to have pity on you!"

He turned and strode on in the dark. She had

heard, but made no reply. She struggled forward, though her steps even now were unsteady.

Mr. Wyville, having first attracted her attention by a slight sound, so that she should not be frightened, rode up to her, and spoke in a low voice.

" I am the Comptroller-General — do not speak. Give me your burden. You will find it when you arrive at the inn at Pinjarra."

She looked up and recognized Mr. Wyville; and without a word she slipped her arms from the straps of the heavy load, and let him lift it from her.

" God bless you, sir ! " she whispered tremulously; " I can walk easily now."

" Here," said Hamerton, handing her his wine-flask, "keep this for yourself, and use it if you feel your strength failing."

" Where is your husband going ? " asked Mr. Wyville.

" He is going to the Vasse, sir. A whale-ship has come in there, and he thinks she will take us off."

They rode on, and soon overtook Draper. Mr. Wyville addressed him in a stern voice.

"If your wife does not reach Pinjarra to-night in safety, I shall hold you accountable. I overheard your late speech to her."

The surprised caitiff made no reply, and the horsemen passed on. They arrived at the little town of Pinjarra two hours later.

Next morning, they found that Draper had arrived. Mr. Wyville arranged with the innkeeper and his wife for Harriet's good treatment, and also that a stockman's team, which was going to Bunbury, should offer to take them so far on their way.

It was a long and fatiguing ride for the horsemen that day, but as the night fell they saw before them, across an arm of the sea, the lights of a town.

" That is Bunbury," said Mr. Wyville, " the scene of our friend Sheridan's sandalwood enterprise."

They stopped in Bunbury two days, Mr. Wyville spending his time in the prison depot, instructing the chief warder in the new system. They found Ngarra-jil there, with fresh horses. He was to ride with them next day towards the Vasse.

As they were leaving the town, on the afternoon of the third day, they met a gang of wood-cutters, carry-ing bundles on their backs, coming in from the bush.

"Are you going to the Vasse?" asked one of the wood-cutters, who was resting by the roadside.

"Yes."

"Well, keep to the eastward of the Koagulup Swamp and the salt marshes. The fire is all along the other side. We've been burnt out up that way."

They thanked him, and rode on. Presently, another man shouted after them.

"There's a man and woman gone on before you, and if they take the road to the right of the swamp, they'll be in danger."

They rode rapidly, striking in on a broad, straight road, which had been cleared by the convicts many years before. Mr. Wyville was silent and preoccupied. Once or twice Hamerton made some passing remark, but he did not hear.

The atmosphere was dense with the low-lying smoke, and the heat was almost intolerable.

A few miles south of Bunbury, the road cut clear across a hill. From the summit, they caught their first sight of the fire. Mr. Wyville reined his horse, and Hamerton and the bushman followed his example.

Before them stretched a vast sea of smoke, level, dense, and grayish-white, unbroken, save here and there by the topmost branches of tall trees, that rose clear above the rolling cloud that covered all below.

"This is Bunbury race-course," said Mr. Wyville; "the light sea-breeze keeps the smoke down, and rolls it away to the eastward. This fire is extensive."

"Where is our road now ? " asked Hamerton.

"Through the smoke ; the fire has not yet reached the plain.   See : it is just seizing the trees yonder as it comes from the valley."

Hamerton looked far to the westward, and saw the sheeted flame, fierce red with ghastly streaks of yellow, hungrily leaping among the trees in waves of terrific length.   For the first time in his life he realized the dreadful power of the element.   It appalled him, as if he were looking on a living and sentient destroyer.

"We must ride swiftly here," said Mr. Wyville, beginning the descent; "but the plain is only three miles wide."

In a minute they had plunged into the murky air, and with heads bent, drove their horses into a hard gallop.   But the animals understood, and needed little pressing.   With ears laid back, as if stricken with terror, they flew, swift-footed.

The air was not so deadly as the first breath suggested.   The dense smoke was thickest overhead ; beneath was a stratum of semi-pure air.   The heat was far more dangerous than the fumes.

At last they reached the rising ground again, and filled their lungs with a sense of profound relief.   The prospect was now changed, and for the better.

The fire in their front appeared only on the right of the road.   It stretched in a straight line as far as they could see, burning the tall forest with a dreadful noise, like the sea on a rocky shore, or like the combined roar of wild beasts.   The wall of flame ran parallel with the road, and about a mile distant.

"It is stopped there by a salt-marsh," said Mr. Wyville ; "but that ends some miles in our front."

"Koagulup there," said Ngarra-jil, meaning that where the marsh ended the great swamp began.   The wood-cutters had warned them to keep to the left of the swamp.

"We must surely overtake those travellers," said Mr. Wyville to Hamerton, "and before they reach the swamp. They might take the road to the right, and be lost."

They galloped forward again, and as they rode, in the falling dusk of night, the fire on the right increased to a glare of terrific intensity. They felt its hot breath on their faces as if it panted a few yards away.

Suddenly, when they had ridden about two miles, Mr. Wyville drew rein, looked fixedly into the bush, and then dismounted. He walked straight to a tall tuad-tree by the roadside, and stooped at its base, as if searching for something.

When he rose and came back, he had in his hand a long rusty chain, with a lock on one end.

"You have keen sight, sir," said Hamerton, astonished.

"I did not see it," he answered quietly; "I knew it was there. I once knew a man to be chained to that tree."

He tied the chain on his horse's neck, and mounted without more words. From that moment he seemed to have only one thought — to overtake and warn those in front.

Half an hour later, they drew rein where the roads divided, one going to the right, the other to the left of the swamp. The travellers were not yet in sight.

"Which road have they taken?" asked Hamerton.

Ngarra-jil had leaped from his horse, and was running along the road to the left. He came back with a disappointed air and struck in on the other road. In half a minute he stopped, and cried out some guttural word.

Mr. Wyville looked at Hamerton, and there were tears in his eyes. He rode to him, and caught him by the arm.

"Take the other road, with Ngarra-jil, and I will

meet you at the farther end of the swamp. It is only
twelve miles, and I know this bush thoroughly."

Hamerton answered only with an indignant glance.

"Do not delay, dear friend," and Wyville's voice was
broken as he spoke ; "for my sake, and for those whose
rights are in your hands, do as I say. Take that road,
and ride on till we meet."

"I shall not do it," said Hamerton, firmly, and striking his horse. "Come on ! if there is danger, I must
face it with you."

His horse flew wildly forward, terrified by the tremendous light of the conflagration. Wyville soon
overtook him, and they rode abreast, the faithful
bushman a horse's length behind.

On their left, a quarter of a mile distant, stretched
the gloomy swamp, at this season a deadly slough of
black mud, with shallow pools of water. On their
right, a mile off, the conflagration leaped and howled
and crashed its falling trees, as if furious at the barrier
of marsh that balked it of its prey. The bush between the swamp and the fire was brighter than day,
and the horsemen drove ahead in the white glare.

They saw the road for miles before them. There
was no one in sight.

Five, seven, nine of the twelve miles of swamp were
passed. Still the road ahead was clear for miles, and
still no travellers.

As they neared the end of the ride, a portentous
change came over the aspect of the fire. Heretofore it
had burned high among the gum-trees, its red tongues
licking the upper air. There was literally a wall of
fire along the farther side of the salt-marsh. Now, the
tree-tops grew dark, while the flame leaped along the
ground, and raced like a wild thing straight toward the
swamp.

"The fire has leaped the marsh !" said Mr. Wyville.

The whole air and earth seemed instantly to swarm

with fear and horror. Flocks of parrots and smaller
birds whirled screaming, striking blindly against the
horsemen as they flew. With thunderous leaps, herds
of kangaroo plunged across the road, and dashed into
the deadly alternative of the swamp. The earth was
alive with insect and reptile life, fleeing instinctively
from the fiery death. Great snakes, with upraised
heads, held their way, hissing in terror, toward the
water, while timid bandicoot and wallaby leaped over
their mortal enemies in the horrid panic.

The horses quivered with terror, and tried to dash
wildly in the direction of the swamp.

"Hold on, for your life!" shouted Wyville to Hamerton. "Do not leave the road."

As they spurred onward, their eyes on the advancing
fire, their hearts stood still one moment at a piercing
sound from their rear. It was a woman's shriek — the
agonized cry reached them above all the horror of the
fire.

Hamerton did not know what to do; but he saw
Mr. Wyville rein up, and he did so also. They looked
back, and a mile behind saw the two unfortunates they
had come to warn. They had strayed from the road,
and the riders had passed them. The fire had now
closed in behind them, and was driving them forward
with appalling fury.

"For God's sake, ride on!" shouted Mr. Wyville to
Hamerton, his voice barely heard in the savage roar
of the conflagration.

"And you?" cried the other with a knitted brow.

"I am going back for these — I *must* go back. God
bless you!"

He struck his spurs into his horse, and the animal
sprang to the front. But next instant he was flung
back on his haunches by Ngarra-jil, dismounted, who
had seized the bridle. The bushman's eyes blazed, and
his face was set in determination.

"No! no!" he cried in his own language; "you shall not! you shall not! It is death, MOONDYNE! It is death!"

Wyville bent forward, broke the man's grasp, speaking rapidly to him. His words moved the faithful heart deeply, and he stood aside, with raised hands of affliction, and let him ride forward.

Hamerton did not follow; but he would not try to escape. He sat in his saddle, with streaming eyes following the splendid heroism of the man he loved dearest of all the world.

It was a ride that could only be faced by audacious bravery. The hot breath of the leaping fire was moving the whole bush through which Wyville rode. The leaves on the trees overhead shrivelled and smoked. The cinders and burning brambles floated and fell on man and horse.

But the rider only saw before him the human beings he meant to save. Nearer and nearer he drew; and he shouted, as best he could, to cheer them; but they did not hear.

He saw with straining eyes the man throw up his hands and sink to the earth; and he saw the woman, faithful to the last, bending over him, holding the wine-flask to his parched lips. He saw her, too, reach out her arms, as if to shield the fallen one from the cruel flame that had seized them. Then she breathed the air of fire, and sank down. Next moment, Wyville leaped from his horse beside them.

It was too late. The woman had fallen in front of the flame, as if to keep it from the face of the man who had deserved so little of her devotion; and still the hand of the faithful dead held to his lips the draught that might have saved her own life.

One moment, with quivering face, the strong man bent above her, while his lips moved. Then he raised his head, and faced his own danger.

Already the fire had cut him off; but it was only the advanced line of the conflagration that had reached the water. It was possible to dash back, by the edge of the swamp.

The awful peril of the moment flashed on him as he rode. The horse bounded wildly ahead; and the skilled hand guided him for the best. But, as he flew, other scenes rose before the rider even brighter than that before him. The present was filled with horror; but the past overtook him and swept over his heart like a great wave of peace.

A tree crashed to the earth across his path. He was forced to drive his horse into the fire to get round the obstacle. The poor animal reared and screamed, but dashed through the fire, with eyes scorched and blinded by the flame, now solely dependent on the hand of its guide. The rider felt the suffering animal's pain, and recorded it in his heart with sympathy.

It was that heart's last record, and it was worthy of the broad manhood that had graved it there. He had given his life for men — he could pity a dumb animal as he died.

By the side of the swamp he was stricken from the saddle by the branch of a falling tree. His body fell in the water, his head resting on the tangled rushes of the swamp.

Once, before he died, his opened eyes were raised, and he looked above him into the sea and forest of fire. But he would not accept that; but upward, with the splendid faith of his old manhood, went the glazing eyes till they rested firmly on the eternal calmness of the sky. As he looked, there came to him, like a vision he had once before dimly seen, a great Thought from the deep sky, and held his soul in rapt communion. But the former dimness was gone; he saw it clearly now for one instant, while all things were closing peacefully in upon him.

Then the man's head sank peacefully to its couch, the limbs stretched out for their long rest, the strong heart stopped its labors.

He was dead.

They found his body next day, unscathed by the fire, preserved by the water in which he had fallen. Reverent hands lifted the burden and bore it into the dim recesses of the bush, followed by numerous dusky mourners.

One white man stood among the children of the forest; but he had no claim higher than theirs. Above the dead stood the white-haired Chief Te-mana-roa, bowed in silent grief. A spearwood litter was made, and the body placed on it. It was raised by the bush-men, who stood awaiting the old chief's orders.

Te-mana-roa turned to Hamerton, who alone of all the assembly belonged to the dead man's race. The old chief read profound grief in his face, and drew closer to him.

"This man belonged to us," he said, laying his dark finger on the wide brow of the dead; "he was true to my people, and they understood and loved him better than his own. We shall bury him in the Vasse."

The litter-bearers moved slowly forward, the old chief took his place behind the dead, and the bush-men with trailed spears followed in sad procession.

Hamerton's heart went strongly with the mourners; but he could not question their right. Two strange spearmen stood near him, to guide him safely through the bush. The faithful Ngarra-jil was gone, to mourn by the lonely grave of the MOONDYNE.

THE END.

MOONDYNE JOE

A STORY FROM THE UNDER-WORLD

By JOHN BOYLE O'REILLY

OPINIONS OF THE PRESS

From the New York Sun.

"Regarded merely with a view to its artistic merits, this is a narrative which no lover of novels should neglect to read. Whether we look to the strange and impressive nature of the scenery portrayed, and the abnormal conditions of life studied—to the novelty of incident and the skilful construction of plot, or to the vigorous strokes by which the persons of the tale are made to stand forth from the canvas—we cannot fail to recognize in this work a strong and captivating performance. . . . We do not know whether the author, as a matter of fact, has visited the penal colony in West Australia, or has made a study of British prisons, but certainly his account of convict life under these diverse conditions bears the marks of authenticity. What is more to our immediate purpose, his analysis of the principles which lie at the roots of the systems of confinement and transportation, is profound and fruitful, and his practical suggestions, enforced, as they are, by the experience of penal settlements, where, after a certain period of probation, the outlaws and the victims of a highly organized society are suffered to begin life anew, deserve to be closely scanned and maturely pondered. . . . Such are some of the problems forced upon the reader's attention by this remarkable book, but which are rather hinted than expounded—

not so much dissected by argument as commended to our sympathies by the poignant spectacle of suffering and the winning accent of conviction. The author seldom overlooks the limitations of his artistic purpose, and the thread of his story may be followed with eagerness by those who would hear with indifference the teaching of the student and the philanthropist."

From the Chicago Times.

"*Moondyne* is remarkable in more respects than one. It has plot enough for half-a-dozen strong romances ; it is written with crispness and simplicity, and in pure and nervous English ; its morality is orthodox ; its scene and characters are wholly novel and unique, and the interest is keenly—even painfully—sustained . . . and no one can read *Moondyne* without loving virtue more, pitying distress, abhorring injustice, and detesting vice. It is one of the few American novels which, while intensely romantic, is lofty in its aim, eloquent and noble in its argument, and healthy and refining in its effect. It is characterized throughout by the highest dramatic intuition, and ought to find its way speedily to the boards."

From the New Orleans Morning Star.

"This fine novel is really a treat, refined in diction, high toned in sentiment, and instructive in details. There is no religious controversy in its pages, no tedious theological arguments in the fabric of its story, but the whole book affords its readers only pleasure and profit. The spirit which animates the work is that of philanthropy, and the dedication, 'To all who are in prison, for whatever cause,' gives the clue to the object of the writer. The characters are well drawn, although we think the hero is overdrawn—that is, he is too perfect—but as a model to youth, the exemplar must be, as far as possible, faultless. The interest of the story is splendidly sustained, and the life of 'Moondyne' is thrilling, grand and beautiful. The lessons conveyed are very noble, and we think this expression in the mouth of Mr. Wyville, under the attendant circumstances, is the one grand lesson of the book, '*Authority must never forget humanity.*' We would like to quote several passages from the book, which for strength and pathos approach very near to the sublime—but we can only name the many striking points, and leave to the reader the pleasure of reading them in full."

From the Boston Daily Advertiser.

"Mr. O'Reilly has made a wonderful story of the convict-labor in Australia. The whole tale is on as magnificent a scale as Dumas' *Monte Cristo*, and more lofty in aim and sentiment. The vast natural wealth and bewildering beauty of the country are made the mere setting for a group of men, who answer every demand of heroism, and for two sweet women. The villain is as bad as the heroes are good ; through the whole book the interest never flags, the enthusiasm never cools, the intense dramatic and emotional power never breaks. With the same glowing ardor the eloquent author tells of superhuman courage, hair-breadth escapes, experiences in the bush, and in the convict camps, discusses the penal code of Australia, the responsibility of England, the abstract principles of liberty and the rights of man, the origin of crime and the deepest and most tender love of man and woman. The rapid and high-wrought fiction of the story is enhanced by the rush and color of the style and the air of reality that is given to the most romantic incidents and to the wildest horrors. *Moondyne*, the title of the book, means something more than manly or kingly, and although it is applied especially to the chief god-like hero, it belongs properly to the whole group of men who are represented as lifting Australia from sin and darkness into virtue and glory by the greatness of their own souls, the strength of their own wills, and their own passion of unselfishness. And all through this gorgeous fabric runs the thread of faith in man, faith in the root of good to be found even in the worst of convicts, and in the law of kindness and encouragement, to replace in all penal colonies the law of force. Mr. O'Reilly dedicates his book 'to all who are in prison for whatever cause.' And prisoners never had a more gallant and chivalrous champion."

From the Boston Herald.

"As a novel, we cannot but regret that the ending is so tragic, but we do not regard this volume as simply a novel. From beginning to end it is a satire upon British institutions, and we have seen nothing to surpass it since Bulwer's novel of *Paul Clifford*, where, under the guise of a love story, the author demonstrated that the prison system of England was an encouragement to crime, and that 'the worst use you could put a man to was to hang him.' Mr. O'Reilly's book has been favorably noticed in most of the leading journals of the country, but very many newspapers criticize it very sharply, although they profess great respect for the author, and to love him sincerely. Mr. O'Reilly is not only a man of talent, but one of real genius. He is in the prime of life, and is abundantly able to take care of himself. He has written some of the best lyric poetry in the language, and although his first novel is not faultless, he has no occasion to be disturbed by any of the flies, gnats, or other dipterous insects which buzz about him."

From the Cambridge Tribune.

"We think the book superior to Charles Reade's book with the same object, that of calling attention to the wrongs inflicted upon convicts, and as a work of fiction it impresses one more agreeably than that."

From the Bookseller.

"A powerful and fascinating tale, illustrating different systems of treatment adopted towards criminal convicts. The story belongs to the time when Western Australia was a penal settlement, governed by laws of Draconic severity. The regulations of our prisons at home were far from satisfactory, as was proved by their frequent changes, none of which long recommended themselves to practical men. Like Jean Valjean in Victor Hugo's story, the hero of the tale under notice was a convict, who, by a turn of the wheel, rose to a position of trust, and distinguished himself as a philanthropist, and a reformer of the present system. No one who begins the story will be able to stop till it is finished."

From the Boston Journal.

"There is power in the book, and pathos, and passion of a noble sort; and there is an abundance of exciting incidents and some bits of stirring and graphic description. The most jaded novel reader will find that there is something more than commonly fresh and inspiring about the story. If there are some faults of construction, and a little lack of symmetry, these are more than atoned for by the virile strength and intensity which hold the reader to the end."